For Laura Manuel with thanks and best wishes

DIAMOND IN THE SKY

Margaret Bailey

DIAMOND IN THE SKY

MARGARET BAILEY

FIVE STAR

An imprint of Thomson Gale, a part of The Thomson Corporation

Detroit • New York • San Francisco • New Haven, Conn. • Waterville, Maine • London

THOMSON
GALE

™

LIBRARY OF CONGRESS CATALOGING-IN-PUBLICATION DATA

Bailey, Margaret, 1938–
  Diamond in the sky / Margaret Bailey. — 1st ed.
    p. cm.
  ISBN-13: 978-1-59414-566-7 (alk. paper)
  ISBN-10: 1-59414-566-0 (alk. paper)
  1. Colorado—History—1876–1950—Fiction. 2. Leadville (Colo.)—Fiction. I. Title.
PS36023.A547D53 2007
  813'.6—dc22

2007005543

Published in 2007 in conjunction with Tekno Books.

Printed in the United States of America on permanent paper
10 9 8 7 6 5 4 3 2

To the hardy people of Leadville, then and now

ACKNOWLEDGMENTS

My most humble thanks go to the following friends in writing, without whose critical insights this would still be an unpolished tale cluttering up my hard drive: Jameson Cole, Janet Lane, Gail Rowe, Karen DuVall, Shannon Dyer, Vicki Kaufman, Michael Phillips, and Linda Sparks. Thanks also to my editor, Alice Duncan, for her sharp eye and wonderful enthusiasm.

I would like to acknowledge Darlene Godat, whose definitive book on the Ice Palace provided invaluable information for setting and detail in my story.

I thank Marcia Martinek, editor of the Leadville *Herald Democrat,* for her kind permission to quote from its 1895–1896 issues.

Although the setting and the events of 1895–1896 are depicted as accurately as I could make them, the story is fictitious. No one sabotaged the construction of the Ice Palace. It was a spectacular structure built in an astonishingly short time. The names of the promoters and officials of Leadville are accurate, but I have put words in their mouths.

CHAPTER 1

August 30, 1895

The old Seth Thomas clock sounded the first of its six bongs into the silence of Thaddeus MacElwain's store. Thad sighed. Closing time. There'd be no more customers, and he'd barely taken in enough to pay a day's worth of the mortgage—in fact, hardly enough to make a trip to the bank worthwhile.

He straightened up from the newspaper spread next to the cash register and surveyed his livelihood. The gold rays of sunset highlighted a few streaks in his show window, pinpointed floating dust motes, and suffused the room in the bronze of a faded tintype. Suddenly the store looked like a relic from another age, left behind, dusty and dying. The last bong died and the clock ticked away again, gently, as it always did, chipping away the seconds of his life, heedless of his fears.

He slid the garters off his sleeves and hung them on a nail near the back hall. He started toward the front to lock up, the floorboards squeaking loudly in the lonely silence.

A shadow crossed the window. Noah Ralston banged the front door against the notions counter, nearly knocking the bell from its hook above the frame. Thaddeus held his breath, fearing for the glass in the top half of the door.

Noah never waited for the bell to silence. "Sorry to bother you at closing time, Thad. Cut me about a pound off that cheddar wheel, will you?" he boomed through the heavy salt and pepper mustache that matched his bushy hair. "I don't know how that cook of mine thinks he can keep potatoes *au gratin* on the menu when he forgets to order cheese!"

Thad smiled at his friend. "Glad to help out, Noah. If your hotel is limping along like my store, you know I'm grateful for any business." He turned to the icebox on the back wall and lifted out the remains of a large wheel. He took the long cheese knife with the elk antler handle from above the wash pan and sliced off a wedge.

" 'Limping' is a good way to put it," said Noah, resting his arm on the counter. "Hard to believe how the town's gone down. Did you read in today's paper about the number of people we've lost?"

Thad nodded, checking the cheese for mold. "Sad to think of Leadville turning into a ghost town like the clapboard towns up in the gulches. If this keeps up, we'll all be wiped out."

"Well, I won't have to worry about the money for a while. Still, a few more guests in the hotel would at least keep me busy. Get my mind off Fiona and the baby." He traced the raised design on the cash register with his fingers. "I know it's only been half a year, but I have to find a new wife, Thad."

Thad looked at him in sympathy but tried to steer the conversation from quiet, pretty Fiona, who'd seemed unhappy within a few months of her marriage and had rarely spoken in Noah's presence. She'd died in the middle of a miscarriage and left her small fortune to Noah. Thad wrapped the cheese in waxed paper and laid it on the scale. "Well, if *I* don't do something, I'll go under before another year passes."

Noah frowned at him with concern. "Won't your past profits carry you for a while?"

Thad shrugged. "I don't have that much of a reserve built up. I did pretty well the first year I owned the store, but since the Silver Panic, things have gone down so fast I'm barely breaking even now."

Noah paid for his cheese and trod back across the protesting floorboards. Through the jingling of the bell he called, "Come on over to the hotel after the supper hour. We'll talk some more over a beer."

"Thanks, I'll do that."

Thad followed him out onto the boardwalk, and leaned against the doorframe with one foot drawn up against it. He watched Noah stride up Harrison in the aura of male heartiness that always surrounded him.

Noah stopped for a minute to shake his head over Williams' Haberdashery in the next block, the latest shop to be boarded up. He turned and put out a hand in a gesture of helplessness.

Thad nodded back across the distance. He'd met Noah and Fiona in the haberdashery shortly after they'd come to Leadville, newly married. They'd been discussing the length of a suit jacket while Thad was looking for a black belt. They'd turned to him for a third opinion. He'd agreed with Fiona, but they'd all laughed about it. They'd become friends, and Thad had helped Noah through the opening of the hotel and the sorrow of Fiona's death.

Noah shook his head again and strode on past the imposing two- and three-story Victorian brick fronts of Harrison Street toward the Ralston Hotel. The air on Harrison seemed to sag when he disappeared.

There's just so much of him, Thad thought, smiling. *He always leaves an emptiness behind.* Thad felt his mind shy from the word.

Empty, he mused, taking the thought out to look at it squarely: the store was usually empty these days, and he spent most of his time dusting the old merchandise or just standing behind the counter thinking about ways to generate business. But it was the other emptiness that he could no longer ignore. What was this all for? Of course, he knew why he'd come to Leadville, and there was no going back to that. A memory shot through him like lightning, a voice that screamed his name and stopped his breath. With an effort of will, he pushed it back in the recess of his mind and looked up the empty street. Yes, there had to be more to living than livelihood. Something to make a twenty-six-year-old feel his life made some sense. Someone to love. A wife. Even Noah admitted his need for a wife.

Of course, compared to Noah . . . Thad ran his hand through his thick sandy hair, parted just to right of center, and fingered his full handlebar mustache. No great Adonis. If he ignored the slight cleft in his chin, he was probably nice-enough looking for most women, but that was the trouble. There weren't many women in Leadville, and none at all who interested him. All too young, too married, or too loose. Just as well; he couldn't afford a wife, anyway. Someday, perhaps . . .

The old guilt rose to remind him he didn't deserve a wife, but a mechanical shriek interrupted the thought. He watched the 6:15 train chuff and clank and whistle into the Colorado Midland station at the bottom of Third Street, shattering the silence like a metallic avalanche. As the quiet settled in again, he pushed aside thoughts of a wife and focused on Mount Massive across the valley, its peak coral red in the last sunlight. Absently, he rubbed the back of his thumbnail through the cleft in his chin. If his business failed and he had to leave this place, his eyes and heart would always ache for the mountains.

The wind stirred around Thad's face, clearing some of the smoke and dust that rose from the mills, and he breathed deeply, a breath that turned into a sigh. He shoved himself away from the wall and turned to go back in the store, but something caught his eye.

Down the hill a woman in a blue traveling coat and a slight man in black emerged from the station. Another man with a carpetbag followed them. The woman turned briefly to look at the other man, almost nervously, Thad thought, but they were

14

too far away to be sure. He glanced at the man with the carpetbag. There was something unpleasant and vaguely familiar about him. The man stopped, dropped his bag, and appeared to study something he took from his pocket.

Thad focused on the woman. She was slender and graceful in her walk, even carrying a valise that dragged at her arm. She caught her companion by the hand. They stopped and argued before starting up the hill. The woman struggled now with both valises. The man's gait was labored and awkward.

Thad started toward them to help her, but before he had gone half a block, they stopped, talked a minute, and turned into a yard. He went back to the store to put away the cheese wheel. It was almost completely dark in the back of the store now. He reached up and pulled the chain on the electric light he'd had installed two years before, when the town was still booming and he'd been full of confidence. The hanging lamp swung a pool of light up and down the tobacco counter and over the dried food bins below the clock.

He'd just turned it off again when the light coming in the front of the store dimmed suddenly. He glanced up. The woman from the station knocked at the door and peered through the glass, her hands cupping her face. He hurried to open the door for her.

The slight man with her was leaning against the wall between the door and the show window, wheezing. After the exertion of the hill, his cheeks were bright red in his pale, freckled face.

"I'm terribly sorry to bother you," she said. The accent that tumbled out with her struggle for air told him she was from the flatlands, much farther east than Denver. "I know you're closed this late in the day . . ." She stopped to gasp. ". . . but your light was the only one I saw coming up the hill . . ." Another gasp. ". . . except the saloon over there." She paused a minute, completely out of breath, gesturing toward the Silver Dollar across the street.

"Please, come in and sit down a minute," said Thad, moving back and holding the door open. "It takes a few weeks to get used to our altitude. Are you here visiting someone?" He turned on the light again and brought out a chair for her.

She forced the young man into it.

Thad could see her face clearly for the first time. Not a woman's face, barely more than a girl's, it was almost the image of her companion's: pale and slightly freckled, with small features—except for her eyes. Warm and ingenuous, they were the same shade as the dark-honey of her hair, a few strands of which had escaped her plain blue straw hat. Her face radiated such sweetness that Thad's breath faltered.

"No," she answered. "We've come out for . . ."

The young man jumped into the pause. "Because of my lungs, she means to say. That's why . . ." He took a breath. ". . . she wouldn't let me carry my own valise . . . up the hill . . . I saw you start toward us." He reached up to Thad and they shook hands. "I'm Larry Corcoran, and this is my sister Juliet."

"Thaddeus MacElwain. So you came out for the drier climate. Where are you from?"

"Baltimore," said Juliet.

"And the doctor said," Larry continued, "if I didn't get away from the east coast, the consumption would get me before my nineteenth birthday. So Lettie gave up her prospects in Maryland to come with me." He coughed and looked at his sister with a mixture of love and guilt.

"What prospects?" asked Juliet, whose breathing had almost returned to normal. Her voice was soft and musical. "A tailor can make a living anywhere." She turned to Thad. "That's what I want to do, set up a tailoring shop. But right now we need to find a room for the night. The boarding house we tried near the station was closed. So when we saw your light, we thought you might be able to guide us to a hotel." Her face reddened. "One that's not expensive."

Thad blinked hard to dispel the resurfacing thought of a wife, but it only rose and blossomed in the gentle warmth that came from Miss Corcoran's eyes. "Well, welcome to Colorado. I'm sure you'll love it here when you adjust to the altitude. I can take you to my friend Noah's hotel. He'll give you a good price."

For a second Thad regretted the suggestion, remembering Noah's need for a wife, but he couldn't take it back now. All he could do was find a way to see her again. His tongue barely under his command, he said, "Tomorrow, if you like, I can help you get settled into a boarding house. I never have any customers before nine o'clock, anyway."

"You're very kind," she said, and warmed him again with her smile.

He took the two valises and they started up the four blocks to Noah's hotel. He hadn't reached the corner of Fourth before he noticed they were lagging behind. He grinned sheepishly and walked back.

"Forgive me," he said. "It was thoughtless of me to set such a furious pace for newcomers. I remember my first few weeks and should know better."

Breathing hard and running her hands up and down the sleeves of her thin coat in the chill of evening, Juliet smiled and turned to her brother. He had stopped and braced himself with his hands on his knees, his back heaving with his struggle for breath.

"Just give me a second," he said, looking up at them. "I'll be all right." He tried to smile.

In a minute they set out again more slowly. As he turned, Thad caught a glimpse of the other man from the station, crossing Harrison in the dusk, carrying the carpetbag on his left.

Something about the man nagged at him, but Miss Corcoran captured his attention again.

She was looking around at the fine brick buildings of Harrison Street. "Why did they call this place Leadville? Such an ugly name for such an imposing town," she said as they crossed Fourth.

Thad stopped her in the middle of Fourth and pointed down at the mining operations along the headwaters of the Arkansas River. "You can't see them well in this light, but down there are huge piles of slag from carbonate ore."

"Oh, yes," said Larry. "We saw them from the train."

Miss Corcoran nodded. "We kept exclaiming about how dreadful they look in this beautiful valley."

Thad considered a minute. "I suppose they do, but the ore was so rich in lead and silver that in less than twenty years the town went from a collection of shacks to what you see now. So they named it Leadville."

"Hmm," said Miss Corcoran, "Silverville would have been a lot prettier."

Behind them, the man with the carpetbag stepped up to Thad's store and peered in the window, breathing hard. He glanced up Harrison after the three retreating figures, tried the door, and found it locked. He turned back toward the Silver Dollar but stopped in the middle of the empty street and looked up and down its length, distaste drawing his features into an ugly frown. "Pathetic," he said aloud, shivering. "Might have known he'd choose a place where you freeze your damn ears off in the middle of August." He hurried into the saloon.

CHAPTER 2

August 31, 1895

Thad slept hardly at all. Juliet Corcoran's face dominated the night, and the smile that had warmed him earlier now made him throw off his quilt. He wanted to get to know this girl. Every man in Leadville would. Noah already did. His eyes had widened in interest the minute Thad had introduced them.

He had to do something to keep her near him. He threw himself onto his left side and looked past the marble-topped dresser into his sitting room. Rooms! Of course. She and her brother could live here. Mrs. Eskitch still had a room upstairs. No. The brother would never manage the stairs, and the room was too small, anyway.

A shop. She wanted to open a shop. Nothing on either side of his store. His store! Why not? He could give her space in the front. She'd want to pay rent.

Suddenly a possibility was before him. He could rent part of the store to someone and help pay off the mortgage. Miss Corcoran was just starting out and wouldn't be able to pay much. He'd have to find someone else. His mind chased that thought into the blind alley of diminishing population and failing businesses. Nothing new in Leadville for months. Perhaps share with someone else who was still holding on. But then, Miss Corcoran . . .

He threw himself flat on his back and stared at the ceiling he could barely see. Mrs. Eskitch's empty room was directly above him. He'd seen it. Too small under the sloping roof to be very comfortable, even for one person. If he lived in it, he'd feel too confined. If *he* lived in it . . .

Long before light, he jumped out of bed and tiptoed into the kitchen, where Mrs. Eskitch kept her cleaning rags. He scrubbed and straightened his rooms until dawn.

Thad was waiting at Noah's carved mahogany reception desk ten minutes before he was supposed to meet Miss Corcoran and her brother. The smell of pancakes, syrup, and coffee hung heavy and sweet in the lobby, even though the sliding stained-glass doors to the hotel restaurant were closed.

Noah came down the hall from the kitchen and stationed himself behind the desk.

Thad shoved the paper he'd been reading toward him and steered the conversation toward the latest mine closing.

Noah's responses were barely relevant. In the first pause, he asked, "Where do they come from?"

Thad waited a minute, as if confused. "Who?"

"The . . ." Noah made a great show of pulling the registration book over where he could glance in it. ". . . Corcorans. The people you brought in last night."

"Oh, the boy and his sister? Out East somewhere, the coast, I think." Thad almost smiled at his own reluctance to tell Noah anything about them.

Juliet came down the steps alone and approached them. Both men smiled and stood straighter. She smiled at both but walked directly to Thad and offered her hand.

"Good morning, Mr. MacElwain. Mr. Ralston."

Thad felt his chest expand as Juliet kept her eyes on him. Out of the corner of his eye, he saw Noah's smile fade. He heard the miffed note of Noah's "Good morning."

"Hello, Miss Corcoran," he said. "How is your brother this

morning?" He held her hand in both of his a second longer than etiquette required. He barely sensed Noah's frown and his movement to the key rack down the counter.

"Still sleeping. It was a long trip, and then the steep walks. I'm afraid they exhausted him. He had a nose bleed, and we both had terrible headaches by the time we went to bed."

"I'm sorry to hear that. It's the altitude. The nosebleeds will go away in a day or two. I hope *you're* feeling better."

"The headache's gone now. Probably Larry's is, too, but he had a bad night, and I decided not to wake him."

"You were quite right to let him sleep. You should take things slowly for a while, too. Shall we go? I promise to set an easy pace."

They stepped out into the fresh, chill air of a mountain morning.

"Oh," she said, "perhaps I should go back for a jacket. I had no idea it would be this cool."

"No need, all we have to do is get out of the shadow of the building across the street." Thad took her arm and steered her into the sun. The warmth of her forearm under the thin, white cotton sleeve flowed pleasantly into him. He looked down at her hat and was suddenly aware of her skin, her shoulder, her thin frame under the dress. His heart bounced happily.

She stopped and smiled into the sun with her eyes closed. "My goodness, I had no idea there could be such a difference between shade and sun."

"It's the dry air," he said. They waited for a passing ore wagon and then stepped through its dusty wake across Harrison. Thad was careful to settle into a slow walk for her.

Juliet looked up and down the main street with the sun still half in her eyes. "All these fancy buildings. I expected Leadville to look like the clapboard towns we came through on the train."

"Oh, no. In fact, this is one of the finest cities in Colorado."

Thad wondered vaguely whether she'd noticed the shops that were abandoned, but he was practicing what he would say next.

She looked at him in surprise. "Well, it's certainly finer than our uncle led us to believe when he suggested we come here."

"Miss Corcoran, I've been thinking. There's a room in the house where I live. It's on the second floor, and I . . . I'd like the view of the mountains from up there much better. I'm sure you want rooms on the first floor because of your brother. You could have my two. The front one has a fine southern exposure—very important in the winter—and I know the price is reasonable."

"Why, Mr. MacElwain, I couldn't possibly allow you to move rooms on our account."

"It's a move I'd like to make. I'm sure Mrs. Eskitch would be happy to have you. She can use the rent. And she sets a fine table for supper."

Juliet hesitated.

"It won't hurt to look at the rooms, will it?" he asked, annoyed at the nervous edge to his voice. "They really would be ideal for you and your brother."

"Well, all right, I'll just look at them." She stopped in front of Mrs. Marechal's yard with its waning display of columbines. "Mr. MacElwain, could we slow down just a bit? I confess, I'm all out of breath again."

Thad stopped and grinned down at her. "There, you see? You definitely want first floor rooms. You don't want to add even ten more feet to our ten thousand, now do you? I know my rooms would be right for you, and I'm sure you'll like Mrs. Eskitch. I have to warn you, though, she'll talk you glassy-eyed." When they set out again, he took her arm as they crossed several intersections, enjoying the touch more each time.

After they had seen the rooms and Juliet had agreed on the

price with Mrs. Eskitch, they started back to the hotel.

"My goodness, Mr. MacElwain, you were so right about her! Such verbal stamina!" said Juliet as they rounded the corner and walked slowly toward Harrison. "I'm positively wall-eyed."

Thad laughed. "Maybe you'll be able to do that when you've been here twenty years, too."

"Never. In a whole lifetime, I don't think I could squeeze that many words into a single breath!"

"She does fill a room with talk, doesn't she? But she's as kind a lady as you'll find in Leadville."

"I can see that. Oh, isn't this lovely—downhill."

Thad hardly felt the sidewalk under his feet, but he was intensely conscious of her hand in the crook of his elbow. She'd be in the house where he lived every night. They would sit together in the parlor. It was a pleasing thought.

Before he could stop himself, the words tumbled out:

"There was one other thing I was thinking about, Miss Corcoran. You said you wanted to set up a tailoring shop. Perhaps you would consider the front of my store. You'd be in the window overlooking Harrison, where everyone passes by. They'd see the quality of your work, and customers coming into the store couldn't miss you. What do you think?"

Juliet stopped and looked up at him. For a second he could read the questions in her mind as they registered in her eyes: why was he doing this? What did he want in return?

Thad smiled into her eyes and the questions faded. He hoped his own doubts were hidden. This was not what he'd intended. But perhaps it could work. If she made a little money, and if his business picked up and he saved on rent in the upstairs room . . .

"The offer overwhelms me, Mr. MacElwain. It would make things far easier than I ever imagined. But I can't do it. I'd crowd you too much."

"Nonsense." They reached the corner of Harrison. To the

right was the hotel. "Would you like to take a look before making up your mind? It's right down here." He pointed to the left.

"But your store seemed quite full last night."

"Only because of all the dry goods that have been lying around since I bought it. All I do is dust them. I'll put them on special sale, which I should have done months ago. And I could move anything that doesn't sell into the back room."

"Well, if you're sure . . ." She followed him down Harrison.

"Quite sure. There just isn't that much trade anymore. I don't think you realize you've stumbled onto a dying town here. Just yesterday the report was in the paper. From forty thousand two years ago to just fourteen thousand today."

Juliet paled and stopped dead in front of the apothecary. "Mr. MacElwain, I had no idea. Will I even be able to make a living here?"

"I hope so. There's *some* money because the gold mines are still operating at a profit, but those who were in silver, actually most of the miners, are going under."

She saw the boarded-up millinery across the street now and stepped off the boardwalk to count the empty stores. She came back with her hand over her heart, and her voice quavered. "My, this is very discouraging. If I worked in your store, how much rent would you want?"

Thad looked into her serious face and knew that if he didn't charge her any rent, she wouldn't even consider his offer. An image flashed through his head: himself throwing his coat down at his door and begging her to enter. Stifling a grin, he frowned, as if calculating complex figures of profit and loss. He ran his hand through his hair, down his neck, and over his chin, covering the cleft. "Shall we say five dollars a month until we see how your business goes?"

Her eyes filled with tears. "You're too kind, Mr. MacElwain. If it were not for my brother, I wouldn't even think of accepting such a charitable offer. But I have no idea what kind of medical expenses we may be facing." Her face reddened and she took a deep breath. "I'll be honest with you. We haven't much. Our father died in a shipwreck about three years ago. Our brother, who's a sea captain, too, has been supporting the family ever since. He'll send us something every month, but it won't be enough to live on. So I thank you." The tears nearly spilled over. She lowered her head and wiped her eyes with a handkerchief. "I'm sorry. I certainly didn't mean to weep in front of a perfect stranger. And right on your main street, too."

Thad looked down at the top of her hat, stunned by a sudden need to hold her, protect her from worry. "I hope we won't be strangers very long. And there's nothing to thank me for, I assure you." He cast about for a way to make her smile again. "Look at it this way—people who come in for your services will buy from me, too, and with such a lovely lady working in my store, who could resist coming in?"

She looked up, and her face softened.

"In fact," he rambled on, in full swing, "I was just thinking about renting out some of my space, but it never occurred to me it might even bolster my business. To tell the truth, I think you might be doing me a great service," he said, trying to convince himself as well as her. "Why, I should probably pay you!"

Juliet laughed, a wonderful laugh that sounded like sleigh bells.

Thad wanted to hear that laugh often. "I have several bolts of fabric you could use to start with. You tailor up something and we'll hang it in the window till someone buys it."

"There's no need to give me fabric. I brought some with me. And the sewing machine will arrive tomorrow or the next day." The smile faded and she looked directly into his eyes. "I don't know how to thank you for all this, Mr. MacElwain." Biting her lower lip, she put her hand in his arm and they walked on.

His conscience tweaked at him. She'd just been so honest with him. "Miss Corcoran, I have to be honest with you, too. I only said five dollars rent because I knew you wouldn't set up your business in my store if I didn't say *some*thing."

She looked away. "I know that."

A sweetness flowed through the silence between them.

Lightheaded now, Thad said, "But I was serious about your being good for my business."

They walked the last block to the store. They settled on the best place for her sewing machine, directly in front of the show window, where she would have plenty of light and passersby would see her. Then he escorted her back to the hotel, asking about her life in Baltimore and telling her of his love for the mountains.

Thad walked back to the store in an aura of happy purpose he'd never felt before, only vaguely aware of a man behind him.

The man caught the door and entered before the bell jingled a second time.

Stepping behind the register, Thad heard the man's heavy breathing over the creak of the floorboards. He opened the cash drawer to slip the money in, and turned his attention to the customer. His own face stared back at him.

"Zeb!" he gasped.

The face contorted into a sardonic grin. "That all you got to say to your loving brother?" Zeb let his carpetbag drop to the floor and put out his left arm in a mock embrace.

"I . . . I wasn't expecting you. My God, I saw you last night. I just didn't recognize you." Zeb had gained at least twenty pounds since Thad had left home.

Zeb ran his hand down his rounded stomach. "Yeah, I guess I went all soft after you left. Happens when you have no . . . well, what shall we call it? Competition? Enemy?"

Thad felt his face flush. The smell of smoke was in his nose again. The white flame of anger swirled around the black fist of guilt, searing as always, but not consuming. The voice rushed at his ears, Zeb's voice, but he made himself deaf to it. He grasped at normality. "How are Mother and Father?"

Zeb shrugged. "Fine, unless a hurricane washed them out to sea since I left." He straightened and his suit coat parted at the middle, revealing the gold chain of his watch and the fob he'd had almost since Thad could remember. It was a tiny shark carved in black onyx, its back arched as if in attack.

Thad glanced at the shark and remembered where he himself had found it, amid planks and a partial keel that had washed up on a beach near home. He'd held it in his hand for barely a moment when Zeb appeared beside him, snatched it away, and claimed it for himself. When Thad started to protest, Zeb grabbed him and pinched and twisted the inside of his upper arm until Thad cried out and fell to his knees.

The little shark disappeared beneath the gray serge of Zeb's suit again. Thad held on to the counter and drew a deep breath. "Why didn't you write me you were coming?"

"Didn't have time." Zeb was still panting. "Damnation, brother, leave it to you to settle where a man can't even breathe. Nearly bust my lungs coming up that damn hill from the station. You were obviously busy by that time."

"Busy?"

Zeb winked and leered. "Watched you from across the street," he said, pointing over his shoulder with his thumb. "Never knew you to work so fast with the ladies, I must say. Another day on the train with Sweet Miss Blue Bonnet and I'd have had a go at her myself." He gave Thad a small salute.

Thad started to swing but his wrist crashed into the open cash drawer and slammed it shut.

"Whoa, there," said Zeb. "You can have her. Even this

backwater mining town has ladies more to my taste. Found one for a memorable evening in your fancy Vendome Hotel, if you know what I mean. A sort of last fling before going to work in your . . . fine emporium." He glanced around. His lips drew up into a sneer.

"You want to work for me?" Thad felt the blood drain from his face. This was not a visit. "Zeb, with the best of will, I couldn't afford to pay you anything. For a while I made good money, but now the town's so depressed no one is making much. Maybe I can help you find something, but there isn't enough work here for two."

"I see." Zeb used his left hand to lift his right arm onto the counter. The sleeve of his suit slid up, revealing a scarred, badly deformed hand and wrist. "So much for brotherly love."

Thad turned away from the forearm, its skin mottled and grotesquely folded on itself like melted wax. Unconsciously he focused on Mount Massive, barely visible from the back of the store. "I told you I didn't . . . How long must I keep apologizing for that?"

Zeb's voice was low and bitter. "As long as I have to live with it."

"Is that why you came here, Zeb? To keep reminding me?"

"Ha, don't imagine yourself that important." Zeb shrugged and grinned. "There was some ugly talk about that drab little Gracie Singer and me."

Gracie. Thad saw the narrow face, the gray eyes, and the lifeless light brown hair. Mousie Grousie the boys had called her behind her back. She had been too shy to look any man in the face.

With his right arm still on the counter, Zeb bent and looked casually at the display of tobaccos. "You remember Gracie, don't you? Seems she got herself pregnant. Her father wanted the whole town to believe I seduced her. Not a very fine assortment of tobaccos, is it?"

"Zeb, not Gracie."

Zeb blew out a small, disdainful breath. " 'Raped' was the word they were all whispering behind their lace fans." He straightened up and waved his hand, dismissing the girl. "Little dull, gray Gracie. She practically begged me for it."

Thad closed his eyes to the lie and opened them again to the useless hand of his brother. He mourned for Gracie. The old knot in the pit of his stomach and the weight on his heart returned. He'd been nearly free of them in Colorado. Why had Zeb come here? To put their old resentments together in one place again?

He looked at his brother over the cash register, conscious of yesterday's small profit. "You'd have a lot better prospects down in Denver, or out in California, but I'll give you a week's rent, and try to help you find work here. That's all I can do. Have you learned a different trade since I left?"

Zeb snorted. "Father offered to take me on in the warehouse. I don't know what he thought I could do there. Shove cotton bales around?"

"Couldn't you have learned the office work?" Of course not. Zeb had never been good at math after he'd had the fever and had to start school all over. It was a stupid question.

The door jingled open and Old Marsh came in.

"What, with this?" Zeb lifted his right arm again. "I can't even write legibly with my left hand, much less keep a ledger. Or have you managed to forget that, too?"

Old Marsh pretended to inspect the plaid shirts on their shelf in the middle of the floor, but Thad could sense that his concentration was on Zeb's caustic tone.

He made his voice as neutral as he could manage. "I haven't forgotten anything. Morning, Marsh." He watched the old man approach the counter.

Zeb stood next to Marsh for a second, then grimaced and moved away, staring at the old man's filthy suit coat with the mangy velvet collar, his badly bowed legs, his stringy gray hair, and tobacco-streaked beard.

"Gimme some of that tobacco." Marsh watched Zeb back away and drew his lips back over his yellowed teeth in a smile that might have been a snarl. "And some papers to roll it in."

Thad took a small sack of tobacco and the cigarette papers out of the case. "That'll be ten cents, Marsh."

"Ten cents! I could ransom King Midas for the damn prices you charge here."

Thad tried to smile at the old man. "Same price as last time, Marsh, and the time before that, and the one before that. If you can find it cheaper anywhere in Leadville, then buy it cheaper. I can't give it away, you know."

Marsh flipped a coin onto the counter and it rolled to the floor. He turned and stumped toward the door. "Damn fancy store owners. I coulda bought out the whole bunch of 'em ten years ago," he muttered, banging the door behind him.

"I wouldn't let any stinking old man like that in a store of mine," said Zeb, coming back from the knife display case.

Thad retrieved the coin and dropped it in the register. "In times like these, you take every dime you can get and hope the customer comes back, even if he smells. Old Marsh used to be as rich as any in Leadville, they say."

"That old flea haven?"

"He made hundreds of thousands, spent a lot and lost the rest in the Silver Panic two years ago."

Zeb turned to the window. Old Marsh was leaning against the glass with one leg up, sprinkling tobacco onto the paper he'd laid on his knee. The flimsy paper blew away, scattering the tobacco. Marsh shook his fist at the air and started up the street without trying a second time.

Zeb stepped to the window to watch him. "Maybe he's got a stash of gold somewhere."

"I doubt it. Now all he has left is a trickle of cash from the mine and, I think, some lots up there on Capitol Hill where he was planning to build his mansion." Thad pointed north and west across Harrison to a bluff overlooking the south end of town and the valley to the west.

Zeb shrugged. "Well, I'm going out for a walk around this pathetic city."

The bell jingled again and Noah burst in.

"Miss Corcoran tells me she's checking out tomorrow," he shouted. "She said she's moving into your rooming house."

Zeb stopped and turned around.

"Noah, this is my brother Zeb."

Noah looked sharply from Zeb to Thad. "I didn't know you had a brother." He offered Zeb his hand, and when Zeb took it with his left, Noah glanced down at it and then looked away.

Zeb sneered at Thad. "Now why wouldn't you mention a thing like that?"

Thad ignored the question and went back to Noah's news. "I offered Miss Corcoran my two rooms because they're on the first floor and her brother can't manage stairs with his lung condition. I'm moving upstairs."

Zeb grinned knowingly.

Noah sputtered. "I could have let her have a room on the first floor."

"I don't think she can afford a hotel room, Noah. She'll have meals at the house, and . . ."

"Yeah," Zeb interrupted, "you can take her under your noble wing." He laughed.

"Well, if you must know, I've offered her space there by the window for her tailoring business. I see no reason why I shouldn't help her out."

Zeb smirked. "And no doubt you can think of several why you *should*." The door clanged and he was gone before Thad could respond to the implication.

Noah stared at him.

"That's the sort of thing Zeb *would* think," said Thad. "You ought to know me better than that."

"You sweet on that girl?"

"Come on, Noah, she just got here last . . . All right, I am. Absurd as it seems. Just yesterday I was standing out there after you left, thinking about a wife, too. And now . . ."

"Well, I'm going to tell you right out, I find the young lady mighty attractive. I want sons. You know there aren't many decent women left around Leadville. So be warned, I'm going to court her, and I've go a lot more to offer than you."

Thad felt his hackles rise. "Now see here, you may be financially . . ."

Noah cut him off. His face became utterly serious. "Also, I don't lose, Thad. Maybe that's a side of me you haven't seen. Call it a failing of mine if you want. I know Fiona did. But when I want something, I go blind to everything else. I'll stop at nothing to get it."

It was a long minute before Thad answered. "Fair enough, Noah."

"I'll send someone from the staff to help get their things to the rooming house. But that doesn't mean I'm going to forget her."

Thad clenched his teeth. "Right."

"You mark my words," Noah said with his back to Thad, reaching for the door and sharing a jangling of the bell with Mrs. Eskitch. Thad had no time to contemplate his sudden anger.

Harriette Eskitch tucked strands of silvery hair back under her wide straw hat and began talking before the bell had stopped. "Did you see the *Herald Democrat* yet this morning, Mr. Mac?" She pulled the paper from her shopping basket and waved it at him.

"I haven't even had time to open the store properly. Is there something special in it?"

"An article about the meeting at the Vendome last night. You know how these high-and-mighties are, they meet and decide things all the time without giving us plain folk a chance to mouth an opinion." She smoothed down the brown pleats that billowed around her ample hips. " 'Course, I'm sure they know better what the town needs . . ."

Thad sighed imperceptibly. "Why don't you tell me about it while I get my register open?"

". . . and we're all so worried about the town going downhill like it's doing. My Mr. Es, God rest, I'm thankful he didn't live to see me running a boarding house. He always said he was going to give me the best of everything. He really did, you know. Says here there was talk again about building an ice palace."

Thad looked up from the nickels he was sliding into their compartment. " 'Again'?"

"Oh, yes, there's been talk of that around here for years. You know, they have them in Canada all the time, and here in the States, too, I think in Minneapolis or Minnesota or someplace."

"Why would anyone want to build an ice palace?"

"Well, says here they'd make a regular winter festival out of it, get visitors to come here instead of everyone in Leadville who can afford it heading to other climes for the winter and the rest of us sitting around our stoves, blowing on our hands and wishing for summer. I tell you, my Mr. Es, he just hated the winter. Came from Texas, you know, and he was always talking about spending the winters in Galveston when we got a little ahead. 'Course, then that stick of dynamite they thought was a dud went off in the shaft, and he got buried in the rubble . . .

Well, that's a long time ago, now. They say a winter carnival would boost business."

"I imagine it would, if anyone came."

"There's that new man came here last winter, that Edwin Senior, he seems to be promoting the idea. What do you think, Mr. Mac, would it save the city?"

"It might. For one winter anyway. I expect they'll be around polling the businessmen about it soon if the idea catches on."

Another customer came in.

"Good morning, Mrs. Kelly," Thad said. "Did you want something, Mrs. Eskitch?"

"Let me see your curtain fabric. Mornin', Mrs. K. I may make some new ones for that nice Miss Conklin you brought over."

Thad grinned. "Corcoran, Mrs. Eskitch." He brought several bolts of muslin from the storeroom and turned to Mrs. Kelly.

Mrs. Kelly was focused on Mrs. Eskitch. "What, you have a new boarder? My dear, how exciting. What's her name again, Mr. MacElwain?"

"Corcoran. Did you want something, Mrs. Kelly?"

"Oh, yes, a pound of oatmeal. And I need a card of white buttons," Mrs. Kelly answered, but she was looking at the bearer of the latest news. "I declare, that husband of mine can't keep buttons on his . . . Do tell me all about this newcomer."

"Oh, she's a dear person, isn't she Mr. Mac? From out East somewhere. She has a brother, too, so I'll have every room in the house occupied. Isn't that lovely?"

Thad measured out the oatmeal, packed it and handed it to Mrs. Kelly.

She turned to leave, stuffing it in her shopping bag. "We haven't had any new blood in Leadville for the longest time, have we?"

Mrs. Eskitch was right on her heels. "And did you see this,

Mrs. K.?" she asked, following her to the door, jabbing at the newspaper, the fabric forgotten. "About the winter carnival we're going to have? They're going to build an ice castle and . . ." She trailed her out the door.

Thad held a card of buttons toward the door, then smiled after them and entered the oatmeal on Mrs. Kelly's bill. He replaced the bolts of muslin absently. A winter festival. Maybe it would boost his income, make him more acceptable to Juliet— Miss Corcoran. He could put most of the old merchandise on sale to get rid of it, buy more modern things. And dozens of warm scarves and mittens. The kinds of things that people coming to Leadville for the first time always needed. And souvenirs. Visitors to attractions like an Ice Palace always wanted souvenirs—pennants, pewter replicas of the attraction.

The daydream faded and he found himself standing alone behind his cash register, remembering the warm sensation that flowed in with Miss Corcoran's smile, the feel of her hand on his arm. It made his whole body tingle. She would be at work in his window tomorrow, at the house tomorrow night. With a rush of enthusiasm he began shoving racks and counters away from the window.

CHAPTER 3

September 12, 1895

Thad leaned against the tobacco counter with his ledger spread out before him. The figures were disappointing again, and he would need enough money to order in some winter clothing soon. But his concentration would not stay on the neat black numbers that marched down the lined pages to eventual ruin. Like his eyes, his mind strayed again and again to Juliet.

At the window she was sewing on the machine that had arrived two days after she did, while Larry, leaning against a table behind her, cut out a pattern.

Juliet began whistling softly, a lilting melody that Thad didn't recognize. In a minute Larry chimed in, pausing occasionally for a deep breath. They whistled a canon.

Thad stood enchanted. "Please, don't stop," he said when they fell silent again. "That was beautiful. What were you whistling?"

Juliet looked at him and blushed. "That was one of the tunes our grandmother taught us when we were small, before she died. She brought them with her from Germany as a girl. Sometimes we even sing them in our awful German. I'm afraid we'll plague you with them often enough."

"I hope you do." Thad smiled.

"Wonderful melodies, aren't they?" she said. "Oma called them *Ohrwürme,* 'ear worms,' which was her way of saying you couldn't get them out of your head."

Juliet turned back to the machine and drew up the hem of her skirt to keep it free of the treadle. Thad returned to his bookkeeping, but it was not long before his eyes wandered to Juliet again, to her shoulder blades pressing against the plaid fabric of her dress as she worked, the pink of her neck above the white collar, her delicate ankle in the thin white stocking . . .

The clackety rhythm of the sewing machine had become music sweet to his ears and indispensable to his heart. He watched as Juliet reached the end of a seam, cut the threads, and tied them off. Slowly, she straightened her back and stretched for a few seconds, gazing out at the mountains in the morning sun, before sliding the fabric under the presser foot again. She shifted the right foot to the treadle, and the lovely left ankle disappeared behind her skirt.

Thad looked at the last few figures in the ledger. They were a little better than the week before, but it was too early to tell whether her presence brought him any customers. He crossed his fingers for a second and asked, "What is that you're working on, Miss Corcoran?"

She stopped the machine and turned toward him, smiling through straight pins in her mouth.

"Oh, pardon, I didn't realize . . ." he said.

She dropped the pins into the palm of her hand. "It's all right. It's a dreadful habit anyway, keeping pins in my mouth. I'm making the jacket Mrs. Lambert ordered. I have enough cloth to finish this, but that's all. Could you send for some more gray flannel with this week's order, Mr. MacElwain? I'll give you the money before you close the register."

"Certainly." Thad moved to the front and stood next to the sewing machine, his heart on a level with his Adam's apple. "Miss Corcoran, could we call each other by our first names now? That is, all three of us?"

Larry looked up and smiled. "I vote yes," he said.

"Well, then," said Juliet, "we're all in favor . . . Thaddeus."

"Thad. My friends all call me Thad."

"Then you'd better call Juliet Lettie, like I do," said Larry.

Juliet smiled at her brother. "Larry couldn't say Juliet when he was small. He's always called me Lettie. Everyone in my family does ever since."

"Which do you prefer?"

Juliet moved her smile to Thad. "Lettie," she said after a pause. She laughed. "Otherwise you'd have to call Larry Laertes, which *I* couldn't say till I was ten."

"Laertes?"

"Our father spent a lot of his sailing time with a huge volume of Shakespeare," Larry explained. "We have a brother named MacDuff and a sister named Desdemona. So they're Duffy and Mona. Unless we're mad at her, then she's Demon."

"What about your family, Thad?" asked Lettie.

"I have just the one brother and the standard complement of parents. You met Zeb when he came in last Saturday after he'd finished delivering the mail."

Lettie's smile faded. "He's so different from you, even if he is the spitting image."

Thad hesitated. This was dangerous ground, but at least she thought he wasn't like Zeb. And if he wanted her to know him, he couldn't hide the past. He swallowed to get his saliva flowing and said, "I've only ever known Zeb the way he is now, but my parents have often told me he was a sweet child until he was six and I was four. He had mumps then, and that went into scarlet fever and then a low fever that dragged on for a long time."

"I don't understand," said Lettie. "Larry's had fever with the consumption for four years. Why would that make *Zeb* so bitter?"

"Mother said it was the scarlet fever that changed his personality, as if it burned all the sweetness out of him."

Lettie frowned slightly but waited.

"He missed most of the first year of school and so much of the second that when I started school we were in the same grade. He hated that, and although he's smart enough, he never did as well in school as I did. His resentment has only grown since then." Thad looked out the window, seeing the anger that had been on Zeb's face ever since he could remember. "I'm sure a lot of it was my fault. When he lashed out at me, I taunted him. Usually that resulted in a fight, and he was always bigger, of course."

"Do you mind if I ask what happened to his arm?" asked Lettie.

He looked back at her and then at Larry. Maybe it would be a relief to get the guilt in the open. "No, I'm glad you asked. I've never told anyone in Leadville about this, but Zeb may spread it around town, and I'd rather you heard it from me. There was an accident, a fire. He blames me for it." Thad stopped, reluctant to let the angry, painful tableau play before his eyes again.

Lettie reached up and touched his hand for a second. "You don't have to go on," she said.

"No, I want you to know. This was shortly before I came here. We had a boathouse in Savannah. One day I had our skiff up on the lift, removing the paint from the bottom of it. Maybe I did something to cause a spark. I don't know, but suddenly the boathouse was on fire."

Lettie drew in her breath and put a hand over her mouth. "You were in the fire, too?"

Thad saw the orange flames rushing toward him, reflected in the shadowy water. "It spread so fast, the door was blocked almost instantly. I panicked, shoved at the boat, and the ropes let go. I think they were already burning. The boat skewed across the walkways and stuck there, above the water. I ran to the open end of the boathouse, dove into the water and swam for help."

"Was Zeb helping with the boat?" asked Larry.

"No, I didn't even know he was there. But when the boat rammed the walkway, it broke his right arm and pinned it against the burning wood. I don't know whether he was already in the water or the boat threw him off the walkway, but the water saved him from getting any more badly burned than he did. Either the walkway finally collapsed or he managed to pull free and get to open water."

He felt Lettie's hand in his, but the images did not disappear. He shut his eyes. The sounds crashed in. The roar of flames. Crackling wood. His own splashing in the water. And the harrowing voice that screamed his name.

"Thad . . ."

He let her hand go and turned away, his head low. He had to force the words out now. "I think I heard him scream. I'm not sure anymore. I must have heard him. Or he convinced me I did. Or I didn't hear him at all. I just don't know. But I swam away."

He heard her chair scrape the floor but hurried on before she could say anything.

"After the accident, he said he'd screamed my name and I had deliberately left him there." He faced her again. "I'm being very honest with you, Miss Corcoran. Everyone knew we didn't get along, and I guess people were ready to believe I'd finally hurt him. I might have been arrested if I hadn't left town." Thad took a deep breath. "I did my share of fighting with him before that, but I swear to you, I didn't know he was there. If I did leave him screaming, I accept my guilt. And I'll never raise a hand in anger again."

Juliet stood up and put both hands in his. "Thad, you will never have to convince me of that. I don't think you were capable of such spite even then."

"Me either," said Larry.

Thad's breath left his lungs as if he'd been struck. The dark fist lifted from his heart, and suddenly he knew this one minute of their faith in him would make the guilt bearable, even if the voice screamed at him forever. "Thank you," he said, choking. "Thank you both."

Larry turned away, saying, "I think you two . . . I'll just check something in the storeroom."

Thad and Lettie stood smiling into each other's eyes, hands joined.

"You're not guilty of anything," Lettie said.

Even as he let her faith in him wash through the dark places in his mind, Thad knew there was no use hiding the rest of the guilt. "I'd like to think so, but that's too simple. Looking back on it now, I know I created my own share of the bad blood. I could have tried harder. If I'd done better by him, maybe he'd have grown up differently. But I was too young and angry or too close to him to see that."

Lettie looked puzzled. "How could you have done better?"

"I could have made worse grades, something . . ."

"That's the grown Thad speaking. It's too much to expect of a child. And do you really think that would have made a difference?"

Thad shrugged and sighed.

"Maybe he's changed now," she said.

Thad tried to dispel his doubts, but the bitterness on Zeb's face when he'd first come in the store made it difficult. "I suppose there's always hope. He has been—well, if not exactly nice, at least better than before. But I wouldn't tell you he hated me if it weren't true. And I nearly matched his enmity before I left home. To be honest, I wish he hadn't come here, but I'm determined to get along with him now." Thad looked down at the hands in his. Perhaps there was worth in him if she thought

41

there was. "It means a lot that you believe in me," he said, keeping his head down because there was more feeling in his eyes than he dared show her.

"Thad . . ."

The doorbell startled them. Lettie jumped and sat down quickly at her machine. Thad moved away from the door that had hit him in the back.

Noah strode in and stopped, looking from one to the other and at Larry emerging again from the back of the store. For a moment no one said anything.

Noah finally boomed into the silence. "I seem to be interrupting something."

"We were just talking about . . . life back home," said Thad, backing away, annoyed. He returned to the register.

Noah stared at him and then at Lettie's face, flushed now from the neck up. "I see. Well, I found something in the hotel's lost-and-found that I think your brother might be able to use, Miss Corcoran." Holding out a sable hat with a fold-down flap for neck and ears, he stepped awkwardly toward Larry. "Here, Larry, I couldn't help noticing you don't have a proper hat for our climate. I hope this might help."

The red of Larry's cheeks spread to his whole face. He looked at the floor and then at Lettie.

She shook her head almost imperceptibly, as if to say, you don't have to accept it.

Larry had already put out his hand. "Thank you, Mr. Ralston. I'm sure it'll be a great help."

Clapping him on the shoulder so hard that Larry bumped into the table, Noah smiled and turned to Lettie. "Miss Corcoran, I'd like to order a suit from you. Something in light gray. Summer weight. What would you recommend?"

"A pin-striped serge is very much in fashion out East these days, Mr. Ralston. Perhaps Thad could order it for you."

Thad nodded, trying not to let his resentment show. He wanted to hold on to that bright, smiling moment, but Noah had dispelled it completely. Now Lettie's back was turned. He frowned, pressing the end of his pencil into the cleft in his chin so hard it slipped and hit the side of his nose.

Lettie's voice was barely audible, but he had no trouble hearing Noah say, "Fine, you can take my measurements now."

"Certainly. Larry, do you have the measuring . . . ?"

Old Marsh clanged into the store muttering, "Dumbest idea I ever did hear." He waggled his head and made his voice a whining falsetto. "Ice castle. Just as dumb now as it ever was. Might as well build a sand castle." He stumped to the counter and took a minute to scratch at his chin under the long gray beard. "Damn ticks. Ain't even supposed to be alive this time of year. Gimme some of that jerky and some of them cans o' beans."

"Watch your language, please, Marsh. There's a lady in the store." Thad backed away from the smell of the miner's old sweat, watching Lettie out of the corner of his eye, dreading her getting so close to Noah, touching him in his shirt. "How much jerky?"

Marsh looked back at the others and grinned at Thad. "Enough I don't gotta come down here at least a week."

At the window Larry stretched the tape around Noah's chest and Lettie jotted down the measurement.

Thad exhaled a breath he'd been holding unconsciously. He took several strips of jerky from the bin against the side wall, and as he turned back, he saw her look at Larry and then say something to Noah. Her face showed it was an awkward moment. Noah glanced over at Thad, his head high in superiority—or triumph.

The door clanged open again and Officer Woolsley marched up to the register, the billy club that hung from his waist batting his right thigh.

"Schuster's is out of hunting knives," he said. "You got any here?"

"Just a moment, Woolsley, I was waiting on Marsh," Thad said, wishing they would both leave and take Noah with them. "How many cans of beans, Marsh?"

Woolsley brushed at his blue uniform as if proximity to Marsh had soiled it, backed down the counter, and leaned his elbow against the glass, squinting at both Thad and Marsh with a hostile stare.

"Enough for a week, too," said Marsh. He sneered at Woolsley. "And some cheese and a couple of them pickles. An' take your time. I ain't in no hurry."

Thad smiled, hiding his face from Woolsley, but worked quickly, anxious to focus on the conversation at the front of the store. Lettie was smiling now at something Noah had said, but she was looking at Marsh.

Marsh paid for his things with less complaining than usual. "You hear about this dumb ice building they're touting?" He leaned on the counter with his back to Woolsley.

"What's so dumb about it?" asked Woolsley.

"It ain't never gonna work, that's what." Marsh kept his back to the policeman and answered as if Thad had asked the question. "They'll never get it built. Never did in all the times they talked about it before."

Woolsley moved up the counter and positioned himself several feet in front of Marsh, his hand on his billy club. "So what? This Mr. Senior who's promoting it is a real pistol. He's in with Mayor Nicholson and that Wood fellow, and Temple, too, and they've got a lot of backing."

"Seems to me he'd try to get the businessmen of Leadville behind it," said Noah from the front. "Nobody's even been by my hotel to see what I think. If you ask me, that's a poor way to do business, downright underhanded, and I won't support it. Most of the restaurant and store owners feel the same way. What about you, Thad?"

"No one's talked to me about it. Except Mrs. Eskitch." They all laughed.

"So what?" Woolsley demanded again, looking at Noah. "It's obvious you'd stand to gain from it anyway. They don't need to ask your opinion about that."

Marsh counted out coins, gathered up his purchases, and stumped to the door. "You just mark my words. They ain't gonna get it up. An' I'll tell 'em so, too. I'm gonna be at that meeting next Monday like everybody else." He banged out of the store.

Woolsley looked over knives without asking to examine one. "This ain't much of a selection, either, just like Schuster's. You store owners don't keep your stock up, you're going to fail, MacElwain. That Schuster's half out of business already." He glared at Thad before banging the door on his way out.

"Woolsley doesn't seem to like you much," said Noah.

Thad shrugged to kill the topic.

"Well, I've got to get on back," Noah said after a second, and then added loudly, "Good-bye, Juliet. I'll see you at eight o'clock."

"Thank you, Mr. Ralston."

"Noah, we settled on Noah."

"Noah," she repeated, looking down at her hands.

"Well, until eight, then." He smiled at her and left without looking at Thad again.

Relieved to see him go but anxious about the "eight o'clock," Thad watched him pass the window with a hollow feeling in his heart. Normally, Noah would have said, "Let's talk about that ice palace, Thad," or "Come on up to the hotel for a beer after work."

An uncomfortable silence pressed into the triangle of friends. Lettie looked up at Thad. "Why wouldn't Mr. Woolsley like you?" she asked.

"He came in once when I was just working in the store, before I bought it. He asked me a lot of questions about why I'd come here. He said there was just something about me, claimed he could always tell when people were hiding something."

"I don't like him at all," said Larry.

Lettie shook her head. "He's certainly unpleasant. It must be awful to have such a suspicious nature."

"He's also the town gossip. Well, one of them. He carries news around the town the way a flea carries disease from one dog to the next." Thad stopped and looked into her eyes with "eight o'clock" still pricking at his heart. He had no right to ask.

She smiled and went back to her sewing as he returned to the ledger.

"I'll have to iron your good shirt before we go to dinner with Mr. Ralston, Larry," she said.

Thad's heart thumped against his ribs. He pressed his pencil so hard against the ledger he broke the lead.

Lettie began whistling a new tune, but this time it sounded shrill to his ears.

Larry looked from one to the other and chimed in a minute later as he went back to his cutting.

CHAPTER 4

September 16, 1895

The people of Leadville filled the Tabor Opera House early, eager to hear the specifics about rumors that had swirled through the streets like dust devils in a warm breeze. Thad, Lettie, Larry, and Noah pressed in with the rest and searched for seats. In a few minutes there would be standing room only. Noah pushed forward a little to scan the round balcony, then worked his way back and pointed at a row toward the back, the only one that still had four seats together.

Thad held back to let Lettie enter the row first. Noah squeezed through a couple of the town's more colorful ladies, elbowed past Thad, and followed Lettie into the row. Thad stifled the impulse to grab at him, and then let Larry in next. Immediately he regretted it. He couldn't hear what Noah said to Lettie that made her laugh.

He sat down on the gold brocade of the chair and glanced at Larry, who had not acclimated as well as they'd hoped. His breathing was still labored and his cheeks remained feverish. Lettie had spoken of taking him back down to Denver, away from Leadville's altitude, but there was no money for another move, and Larry had begged for a few months to adjust to the mountains he already loved.

Thad turned his attention to the stage. The maroon velvet curtain with its long gold fringe was open. The stage was bare except for the cream-colored backdrop at the rear, a table where several men sat, and a podium.

Mayor Nicholson stepped to the podium and held his arms out for silence. "My fellow Lead-villains," he started. There was a titter of appreciative laughter. "I'm not going to belabor you with my usual rhetoric tonight." The audience clapped good-naturedly. A few of the older boys whistled. "I know you're all anxious to hear from Mr. Senior about the project that's been the talk of the town for the last several weeks. So without further ado, allow me to introduce Mr. Edwin W. Senior."

Edwin Senior, sandy-haired with a mustache over a square chin, rose to enthusiastic applause. He pulled at the vest that was buttoned almost to his shirt collar and addressed the audience from the front of the stage, ignoring the podium. "I see I don't have to explain why we're here. So let me just begin with a few facts." Mr. Senior paused. The last clapping, chatting and scraping of seats silenced. "People have built ice structures for years in Canada and some of our northern states, but we aren't going to grace them with the name *palace*. They're generally small, non-functional buildings. Ours, on the other hand, is going to be enormous, a credit to the natural beauty of our valley and to the ingenuity of Leadville's people." He waited out another round of applause. "It will house a fine restaurant, a dance hall, and a full-sized ice-skating rink. We're going to make it into an attraction that will bring us visitors from all over the United States."

"It ain't never gonna work!" The grating voice of Old Marsh pierced the silence of Senior's dramatic pause.

Every head turned in disapproval of his splash of cold water on the expectant enthusiasm. A few men hissed. Thad turned to look, but Marsh stood hidden among a group of old miners almost as disreputable as he.

"Old crank," commented someone in the front.

"Keep yer bad tobacco in yer own jaw and let us get on with

the meeting," yelled a miner near the door.

Edwin Senior raised his arm and the crowd fell silent again. "Let us hear from the gentleman in the rear," he said with a patronizing smile. "If there really is some reason why we shouldn't build a beautiful ice palace, we ought to find out about it before we start hauling in the ice. Can you tell us . . . sir . . . why you think 'it ain't gonna work'?"

Marsh stepped out from the ranks of the miners and leaned against one of the balcony support posts. " 'Cause even in the winter the sun's gonna melt it down, young fella. Anyone lives around here knows what kind of warm spells we get in the middle of the winter. Fifty degrees some days." He stuck his long scraggy beard out in triumph.

Mr. Senior nodded. "Well, you're right about that. And as it happens, I am aware of warm spells. I've been here since last February, and we've already taken the possibility into consideration. As you well know, the winter nighttime temperature is nearly always well below zero. We plan to spray our Palace every night so it'll refreeze, and if a really warm spell looks to damage it, we'll build a frame for hanging canvas to shade it. Does that answer your objection?"

With an expression of personal triumph, every head turned back to Old Marsh.

His voice a little less confident, Marsh shouted back, "Even if that'd work, who'd ever come to see it? What makes you think even them hoity-toits down in Denver will take the nine-hour train ride to see some building where it's just plain freezing inside?"

"My good sir," Senior said, his face a mask of contempt, "we already have all three railroads one hundred percent behind us. They're prepared to offer special rates to transcontinental passengers who break their trip in Leadville, and discounts to groups of twenty or more. We're planning contests of all kinds—

dancing, skating, sledding, curling. We also plan to present special days for interest groups such as the German *Turnverein* down in Denver, the Freemasons, and so on." He gestured with his palms up, rendering Marsh's comments insignificant, and turned his attention to the rest of the audience. "You must understand, this is not some little igloo we're planning. It's going to be the most beautiful structure you've ever seen. People will hear about it all over the world." He let that sink in.

"But that isn't the most important thing. What matters most is what the ice palace will do for us. It'll put the town back on its feet. We're planning to use only local labor for the construction, creating hundreds of jobs."

Even the miners at the back applauded this time.

"Our visitors will demand housing, fine food, souvenirs. Those of you who are hotel, restaurant, or store owners will benefit."

The more well-dressed men clapped politely.

"They'll be interested in sleigh rides, mine tours, and things that your imagination can still create. Not only that, we plan to build our ice palace with a solid substructure that will last for years. Every winter, all we'll have to do is cover it with ice again, and we'll have a winter festival that will ensure us of good income for the foreseeable future." He raised his arms wide and then put his hands together as if he were cupping something magical and fragile. "Ladies and gentlemen, not only will it sparkle during the day like a diamond in the sky, it'll be lit with colored electric lights at night, like a frozen fireworks display!" His arms flew out again to imitate a rocket.

The women in the theater oohed just before the rush of applause.

"The Diamond in the Sky!" repeated Larry.

Thad looked at his rapt face and then past him at Noah, who was gazing pensively at Senior. Lettie looked back at Thad, smiling in excitement.

The meeting gave Mr. Senior its overwhelming approval to draw up a plan for the palace, find a site for it, and form an executive committee to begin work.

Thad, Lettie, and Larry said goodnight to Noah at Seventh and headed toward Mrs. Eskitch's. Zeb caught up to them before they reached Poplar.

"Well, brother, what do you think of this ice palace idea?" he asked without greeting any of them.

"Zeb, you remember Miss Corcoran and her brother."

They exchanged greetings awkwardly and Zeb repeated his question.

"I don't know," said Thad. "It's a very expensive proposition, and no one said where the money was to come from. Besides, it's the middle of September. A thing like that would take time to build. Months. I can't imagine they'd get it done in time to take advantage of the winter weather." He took Lettie's arm to cross the street.

"Just like you," said Zeb. "You never could take a dare."

"I loved the idea," said Lettie. "Just imagine. It'd look like a house made of crystals."

"Me, too," said Larry. "I wish I were strong enough to work on it myself."

"See," Zeb sneered. "The only ones stupid enough to be against it are you and that smelly old knockabout."

Thad shrugged to hide his embarrassment. They rounded the corner onto Hemlock. "Well, if nothing else, it'd make the winter something besides the dead time up here. None of you have ever been in Leadville in the winter before. It can be pretty dull by mid-February."

"I think you should invest in it," said Zeb.

Thad turned to him in surprise. "Invest in it? I hadn't even thought about that."

"Well, you should. You could make a fortune."

Thad looked at Lettie. Her eyes widened, but she said nothing.

Thad stood at the tobacco counter the following morning, absently placing money in the compartments of his cash drawer. A thought nagged at him. Why would Zeb wish him a fortune? It wasn't like him at all. The few times he'd come in the store to demand money, he'd seemed cold, if not quite as bitter and angry as before. He'd always been one to use, not to help. Perhaps that was it: more money for Zeb if Thad made a fortune.

Whatever the reason, he was right. The promoters would have to find investors for the palace. If the winter carnival was a success, they would make a great deal of money. Lettie's warm smile wavered before him. She was seeing Noah often. *Still,* Thad thought, *she seems to prefer me, somehow. At least I think so. But then there's Larry, and Noah can certainly offer her more help for him than I can.* Suddenly Thad realized the magnitude of the truth he had hit upon: that Lettie would have no choice but to marry someone who could pay Larry's medical bills. And that was Noah.

God, no, he thought, wadding the one-dollar bills in his hand and shoving them into the slot for the fives. *I can't let that happen. I have to get more money. The Ice Palace. I* could *invest. I could also lose my money. I have one chance in three,* he mused. *If I don't invest in the ice palace and keep the $400 I've saved, I have next to nothing to offer her. I dare not even ask for her hand. If I invest in the ice palace and lose the $400, I lose her. If I invest and make enough to compete with Noah, I have a chance.*

I wonder if Noah's going to put any money in it. He doesn't seem to trust that Senior.

Lettie walked past the window, looking across at the peaks,

where the first light snow lay like a dusting of sugar. She passed the door, caught herself, then backed into the store. "Look at the mountains, Thad," she said over her shoulder. "The aspens have turned to gold almost overnight."

Thad laughed. He joined her at the door and suppressed the desire to place his hands on her shoulders. "We don't have the most subtle of autumns, but it's one of the most spectacular. I'm glad we've finally gotten a sunny day. It's been such a rainy September."

"Has it?" asked Lettie.

"For this area, it has. You know, the aspens should be at their peak by Sunday. Why don't we take a ride out of town to see them if the weather cooperates? Larry, too, of course. We could rent a carriage and ask Mrs. Eskitch to make us a picnic."

"I'd love to. Speaking of Mrs. Eskitch, she catch you on your way out this morning and bend your ear about the toboggan slide?"

"What toboggan slide?"

"It seems she and Mrs. Kelly stayed longer at the opera house last night and heard the promoters talking about one they're planning to go with the palace. I can't wait to see all this."

The following Sunday Thad drove Lettie and Larry along the banks of the Arkansas to the one place where the tracked road forded the shallow river. In the warm air, scoured clean by a southerly breeze, they had all removed their jackets to bask in the glorious sunlight that poured out of a sky so blue it was nearly black.

Thad reined the horse at the foot of Mount Massive and helped Lettie out of the carriage. Larry leaned back in the seat and breathed deeply. He coughed but smiled.

"Oh, Thad," Lettie said, spinning slowly in the sun. "Just smell the air up here. It's like . . . like crystal gone to vapor."

"I know. I love to come here, if for no other reason than to get upwind of Leadville. Usually the wind blows all the smoke and dust of the mills right into town." He turned to the direction of the wind. "Does the lungs good, doesn't it, Larry?"

"More than that. It makes me feel . . . clean inside or something."

"This is where we ought to be living," said Lettie. "We didn't realize when our uncle told us about Leadville how bad the air smelled. Of course, he was here . . . when, Larry? Back in the late seventies, I suppose."

"Well, I don't think a bad smell ever killed anybody," said Larry. "And we couldn't get by this far from town. It'd be a long walk to Thad's store."

"Hmmm," said Lettie. "You're right. Thad, you'll just have to move the store up here."

Thad laughed. "I don't think the lodge pole pines will keep me in business long."

Larry lay down on the seat. "Listen, you two, go on and take a walk or something. I'd just like to lie here and soak up the sun. Leave me a piece of that chicken and I'll be fine."

Thad looked down at Lettie. She smiled and nodded.

"All right," he said, "let's walk up a way. There's a beautiful clearing about half a mile up the hill. Think you can make it that far?"

She looked up at the skirt of Mt. Massive. "I love the way you call this a hill. If I begin to gasp and turn blue . . ." She laughed and leaned against the wheel with her wrist across her forehead. ". . . you'll just have to turn the food out and carry me in the picnic basket."

Thad grinned, flexed his biceps, and looked doubtful. He took the picnic basket in his left hand and Lettie's arm in his right to help her over fallen logs in the aspen forest. In a few minutes his hand slid down into hers. He half expected her to pull it away, but she held tightly while trying to keep her skirt from snagging on broken branches.

His left fist tightened around the handle as he tried not to think of setting the basket down and putting both hands on her face, removing her hat, running his fingers through her dark-honey hair.

They reached the clearing, a small meadow of tall, tawny grass surrounded by the glowing yellow light of sun in the aspens. A breeze rippled the grass and sent the aspens into a tremulous whisper.

Lettie squeezed his hand and let it go. She walked into the trees and stood looking at the blue-black sky above the murmuring gold. She placed both hands on a slender, powdery white trunk and ran her fingers down a branch of gold leaves. She turned to him and stretched out her hand.

Thad moved to her and took her hand again.

"Please, don't say anything," she whispered, standing next to him. "I don't even want to breathe. I just want to take in the blue and gold and hear the trees ripple the silence."

Thad looked at her face in the glorious, golden light of autumn and knew he loved her beyond any capacity he had ever imagined. He moved behind her and put his hands around her waist. She placed her hands over his.

"I don't think I ever want to leave here," she whispered after a long while.

Be mine, he begged her silently.

CHAPTER 5

September 24, 1895

Thad ushered Lettie into a row in the middle of the opera house and waited for Larry to follow her. Instead, Larry moved aside, blocking Noah, and extended his hand for Thad to enter. Thad sat down and glanced to his left, expecting to find Noah glowering at him, but it was Larry who sat there, grinning at the sable hat Noah had given him. He hung it on his right kneecap. Three seats away from Lettie sat Noah, red of face. Smiling, Thad turned to help Lettie slip out of her thin blue traveling coat.

Noah leaned around the other men and asked, "You'll allow me to escort you home after the presentation, Juliet?"

"Thank you, Mr. Ralston . . . Noah. Of course, Thad and Larry will be going the same way, but you're welcome to join us if you like."

Noah smiled grimly and frowned at Thad and Larry before settling back in his seat.

"Are you warm enough, Lettie?" Thad asked, pleased that she'd stymied Noah's near-command, but vexed that he would join the group.

"Oh, yes, I'm too excited about all this to be cold. Isn't it going to be wonderful?"

Her excitement caught him up and propelled him into a dream of customers by the hundreds filling his cash register, making him—not rich, perhaps, but well enough off to . . .

The opera house quickly filled with the people of Leadville

and their air of confident anticipation. At the back, the more disreputable miners stood against the wall again. Two rows in front of Thad, Zeb was sitting with several of the State Street saloon owners and three women in gaudy frills. Zeb turned and grinned at him, then put his arm around the shoulder of a frizzy blond.

Thad looked away and focused on the stage. On its left stood an easel, the huge picture on it covered with blue satin cloth; to the right was a table with several stacks of papers. Mayor Nicholson, Edwin Senior, and several men Thad didn't know filed onto the stage and took their seats behind the table. An expectant hush fell over the room. Senior stood and stepped to the edge of the stage.

"Thank you for turning out again tonight, ladies and gentlemen. For those of you who weren't at the last meeting, I'm Edwin Senior, promoter of the project." After a moment's applause he put out his arms for silence and continued. "I know you're all anxious to see the design of Leadville's fabulous Ice Palace," he started, gesturing toward the easel. "But first, let me give you some idea of the size. We haven't settled on the outside dimensions yet, but in the center we're planning an ice skating rink one hundred fifty by two hundred feet. That's a surface of thirty thousand square feet."

The audience gasped.

"You already know of the planned restaurant and ballroom, so you can guess that the Ice Palace will have to be about three hundred by four hundred feet to encompass it all. It will require at least two hundred thousand board feet of lumber for a sturdy substructure and five thousand tons of ice for the walls. Leadville's own Coble and Kerr contractors have agreed to undertake the inner structure, and we have contacted Cole and McCordie Ice Company. They assure us they can make or cut at least two hundred tons a day from Turquoise Lake and the Twin Lakes and haul it up on sledges. With that said, let me introduce you to the Ice Palace. Mr. Temple, if you please."

Another man joined him and they moved the easel in front of the podium.

"Ladies and gentlemen, I present to you the most beautiful Ice Palace the world has ever seen!" Senior looked at the audience for another moment and then ripped the satin from the drawing with a flourish. Seats all over the auditorium squeaked as the audience bent forward to look at the floor plan.

"This will be the main entrance," Senior continued, pointing at the bottom of the plan with a wooden dowel. "On either side of it we have these two open octagonal towers with two doors leading into each. The towers will be about ninety feet high and forty feet in diameter, more than twice as wide as most of your houses, so that will give you some idea of the scale. In the ice walls we plan to display frozen Colorado flora and fauna and Colorado products, for which advertisements the manufacturers will pay a fee. This idea has caught the attention of our state's industries before we even start. We've already been approached by the Coors Brewing Company and Kuner Pickles."

He moved the dowel up the drawing, pointing out the features. "You can see the entrances to the restaurant, the ice rink, and the ballroom. All three will be lighted by beautiful chandeliers and electric lights frozen into the ice pillars."

The ladies in the audience oohed. Thad glanced at Lettie. She tore her gaze from the drawing and smiled back.

"All of the smaller round turrets at the corners and the two larger ones at the back end of the building will house displays like the ones at the front. And now for the sight you've all been waiting for." He lifted the floor plan from the easel and revealed the projected façade. The Palace was more beautiful than Camelot.

Women's hands flew to their throats. Men shook their heads

in amazement.

"We've settled on Norman architecture because it lends itself so well to construction with blocks. As visitors approach from Eighth, they will have the sun behind the Palace. It will sparkle like the castle of the king and queen of fairyland, like a real diamond in our blue sky. Note the many turrets and small spires. They will all have flags flying from them. At the front entrance we will have a statue of 'Lady Leadville' pointing toward the Mosquito Range, the first source of the city's wealth."

He and Mr. Temple moved the easel to the side again and he went to the podium. "Now, I know the first question on everyone's mind is how much all this is going to cost. We're figuring about twenty thousand dollars, but not taxpayers' money. Rather, we're going to create an open stock venture. My associate Mr. Temple and I have already raised two thousand dollars, and we have promises of twenty-five hundred more."

"Put me down for fifty dollars," yelled Roscoe Bardwell, the blacksmith.

A small chorus of other offers arose, and Mr. Temple scrambled to write names and amounts down.

Thad felt Lettie look at him and knew this was his best hope. He leaned forward to jump up and pledge his four hundred dollars.

Zeb turned completely around in his seat to look at him, his face full of challenge and derision.

Thad froze. Why was this so important to Zeb? Suddenly, he did not want Zeb to know how much money he had, or even that he was planning to invest it. And his distrust fed a tiny flame of fear at the bottom of his heart. He would almost certainly invest in the palace and hope not only for a good return, but for a huge increase in business during the carnival. But if he lost, he would have to close his store and leave.

Besides, Noah was withholding his support, and Noah was

shrewd. Thad turned to ask whether Noah had changed his mind, but a voice from among the saloonkeepers surrounding Zeb interrupted him.

"You ain't getting nothing from me. You ain't seen fit to include us in your scheme, so count us out."

Edwin Senior stepped to the edge of the stage. "I know I haven't been in your . . . establishments, gentlemen. I'm just not a drinking man."

"Now I know why I don't trust you!" yelled another voice, and the saloonkeepers guffawed loudly.

The rest of the crowd either laughed or hissed, but only three more men volunteered money.

Lettie was looking at him, but Thad couldn't bring himself to make the public gesture. Not now, not with Zeb staring at him. But soon . . .

Senior waited, obviously hoping the enthusiastic pledges would begin again. He glared at the saloonkeepers. "Well, let me get on to the next topic," he said. "We need at least five acres for the site. We've decided to build on Capitol Hill, on the bluff bounded by Seventh and Eighth and Spruce and Leiter."

"*What?* In a hog's eye you will!" screamed the raspy voice of Old Marsh from the very back of the room.

Mr. Temple flipped hurriedly through his papers and rushed to hand Mr. Senior a note. Mr. Senior looked at it for a second and then looked at Old Marsh.

"Would you be Mr. Lemuel Marshall, sir?"

"I would, and you know it damn well, Mr. Edwin Senior, sir," answered Marsh in a sarcastic imitation of Senior.

"I see. I've been advised by the city that you own lots eleven, twelve, thirteen and fourteen of that plat. Be assured, sir, that the city will compensate you for the use of the land."

"I ain't interested in being compensated. You just find some other place for your crazy project."

"Mr. Marshall, we've tried to approach you about this but were unable to find you. We realize what this land means to you, but we've looked at sites all over Leadville, and none other suits the construction like this one. It is high enough to be visible from all three rail lines, so that even those just passing through can see it shining in the sun. It enjoys spectacular views of the mountains east and west and lends itself ideally to the construction of a toboggan run from the top of Eighth Avenue, around the site, and down the hill on Leiter to Seventh."

"Well, none of that cuts any *ice* with me, if you get my drift," sneered Old Marsh. "It's my land and you'll build a damn ice house on it over my dead body."

With that he stomped out the back door, leaving the assembly in an uproar.

CHAPTER 6

September 25, 1895

Thad leaned over tiny threaded tags and tried to focus on pricing goods that had come in an hour before last night's meeting. It was no good. The meeting kept churning in his mind, along with Marsh's determination to stop the palace, and his own hesitation about the investment. He thrust his fingers into his hair and pulled hard in frustration. *I'm almost* sure it's a good investment, he thought. *But I'm entirely sure that if it isn't, I lose Lettie* and *the store.*

He forced himself back to his tags. He wrote something, then shook his head and stared at his work. He had just priced a tin bathtub at eighteen dollars when he should have written one dollar and eighty cents. Annoyed, he glanced over at Lettie and felt his mood soften. He watched her deft, purposeful movements. The buoyancy of her presence in his heart rose and curved his lips into a smile.

The treadle of her sewing machine stopped its clickety rhythm. She hunched over and rubbed both ankles briskly under her skirt, her blue crocheted shawl falling loose at her sides. She straightened up and looked out the window, rubbing her hands together and then pressing them under her armpits.

Outside, a freezing mist was slowly glazing electric wires and the north sides of street signs and hitching posts. Even the Silver Dollar Saloon across the street, ghostly since opening time, had disappeared altogether.

"Does it always get like this so early in the year?" she asked. "It's not even October yet." She rubbed her ankles again.

"Oh, Lettie, I'm so sorry. I didn't even think about how cold it must be there by the window. Let me see what I can do."

"I'm afraid the cold sinks right to my feet," she said.

Thad threw another shovelful of coal into the stove. He rummaged through the storeroom until he found the dented bed warmer that had never sold, a covered copper dish on a long wooden handle. He lifted a few coals from the stove with a pair of long tongs, threw them in the warmer and laid it in front of her.

"We could improvise something better than this," he said. "What if we took a length of blanket wool, tacked it all around the sides of the machine and put the warmer under here?" He pointed to the open lid that served as worktable. "That would hold the heat of the warmer in. And we could tack some wool across the bottom half of the window. That might help your hands."

"That's a wonderful idea, but I can't let you use your merchandise to build me a tent."

"Don't worry. I have an old bolt that was here when I bought the store. It's too faded around the edges to sell now, anyway."

"Are you sure? Well, thank you, Thad, but I hate being such a bother to you."

He clamped his hands together to keep them to himself. "You are anything but a bother to me," he said, wishing he could add that he wanted to provide warmth for her lovely feet forever. "It's going to get a lot colder than this, Lettie, and we'd better get you prepared for it." He started to the storeroom again for the wool, but the jingling of the bell stopped him. The door slammed again quickly.

"Good morning, Juliet, morning, Thad." As usual, Noah's loud greeting seemed to echo about the store, eddying now with the cold air that rushed in with him. "I just came in to check on my suit. Has the material come in yet?" He stepped toward Lettie, the frozen mist on his mustache already dripping. He took out a handkerchief to wipe at it.

"Yes," said Thad, going to the worktable behind Lettie and holding up the new bolt of pin-striped serge to draw him away. "It came in yesterday's shipment."

Noah followed him but kept his eyes on Lettie. He fingered the fabric without interest.

"This *is* what you wanted, isn't it?" asked Thad, annoyed.

"What? Oh, it'll do."

"Look, I ordered it especially . . ." Thad stopped, realizing he was about to make a scene in front of Lettie. As soon as he stopped, he knew his bile had nothing to do with the fabric.

"I'm glad you came," said Lettie.

Noah gave Thad a gloating smile, puffed his chest out, and strode to the machine.

"I needed to ask you some questions," she continued. "Did you want a vest? A watch pocket? Piping around the lapels?"

"You just make it the way you're used to making suits out East and I'm sure it'll be splendid, Juliet."

The bell dinged and Mayor Nicholson and Edwin Senior hurried in, huffing with the cold.

"Good morning, Miss. Morning, Noah," said the mayor.

"What a morning," said Senior, stamping his feet on the old towel Thad had laid in front of the door to catch mud. He took off his fur hat and shook it, splattering the others with bits of ice. "Oh, I do beg your pardon," he said.

Nicholson tsked with his tongue and wiped at his face. He turned to Thad. "You're MacElwain, aren't you?"

"Yes."

"Nice store you have here," Nicholson continued, unbuttoning his gray overcoat and stuffing his gloves into the pockets. He glanced at the racks and shelves. "I've never been in before. 'Course, my wife does all the shopping." He cleared his throat. "MacElwain, we understand you're the nearest thing Old Marsh has to a friend around here."

Thad laughed. "That's stretching things to the breaking point. He comes in once a week or so and complains about my prices. I don't even know where his claim is."

"Well, nobody else seems to know him at all, except by his foul temper. We were wondering if you could help us influence him on this matter of his land, which we need for the Ice Palace. We've done everything in our power, short of condemning the land, and we don't want to do that if we can avoid it. He refuses to lease it for a reasonable amount. We offered to buy it outright, but he wants a better price than he'd have gotten when Leadville was booming. He insists prices will come back up and we're only robbing him of future value. Can you help us out?"

"I doubt that I have any sway over Marsh, Mr. Nicholson. He's . . ." Thad hesitated to voice his opinion of Marsh.

"Ornery as an old mule and crazy to boot," finished Noah.

"Can't you persuade him how much it would benefit the town, Mr. MacElwade?" asked Senior.

"MacElwain. Sir, if I know Old Marsh, he'll stick to his guns even if it means his own ruin. You heard him. 'Over my dead body,' he said. I expect he meant it."

The mayor and Senior looked at each other.

"Well, when he comes in again, perhaps you could have a word with him. The town would be very grateful," said the mayor. He looked hard at Thad a moment. "Nice store, as I said. Still, I imagine you could use the profit from the Ice Palace. Which of us couldn't use a few more customers?" He leaned toward Thad and lowered his voice. "Perhaps I'll tell my wife to shop here more often." Moving toward the door, he left the sentence trailing as almost a question. "Thank you for your time," he added, closing the door quickly behind him.

Thad stared as he passed the window, heading toward City Hall.

Senior turned to Thad again at the door. "You're two of our established businessmen, Mr. MacElwain, Mr. Ralston. Were you planning to invest in the Ice Palace?"

"No," said Noah.

Thad glanced at him, almost certain he would invest, but reluctant to say so in front of Noah. "I'll have to let you know."

Senior looked darkly at Noah but turned to Thad and said, "You really should think it over, MacElwain. It's a sound investment and promises a fine return. And if you see Marshall again, please do what you can."

When they were gone, Thad asked Noah, "What do you have against the investment?"

"I just don't trust that Senior, somehow. He's never asked me for support, and he hasn't approached the Leadville banks. He doesn't even have an account here. Does all his banking in Salt Lake."

"That doesn't necessarily mean he's dishonest."

"No, but why should I risk anything on this venture? If it's a success, I stand to gain enormously. The beginning of the toboggan run is practically at the entrance to the hotel, and the main entrance to the Ice Palace itself is only two blocks away. If the whole thing fails, I'm no worse off than I am now. If it succeeds, I profit with no risk. I would think the same holds for you."

"Perhaps," said Thad, thinking that if he made a small fortune on the Ice Palace with investment *and* increased business while Noah didn't, Lettie would have no reason to turn to Noah.

Noah looked at the fabric again and out at the bleak fog. "I guess I can wear the suit next year. Well, I've got to get back." He bent to kiss Lettie's hand.

Lettie backed away, blushing.

Noah straightened, bowed elaborately, placed his left hand over his heart, and then described a broad arc with it. "Good-bye, fair Juliet, until tomorrow," he said, even louder than usual. "Order in a good supply of ice skates, Thad," he said as the door closed.

"Already done," Thad called back through clenched teeth.

Lettie watched Noah pass the window and then smiled up at Thad.

"Right," he said, forcing himself to relax and smiling back. "I was on my way to get the wool."

To reach the bolt he wanted, he had to shut the door in the narrow storeroom and stand on a can of kerosene. He pulled at the gray wool. The fabric snagged on the bottom of Lettie's sewing machine crate, which Thad had lifted to the top to get it out of the way, although it was almost too big for the shelf and prevented the door from opening completely. The crate slid forward and teetered on the edge. He shoved it back a bit and left the storeroom.

They worked together to tack the blanket material to the sewing machine. "Why didn't Larry come in today?" asked Thad.

"He was more feverish than usual. I think it's the fog. Makes the air damper. So I left him reading one of those awful novels Mrs. Eskitch has in the parlor. I'll take him something from the lending library on the way home." After a pause and a deep breath, she said, "He thinks very highly of you, you know." She had her back to him, leaning over the other side of the machine, but Thad saw her left cheek go red.

"Did he say that? I'm glad. I'm fond of him, too. He's more like a brother to me than Zeb. I envy you, having a brother like him."

"In a way, he's all I really have. I was six when Mother died, and Larry was two, so I've always been the nearest thing he had to a mother." She turned to face him. Her eyes were very serious. "He's important to me, Thad."

"I see that. And I'm glad you have him." He could not visualize Lettie at all without Larry. The knowledge that Lettie would have to marry a man who could pay Larry's bills hit him again. It was a minute before he could speak. "May I ask why your sister didn't take on the role of mother? Isn't she older?"

"Duffy and Mona are a lot older. My father married a second time after their mother died. When we were growing up, Duffy was away at sea most of the time, like Daddy, and Mona was busy studying and then teaching school by the time our mother died. So when I wasn't in school, I took care of Larry."

Thad tried to picture the small Lettie herding the toddler Larry off to bed, but the grown Lettie walked past in his imagination, herding their own children off to bed. The thought made him reel. He swallowed hard and smiled, saying, "He's so fortunate to have you."

Lettie let go of the wool and looked at him. "Please, don't put me on a pedestal, Thad. It's my fault his health got so much worse."

"How can you even think that?"

"Because I know it's true. I should have brought him away from the coast sooner. But I was afraid to leave home, and Larry didn't want to come. Now I think I should take him out of this altitude. We've talked about it, but he insists he feels better than he looks. He loves it here and refuses to leave. You see? I'm just too weak when it comes to making difficult decisions."

"We all are, Lettie, believe me," he said, thinking of his own dilemma. "Anyway, most girls I've known would have come to resent the person they had to take care of."

"You know Larry. Could you ever resent him? He's had that sunny smile since the day he was born. It's not as if he grew up selfish or grasping."

"No, he certainly didn't. As I said, I'm fond of him, too. Of you both." He took her hand for a second. She squeezed, and then they both realized there was a tack between their palms. They laughed.

Thad opened his hand, took the tack, and then put both hands over hers. "You're still cold," he said, massaging her fingers, pulling her hand toward his mouth against his will.

"Better than I was." She reddened and pulled her hand away.

Confused, Thad went back to tacking the blanket. "Didn't you want to stay with Larry if he was ailing today?"

"He has days like this from time to time, and he refuses to let me make a fuss. He hates being weak and needing help."

"I know. Some days I can see it's difficult for him even to sit behind the register, but he never says a word. I admire his . . . what?"

"My father called it stoicism."

Lettie sat down again with the bed warmer housed under the machine. "Oh, this is wonderful. Thank you so much, Thad."

Thad went back to his new merchandise. In a minute he glanced up again. She was looking at him.

"Thad," she said, "I know it's none of my affair, but are you really thinking of investing in the Ice Palace?"

"I'm sure I will if they get all the problems solved. I haven't much, and I could lose that, but I'd like to have more to offer . . ."

Lettie waited. "I see," she said finally, turning back to the machine. In a few minutes she was whistling one of the lovely melodies her grandmother had taught her.

Thad let the sweet sound wash through him. It was like the lilt of her presence in his heart, and he could no longer imagine life without her. Did she understand how he felt? Why did she sometimes respond to him, sometimes draw away? *Now,* he thought, *say it. Say you'll give her the help she needs, say you love her. Noah would shout it without hesitation. Noah could afford to. Damn it.*

CHAPTER 7

September 28, 1895

Through a good stream of customers responding to the sale sign he'd put out on the boardwalk, Thad had been watching Lettie's back all day. She'd been with Noah last night and hadn't said three words to him since. Between customers there'd been no whistling or singing. Only Larry, nearly invisible in a corner behind the register, had chatted off and on in a forced way, trying to ease the tension with trivia.

Thad had rung up the slightly rusted snow shovel for Old Mr. Paxton, wondering where Lettie had spent the evening. What had Noah done to make her so withdrawn, he'd asked himself as he handed Mrs. Lambert the last four flower-printed sugar sacks and slipped a lemon drop to her son Ralphie. Watching his own hands wrap a dill pickle for Mrs. Marechal, he'd seen Noah's large, determined hand on Lettie's slender arm, guiding her into his apartment, taking her hat, helping her unbutton her blue coat.

The thought of what might have happened next stopped the whisking motion of knife blade against sharpener. He watched her tense back and neck against the evening light, but they gave no clue as to what was wrong. She shivered and pulled the blue shawl over her thin white blouse. He laid the knife on the block, pulled the light chain, and poured a few more lumps of coal into the stove, keeping his gaze on her.

The coals scraped down the spout of the scuttle and thudded

into the fire. She did not turn to look.

Still watching her, Thad went back to the cheese knife, barely listening to Larry's tales of life in Maryland. Withdrawn, Lettie sat staring out at the early snow that had turned Harrison Street to slush. She'd done little sewing since morning, although she had several orders for the gold and gray uniforms of the ice-skating team.

Thad had left her to her own thoughts, a churning fear in the pit of his stomach, and anger—with his own cowardice as much as the present tension. He'd tried several times in the last few days to say how he felt about her, but always the old black fist of guilt opened to show him his worthlessness still lying in its palm, no matter how much faith she had in him. And when he'd been able to shove the fist aside, he'd realized his love was too important to risk revealing. Once it was out in the open, there'd be no turning back, and if she said she couldn't return his feelings . . . He'd lost his nerve each time, fearing she'd say she could no longer work in his store if he felt that way. Perhaps she'd even move from the boarding house.

". . . so after our father decided he just couldn't give up the sea," Larry was saying, "we settled in Baltimore and all of us learned to sail on Chesapeake Bay. Of course, that was before he died. You should see the Chesapeake someday, Thad, it's really . . ." He stopped.

Thad noticed the sudden silence in mid-sentence and turned to look at him, wondering whether Larry had asked him a question. Out of the corner of his eye he saw Lettie turn, too.

Larry smiled, looking at Lettie and then Thad. "I'm sorry, you two, but somebody has to bring this up or you'll have to hack us a path out of the tension with that knife you almost sharpened down to nothing, Thad." He took a deep breath and asked, "How was your dinner with Noah, Lettie?"

"It was a lovely meal," she said and turned back to the

machine. Then in a voice barely audible, she added, "He stated his intentions."

Thad felt a vise choke his throat and constrict his heart. He stabbed the long knife into the chopping block at an angle, snapping off the tip. The angry thud and the clatter of the knife as it bounced to the floor prefaced a heavy silence. Finally, Lettie turned and looked at him, her face drawn. Thad could not tell whether he saw misery or apprehension in her eyes.

Larry stood up. "You know, the dampness has made me feel tired all day. I think I'll go on back to the house if no one minds."

Thad and Lettie remained frozen, staring at each other.

Larry put on his coat and Noah's sable hat and slipped quietly out the back.

"Forgive me for asking, but what did you answer to his 'intentions'?" Thad asked when he could control the fear in his voice.

Lettie turned back to the sewing machine. It was a long time before she responded. She spoke almost into her lap. "I said he wasn't the one I love."

Thad stepped slowly around the tobacco counter and the rack of shirts, watching her hunched, tense back. He knelt at her side and placed his hand on her arm. "Does that mean you care for me? Please, Lettie, say you do."

She curled further into herself and nodded. A tear fell onto her clamped hands.

Thad's breath left his chest in a rush of relief. He slid his arm around her shoulder, rested his head on her fine hair, and spoke into her ear. "I love you, Lettie, I've loved you since I watched you in the gold light of the aspen trees, even since I saw you carrying Larry's valise up the hill. I want nothing in the world but to be with you, to take care of you for the rest of my life."

She turned to him. "Oh, Thad," the words tumbled out

between sobs, "I didn't think you cared for me, at least not that way. I've been so miserable except when I'm with you."

"Lettie . . ." Elation surged through him.

"I've come to love you for your kindness and your honesty," she said. "I only feel at home here in the store with you, as if you're already part of me. I never want to be without you." She put her hands to his face. Still the tears flowed.

Thad dabbed them away with his handkerchief.

Lettie smiled thinly and caressed his cheeks. "I don't want to marry Noah. Of course, he's a kind man, I'm sure. It's just that somehow there's too much of him. He always makes me feel a little squashed."

Thad laughed at her description. "Me, too." And then he was laughing at the fears that had plagued him. She loved him, not Noah. A wave of emotion swept his breath away. "Oh, Lettie, you have no idea how many times I've tried to say I love you." He moved his hand over the top of her hair and down her cheek, barely touching her. He took a deep breath. "Will you be my wife?"

Lettie pressed his hand to her face, and the tears welled again. "I can't marry you, Thad. I think you know that. That's why I've tried not to lead you on."

Thad felt his heart stop, even though he'd always known the truth. Now it was out, definite, no longer deniable, a black void in place of a future. He turned away, taking his hand from her face. She caught it tightly with both of hers, moved it to her lap, and rocked back and forth, as if to ease its pain.

"I would, Thad, I would marry you this minute, if only . . ."

"It's Larry, isn't it?" he asked, kneeling at her side.

"Of course. I may have to marry Noah for his sake. You can see he's not getting better, even with the powders and vapors Dr. Loomis gives him. And I haven't told you this: we received a letter from Duffy yesterday, and a newspaper clipping about a

German doctor who might be able to cure consumption with . . . what did he call it? Tuberculine or something. I don't even know whether we can get it in this country, but it's sure to be expensive." She reached into a pocket in her skirt and laid a clipping on the end of the machine.

Thad reached for it.

"Wait, you can read the article later. That's not all I have to tell you." Lettie took a deep breath. "Duffy said Mona has the consumption now, too. She's not married, so he has to help with her medical expenses and will only be able to give us half of what he's been sending. If the tailoring weren't picking up now with all the uniforms, I don't know what I'd do."

"Can you give me some time, my love? If I invest everything in the Ice Palace and make enough money to help, will you marry me?"

"Of course I will. I just don't know how long I dare wait. I love Larry. I'm responsible for him. I don't want him to . . ." Her throat caught and she closed her eyes. "I don't want him to die." Tears wet her lashes and flowed down her cheeks. "But I love you, too, and I want so much to be your wife." She put both hands to her face. "Oh, Thad, I can't put you in such a position. You could lose everything, and it makes me sound . . ."

"It makes you sound like an angel willing to sacrifice her happiness to the health of her brother, and I love you the more for it. I certainly don't know anyone else who'd give up everything for a brother. I can't imagine myself doing that for Zeb."

"I wouldn't for Zeb either, forgive me for saying so. But with Larry it's different."

Thad leaned his forehead against her shoulder. "Ah, Lettie, I've learned so much from you, from your generosity of heart. All I can do is try to match it." Noah's triumphant smirk appeared against the blue wool of her shawl, and then Larry's cheerful, feverish smile. Thad clenched his jaw and swallowed hard. "I promise you, if you have to marry Noah, I'll live with it somehow, even if I have to leave Leadville, but I'll never stop loving you. As for the money—if I lose you, I've lost everything, no matter how much money I have."

She lifted his head, slid off the chair, and knelt with her head against his heart. Their arms folded around each other.

"I want you so much, Lettie. I want to kiss every inch of you and tell every cell in your body I love it."

She looked up at him, her eyes wide.

Thad realized what he'd just said. "I beg your pardon. That was a shocking thing to say."

She smiled and blushed. "Do you think I haven't had shocking thoughts about you?"

He bit his lips to stop himself from kissing her right in front of the window. His hands ached behind her back with the desire to touch the skin beneath the blouse, to feel it slide under his fingers. In his frustration he took both her hands and kissed the fingertips, the palms, the wrists. She pulled her hands away and her arms encircled his chest. She was fragile next to him, warm and breathless. He could feel so much of her through all their layers of clothing. He kissed her then, and felt her merge into him completely.

Lettie moaned faintly and lowered her head. "I never knew . . . oh, Thad, I want . . ." She shook her head and pulled away. They both glanced at the big window. Two horses struggled to pull a cargo wagon up Harrison through the deepening slush, but the driver kept his eyes forward.

Thad shuddered and let her go. "If I don't stop . . ."

She put her finger on his lips. "I know." She ran her fingers under his mustache then over the hairs and out to the ends. Smiling, she twirled them. "I've always wanted to do that. And that's the least of it," she said, blushing again. She placed her finger for the shortest moment into the cleft in his chin before standing up. "I think I'd better go back to the house. I must look such a sight that anyone coming in would think the very worst. It's getting too dark to work now, anyway."

"Much as I don't want to let you go, I think you're right. At least about the darkness." He stroked her face. "I love you, Lettie. I'll make this work somehow."

She placed her hand on his and held it with her head tilted into it. "I love you, Thad."

Old Marsh banged the door open.

Jolted from their private flood of emotion, they both jumped.

Marsh stomped to the counter and slapped an envelope onto the glass. "Lookit that," he screeched at them. "They condemned my property and took it over 'for the public good.' They railroaded my rights and stole what belonged to me. Go on, read it. I ain't gonna let 'em get away with this." He paced from one end of the counter to the other, growling and slapping his old felt hat against the glass.

Thad slipped the letter from the torn envelope. He and Lettie read it together.

Thad shook his head and tried to hide his elation that the Palace was going forward. "It's too bad, really, Marsh, but there isn't anything you can do about it now. Your compensation seems fair enough."

"You think I care about 'compensation'?" he shouted, banging on the counter with each syllable of the last word.

"Leadville needs this, Marsh," said Thad. "You know yourself what a slump we'd been in until Senior came up with the ice palace idea. We all have a lot riding on it."

"Couldn't you just see it as something you've done to help the city?" asked Lettie.

"I wouldn't give one hair of a mule's tail for this city. What's it ever done for me anyway except shun me and take what I own? I mighta sold the land to 'em if they'd'a offered me a decent price. But no, they couldn't wait, hadda shove me aside again."

Thad held the letter toward him. "Well, as I said, there's nothing you can do. I'm afraid the city has the legal right to condemn property. Don't try to block this, Marsh. It could go badly for you."

"Don't you threaten me!" Marsh reached for the letter but dropped his hand on the counter before taking it. His eyes narrowed. "Here I thought you was one of the good ones around Leadville. You gone and put money in this thing, ain't you?"

Thad hesitated.

"Or you're gonna," growled Marsh. "You go ahead and do that, Mr. Fancy Storekeeper. I'll block this thing, all right. You wait and see." He snatched the letter and envelope out of Thad's hand and banged out again.

Lettie put her hand on Thad's arm. "Do you think he can really stop the Ice Palace?" she asked. "Oh, Thad, this means everything to us."

Thad hid his fear from her. "No, there's no way to do it. He just has to bluster about it. The best thing for him to do would be to take the money and leave town. He hates everybody here, anyway. Why should he stay?"

"He's a sad old man, isn't he?"

"He is, but most of his problems come from his own cantankerous nature. I can't say I feel sorry for him."

"Where do you suppose he lives?"

"Somewhere up on the Mosquito Range, they say, in a shack by his claim."

"I hope he does leave," she said. "He frightens me."

"Don't worry. There's really nothing he can do. I'll see you at the house," he said, kissing her on the forehead. When he'd let her out the back door, he retrieved the newspaper clipping and took it under the electric light to read it.

Robert Koch, a German doctor, had isolated the bacterium that caused consumption, which he was now calling *Tuberculose*. He had developed a serum which he hoped was a cure for the disease, but it was experimental.

Thad's heart sank. Medical experiments were slow, even when they worked. This new drug might take too long for Larry. There had to be doctors at the hospital down in Denver who knew more about this. He would take Lettie and Larry there as soon as he had a little more money. If only Larry could hold on for a couple of months. Clutching hope but fighting a wave of desperation, he put the article in his pocket and began closing out his register.

In a few minutes Zeb came in trailing slushy footprints. The snow on his hat, shoulders, and leather mailbag melted and dripped to the floor. He hoisted the strap of the mailbag over his head and dropped it with a grunt. "Damn, that stupid thing drags on my shoulder. Well, loving brother, how's business?"

The biting tone lurched through Thad's stomach, adding bitterness to his desperation. He tried to hold on to the sweet fullness of Lettie's love. "It's picking up a little." He closed the register drawer again.

"That's good to hear. I need to borrow a few dollars."

"Zeb, you're getting a decent salary. Your room at McGuire's can't cost all that much." Thad rested his forearm on the ledge of the cash drawer and leaned against the register. "And you haven't paid back a cent of the money I've already loaned you. What are you doing with it all?"

"That's none of your business, but I can tell you I don't live the same kind of dull, straightlaced life you do and never will. A man has to have some pleasures."

"If you can't tell me why you need the money, I can't lend you any more. There are other things . . ."

"Things named Corcoran?" Zeb's voice was suddenly honeyed and sarcastic. "You're that sweet on the pretty little thing with the sickly brother? Don't make me laugh. Everyone in town knows Ralston wants her, and he gets what he wants. She's his, brother, you can bet your last dollar on that."

"No!" The word leapt out like a slap. "Miss Corcoran wouldn't mar . . . doesn't want Noah's money."

"Oh, no? She wouldn't enjoy a new gown from time to time? A pretty ring? Well, maybe she'd want to feed and clothe the babies she'd make for you. You think you could offer her even that? With this paltry little country store?" Zeb looked about in the circle cast by the lamp. "Pathetic, that's what this is."

Zeb's judgment angered Thad, and he said before he could stop himself, "I'm going to invest . . ."

"In the Ice Palace? Well, it's about time. Good for you." Zeb took off his dripping fur hat in salute. "Congratulations! Little Miss Priss must be good for something after all, if she put a rod up your spine. I'll just have to see what I can do to push things along."

"Why would you want things to turn out well for me, Zeb? You never have before."

Zeb grinned and heaved the leather bag back onto his shoulder. "Never mind about the loan," he said on the way out.

Thad went out to bring in the sale sign he'd placed on the boardwalk. He watched Zeb enter the Silver Dollar. "For once, Zeb, you'd better keep out of my way," he said to his brother's back. Then he remembered his promise to get along better with him.

CHAPTER 8

October 1, 1895

Thad shed his overcoat, hung it on a wooden peg, and paced in the dark, paneled hall outside Edwin Senior's office. He sat down on the edge of the single chair under the row of pegs but immediately jumped up and paced again. His mind was still caught up in the dream he'd had last night, in which he was preparing to leap over a chasm with no security but a rope from the Crystal Palace Carnival Association. At the bottom lay disaster. On the other side stood Lettie, watching the rope with a hopeful smile, while Noah resolutely drew her away from the edge.

He patted the folded bills in the breast pocket of his good suit coat for the tenth time since he'd entered the hotel where Senior had his suite. He shifted them to the lower right pocket, where he could keep his hand on them. The flat lump reassured and frightened him at the same time: four one-hundred-dollar bills, three tens and a five. In his savings account only seventy-five dollars remained. He would need it if his profits didn't cover the cost of souvenirs for the tourists and the normal merchandise he had to keep in stock.

He leaned against the wall next to Senior's room. The voices on the other side of the door sounded tense, almost fearful. Occasionally he could make out a dollar figure, but the specifics of the conversation were lost on him. Finally he could stand it no longer. At his knock the discussion ceased.

"Come in," he heard.

Senior jumped up immediately when he saw Thad and came around the desk with his hand extended. "Ah, MacElwade," he said with a welcoming smile.

"MacElwain, sir."

"Of course. Have you met W. L. Temple, secretary of the Leadville Crystal Carnival Association?"

Thad shook hands with the tall, graying man.

"Ah, yes. You had an appointment, didn't you?" said Temple.

"Have we kept you waiting?" Senior asked, slapping his forehead with the heel of his hand. "I do apologize."

"No need to. Sir, it's about that investment . . ."

"Yes, indeed. Wonderful." Senior clapped him on the shoulder as they shook hands. "Glad you've decided to join our wise investors. Please, have a seat."

Thad stood, his hand around the money again.

"You don't have any doubts about the success of the Ice Palace, do you?" asked Senior.

"No, not exactly. It's just that this . . . well, to be honest, and I tell you this in strictest confidence, this represents all I've been able to save with the city in such a slump. It's my only ho—It's very important to me. I'd hate to lose it."

"Of course you would. Have a seat, have a seat, MacElwain."

Thad sat down opposite Senior and took in the promoter's sandy hair, watery blue eyes, thin mustache, and broad chin. He did not look away from the scrutiny, and Thad relaxed. The man seemed quite forthright.

Senior's voice became serious. "I assure you, sir, the Ice Palace, the Winter Carnival, the toboggan run, they're all going to be the greatest success. How could they be otherwise? There isn't another structure in the world to compare with our Palace. We have so much backing from all three railroads, which will be the arteries that bring the new life's blood to our town, that we can't fail."

"We've taken into account warm spells, excessive snow, truly every contingency," continued Temple, standing at Senior's side. "We need only a little more financial backing from Leadville's leading businessmen, such as yourself."

A question flashed through Thad's mind: was the general poverty in Leadville the one contingency they hadn't considered? "May I ask what kind of return one can expect on this investment?"

"Well, of course, that depends on the amount invested and the total success of the carnival. The more we have to spend on it, the more successful it will be. How much were you planning to put in?"

Thad tightened his fingers around the bills in his pocket. He swallowed. "Four hundred thirty-five dollars," he said, taking it out.

A look of disappointment passed between Senior and Temple.

"Assuming that the project is quite successful, I wouldn't be surprised if you doubled that by the end of the winter, but you understand, I can't guarantee such a high return," said Senior.

He couldn't have expected anything better than one hundred percent, but Thad looked down at his savings, disappointed. Eight hundred dollars couldn't compare to Noah's fortune. But then, Lettie loved him and would marry him if he could help Larry, not if he could outdo Noah's wealth. Her face, twisted in misery at the thought of marrying Noah, floated for a second before him. Her willingness to sacrifice everything shamed him. "All right," he said, shoving the folded bills across the desk.

Mr. Temple bent over the desk, filled in the stock certificate without moving the money, and signed his name on the left. He handed the paper to Thad.

"Er . . . don't you need to sign this, as well?" Thad asked Senior.

"Oh, no, I'm not on the executive committee. The president is Charles Limberg, whose signature is already on the paper. I'm merely the general manager," said Senior, coming around his desk again. He and Temple shook Thad's hand vigorously.

Senior walked him toward the door, his arm around Thad's shoulder. "This was a sound move for your financial future, MacElwain, and a grand gesture for the benefit of Leadville. You can be proud of what you've done today,"

Thad had hardly touched the doorknob when it turned in his hand and Mayor Nicholson shoved into the room. Thad glanced back at the money just as Temple swept it into the desk drawer. A tense look passed between Temple and Senior. Nicholson's face was lined with distress, as well.

Thad stepped into the hall and the door closed behind him. He reached for his coat and froze in motion. There was no mistaking the tone in the Nicholson's loud voice or the import of the conversation.

"It's going the way I feared, Senior. The local businessmen just don't want to do business with you. I've talked my way up and down the entire length of Harrison and gotten nowhere. Every time I step out of my office, there's a different unemployed miner asking when the jobs you promised are going to material-ize. Every week another mine is abandoned, another business closes, another family leaves town. We need to get this thing moving."

Senior said something in his softer voice that Thad couldn't hear.

Nicholson, more distraught than before, continued. "I hardly need remind you that winter is already upon us. If we don't have this thing in operation by Christmas, we'll have wasted our money, and more important, the money of the people who put their faith in us."

Thad put his ear to the door.

"The money will come in, Nicholson, I assure you. Why, Mr. MacElwain, whom you saw on your way in, just gave us a sizable investment. Isn't that right, Temple?"

"Yes, a goodly sum."

"The Winter Festival will go on as scheduled, I assure you," said Senior.

Thad picked up his stock certificate from the chair where he'd laid it and stared at it, looking for reassurance. There was none. He took a step back to the door, stopped, and shrugged into his coat. He folded the certificate and put it in his breast pocket where the money had been. Rather than replacing the wad, it seemed to gouge a hole in his chest.

CHAPTER 9

October 19, 1895

Thad was in the store earlier than the others. Under the electric light, he read his stock certificate again, an imposing paper edged in a blue geometric design. In exotic script arched across the top, he read, "The Leadville Crystal Carnival Associat'n." His certificate number, 87, appeared in a decorated box in the upper left corner, and on the right, 435 Shares. Under the arch was a half-tone picture of the proposed Palace.

"This is to certify," he continued, "that <u>Thaddeus MacElwain</u> is the owner of <u>Four hundred thirty-five</u> Shares of the denomination of <u>One dollar each</u> of full-paid, non-assessable Capitol Stock in The Leadville Crystal Carnival Association." The embossed gold corporate seal adorned the lower left corner, with Temple's almost vertical but gracefully looping signature next to it, and that of Limberg sloping hurriedly toward the right margin.

With a derisive puff of breath, Thad slapped the paper against his thigh, threw it on the glass, and kicked the drawer at the bottom of the tobacco counter. A fancy piece of paper wouldn't double his money, and nearly three weeks after he'd put up his savings, the Ice Palace site was still in its natural state. He'd been a fool. He would lose everything.

Every day his customers talked about the shortage of funds, about the almost complete lack of new investment since late September. The end of October was nearing; if they didn't begin construction immediately, they would never get the Palace open by Christmas.

The bell jangled loudly into his cloud of despair. The door banged into the notions counter and slammed shut. Noah stood leaning against it, breathing heavily, eyes hard and hostile. Neither man spoke for a moment.

"She put me off for days." Noah's voice grated through clenched jaws. "Half an hour ago she appeared in my office looking as if she hadn't slept in a week. I assume you know what she said."

Thad's heart skipped a beat, as if he'd been caught in some terrible moral wrong. "I'm sorry, Noah. I certainly never wanted to be the rival of my good friend, but Lettie and I love each other."

"Damn you, you should have bowed out, Thad. You know I want her."

"You *want* her. I love her."

Noah slammed his fist down on the top of the notions counter. "I can offer her more." He was shouting now.

"But she loves me," Thad shouted back triumphantly.

"You?" Noah looked at him as if he were a child. "She'll get over that soon enough once she's with me."

Thad felt his hackles rise, and blood rushed to his head. He started around the counter, but Noah's next sentence stopped him dead.

"I could send Larry to the best sanatorium."

Thad's head jerked back and he saw Lettie as she'd been when he'd made the promise, sitting at the machine, tears running onto both their hands intertwined on her lap. Noah had struck the one defenseless spot in their love. Despair took the place of his anger instantly. He clutched at the counter for support. "We know that." He gritted his teeth and balled both hands into fists at his sides. It cost him all his will to say, "If she has to choose you in the end . . ."

"How dare you? She will not 'have to choose' me. She'll *want* me . . ."

"Let me finish. If she *chooses* you in the end, Noah, I *will* bow out and try to live with it. I promised her that. And I promise you that. I hope you can do the same."

Noah strode to the counter and leaned over it with his eyes pinched into slits. "I told you before, bowing out is not in my nature. I'm not going to lose. Just how do you think you . . . ?" His eyes lit on the certificate and darkened with realization. "You put your money into it, didn't you?"

"Yes." Damn it all, Thad thought, checking his impulse to sweep the certificate onto the floor.

"You're going to lose it. I told you that man Senior couldn't be trusted. But it doesn't matter. I aim to have her. Regardless of what it takes. Do you understand?"

Mrs. Eskitch bustled in and crowded Noah at the counter, waggling the *Herald Democrat* in Thad's direction. "Have you seen this, Mr. Mac? I need about three handfuls of lentils, two spools of black thread . . ." She stopped short and glanced at Noah. "Good morning to you, too, Mr. Ralston."

"Seen what?" asked Thad, his eyes on Noah.

"The letter from that Mr. Senior. He's resigned right here," she said, punching at the first page with her mittened hand.

Thad's attention was riveted on her now.

"See this?" Mrs. Eskitch continued. "Right here, it says, 'Board of Dir . . . Crystal Pal . . .' mmmm, yes, here we are: 'Gentlemen: My attention having been drawn to the fact that you gentlemen believe there exists in Leadville today feeling against myself acting in the position of General Manager, by many who would contribute toward carrying the enterprise to a successful conclusion, and while I may differ with you gentlemen regarding the advisability or necessity of securing the support of those referred to, . . .' Well, I declare, I didn't understand a word of that . . . mmm, now where'd it go? I know Mrs. Kelly told me there was a part in here that wasn't all fuzz."

Mrs. Eskitch glanced to the bottom of the column, pulled her mitten off with her teeth, retrieved it with her left hand, and flipped several pages.

Thad kept his fists balled to keep from snatching the paper away from her. If Senior had resigned . . . He could feel Noah's eyes on him.

"Oh, yes, here we go. 'I would therefore respectfully submit for your consideration, should you decide it advisable, that I withdraw my subscription of one hundred dollars, and further pay me the sum of two hundred dollars in lieu of money I have personally expended, and services up to date. Respectfully, E. W. Senior.' I think that says he resigned. Doesn't it? Isn't that awful? Land's sakes, *three* hundred dollars. Such a lot of money. And he has such pretty blue eyes, don't you think? *I* always thought he had the best interests of Leadville at heart. I just don't understand why some people didn't like him. It says here that Tingley Wood is going to take over for him and that a lot more local people will be investing again. What do you think, Mr. Mac?"

"Only the fools," said Noah, more softly than he had ever spoken. He left with such quiet finality that even the bell hardly sounded.

"Well, I never." Mrs. Eskitch watched him pass the window. "Now who put such a bee in *his* bonnet?" She turned back to Thad. "I didn't want to say something of such a personal nature in front of Mr. Ralston, Mr. Mac. After all, he's nearly a stranger, but I need some of those denture plasters, too." Her face reddened.

Grief over the loss of his friend clouded his elation as Thad rang up Mrs. Eskitch's purchases. He saw her to the door as an excuse to look up Harrison after Noah. He had already disappeared, but his anger hung in the air.

A few minutes later Lettie and Larry let themselves in the back door.

"What's the matter?" asked Lettie while Larry hung their coats in the hall.

"Noah was just here. He was . . ." Thad looked down at her worried face and couldn't burden her with the words that really described Noah's attitude or his own fears. ". . . very determined."

"I see. Oh, Thad, I'm sorry." She put her head down. "I shouldn't have gone, but he's been so insistent. He was polite when I told him, but I could tell he was furious. I should have known he'd come." Her shoulders sagged and she spoke barely above a whisper. "I feel so badly about all this. I've made you lose your best friend, haven't I?"

"Never mind, my love," he whispered, and then said more loudly, "Senior has resigned, and Tingley Wood is taking over. It looks as if the money for the Palace will come in after all."

Her face glowed again and she mouthed, "I love you."

Larry came in and leaned against the counter for a moment, breathing with a rattle in his chest.

Thad listened to the rale as he carefully put the stock certificate back in the ledger. It *will* turn out all right, he thought. Now it has to.

CHAPTER 10

November 8, 1895

Hanging horizontal and low into the Arkansas Valley, clouds weighted the air with dampness that promised snow. They sapped the light of color and flattened it into a pre-dawn gray, though the time for sunrise had passed.

In spite of the dreary cold, most of the Leadville's populace lined the streets around the site of the Ice Palace, waiting for the first blasts of dynamite that would begin clearing and leveling the five acres. Construction was about to begin, without speech-making or ceremony.

Thad and Lettie stood in the crowd lining Spruce Street. Thad wore the sable hat he'd borrowed from Larry. Lettie had draped her blue shawl over her head and tucked it into the top of the warm black coat Thad had ordered for her. They allowed their shoulders to touch in the crowd.

Lettie shivered in spite of her clothing.

"You're cold," said Thad. "Why don't we go back?"

"Oh, no, Thad, that was just a vibration of hope. I can't wait to see this."

He nodded and smiled down at her, knowing what lay behind her anticipation. "All I can say is, 'Bless that Mr. Wood.' He's done us a great favor."

They turned their attention again to the three men who were setting the dynamite in the angled holes they'd dug under the stump of a magnificent blue spruce. The tree itself already lay in

91

the dirt, its branches arcing gracefully into its trunk, its tip pointing up Eighth.

Far behind them, at the top of Eighth Street, Old Marsh stood alone on his stumpy, bowed legs, his hands stuffed into the pockets of an ancient sheepskin coat, his head bare to the malevolent airs rising from his lots. The tip of his tree pointed mockingly at him. Bitterness reamed the wrinkles in his face and warped his lips into a frown of hatred.

Above Marsh, looking out of his top-story apartment, Noah waited as well, watching. The emptiness of his rooms drew in the gray of the day and pressed the frustration he wanted to vent back against his chest. He scanned the crowd and spotted the sable hat he'd pulled from the lost-and-found. He knew immediately the person wearing it must be Thad. Juliet stood next to him in the blue shawl she'd been wearing since the early fall. They were standing closer together than the crowd warranted. Noah's mood darkened. If Thad made a good profit from this thing . . .

A yell rose from the blast site, the workers ran, the onlookers put their hands to their ears, and the explosion rocked the entire city. A huge puff of smoke, mud, dirty snow, and fragments of sagebrush shot into the air and then sank again to a rousing cheer and thudding echoes from Mount Massive and the Mosquito range. The stump now stood on its side, its roots clawing at the air, matted with dirt and rocks.

Old Marsh closed his eyes and let the bile rise. "You won't do this to me. By hell, I'll stop you yet," he swore, and turned to leave without looking down the hill again.

★ ★ ★ ★ ★

Noah jumped as the crystal vase on the table behind him crashed to the floor in the blast, but he did not turn. A figure moved in the corner of his vision and he looked through the south window. He watched Old Marsh clomping toward Harrison. When he turned his attention back to the throng, he caught Juliet looking up at Thad. Noah was too far away to see whether she was smiling, but there was no mistaking the aura that surrounded them as they stood while the others moved away. A growl escaped his throat.

He turned, and his eyes fell on the tintype of Fiona in its silver frame. In spite of the coppery color of the picture, he could feel her blue eyes on him, reproaching him for his "overbearance." For the things he'd demanded of her after they were married and his temper when she protested. His anger exploded and he slapped the picture off the table. It flew past the smashed vase and crashed against the south wall. "Why don't you remember the good things?" he shouted at the face-down frame on the Persian carpet. "I loved you, in my way. You know that. But I wanted a son. And I *will have* the sons you failed to give me."

At the blast site, most of the crowd started back toward Seventh or Eighth, but Juliet took Thad's hand as he turned to go.

"Let's watch a minute more," she begged. "I just feel like it's all for us."

"I know. Like watching our hope take shape?"

"Yes, that's exactly what it's like. Nothing can stop the Ice Palace now, can it?"

"No, my love. I just hope Larry's health holds up for a few more months."

Together they moved a little closer to the lots. They stood

with their hands entwined and hidden between the folds of her skirt.

The workers began driving in mule teams to chain up the freed stump and drag it down the hill. When the stump was gone and the men were preparing to blast the next tree, Thad and Lettie headed down Spruce.

Larry had stayed behind to avoid the damp cold and to mind the store. On the streets a stream of happy people headed for the Palace site. The silence of the store, broken only by the ticking clock and the rasp of his chest, made him feel left out, pathetic. He sighed and sat in Lettie's sewing chair at the cold window, trying to feel he was a part of the excitement, until he began to shiver and cough. He started to throw more coal into the stove but found the scuttle empty. He picked it up, switched off the light to discourage customers from coming in for a few minutes, and went out to refill the scuttle from the coal bin in the storeroom.

He was moving a can of kerosene aside when the blast from Capitol Hill threw him off balance. He fell, knocking his forehead on the edge of the bin. The lid slammed down on the back of his head. He slid down the side of the bin and came to rest against sacks of ice-cream salt. He barely heard glass smashing in the store. A wave of black washed over him, and a bolt of maroon flannel rolled from the middle shelf across the bin, covering him like a tent.

Lettie's sewing machine crate teetered at the top of the shelving and settled back into its precarious balance.

Zeb ran out of the Silver Dollar Saloon with the barkeep when the blast went off. He started up Harrison and then noted the darkened store. He glanced up toward Eighth. The barkeep ran in the direction of the blast. Zeb hurried to the store, glanced about to be sure no one was looking, and slipped in.

"Thad?" he called softly. "Thad?" he said louder, stepping around the fallen shirt rack. He looked out again and sauntered over to the knife case before heading for the cash register. He started to punch the no-sale button with his left hand, then grimly lifted his right hand and shoved his fused index and middle fingers down on the key. He slipped three one-dollar bills from the drawer, glancing constantly at both doors. Sliding the money into his pocket, he relaxed, pushed the glass door aside, reached into the counter, and removed a pouch of tobacco and two packets of papers. The dull gleam of a brass knob caught his attention, and he noticed the drawer at the bottom. He slid it open, wincing at its creak. As he lifted the ledger a slip of paper fell to the floor. He held the stock certificate to the weak light from the window.

"Four hundred thirty-five," he muttered. "What a timid little Gracie. There's got to be more. Or maybe not." He turned the certificate over, as if to read some bank balance on the reverse. "It'd be just like him to sink it all in this blithering scheme." He smiled. Thad had played right into his hands. The doorbell jolted his thoughts.

Old Marsh banged in looking like an angry vulture.

"The store's closed," snapped Zeb.

Marsh glared at him for a second. "Then what're you doin' at the cash register? How much did you take outta there?"

"What do you want, old man?"

Marsh hesitated and then stuck his bearded chin out. "Kerosene. Matches."

Zeb looked at him sharply. "What for?"

Marsh put both forearms on the counter and leaned so far forward his face was only a foot away. "None o' your affair, you dandy young pup."

Zeb backed away. "You going to build a fire someplace?"

"Mebbe."

"I like a good blaze. When it's not too close." Zeb felt the
blood drain from his face at the thought of fire, but ideas were
forming in his head, rapidly becoming plans he could use. "And
I can imagine where you'd like to set one. You know where my
brother keeps the kerosene?" He grinned conspiratorially and
began looking around, stepping over spice boxes that had fallen
in the blast and a couple of broken canning jars.

Larry awakened to the sound of hostile voices. He lifted the
fabric aside, struggled quietly to his feet and moved to the door.
His ears buzzed and his head felt light. Peering around the
jamb he could see the two men silhouetted against the window.
He tried to concentrate, but his brain seemed to be on a rocking horse. His vision blackened from the outside edges toward
the center and then cleared again. He forced himself to listen to
the voices. One of them was Zeb's.

"It's how you got that arm, ain't it?" asked Marsh.

Zeb felt the taut, hideous skin beneath his sleeve, winced at
the remembered agony. "So?"

"I hear tell you let him take the blame for it."

"Listen, old man, I don't make any secret of it, I waste no
love on that brother of mine, and if he got the blame for a fire I
set because . . . well, he had it coming." Leaving the stock
certificate on the counter, Zeb went to rummage behind the
knife display case, looking for kerosene. "He's been standing in
my way since I can remember, getting every damn thing that
should have come to me." He straightened up and glared at
Marsh. "But you better mind your own business. I know what
you're about, and if I hear you've been spreading tales about
me, well, you just let your imagination do its worst, and I'll
start from there when I get my hands on you."

Marsh vibrated his lips in imitation of a mother tickling a baby's stomach.

Zeb returned to the tobacco counter.

Marsh's eyes followed him and then he spied the certificate lying next to the cash register. "Your brother put his money in that ice house?"

"What's it to you?" Zeb grabbed the certificate, threw it on top of the ledger, and kicked the drawer shut.

"If he did, he ain't no friend of mine." The two men stared for a moment, sizing each other up.

Thad and Lettie walked in.

"What are you doing here, Zeb?" asked Thad. "Why is the light off?"

"That's just what I asked myself when I noticed it right after the blast." He glanced down to be sure the drawer was completely shut. "I came in to hold down the fort till you got back. Then Marsh came in and I was trying to help him."

Larry turned and leaned against the wall of the storeroom. The movement made him dizzy. There was something he should tell Thad. Zeb lied about something. What was it he should he tell Thad? He put his hand on the back of his head, where a painful knot was swelling. Another wave of dizziness clouded his vision and cleared. There was something he had to do for Thad.

"If this is all the thanks I'm going to get," Zeb continued, "I won't ever bother again." He started toward the door. "Marsh wants some . . ."

"I can get it later," said Marsh and followed Zeb out.

"Zeb . . ." called Thad, but Zeb was already out of earshot. "Where do you suppose Larry is?" he asked, watching Marsh trail Zeb toward the saloon.

"Maybe he got worse," said Lettie. "I'd better go over to the house to see if he's all right."

"I'm fine," called Larry, supporting himself on the wall as he emerged from the storeroom. "I just came back to get some coal. At least, that's what I think I did. And then the blast went off. It knocked me down and I guess I blacked out for a few minutes. I'm sorry, Thad."

Lettie rushed to him. "Oh, Larry, you've such a bruise on your forehead. Or is that coal dust? Let me look at you. Thad, could you turn the light on?"

"It's nothing. You know how hardheaded I am." Larry rubbed the back of his head and grinned. "And you should see the coal bin lid. It's so skewed I doubt if it'll ever fit right again. Can you just give me a little piece of ice, Thad? I'll be fine."

Lettie wrapped a cloth around the ice for Larry. "Oh, do I ever need that bed warmer," she said when he was holding it to his forehead. "My feet are freezing. I'm going to take to wearing some of those big miners' boots, after all." She added coals to the warmer, placed it at her feet, and opened her machine.

Thad filled the scuttle and added coal to the stove. He swept up the broken canning jars and set spice boxes and fallen racks to right on the shelves above the dried food bins.

Larry shifted the ice to the back of his head and watched Thad for a minute. He opened his mouth to say something, and then stopped. What was it he was going to tell him? A fire. Something about fire? Had Zeb started the fire in Savannah? Zeb is that ruthless, he thought. Adrenaline shot to his heart and made it bounce. If he knew I'd heard . . . Larry watched the looks that passed between Lettie and Thad. They were so happy. What good would it do to tell Thad about it now? He could tell him later, when he was sure he remembered right. Besides, there was something brewing between Zeb and Old Marsh. If he kept his suspicion to himself, he might be able to use it to prevent whatever they cooked up. He looked from his sister to the man he hoped would be his brother and smiled. In a few minutes he joined Lettie's whistling until it made him cough.

Zeb handed the barkeep a tin flask and waited, surveying the empty saloon in the mirror. "You need to air this place out, George," he said, avoiding a sticky-looking glass circle when he put his elbow on the bar. "Stinks of stale beer and tobacco."

George shrugged and filled the flask, spilling a little of the whiskey.

Zeb threw a coin on the bar and turned to eye the collection of mule-deer heads that lined the back wall of the saloon. "You ought to get a new zoo, too." Moth-eaten and dusty, the trophies always reminded him of fleas, and he avoided them unless someone buying him a drink happened to be sitting under them.

George turned to put Zeb's money in his register. "You don't like them, you can do your drinking elsewhere."

"Kinda early for drinking, anyway, ain't it?" Marsh asked, suddenly appearing at Zeb's elbow.

Zeb turned to stare and moved away far enough to escape the old man's unwashed odor. "Not that it's your concern, but I like to take a little in a flask to work. Damn cold in that post office, with the door flying open every two minutes. Not to mention dragging myself up and down these mountains with a heavy mail sack weighing me down."

"How much you take outta your brother's till?"

Zeb glared at him. "You're on the wrong track, old man."

"I don't know what you're so defensive about. Like I said, he ain't no friend of mine. Sure as hell not after he invested in their scheme to ruin me." Marsh gave him a smile that showed his tobacco-browned teeth. "So I ain't *necessarily* aiming to tell him about the money you stole. Maybe I'll even keep quiet about the fire. 'Course you could do something to help me, too.

Might even get a thrill outta doing it."

"Like what?" Zeb asked, though his stare remained cold.

"Get me that kerosene."

Zeb let a minute pass, studying the ingrained bitterness on Marsh's face. The old man was useful. "If my brother's really made an enemy of you, I'll do better than that," he said, smiling. *A lot better than kerosene,* he thought. *A lot better than a mere fire.*

CHAPTER 11

November 13, 1895

All morning Thad listened happily to the clink of coins in the cash drawer, and the occasional rustle of bills sliding in when the few customers who had paper money bought enough to use it. The sandwich board he'd kept outside to advertise his sales had given his business a boost.

More than the sales, however, the optimism that had taken over Leadville had infected him, too. For five days now they'd watched mule teams drag stumps away and haul dirt up the hill to level the site where the Palace would be built.

Between customers he watched Lettie and listened to the lilting tunes she whistled or sang with Larry, who had been breathing better the last few days. Lettie was busy all day now, and even her small sewing motions were full of swing and grace.

"They're bringing in the first load of lumber for the substructure," she called suddenly from the sewing machine.

Thad joined her at the window, with Larry, Mrs. Lambert, and Ralphie.

Lettie got up and joined him where he stood behind the others. They edged closer to each other, their hands joined. Together they watched the mules struggle to pull the first wagonloads of boards and beams up Spruce Street two blocks away.

"I don't know," said Mrs. Lambert. "Here it is the middle of November." She tucked the can of tooth powder and the liver pills she'd bought into her shopping bag. "I don't see how they think they can have that thing finished by Christmas."

"But they've hired several hundred people, haven't they?" asked Lettie.

Mrs. Lambert nodded. "My husband is one of them. He says they'll work into the night if they have to. Even so, they'll need some kind of miracle."

"Night? Brrr," said Larry, twitching. "That sends goose feet slithering down my spine. Imagine working out there with *ice* when the temperature is freezing even during the day. It's a daring venture."

"Breathtaking," said Lettie.

"Tremendous," said Mrs. Lambert.

"Stupendous and . . . propitious," said Thad, squeezing Lettie's hand.

"*I* just can't wait for the toboggan," said eight-year-old Ralphie, his nose pressed against the glass.

In the noonday lull, Thad stepped behind Lettie as she stood from the machine and put his arms around her waist. "I have something for you," he said into her ear.

She turned in his arms, and after a glance at the window, stroked his face. She cocked her head. "I can't think what it could be. I have your heart. That's all I'll ever need from you."

He pulled something from his pocket but kept it hidden in his hand. He smiled deviously. "My dear lady, if you don't need this, perhaps I should find one who does."

Giving him a Roman candle of a glare, she reached for it. "Oh, no, you don't."

He slipped it behind his back.

She put her hands on her waist. "My good sir, the lady will simply perish of curiosity if you don't hand that over."

Thad opened her hand and laid his gift in her palm—a heart-shaped medallion with an image of the Ice Palace in *alto-relievo*.

"It's just a souvenir, and they'll probably be selling them all over town in a few weeks, but I wanted you to have the first one."

Lettie gasped. "Thad, it's beautiful." She read the inscriptions: " '1895, 1896, Crystal Carnival and Ice Palace, Leadville, Colorado.' " She looked up, her eyes shining with sudden tears. "It's so perfect—our hearts holding the Palace."

"It's not gold, Lettie. Probably just brass. I wish I could afford to give you gold and diamonds."

She threw herself against him with a sob. "I don't want diamonds, Thad. All I want is you, and you've given me that in so many ways. This is just the perfect symbol for us. Thank you so much, my love."

Thad held her with the medallion between their hearts.

She broke from his embrace. "Wait. I have some ribbon. I knew I was saving that scrap of ribbon for something special." She rummaged in her sewing kit and drew out about a yard of green satin ribbon. "I'll wear it on this. It's the color of hope."

They threaded the ribbon through the link at the top of the medallion and Thad tied it around her neck.

In the Silver Dollar that evening, Zeb found himself edging toward the end of the bar as one rough-clad ex-miner after another crowded him, shedding dust and smelling of old sweat and new labor.

"Sledgehammer" McAllister elbowed him aside and hoisted himself so that he was sitting on the bar facing the crowd. He reeled and nearly slipped off the bar before he righted himself.

Zeb knew Sledgehammer's usually sad face and brawny form because when the post office opened every day the miner was waiting to check a box that was always empty.

"Listen here, me laddies," Sledgehammer yelled in a thick

brogue. "We done good, did we not? Let's have a toast to strong backs!"

"Hear, hear," chorused the other workers.

"I say let's drink to a paycheck!" shouted Rusty Jackson.

"First one in eleven months, I'll drink to that!" called another miner from the back of the crowd.

"Let's have a toast to Tingley Wood," said Rusty.

"Right you are. To the man who got us going again," cried Sledgehammer.

They boasted about the foundation they were digging, the substructure they were going to build on it, and the money they would all make on the carnival. They toasted the mayor, the future, and even the departed Edwin Senior for coming up with the Palace idea. Most of all they toasted themselves.

Nursing a double straight whiskey, Zeb listened to their prattle with a small smile on his lips and a feeling of secret power in his heart. At first he enjoyed the sensation, but the false smile made his face tired, and his frustration built with the knowledge that he would never be able to brag of the part he would play in the stupid ice house.

He waited till most of them had straggled out, leaving only a couple of men with their heads on the tables. He checked the clock between the mangy deer heads on the back wall. "Well, George," he said loudly, "time for me to head for bed." He grinned broadly and winked, evoking a halfhearted, distracted smile from the barkeep, who was already turning chairs onto the tables. The clock bonged once for the half hour between eleven and midnight as the door swung shut and Zeb stood on the dark street.

When he left the boardwalks of Harrison and began stepping into ice-glazed puddles or tripping on stones, he cursed the dark. The overcast sky had kept the air slightly warmer than usual, but left only a few curtained lanterns to light the inky side streets.

They would need light, and stupid Old Marsh probably wouldn't have the good sense to refill his miner's lantern, even if he thought to bring it. Zeb would have to take his own, the one he'd bought for getting around town at night while keeping his one good arm around a woman.

He shook involuntarily at the thought of the fire he was about to set. He heard the roar of flame and for an instant the massive scar that was his right arm burned in agony again. But he had to do this. It was exactly what Marsh *would* do, old fool, and nothing else would give Thad such a clear motive for revenge. He put his fear aside before it turned to panic and focused on the benefit of getting through the deed.

Climbing the stairs to McGuire's, he looked up into the blackness and hoped the snow would hold off till they were finished. In his room he waited till midnight to change into old clothes. He checked his miner's lantern for oil and slipped it on over his cap. As he left, he picked up the can of kerosene he'd bought from one of Thad's competitors.

In the dark, Zeb smelled Marsh almost before he could make him out at the corner of Eighth and Spruce. The old man's back was to him, and Zeb poked him between the shoulder blades. Marsh spun around and made a sound that might be grunt or a growl. Neither man spoke a word of greeting.

Zeb set down his can of kerosene and shoved the miner's lantern under his right arm. He struck a match with his thumbnail to light it.

"What d'you think you're doin'?" rasped Marsh, slapping the match from his hand. "You want the whole town to see us?"

"You think you can make it through this muck without a light? You'll break your old fool neck. Anyway, the whole damn town's asleep. You see a soul on your way here? A single light in a window?"

Marsh looked around at the nearest buildings. "No."

"Well, then."

The old man reluctantly lit the lantern, keeping both their bodies in a position to block the light from the houses behind them.

Zeb fixed it over his hat, bent his head to light the mud directly in front of them, and picked his way across the Palace site with Marsh disgustingly close to his side. The smell of fresh lumber met them before the light hit any of the stacks. He aimed his lantern at two of the four piles of beams while Marsh doused them, then opened his can and poured his kerosene on the other two. When the cans were empty he carried them to the edge of the site and waited.

Marsh joined him, stumbling through the mud. "Well, go on, get 'em going."

The smell of the kerosene made Zeb panicky. "Listen, I said I would help. I did that." Searing flames slammed into memory. Pain. He could hardly breathe and his words came in snatches. "I'm not going anywhere near that lumber with a lighted match in my one good hand. You're going to have to do that part yourself." Zeb fought the compulsion to flee. He had to be sure this part of the plan worked.

"Well, you ain't much use, you namby-pamby kitten."

Zeb grabbed him by the beard and pulled him close. "Just go do it, and I hope you get your hand caught in it. Then you can tell me about namby-pamby."

Marsh let out a foul puff of breath, struck Zeb's wrist with surprising force, and shoved him away.

Zeb watched the old man light two matches and throw them quickly on two of the stacks. The kerosene caught with a loud *whoosh* and a fireball that nearly threw them both off their feet. Instantly the smell of singed hair mingled with the kerosene fumes, and Zeb laughed when Marsh slapped at his beard.

"Go on and do them all," whispered Zeb as loudly as he dared, but he didn't wait to see what Marsh did. The heat of the fire reached him now, and panic shot though him. He turned and rushed toward Eighth, slipping and stumbling in the mud cast into lumps and shadows by the light of the fire.

Marsh turned to share a moment's gloating, but all that was left of MacElwain's brother was his headlight bobbing around the corner of Leitner. "Stupid sissy," he hissed. He grabbed the two cans and ran as fast as his bowed legs would carry him down the treacherous terrain toward Seventh.

Noah switched off his light and changed into his nightshirt. He opened his window for a breath of fresh air before going to bed. He stared out at the darkness for some minutes, hardly conscious of the cold, almost smelling the lumber on the Palace site. Thad's hopes for the future. Noah could not let them materialize. The Palace would fail, of course, but if Thad even made enough profit to send Larry to a good sanatorium . . .

Suddenly a light moved on the construction site. Noah leaned out the window and stared down Eighth. In the bouncing, swinging light beam he could see a figure moving among the piles of lumber. He felt his way to a cupboard and took out a pair of binoculars.

There was no mistaking Old Marsh with his bowed legs. He was pouring something on the lumber from a can. Was he going to set the thing on fire? Who was the man with the lantern on his head? Noah adjusted the binoculars more finely, but suddenly they weren't necessary. He realized with shock that the other man was using only his left arm. He frowned. It was that brother of Thad's. Why would Zeb, with his arm already crippled by one fire, risk another? Then realization struck. Zeb was doing this to ensure Thad's ruin. But Marsh would get the blame for this, not Thad. Zeb had more in mind. He wouldn't stop with this. He would bear watching.

The men stopped, set the cans to the side of the site, and then seemed to argue about something. Old Marsh shoved at Zeb and turned back to the piles of lumber. He set a match to two piles. They flared up. Zeb backed away and ran. In the light of the fire, Marsh ran in the opposite direction, taking the cans with him. The two piles of lumber blazed high into the darkness for a minute and settled into a slow burn.

Laughing aloud, Noah shut the window and started to put the binoculars away. He glanced down at the site again and left them on the sill. One vengeful young fop and one bitter old codger—they were the worst that the town had to offer. And they had allied themselves to do the one thing Noah wanted done: assure Thad's failure while his own hands stayed clean.

Smiling, Noah watched the blaze until the fire bell rang almost twenty minutes later and the truck arrived.

CHAPTER 12

November 14, 1895

Most of Leadville's population lined the edge of the site, staring at the damage and hunched against the cold that had sunk into the valley after a light dusting of snow. Weak sunlight had just begun inching down the side of Mount Massive and wouldn't reach the construction area for another quarter hour.

Thad stood with his hands jammed into his jacket pockets, hardly conscious of his bare head and cold feet. The acrid smell of a doused fire stung his nose, as acidic as the hatred that seethed in his stomach. All around him the name "Old Marsh" hung in the puffs of angry breath that dotted the frigid air. Of course he had done it. Who else had any reason to?

Two of the piles of lumber had burned down to saddle-shaped heaps of coal, only their lowest boards still showing undamaged wood on the ends. But Marsh had soaked both of the other piles as well, and the beams would have to be replaced, since no one seemed to know what the combination of kerosene and ice would do. Thad ground his teeth at the thought of the churlish old miner who didn't care if the town went under.

Larry and Lettie joined him in the crowd, along with Mrs. Eskitch. Lettie stared at the damage with one gloved hand over her heart and the other covering her mouth.

"I didn't think he'd go this far," said Larry.

"He's just an evil old curmudgeon," said Mrs. Eskitch. "I declare, I never could find it in my heart to like that man. He used to be partners with my Mr. Es, God rest, when we first came here, and you never knew a man to be shiftier."

Thad turned and stared, as did the others.

"Oh, yes," she assured them. "He hired slipshod laborers because they were cheaper, and, my dears, he even tried to get Chinamen from the west coast down there in the shafts for a while. Of course, everybody knew Chinamen were barred from Leadville."

"No!" said Lettie.

"Oh, yes. That's the God's truth! Got my Mr. Es in trouble with the city, and when Mr. Es called him on it, he said things to him that a lady can't repeat." Her mittened hand fluttered up and fanned her round red cheeks. "Well, that was the end of the partnership. I declare, he hasn't changed one iota since then and that's been, let's see, my Mr. Es, he died in eighty-nine, so you can see, it's been a long time."

"I just hope they caught him in the act and he's sitting in jail this very minute," said Thad.

Mrs. Eskitch had hit her stride. "They say he was in the Frodsham gang back in seventy-nine. 'Course, my Mr. Es would never have hired him if we'd known, but the gangs were pretty well banished by the time we came out. And anyway, he was already too old to be mixed up in that kind of thing if he'd had the sense God gave a goose."

"I've heard of the Frodsham gang," said Thad, staring again at the charred lumber. "Marsh's crimes go back that far?"

"We haven't heard of any gangs," said Lettie.

Mrs. Eskitch nodded knowledgeably. "Lot jumpers."

"Lot jumpers?" echoed Larry.

"Back then," she continued, "when the Leadville boom was in full swing and they were clearing land to move the main street from Chestnut to Harrison, the price of lots soared to the very peaks."

"They moved the main street?" Thad said, stunned. "I didn't know it wasn't always Harrison."

"Why, yes, it used to be Chestnut. 'Course, that was before a goodly part of it burned, and that was in eighty-two. Or was it eighty-three? Now, let me explain. You two newcomers probably know what claim jumping is."

Lettie and Larry nodded.

Mrs. Eskitch pulled her cloak closer, settling in for a long story. "Well, in town it was lot jumping. If you got a good lot and started building your business or house, these gangs would just come along, drive the workers off, throw your materials in the street, or steal them, and take over."

"Why, that's awful," said Lettie.

Mrs. Eskitch nodded and put her hand on Lettie's arm. "Well, my dear, the Frodsham gang was the worst. Finally, the town got sick of it and the police didn't seem to be any use. So they got Frodsham, took him to one of the unfinished buildings on a lot he'd jumped, and hanged him right from the rafters. Then they went back and got that Stewart person—now what was his first name again? 'Course, he wasn't a lot jumper, just a footpad. They hanged him right next to Frodsham."

"Hot dingers," said Larry. "Without a trial or anything?"

"Oh, yes, my dear. The ones who did it left a note pinned to Frodsham's trousers. Claimed there were seven hundred of them and that any other lot jumpers and footpads could reckon with the same fate. Why, the very next day, it was like the town had gone to war. Everybody was scared to death the gangs would fight back. The police tried to gather all the law-abiding citizens in Tabor's Opera House, where they'd be safe. But nobody wanted to venture outdoors, and anybody who had property stayed home to defend it. I know my Mr. Es stayed by the front window almost all day, with his rifle cocked. But the day passed, and whoever they were, the seven hundred, they turned the town around. They had to do something, you know. Back in those days, Leadville was a rowdy place. There were so many footpads about that no one dared venture out at night."

"What's a footpad?" asked Lettie.

"A thief who'd knock you down, or worse, to take what you had," answered Thad.

"Sounds like Old Marsh," said Larry. The others nodded.

Near the top of Eighth Zeb stood and watched the reaction of the crowd. As the people came back toward Harrison, he caught the name Marsh several times. He smiled.

When he'd walked past the site on his way up, the smell of last night's fear overpowered any other coming from the mess left by his fire. But now there was something else rushing through his veins. Satisfaction. No, more. Thrill. He'd done it. He'd thwarted Thad just like the last time. He'd gotten past the fear and discovered—what? Fascination. Those two great towers of flame. Destructive. Painful. His handiwork. His power. His secret.

Noah came out of the hotel and stood beside him.

"Nice blaze," Noah said. "Wonder who could have started it," he added, his voice edged with sarcasm.

Zeb stared at him, at the shrewd smile that was playing around Noah's lips. He looked the man squarely in the eyes. "Dangerous thing, fire," he said. "You want to keep away from it." He turned on his heel and walked off toward the post office.

All morning Thad's customers complained about Old Marsh. As the day wore on, the magnitude of the setback he'd caused to the Palace grew with each new telling. Each customer had a different story to tell about the old miner's despicable nature; each hoped he would rot in the basement of the town hall forever. And each discussion added another coal to Thad's burning anger.

An hour after lunch, the store had almost returned to normal. Lettie was cutting out another uniform for the skating team while Larry stacked the pinned pieces for her. Thad was ringing up half a pound of coffee beans and a smoked sausage for Mrs. Marechal, when Officer Woolsley walked in.

"Afternoon, Miss, Mrs. Marechal, MacElwain," he said.

Thad looked up and barely returned the greeting. "Did you catch Old Marsh?" he asked.

"What a terrible thing to do," Mrs. Marechal said before Woolsley could answer. "That old coot. No telling what he might try next. You keep him in jail till the carnival's over, you hear me, Clyde?"

Woolsley glared at her.

"Oh, for goodness' sakes, Clyde, you're my next-door neighbor. Now, did you arrest Marsh or not, *Officer* Woolsley?"

"We picked him up, all right. He denies having anything to do with it. No one seems to have seen anything."

"Are you saying you let him go?" Thad shouted, his voice shaking with anger and disbelief. He slammed the register drawer. "You know perfectly well he did it."

"You watch your temper, MacElwain." Woolsley glared at him for a second and then turned to the others. "Look, we questioned him all morning. But we got no proof. Can't look for footprints in that muck, and anyway, the site is nothing *but* footprints in the mud. No point looking for muddy boots. Everybody in town has muddy boots from the site." He put his hands up in a gesture of helplessness. "I had to let him go. Still, I think sitting in jail a few hours put the fear of God in him. I don't believe he'll try anything else, *Mrs. Marechal.*"

"Then you don't know Marsh," said Thad.

"And you do?" Woolsley put his left hand on the billy club

hanging at his waist. "Then I suppose you know he filed a complaint against you?"

"He did *what?*"

Lettie and Larry joined him behind the counter.

"That's ridiculous," said Lettie. "Whatever for?"

"He says you threatened him."

"Threatened him?" Thad laughed, but his anger was about to boil over. "I haven't even seen him since he came in here ranting about the city condemning his property."

"That's when he says you did it."

"I did no such thing."

"He certainly didn't," said Lettie. "I stood right here the whole time Marsh was in the store."

"Marsh stomped up and down in a real fury, banging on the glass." Thad pointed down the tobacco counter. "I doubt he even heard what was said."

"Oh, yeah? He says you told him not to try to block the Ice Palace or it'd go badly for him."

Thad was stunned. "That's exactly what I said. I meant it'd be a legal battle he couldn't win."

"That's not the way he understood it. Anyway, everybody knows you've put all your money in the Palace, MacElwain." He glanced at Lettie with a half-smile playing around his lips.

Furious, Thad stepped between her and Woolsley. "That's true, but I didn't invest any of it until after Marsh had been here. I had no reason to threaten him."

Lettie stepped to Thad's side again, put her hand on his arm and squeezed it.

Thad glanced at her, knowing she was trying to calm him down. She was glaring at the officer.

Woolsley looked around at the store. "What about your business? That's picked up, hasn't it?"

"Yes, of course, but . . ."

Mrs. Marechal clicked her tongue and put her hands on her hips. "Well, really, Clyde, every business in town . . ."

He silenced her with a gesture. "So Marsh is a hindrance."

Thad looked him straight in the eye. "The fire he set is certainly a hindrance, to the whole town, not just to me."

Woolsley's mouth opened but the slap of Larry's hand on the counter stopped him.

"You obviously don't know Thad, Woolsley, so maybe there's some excuse there," said Larry. "But you ought to know better than to take the word of an old lout against the word of a respected businessman. If there's anyone in Leadville who ought to know Old Marsh, it's you."

"I'm just telling you, a complaint's been filed. So watch your step, MacElwain. I'm keeping my eye on you."

"Keep it on Marsh. He's the guilty party," said Lettie.

In the late afternoon Thad was writing an advertisement he wanted to run in the paper and grinning, glad of the distraction provided by several thirteen-year-old members of the ice skating team. They were browsing through the store with voice-changing clamor, waiting to try their uniforms on in the back room. They crowded in front of the knife case and the new ice skates, pushing and jostling each other. One of them picked up a box of piles ointment from the small medication display and showed it around, setting off a round of laughter. Thad watched them, smiling and leaning on the counter with the back of his index finger in the cleft in his chin, absently doodling on the paper.

Lettie, who probably couldn't see what had set them off, looked at Thad and grinned, too. "Boys," she called, "Mr. MacElwain is kind enough to let me use part of his store for my tailoring." She lowered her voice as they shushed each other. "I don't think he counted on my bringing in such rowdiness. Couldn't you quiet down, please?"

Some of the boys turned half-smitten faces to her, the rest to Thad, and apologized in a confused chorus. They went back to the displays they'd been handling, and slowly the noise rose again.

Old Marsh stumped in, reeling.

Instantly, the boys' banter stopped and everyone stared at the old man.

Thad grabbed the paper he'd been writing on, balled it up, and threw it on the floor, speechless with anger.

Lettie looked at Marsh with distaste and stood up, watching Thad. Larry put aside the book he'd been reading.

"What're you all looking at?" Marsh asked, turning to stare spitefully into each person's eyes. "Ain't you never seen a rich miner before?" His exaggerated motions carried him too far and he made a full turn before focusing on Thad. "Or is it my fancy barbering?" He stroked his beard, shorter by two inches than anyone had ever seen it.

Thad rushed forward until he felt Lettie's hand on his arm. "You're not welcome in this store anymore, Marsh," he said loudly. "In fact, you have a lot of gall to come here."

One of the skaters added, "You got a lot of nerve showing your face in town at all. You think anyone's grateful for what you did?"

"You ought to be tarred," said another team member.

"And feathered, too," said another, his voice cracking on "feathered."

"What? What did I do?" Marsh asked, his face a mask of offended innocence.

"I suppose you want us to think you were drunk when you set the fire," said Larry.

"That would be no excuse," said Thad. His hands itched with the desire to grab the old man, but Lettie's hand pressed into his arm.

"I never set that fire. But that don't mean I'm taking this Ice Palace nonsense lying down. I'm gonna stop it yet."

Lettie stepped in front of Thad. "Mr. Marshall, don't you see? A lot of people have pinned their hopes on the Ice Palace. If it fails, everyone will suffer."

He leered into her face and flipped the medallion on its green ribbon. "I wonder where you got that," he said, leaving little doubt about his sarcasm. "From your rich suitor or your poor shopkeeper?"

She backed away from the smell of alcohol mixed with his usual odor. He grabbed her wrist and pulled her back. Thad stepped between them and shoved him. Larry started forward. The skaters made a circle around them all.

"Take your filthy hands off her," said Thad slowly and quietly.

Marsh let go but leaned around Thad to say, "I know what kind of hopes *you* got pinned on it, missy," he said. "The kind that don't come true."

"Get out, Marsh," said Thad, grabbing his shoulders and shoving him toward the door.

"As for you, Mr. Shopkeeper, you better look closer to home for who's doin' you harm," he said, clawing at Thad's arm to free himself.

Thad shoved his shoulder harder. "What's that supposed to mean? I didn't threaten you when you came in here with that letter, and you know it. Now get your foul presence out of here or I'll . . ."

"You'll what? Is that a threat now?"

"Most assuredly. You stay away from that Ice Palace or you'll be sorry. I have a lot riding on it, and so has the whole town."

He pushed Marsh out the door, and the skaters bounced out after him. They pranced in a circle around him, taunting him and imitating his bowlegged walk as he stalked up the middle of Harrison.

Thad, Lettie, and Larry watched them out of sight, all shaking in the darkening store.

"You shouldn't have said that," said Larry.

"I know. I lost my head."

Lettie put her hand in his.

This is not going to be the end of it, thought Thad, and a sense of foreboding shook him to the marrow.

CHAPTER 13

November 25, 1895

The last scraps of cloud drifted south along the Arkansas Valley. In their wake the slanting afternoon sun cast its blinding light on the broad white shoulders of Mount Massive, the Mosquito Range, and the snow-covered valley between them. The people of Leadville bunched their scarves over their noses and pulled their hats low to protect their eyes from the glare.

Winter had sunk into the valley for its six-month stay. Sleighs and mule-drawn sledges now plied the streets in place of the wagons and stagecoaches of autumn, and pedestrians wore boots or snowshoes to go about their daily business.

At the bottom of Third Street, sledges of Cole & McCordie hauled in covered ice blocks, delivering the contracted two hundred tons per day. Few people paid them much mind now, but the progress on the Palace gave Leadville a solid underpinning it hadn't had for two years.

Thad went out to shovel the new snow and spread his salt/sand mix on his part of the boardwalk. From time to time he stopped to watch the sledges and smile, as if their cargo were his personal property. His chances for happiness grew with each load, each block that would go into the Palace. Still, no one had said exactly when the Palace would open, and when he thought of his own present finances, the solid underpinning felt more like quicksand.

Before going back into the store, he lowered the black wool

he'd draped over hinged rods as an awning for Lettie against the afternoon sun, and set out his sandwich board, advertising lentils on one side and mousetraps on the other. Back in the store, he found Lettie facing almost completely away from the show window. Larry had retreated to the corner behind the register and sat with his eyes closed, head resting against the storeroom wall.

"The sun's still blinding you, isn't it?" Thad asked Lettie, peering out at the awning.

"Actually, no. Right now it's the light bouncing off the snow. But the shade helps when the sun gets a little lower. Thank you, Thad."

"I could cover the window completely," he suggested.

"Good heavens, no. We'd all go stir-crazy. Actually, this isn't bad. It's good light for sewing. The only thing I miss is watching the ice go up the hill." She smiled up at him.

Thad nodded. He put his hand on her face before going back to the counter.

Mrs. Eskitch bustled into the store in the middle of a sentence. ". . . happened this morning? They laid the first ice block. You'd think there'd be something in the paper so a body could go and watch, and there'd be a ceremony or something, like a cornerstone, wouldn't you? But no. I just happened to walk up there. They've already got a whole row done on this side." She put one hand on her cheek and pointed with the other vaguely in a northwesterly direction. "Let's see, that'd be east, wouldn't it? Or is it north? And started a second row." She pulled her scarf away from her eyes and tucked it under her second chin.

Thad visualized a trail of words still hanging in the air from her house to the Palace and the store. "That so?" he asked, not daring to look at Lettie or Larry, who'd sat upright again, knowing they'd all burst out laughing.

He needn't have worried. Mrs. Eskitch was in full swing and probably wouldn't notice if an ice block fell on her head. "You know how they do it? One of the workers told me. The blocks are all different sizes when they come up from the lakes, depending on how thick the ice is where they cut it. So they put the blocks in those wooden forms that we were all wondering about and fill them up with *hot* water so they'll all freeze at the same size. Then they lay a block on top of two others, like they do bricks, then they pour *hot* water between them. I asked one of the workers about that, 'cause it doesn't seem sensible to me, but he said they did it because hot water freezes faster than cold. Now that's the silliest thing I ever heard, but he seemed real sure of himself, got right snappish with me, as a matter of fact." She stopped for breath.

Thad bit his lip as he bent to move tobacco pouches aimlessly about. Larry grinned at him, and he barely managed to turn back to Mrs. Eskitch with a straight face.

"Well, that's wonderful that they've started on the walls," said Lettie.

"Yes," said Thad. "Did you want something, Mrs. Eskitch?"

"Want something?" She shook her head as if to clear it. "Oh, why yes, I did. I ran into that nice Mr. Wood. He talked to me for ever so long. Such a handsome face with that goatee, don't you think? And he asked me to tell you the investors are having a short meeting at five o'clock today if you want to come. He said it's not terribly important, but you might want to know. Just wants to say something about . . . now, what was it he said? Oh, yes, 'future finances.' Those were his exact words." She beamed at Thad and gave him a short, satisfied nod.

Thad's heart beat a little faster. How could future finances not be important when Old Marsh had forced the replacement of so much lumber? "I'm afraid I'll have to read about it in the paper," he said, trying not to let the dread he felt show in his voice. "I can't get away a whole hour before closing time, but thank you for telling me."

"Oh, you're very welcome. It's so exciting. The workers over there say we'll have the Ice Palace ready for Christmas no matter what. And I heard Mr. Wood say all the restaurants and hotels and shops are decking themselves out for the best season ever. What are you going to do here, Mr. Mac?"

Lettie set her sewing down and turned to him. "Oh, yes, Thad, let's decorate the store so it looks grand even from down at the station and people are drawn right up the hill to it. I can sew bright ornaments and garlands to put around the window and the door."

"That's a wonderful idea," said Larry. "I'll cut them out for you."

Thad looked from one to the other and felt the idea bubble in himself, too. "There's some old felt in the back. Let's look and see what colors I have."

"Well, I have to go on home," chirped Mrs. Eskitch. The clock bonged once for a half hour. She drew in a great breath. "Good heavens! Four-thirty. The water's probably boiled out of the pot by now. Or the fire's gone out. And you know how long corned beef has to cook. I'll have to see what can be done to revive it. Supper may be a few minutes late. My dears, I simply had no idea Mr. Wood had kept me so long with all his talking," she said as the bell jingled her exit.

Biting their lips, Thad, Lettie, and Larry waited till she was past the show window before collapsing into laughter.

When he could function again, Thad said, "I can't imagine where she got her lung capacity."

"If we could bottle it, I'd sure buy some," said Larry.

Thad and Lettie looked at each other and then at him, suddenly sad.

Larry's face fell. "Oops, sorry, you two. I didn't mean to

122

throw a pall on things. Anyway, I think you should go to the meeting, Thad."

"I do, too," said Lettie. "We can look for the felt in the morning."

Larry stationed himself behind the counter. "I can take care of the register and close up for you."

Lettie took up her sewing again. "I'll help if anybody comes in. I know where everything is."

Thad tried to focus on what Mrs. Eskitch had said. The meeting wasn't "terribly important." Perhaps that was an indication that there might be good news for a change. "Well, if you're sure you don't mind . . . I'll start clearing the register before I go. Then I can tell you at supper what the meeting was about."

A few minutes after Thad left, Zeb sauntered in, his empty mailbag hanging like a deflated leather ball at his side. He dropped it next to the door and unbuttoned his overcoat and suit coat. He stopped at the machine, where Lettie was folding a pair of uniform pants she'd just finished. "Well, good afternoon to you, Miss Corcoran. Where's Thad?"

Lettie hesitated, her eye caught by the tiny black shark that dangled from his watch chain. Like him, it looked rapacious. The danger she'd felt when she'd first laid eyes on Zeb in the train—no, when *he'd* first laid eyes on *her*—had never abated. "At a meeting," she said.

"Aha. The look on your face tells me you think that's none of my business."

Lettie felt her face flush. She turned away and laid the pants on top of the finished jacket.

"Come now, Miss. You mean I can't take a little brotherly interest in Thad?"

She turned to face him, angry now at the blatant sarcasm in his tone. "I beg your pardon, Mr. MacElwain, but brotherly love isn't something you seem to have in you. We all know you only came here to use Thad." Zeb's mouth opened, but she rushed on before he could say anything. "And don't tell me about the accident in the boathouse as an excuse for your behavior. I *know* it couldn't have been his fault."

Zeb's eyes narrowed and he glared for a minute. "You know nothing at all," he said through clenched teeth. He turned and strolled around the store, stopping to bend over the showcase with the hunting knives, glancing back at her from time to time.

The floorboards creaked and the clock ticked into the hostile silence.

Lettie began pinning a new pair of pants together, pointedly ignoring Zeb.

Zeb continued his tour, fingering ice skates, Palace souvenirs, and pom-pommed hats. He started down the side wall toward the rear of the store.

Behind the cash register Larry shifted in his chair to put himself more in shadow, watching Zeb's progress. He wasn't just idly eyeing the displays. He seemed to be looking for something, and his uncharacteristic control in the face of Lettie's insult was puzzling. Larry had heard his answer and seen the clenched fist behind his back. He was reining himself in for some reason. As Zeb turned in his direction, Larry sat perfectly still.

When Zeb reached the long counter at the back, his eyes lit on the cheese knife with the antler handle hanging above the washbasin. He stopped dead and hardly seemed to breathe for a minute, as if memorizing the hole drilled in the antler handle, the leather thong strung through it, and the exact position of the nail on which the knife hung.

Larry watched the change in his face and frowned.

Zeb glanced at Lettie. She had her back to him. He turned from the knife after another look, walked casually to the front

124

and leaned against the door.

Larry's back began to tire, tilted as it was to keep him in shadow, but he dared not move lest the chair squeak or scrape the floor and give him away. Why would Zeb be so fascinated with Thad's old cheese knife? Turning only his head, Larry listened to the conversation at the front.

Zeb looked down at Lettie with the scornful twist of face that was his smile. "Oh, by the way," he said, "Mrs. McGuire asked me to see if Thad has any ice cream salt."

Lettie flinched involuntarily. Why was it that the most innocent things Zeb said took on the air of evil? "She wants to make ice cream in the middle of winter?" The pin she was shoving through the fabric pricked her middle finger and she winced.

Zeb grinned patronizingly at her. "Maybe she wants to use it on the front steps. I nearly broke my neck coming down them this morning."

"It's in the storeroom. Do you want to take it with you now?"

He laughed and leaned toward her. "I'll just let her know." He made no move to leave.

"I think Thad's going directly to Mrs. Eskitch's after the meeting," said Lettie.

"No matter. Where's your brother today? I thought he was attached to you like a leech."

Lettie glared at him and looked around. "I . . . don't know. He was here before you came in." Her voice sounded unsteady now, and made her feel even more vulnerable and alone in Zeb's presence. "I . . . I'm sure he'll be back in a minute."

Zeb leaned against the doorframe again. His cheerful tone showed he was enjoying himself. "He's what's got you so nervous, isn't he?"

"I don't know what you mean. I'm not nervous."

"Oh? You always prick your fingers when you're calm? Of course you're nervous, what with wanting one man and having to marry another. A genuine tragedy of nerves." He plucked a pin from the red pincushion on her wrist and handed it to her with a small bow.

Lettie ignored the pin, her mind on what he'd just blurted out. It was a blessing Larry had stepped out. She didn't want him upset about all this. "Whatever you think you know, Mr. MacElwain, I'll thank you to keep it to yourself. It's really none of your affair."

"Of course not. Just get used to the idea of being Mrs. Noah Ralston. That's how this is all going to end, you know." He jabbed the pin back into the cushion hard enough to knock her wrist onto the work table but not quite hard enough to jab it into her skin.

Lettie jerked her arm away and put both hands in her lap. She looked up at him with what she hoped was a glare. "Why are you so spiteful, sir? My brother and I have never done you any harm, and I doubt that Thad has ever done anything so bad it would justify your hatred, either."

"I told you, you know nothing." The bitterness disappeared as if he had wiped it off his face, and Zeb smiled at her with something like real apology as he turned to leave. "Let's just say the hatred's in my nature." He looked up at the top of the door. "I hate this bell, too." He lunged up, slapped it hard and walked out.

"Lettie, how . . ." said Larry from the shadows.

Lettie jumped and immediately her heart sank. Had he been here all along after all? " 'How' what?"

"How could Thad have such a brother?"

She heard the strain in his voice and knew he had heard. He was stalling to keep himself calm. His protest was coming, but she followed his lead, hoping he'd let the subject of Noah pass. "I don't know," she said, nervously sticking pins in the fabric without reference to the pattern. "There's no excuse for him, no matter how sick he was. Ever since he's been here . . ."

"I heard it all, Lettie," Larry said, his voice angry now, barely controlled. "Is it true what he said about you and Thad and Noah?"

Lettie turned toward the back and started to say something.

"I know you, Lettie." Larry slapped himself on the forehead. "My God, I should have seen it. How could you make a decision like that without telling me?"

Lettie got up and walked back to where she could face him. Larry glared up at her, his face flushed.

"Larry, nothing's really been decided yet. I do love Thad, but you know how things stand with him financially."

He jumped up from the chair. "I also know you don't want his money. Are you telling me Thad invested his entire savings in the Ice Palace on *my* account?"

"No, on my account. It's me he wants to marry."

"You and my lungs, you mean." He grabbed her shoulders. "I will not let you marry Noah because of me, Lettie. You hear me? I'd rather die first. I mean it."

"But *I* don't want you to die, Larry, don't you understand that?" Lettie put her arms around her brother. He shook her off, grabbed his coat from the peg in the hall and slammed the door on the way out the back.

Lettie took off her apron and hung it on a nail as she left the kitchen to join Thad in the parlor. She should tell him about Larry's anger and his determination that she not marry Noah. She owed him that much honesty, but the change in the situation would only lay that much more burden on him. She stopped for a second at the door and looked at him, sitting in one of Mrs. Eskitch's blue chintz chairs reading the *Herald Democrat*. Suddenly a whole life with him flooded through her and she knew she would love him still in fifty years if she came in from their own kitchen and found him reading the paper.

He glanced up and smiled. "You don't have to do that, you know," he said, folding the paper and laying it on the table beside him. "Wiping dishes isn't part of your rent."

She smiled back and let the short reverie go. "I know, but it's such a little thing to do. You didn't get a word in edgewise at supper once Mrs. Eskitch got started on the toboggan. How was your meeting?"

Thad smiled back at her. "I've been so excited about it, I'd have insisted you take a walk with me so I could tell you if Mrs. Eskitch hadn't herded us right to the table. He grinned up at her. "Of course, now that I've waited so long, I think I'll just go up and get the last of the corned beef out of my teeth." He rose and started to step away from the chair.

Lettie put a single index finger on his shoulder and shoved him back into the chair, a terrible frown on her face. "My good man, I've been about to burst with questions. I think you'd better tell me right now or I'll . . ."

Thad laughed. "You'll what?"

Lettie thought for a second. "I'll bring you another huge helping of the corned beef and you'll have it stuck . . ."

Thad threw up his hands. "Horrors. Pray, don't fill in the details! Come, you'd better sit down first." When she'd taken the chair in the other half-circle of the lamplight, he leaned forward and said, "Oh, Lettie, it's the best news possible, but hardly believable. Tingley Wood has promised to supply all the funds for the construction of the palace above the twenty-thousand-dollar stock sale. Out of his own pocket."

Lettie gasped. "His own money?"

"That means that it'll be done right, no cutting corners because of lack of funds. It's going to be such a success, my love," he whispered. "Nothing will stand in our way anymore."

Looking back at the kitchen door, she leaned across and stroked his face. Zeb's horrible behavior and Larry's words about his own death echoed in her head, but she couldn't ruin Thad's happiness by bringing them up just now. She looked in his eyes and knew he, too, felt the house around them as theirs, a private world, until Mrs. Eskitch bustled in babbling and took up her tatting.

CHAPTER 14

December 1, 1895

Zeb stood on the porch of Mrs. McGuire's just after midnight, cursing the full moon that lit the town like the noonday sun. It was so cold the little moisture in the air condensed and fell to earth as twinkling ice crystals. His eyes watered and the tears that drained into his nose froze there. He wiped his eyes with a handkerchief and started down the stairs. His right hand, useless though it was, still stung with the cold. He reached around with his left and jerked at his coat until he managed to get the right hand in the pocket, almost reveling in the anger that always came with consciousness of the injury. "Now, brother," he said softly. "Tonight."

He stepped off the porch. His shoe hit ice on the first step, and the crack seemed to echo through the whole city. He backed up, considered a moment, and then climbed over the railing into the snow, sinking up to his shins. Snow packed into his boots as he post-holed the three steps to the sidewalk, and he filled his fogged breath with silent swearwords.

At Harrison he started toward Thad's store. Two late workers were weaving toward him, waving bottles through the air, trying to sing different songs and shushing each other as they came. Zeb spun back under the toboggan and moved around a post as they passed. He waited a few minutes, checked the street, and crossed Harrison. He was going to be late getting to the site, but Old Fool Marsh would just have to wait. Maybe he'd freeze.

130

That would make it even easier. Before going to the back of the store, he checked Harrison again. It was empty now, even the Silver Dollar across the street dark and silent.

He cursed again when he saw the back door in shadow, made all the darker by the bright moonlight. He took out a screwdriver and went to work on the fixed side of the padlock's hardware. His hand was freezing, the metal was rusty, and in the shadow he had to feel for the slot in the screw. Very slowly, he turned the screwdriver, shoving his weight against it to steady his awkward left hand. The screwdriver slipped and scraped loudly. The padlock jumped and banged back into place. Zeb started, looked around, and waited a few seconds before going back to work.

The screw loosened on the second try, and he removed it, taking care not to let it fall in the snow piled on the side of the path Thad had shoveled. He put it in his pocket and removed the remaining screws.

When the door swung open, he went in and waited for his eyes to adjust to the dark. He stepped into the storeroom, closed the door, and lit a candle he had brought with him.

The salt was stacked in twenty-five-pound cloth sacks next to the coal bin. He grabbed the top one and dragged it toward the hallway, snuffing the candle at the door. He went into the store, felt around on the wall above the washbasin until he found the cheese knife. Lifting its thong off the nail, he tested the blade with his thumb and smiled. Sharp as pain.

Zeb wrapped the blade in the rag hanging on the side of the tin pan and slipped the knife into his coat pocket. He dragged the bag of salt out the back door and replaced the screws in the padlock. With a grunt, he lifted the salt onto the packed snow at the side of the path and then clutched it to his chest.

From the top of Third Street he could see Old Marsh pacing and slapping his hands against his arms in that old mink-lined coat that looked more like mangy rat. Probably felt that way, too. Zeb wished he had a second hand to pinch his nose shut as Marsh started up the hill toward him almost at a run, scowling, his breath trailing in angry clouds behind him.

The old man stopped halfway up the block and waited. His whisper grated through the space that separated them. "What took you so long, you stupid dandy? I coulda froze to death waiting on you."

Zeb sneered at him. "So do the hard part yourself next time. Let's see you remove and replace a padlock without leaving any traces of forced entry. It took time."

"That all you brought? Twenty-five pounds? How far you think we're gonna get with that little bit of salt?"

"It's all I can carry with one arm. You go back and get some more if you want it."

"Jesus!"

"Listen, old fool, no matter how thin we spread it, they're going to have to replace the ice. They can't take any chances."

Marsh put his hands on his waist. "D'you bring me a pail or something to put it in? No. Don't you ever think ahead? I oughta let you go on and do the whole thing yourself. Too damned cold out here anyway."

"All right, I will do it myself," Zeb bluffed. He did not want to kill the old cur here. The site would be much better. "Of course, you're still going to get the blame for it, you know."

"No skin off my nose. I'm gettin' out the minute we finish. Got my mule hitched right down there."

Zeb glanced at the corner, where the packed mule waited, tied to a street sign.

"Well, you probably want to hurry, then," Zeb said, hardly able to disguise the desperation in his voice. He had to get Marsh up to the ice walls. The salt began to slip down his hip. "Only you'd better help me carry the sack up to the walls.

Otherwise it might not get done at all. Come on, old man, my hand's freezing."

Marsh glared at him over his ice-caked mustache and beard and grabbed the sack out of his arm. "That's all I'm doing," he snarled.

They worked their way slowly and erratically up the hill, trying to avoid ice patches that would crack under their weight in the quiet town. The walls of the Ice Palace were almost shoulder height, gleaming at them like frozen bile in the baleful light.

"Stupid fools think that thing can't melt," said Marsh. "I'll show them." He set the sack on one of several waiting blocks, where it slumped over itself like a sleeping old man. "All we're doing is what the sun is gonna do anyhow. How you gonna open this sack?"

Zeb pulled the knife from his pocket. "With this."

Marsh grinned. "Well, at least you done one thing right."

Zeb nearly laughed aloud. "The best part, in fact."

"That's your brother's knife, ain't it?"

"Yes."

"Nice touch."

Zeb stabbed into the top of the sack, anxious to judge the force he needed to make a hole with the chipped blade end. The knife slashed right through the burlap, leaving a gash of frayed threads. Zeb blinked, surprised and pleased at how easily it had gone through. Thad must have sharpened the broken tip, too. Idiot.

The sack fell over, and some of the salt ran out and fell to the ground.

"Stop wasting it!" Marsh shoved the bag so that all of the salt would run onto the block. "Hell, I can't resist spreading some around. Come on, make the hole bigger." He cupped his hands, filled them with salt and turned toward the wall.

Zeb started after him, raising the knife. The blade flashed in the moonlight. His stomach wrenched. He raised the knife higher, straining, but his arm dropped to his side again. He turned back and leaned against the block, breathing hard. Then everything came in a flash: the years of living in Thad's shadow when he should have been first in everything, of always coming out worse, of looking at him across the dining table and wishing he'd choke on his food, of suffocating under that self-righteous innocence Thad always hid behind.

Suddenly Zeb's arm was burning again, rammed under the full weight of the boat. The walk collapsed, he sank under the boat and managed to get into the open, half swimming with his left arm, half pulling himself from post to barnacle-encrusted post, slicing his hand, his right arm an agony of seared flesh in the murky, salty water. He looked down at his hideous right hand. Hatred burned up his arm and shot into his heart, his brain.

"You gonna do this or not?" Marsh's raspy whisper mocked him suddenly from behind. The old man grabbed more salt and turned back to the wall. The old man everybody hated. He deserved to die. He was miserable anyway.

"Yes," hissed Zeb, turning to follow him. The knife seemed to yank his hand up. He brought it down with all his force. It hit Marsh's back right where he wanted it to, above the heart. Then it stopped. Marsh fell forward onto the frozen ground, and the breath went out of him, his salt scattering about the mud. The knife clattered onto a patch of ice. Zeb was on him immediately, snatched up the knife and plunged it in again, using his weight to force the blade through all the layers of clothing. Marsh gasped, twisted his arm back and fought to get a hand to the knife. Zeb sat on him, pinning him to the frozen ground. Marsh gave up on the knife and thrashed at the mud and ice, trying to pull himself away. His head came up, trying to look Zeb in the eye.

"You ought to thank me for this, you smelly old cur," said Zeb.

"You . . ." Old Marsh's breath rattled. His face hit the frozen mud again.

Zeb rolled off him and knelt on the mud, breathing in great gulps that filled his lungs with icy shock. He bent low over his knees for a few seconds and then went back to the salt bag. He grabbed it by the hole and carried it to the wall, stumbling blindly over the uneven ground. He threw salt over the tops of the blocks, not worrying about whether it spread evenly or fell into the building. When the sack was nearly empty, he threw the rest over the blocks waiting on the ground. He dropped the sack on the last block and left. He did not look at Old Marsh again.

Noah shoved his ledger aside, stood and stretched in front of his ice-framed window. He took up the binoculars and scanned the Palace site, as he did most nights, watching for Old Marsh and Zeb. They would be back, of that he was sure. Marsh wouldn't give up with a fire. And Zeb—well, Zeb wouldn't abet Marsh unless he had his own motives. There was nothing going on down there tonight, though.

Noah set the binoculars back on the sill and gazed absently at the moonlit frozen whiteness of Mount Massive, seeing in it Juliet's polite coldness. She was obviously sweet on Thad. Noah's resentment welled to the surface. Why couldn't Thad just leave town, make it simple for all of them? His situation was hopeless anyway. The Palace was a lost cause before it even opened.

Below him the rime of frost on the skeleton of the toboggan scaffold sparkled like milky diamonds running down Eighth, ending in a tiny sharp gleam near the Palace. The gleam disappeared and he realized it had been a flash. He grabbed the binoculars and was looking for the spot where he'd seen it when there was another flash.

Noah's breath rushed out of his lungs. It was what he'd been waiting for: Zeb and Marsh, and the flash had been near Zeb's raised hand. Marsh fell, and Zeb jumped on top of him. Noah watched Zeb grab at something glinting on the ground, then raise it and bring his full weight down on Marsh. Noah's mouth fell open. Zeb had stabbed the old man. He knelt in the mud for a minute, then got up and moved along the partially completed ice walls and among the blocks that hadn't yet been set. Marsh lay on the ground, the knife handle sticking out of his back, barely visible. Noah frowned. Zeb would not be doing this unless he could use it against Thad somehow. Noah's frown gave way to a broad smile. It was so easy when your enemy's enemy did everything for you.

CHAPTER 15

December 1, 1895

Thad turned his lathered face to the left, to glean more of the unsatisfactory light coming through his dormer window, which was completely frosted over. He thought of the south window he'd had downstairs, where he'd stood to shave on days like this, his mirror dangling from a small nail at the top of the frame. Here, the dormer floor was crammed with boxes of his things, blocking his access to the window. He mentally inventoried the small room behind him—the narrow metal bed with its puffy down quilt, the tiny washstand, the stove, the small coal box, and the single chair. There was no other space for the pile of boxes. And he had to bend over just to see in the mirror that hung at an angle from the slanted wall.

He sighed. When they were married, he could move back downstairs with them. He and Lettie could have the larger room with the spool bed. His hand stopped pulling at the razor as he let himself visualize lying in the big bed with her in his arms. Her hair soft in his fingers, her lips . . . The face in the mirror smiled at him like gibbering lunatic. He pulled his thoughts back to the present. When his profit from the Palace came in, they would send Larry to a sanatorium for a few months until he was well. They'd have some real privacy. Lettie would miss Larry, of course. "Well, I'm sure I would too," he said aloud. "But to have Lettie all to myself for a while—I'll cope with the grief."

Smiling idiotically again, he wiped his face, rinsed the last of the shaving soap from his brush and mug, and stropped his razor for the next day. The last few swipes mingled with the sound of Mrs. Eskitch downstairs turning the coffee grinder, and Thad could see it clamped between her knees where she always steadied it. Already the smell of the coffee grounds penetrated the house, overpowering even his shaving soap. Someday it would be Lettie he'd hear in their own house.

Suddenly there was a rapping sound. The grinder stopped as Mrs. Eskitch probably tried to decide whether someone could really be at the door so early in the morning. The grinder started up again. The rap became a knock, loud, and definitely at the front of the house.

"All right, I'm coming, don't get your liver in a quiver," Thad heard her call as she stepped through the hall. ". . . fly off the hinges . . . wake the whole house . . ."

Thad had one arm in his vest when he heard Woolsley's voice.

"Where's MacElwain's room?" the officer asked loudly.

Thad forgot the vest. What on earth would Woolsley want with him at this hour? The store. Someone had broken into the store. He grabbed his suit coat from the back of the chair, shoved his arms into it, and went out onto the landing.

Lettie was just stepping out of her rooms, and Mrs. Eskitch was still standing open-mouthed at the front door, winding up for speechlessness, and pointing toward the stairs. Woolsley was already on the way up.

Thad started down. "Woolsley. What're you doing here? Is something wrong at the store?"

"As if you didn't know what was wrong, MacElwain. You're under arrest."

"*What?*" Thad missed a step and grabbed the banister for support.

Lettie and Mrs. Eskitch gasped.

"You heard me," said Woolsley.

"For what?" asked Thad, his heart thudding against his ribs.

"For the murder of Lemuel Marshall, of course."

"Old Marsh is dead?"

"You know perfectly well he is."

Thad could hardly breathe. "How would I know that?"

Woolsley cocked his head and waited for Thad to answer his own question.

"You think I killed him?" The steps seemed to turn to water and Thad struggled not to slide beneath it. He made it to the bottom of the stairs without being conscious of movement.

Woolsley shoved both thumbs into his belt. "I know you did."

"That's not possible," said Lettie. She moved next to Thad. "He was here all night."

"You telling me you were in his room? All night?" Woolsley leered at her.

"Lettie, don't," said Thad. "Remember the fleas carrying disease all over town."

Lettie looked puzzled and then seemed to remember the comparison he'd once made to Woolsley.

Mrs. Eskitch joined them at the bottom of the stairs, her hand fluttering up to her bosom. "Oh, my dear, you know I can't have that sort of thing in my house! Why, this is not . . ."

Lettie flushed. "No, of course not. He was upstairs."

Woolsley freed his billy club from his waist and batted it against his thigh. "Upstairs alone. That's a lie. Was anyone with you?"

"It is not a lie. And no, no one else was there. *Certainly* not Miss Corcoran. I was working on my books until late."

"Then no one saw you. You sneaked out in the middle of the night."

"What makes you think I killed him? I don't even know where he lives." Over the initial shock, Thad began to focus on the absurdity of the charge. "I couldn't find his place in broad daylight."

"How can you possibly think such a thing of Thad, Mr. Woolsley?" Lettie asked, and the hand she placed on Thad's arm trembled as angrily as her voice.

Woolsley ignored her and kept his belligerent eyes on Thad. "It was your knife did it. Over on the Palace site. Mr. Ralston came down not long after Marsh was found this morning and identified it. Said it was the knife you use to cut cheese."

"What?" Shock struck again and yanked everything from his senses but an unspeakable premonition. "Noah said that? It's ridiculous. My knife's in the store. Big cheese knife with an antler handle."

Woolsley smiled, his head high. "You better keep your mouth shut, MacElwain. You just described the murder weapon."

Thad's mouth fell open. "It can't be. I left it where I always leave it, hanging above the wash pan. If it was mine, someone must have broken in and stolen it."

"Well, let's just go on over and see if the knife is still there. If it is, you're in the clear."

Thad took his coat from the stand near the door and started to pull it on, his mind struggling for belief.

"Oh, my dear, we can't have you going out on the street with your vest hanging out of your suit," said Mrs. Eskitch. "Now you get out of that jacket and let's get you dressed like a gentleman!"

Lettie held the suit coat for him while he put the vest on properly. Then she reached for her own overcoat.

"Don't, Lettie, this is all a mistake. Don't worry about a thing. Stay here and eat. I'll be back in a few minutes."

She hesitated.

"Please," he said. "I won't have you being part of anything so humiliating. Stay here."

As they left, Thad turned and tried to smile at Mrs. Eskitch and Lettie, who were staring out the parlor window after them. He wanted to run, lag behind, walk on the opposite side of the street, anything not to be seen in the escort of the officer. Finally they reached the back of the store. He took his key out and opened the padlock with shaking hands.

"The lock's just fine. I don't see any signs of a break in, do you?" prodded Woolsley.

Thad glanced down at the lock. "No. Maybe someone broke in the front."

They went through the building and checked the front door. "Looks fine to me," said Woolsley. "You see anything amiss?"

"No."

"So, where's the cheese knife?"

Thad pointed almost without looking at the nail where the knife usually hung.

"Well, where is it?" asked Woolsley, triumph riding on his voice.

Thad looked again. He searched the entire space around the icebox, cutting block, and wash pan, then started to widen the hunt, his panic rising.

"No use doing that," said Woolsley. "It's gone. And you know *where* it's gone."

Thad's head throbbed. "I don't understand. I left it here last night, just as I always do." Fear burned in the pit of his stomach. "Believe me, Woolsley, I had nothing to do with this. I didn't know Marsh was dead until you said so."

"Sure you didn't. Come on, you're under arrest. Give me your hands."

"You don't need to shackle me. I'm not going to run. You have my word. I didn't do it."

"Police regulations, MacElwain. Far as the law is concerned, you're a murderer. I got to put the cuffs on."

"I am *not* a murderer," Thad shouted, shaken to the center of his being that anyone, even Woolsley, could believe such a thing of him.

By the time they left the store again, Harrison Street was alive with businessmen and schoolchildren. They turned to stare as Woolsley shoved him through the glassy, smoke-laden cold. The county courthouse a block from the store, with its tower above the entrance and the stone cornices over its windows, had never looked so forbidding, so inescapable.

CHAPTER 16

December 1, 1895

Thad stood in the middle of the stone floor avoiding the cot in the corner with the bare, discolored pillow on one end and a thick gray woolen blanket folded at the other. Afraid of the lice that almost certainly nested in the flattened straw mattress, he'd been pacing since Woolsley locked him in, though he had no idea how long ago that was. For the hundredth time he looked around the dim, cold cell, locked in a place he'd thought as far removed from him as the moon, the realm of those who were not honest, not hardworking. Those who didn't care. Those who didn't have Lettie.

Her face came into consciousness, and wave after wave of horrified disbelief gave way to realization that someone had done this to him, and done it well. Someone had taken away his life. His hopes for the future. Who would do this to him? Eddies of darkness passed through his mind but refused to become specific suspicions. He'd never done anyone enough harm to warrant this.

He paced again, feeling that if he rammed his body into the scratched and grimy walls, it would ease the pain and fear inside him. But no amount of ramming would break through the wall that separated him from his hopes. *The shame of a trial will ruin me,* he thought, *even if I'm acquitted. No one ever really believes in the innocence of a person who's accused of murder. And if that doesn't ruin me, the cost of a trial will. It'll eat up everything I make on the*

Ice Palace. I'll never have anything to offer Lettie, other than my love.

Blackness washed over him. He could not allow Lettie to hope anymore. It would force her to choose between him and her brother. He could not make her live with such a choice. She would have to . . .

Somewhere beyond the heavy wooden door a key clinked in a lock and Thad heard the light tap of Lettie's step. He was at the door before her face appeared in its small barred window. An officer opened it for her and she stepped in. After the officer had locked the door and disappeared, she threw her arms around him and they held each other tightly for a long time.

"Lettie, Lettie, you feel like a ray of sunshine in a grave. You can't know what it means to see you, though God knows I never would have wanted you to come to me in jail."

"You're here because of some mistake, my love. This is only where you are, not who you are."

He cupped her face in his hands and tried to swallow the lump in his throat. "My God, I love you."

She reached up and kissed him long and softly on the lips. He let the warmth of her love surge through him, but it only increased his despair.

"Don't lose heart," she said, putting her arms tightly around him and her head against his chest. "We'll have you out of here as soon as we can."

The rasp of a key turning in the lock drove them to opposite sides of the small cell. An extremely thin man with a pasty face and cold black eyes joined them.

"I'm Josiah Grimes, MacElwain," he said. "Lake County prosecutor. I've been called in to try you because the Leadville district attorney knows you."

"Then he knows I couldn't possibly kill anyone."

"He may believe that, but it would be his job to prove you

did, and we can't risk any prejudicial treatment, especially since a murderer might go free."

Grimes laid a thin folder on the rough wooden table that stood in front of the cot. He took out a single sheet of paper and perused it as he spoke. "You may as well know, MacElwain, this sort of thing is going to complicate the case right down the line. Judge Wyeth has already disqualified himself from the trial, even refuses to sit at the arraignment, because of being an investor in the Ice Palace. Which means you won't appear before a judge for at least two weeks, when Dickson returns."

Thad felt his insides shrink into a tight knot, ready to explode. "Two weeks! Then let me out. I'm not going to run. I've nothing to run from. I haven't done anything. I swear I'll be here in two weeks."

"Can't do that. This is a murder investigation, not some footpad's theft, MacElwain."

"I can't sit in this cold cave for two weeks," Thad shouted at him. "I have a store to run. I'll go bankrupt in two weeks if I can't tend to my business!"

"Watch your tone, MacElwain. And seems to me you should have thought of that before you killed Mr. . . ." he checked his document, "Lemuel Marshall."

"I didn't kill that old . . . I didn't kill him, Grimes, I swear it."

"He didn't kill him," Lettie added. "I . . . I can . . . prove it."

Grimes looked at Lettie for the first time. "What are you saying?"

"I was with him . . ."

"Lettie, don't."

". . . all night." Lettie's face flushed, but she looked Grimes directly in the eyes.

"No, she wasn't, Mr. Grimes. I was in my room alone. I was going over my books, like I always do on the last day of the

145

month. Miss Corcoran was probably downstairs. We live in the same boarding house. But I didn't see her again after supper."

Lettie stepped forward, her hands clasped at her waist. "Mr. Grimes, please, look at Thad. You can see in his eyes what kind of man he is."

Grimes looked hard at Lettie, then at Thad and the paper in his hand. His face softened slightly. "The evidence against you is pretty damning, MacElwain. There's no doubt the murder was committed with your knife. And you threatened the victim on more than one occasion, once publicly. You could save us all a lot of trouble if you'd go on and confess."

Thad shouted before he could stop himself. *"Confess?"* He felt Lettie's hand on his arm and checked his anger. "I can't confess to something I didn't do. I don't care what the evidence is, I did not kill Old Marsh!"

Grimes gazed at him a moment and shrugged. "It's my job to prove you did, and it won't be hard. Get yourself a good lawyer." He returned the document to the folder and shoved it under his arm. "For the moment there's nothing you can do but wait till Dickson returns. That at least gives you time to prepare your case." He banged on the cell door for the officer to open it and turned back to Lettie as he waited. "I won't damage your good name by repeating what you just said, Miss," he added, more gently than he had spoken before, "but don't let me hear you perjure yourself again to try to save your friend. If he's innocent, it'll come out at the trial." The door closed behind him and the key turned again.

"Lettie, don't you . . ."

"I'm sorry, I just can't bear the thought of you taking the blame for something you didn't do. I don't care about my reputation. I'd throw it to the winds for you."

He put his arms around her again and held her so close he feared breaking her ribs. "Oh, Lettie, I love you so much. I'd give my life for you and smile doing it." His breath caught. He felt her begin to shake with sobs. "I've been pacing though a nightmare here, helplessly waiting for something to happen, thinking what all this means for us. There's no hope anymore. You know that, too." He put his hand behind her head and pressed it closer, bending to her as if to shield her from his own words. "There's Larry. I love him, too, you know. I'll have to sell my shares to hire a lawyer, and that means everything's gone. I can't ever offer you any help for him."

Her arms tightened around him. "No," she choked out, "don't say this."

He lowered his head even more and forced the words out of his soul and into her ear. "Marry Noah. I know it has to be." He clenched his jaw hard to keep from sobbing aloud.

Lettie pushed away to smile at him through tears. "I can't bear the thought of not being with you, of leaving you at all, much less when you're trapped here. Anyway, Larry refuses to let me marry Noah for his sake. He's already said so. I'm afraid he'll leave or do something desperate."

"Then you'll have to pretend for him that you really love Noah."

Lettie shook her head and led him to the cot. When she started to sit down on the flattened straw mattress, he stopped her, took off his overcoat and laid it out for her to sit on. He sat next to her, almost feeling the crawling lice under him, resigned to the fact that he couldn't avoid the mattress for two weeks. He put his arm around her shoulder.

She leaned into him. "I can never pretend that, Thad. And even if I could, Larry would never believe it. He knows how I feel about you. Let me wait the two weeks till the judge gets back." She sat up straight again and looked up at him. "Maybe I can find out something. Someone out there killed Old Marsh and knows you didn't. Maybe he'll make a mistake."

"Who would want me to take the blame for it?"

Lettie looked away and bit her lip. "Forgive me for asking, Thad, but would Zeb do a thing like that?"

Thad blinked and frowned, giving himself a moment to think. The darkness that had swirled in his head condensed into a knot, shiny and clear as a black marble. Zeb? Thad shook his head, half in refusal to believe the suggestion and half in answer to her question. "No. He's my own brother. I don't think so. I know he's not the best brother in the world, but he's been trying to get along, hasn't he? In his way?" Thad breathed out a short laugh. "Besides, if I'm in jail, where's he going to go for interest-free, non-repayable loans?"

Lettie hesitated. "I suppose you're right. But who wants you out of the way?"

They looked at each other, eyes wide, as realization dawned.

"Noah," they said together. They stared into the ramifications of that knowledge for a minute.

Thad jumped up and headed for the door, as if the knowledge would free him. "It has to be him." He pulled on the bars of the door for a second and turned back to her. "My God, I just told you to marry him."

"Maybe I can talk him into admitting it," said Lettie.

"No, stay away from him. I didn't realize he was that dangerous. He might harm you."

"Never. I'm what he wants." She put her hand to her mouth. "It makes me sick even to think about marrying him."

"We can't prove he did it. We're just assuming it. How did he get my knife?"

"Are you sure you've used it since he was in last?"

"Of course. Noah hasn't been in the store since . . . when? Since that day when Tingley Wood took over the Palace. That was weeks ago."

"Do you remember what you did with it last night when you

closed the store?"

"The same as usual, as far as I know. I didn't pay any special attention, but I always wash it thoroughly at the end of the day and hang it on that nail. I do know I was the last person in the store and both doors were locked when I left." He ran his hand through his hair. "That's the strange thing. There wasn't any sign that anyone broke into the store."

"Are you sure the knife was still there when you left?"

"I *think* I'd remember if it wasn't."

"Well, Noah knows how it was done. I'll try to get it out of him."

"Lettie, please, promise me you'll stay away from him till this is all cleared up. If he did kill Marsh, he's capable of killing you, too, especially if he thinks he can't have you."

"But . . ."

"Please, my love, I'll be sick with worry about you and power-less to protect you."

"Oh, Thad, of course. I wasn't thinking about you at all. I'll do what you ask. And don't worry about the store. Larry and I can run it if you trust us to."

"Trust you? Of course I trust you. But I can't let you do it. What about your own business?"

"We'll manage both, don't worry. Please, Thad, I really mean that. You've enough to worry about, being in here. We'll be all right and keep things going for you." She stood to go. "Can I bring you anything next time I come? Surely you'll need fresh clothes, your razor."

"Whatever you can bring would help."

"Maybe a quilt. It's cold as the bottom of a well in here." Lettie looked around. "There's no stove!"

"And that one little window is in the shadow of the building across the street and doesn't get any sun at all. I guess they as-sume prisoners can survive in cave temperature."

When the door closed behind her, he heard the sound echo dully about the basement of the courthouse. He turned away from the door and paced the narrow space of the cell again, trying to outrun the black desolation, to find hope in the cold walls. There was none. He sat on the bunk, heedless of the lice now, rested his elbows on his knees and his head in his hands.

CHAPTER 17

December 2, 1895

Lettie stood at the front window of the store with her blue shawl wrapped tightly around her, rubbing her shoulders against the chill. Somewhere behind her Larry sat waiting for customers, but if she talked to him, she would only give word to fears she didn't want to acknowledge. She drew both lips between her teeth and pressed hard to hold back the tears. The old wall clock ticked into the silent store, its sound like water dripping into the meaningless flow of hours. The sewing machine stood open next to her, a stack of basted gold felt pieces ready to sew, but she hadn't the will to start on them. The store was a foreign, empty place without Thad, empty as her heart.

Through the smoky, frigid air she watched the ice sledges moving past at the bottom of Third Street, like the activity of Eskimos somewhere far away. It had nothing to do with her anymore, nothing to do with hope or happiness. It certainly wasn't related to a good man sitting in jail for something he didn't do. She closed her eyes, wishing herself two days back, or fifty years hence, when lost love might not hurt so much.

Behind her Larry's chair scraped across the floor, startling her back to the unbearable present.

"I think I'll move up where people can see me," he said from in front of the tobacco counter. "Do you think they're boycotting the store with Thad in jail?"

Lettie shrugged but couldn't bring herself to answer.

Larry coughed before he went on. "It's half past eleven and not a single soul has come in all morning. You know how gossip flies around Leadville."

A tear fell and she wiped it away, angry at herself for her weakness. "I don't know," she forced herself to say, "but if his customers are staying away and if we don't do something, Thad will go bankrupt even without the expense of a lawyer's fees."

"What can we do?"

"Maybe put a sign in the window, some kind of price reduction. Does Thad still have any old things that haven't been on sale yet?"

Before Larry could answer, the door jangled open. Zeb stepped in and shut the door quickly against the blast of icy air that blew in with him.

"Well, hello, Miss Corcoran, Larry," he said, taking off his fur hat and throwing it onto the notions counter.

Lettie frowned. What would Zeb be doing here at this time of day? She glanced around at the clock and back at him.

Zeb followed her glance and then stared at her with his jaw out. "I don't know that it's your concern," he said, "but, no, I'm not playing hooky from that pack mule's job at the post office. In fact, I quit. What with Thad being in jail and all, someone's going to have to mind the store for him."

Lettie felt a cold knot of anxiety draw up her heart. "You'll pardon me for saying so, Mr. MacElwain, but that seems a bit out of character for you."

"No, I won't pardon you, but yes, I suppose it does." He gave her a brittle smile. "You see, somewhere in the dark recesses of my heart, even I know that kin is kin."

Lettie started to answer, but Larry spoke first. "We're taking care of the store," he said coldly. "He wants us to. He already said so."

Zeb looked at him with the intense stare of a stalking cat.

"You aren't his brother. I am. And I'll take care of him."

Lettie looked nervously at Larry, wondering whether Zeb had any legal right to take over the store. His answering look said, *let's talk about this later.*

They both watched Zeb stroll around the store with the air of new ownership. He fingered the shirts on the shelf between the sewing machine and the stove, straightened the reading glasses, and headed toward the back. For a second he glanced at the place where the knife had hung, and a hint of a smile crossed his face. He looked away quickly and bent to peer through the glass of the tobacco counter at a few Meerschaum pipes.

He knows something, Larry thought. He watched Zeb, sensing the deep-seated malice that rendered his morals as hideous as the scars rendered his hand. *I have to find out what he knows about the knife,* Larry said to himself. *And I can't let him take over the store. I'll demand that he leave.* He opened his mouth, but no sound came out. He felt himself go pale at the thought of confronting Zeb.

Zeb glared at him. "You got something to say?"

Larry stood up, cursing his lack of courage. He stepped behind the cash register. "You can't work here, Zeb. You know Thad can't afford to pay you anything." Even to him, his voice sounded more like begging than commanding. *Pathetic,* he thought. *I'll never have the nerve to cross him. I need to work at him from the inside. I'll have to get closer.* The thought made his stomach turn.

Zeb continued to stare at him. "Oh, quite. I'll manage, don't worry."

Larry tried again. "There hasn't been a customer all day." He pictured himself spread-eagle over the register, blocking it from Zeb's grasping hand.

Zeb's eyes seemed to turn him to stone. "Well, what business doesn't have its dull days?"

The door opened again and Mrs. Eskitch entered in a flurry of scarves and wool strings tied to earmuffs and mittens, her nose and cheeks red and raw.

Zeb grinned down at him. "There, see?" His words were lost in Mrs. Eskitch's instant chatter.

"The whole town's talking about it. As if anyone could really believe our Mr. Mac would do such a thing. Well, I declare, it's our other Mr. MacElwain. I'm so sorry to hear about your brother's trouble, Mr. MacElwain. I'm sure it's all going to turn out all right in the end. Anyone who knows him knows he couldn't kill a fly. And I told everybody I met the same thing."

"Well, he *was* heard to threaten the old fool," said Zeb. "Anyway, everybody wanted that mangy cur out of the way. I think Thad ought to get a medal."

Larry stared.

Lettie gasped. "How can you take sides like that against your own brother?"

Zeb raised both shoulders and extended his left hand, palm up in a gesture of helplessness. "I'm only repeating what's common knowledge."

Larry looked hard at Zeb. He looked back at the place where the knife should be hanging and remembered Zeb's face the first time he'd spotted it. The danger that always emanated from Zeb struck him again.

"Well, my dear," Mrs. Eskitch interrupted his thoughts, "let me have a jar of tomatoes. I canned my own beans and peas last summer and I have enough potatoes in the root cellar. They keep so well, don't they? And apples, too. You can eat them all winter. But my tomatoes are all gone. I think I'll make Mr. Mac a nice pot of vegetable soup and take it over for his supper. I'll stop by the butcher's and pick up a soup bone. I'm sure they won't give him anything like a home-cooked meal in that awful place."

Lettie stood and hugged her. "Oh, Mrs. Es, that's so kind of you. I know he'll be grateful."

"Especially for your faith in him," said Larry, looking pointedly at Zeb.

"Oh, I'm just sure he's innocent, too," he said, smiling.

Larry started toward the shelves in the back corner to get the tomatoes.

Zeb grabbed his shoulder with fingers like railroad spikes. "I'll get it. You sit down, Larry. We don't want you getting sick on us again, now do we?" A benevolent smile on his face, he steered Larry to the chair, forced him into it, and turned toward the shelves. "I'm taking over the store, Mrs. Eskitch, coming to my brother's aid," he said over his shoulder.

A look of alarm flitted across Mrs. Eskitch's face.

Even she knows, thought Larry, getting up and stationing himself behind the register to ring up the sale. The whole town knew by now what a cad Zeb was.

Mrs. Eskitch smiled at Zeb's back. "Well, now, isn't that nice? You see, with all of us believing in him and helping out, how could it possibly turn out badly? I just know they'll set him free soon as they find the real killer."

Zeb turned and stared wide-eyed, his raised hand around the neck of a jar.

Mrs. Eskitch opened her mouth, but no sound came out.

Zeb's stare glided into a smile that froze his face. He set the tomatoes on the counter, grabbed Larry's forearm to shove him aside, and opened the register.

Larry joined Lettie at the sewing machine, rubbing his arm to rid himself of the cold of Zeb's touch.

CHAPTER 18

December 7, 1895

Lettie opened the cash register under the electric light, glancing nervously toward the door for Zeb's return. For days he had nearly snarled at her and Larry if they approached the register. Now she had made up her mind to find out why. Checking the door once more, she took the money from the drawer and began counting it. There was not much to count. Seventeen dollars in bills and two dollars and eighty-eight cents in coin. She put it back in the drawer and leaned against the cash register. All day she'd kept her ears open when Zeb quoted prices to customers, keeping an approximate total in her head. There should be at least eight-fifty over the fifteen that Thad always started with. She could have figured wrong, but she'd hardly be that far off the mark.

She looked toward the Silver Dollar Saloon, where Zeb always went for a few minutes just before closing time, but saw only her own reflection in the window against the deep dusk outside. Now it was clear where he was getting the money for the visits. She held on to the top of the cash register with both hands and bowed her head until it rested on her right arm. She had no proof he was stealing money.

Zeb would be back any minute and could see her in the lighted store as soon as he left the saloon. The thought of meeting him now revolted her, of having to look at his cold, vindictive eyes. She had to leave, even if her leaving meant he could clean out the cash drawer for a Saturday night spree. She grabbed her coat from its peg in the hall and walked out just as he came in.

"Leaving so soon, Miss Corcoran?" he asked, his tone neutral for once.

"I'm going to visit Thad before it gets too late," she mumbled, her mouth dry.

She started up the boardwalk toward Fourth in case he was watching but knew she couldn't visit Thad right now. She was too upset about Zeb's theft. She'd surely blurt it out if she saw Thad, and she hadn't told him specifically that Zeb had taken over for fear of worrying him. At the corner of Seventh Street she sat down on the steps of the boarded-up apothecary. Exhaustion overcame her, and she realized how drained she was after a week of being in the same room with Zeb, worrying about Thad, trying not to look into a bleak future. And now this.

The weather, at least, had turned warm and pleasant, a complete change from the week before, from the night Old Marsh had died and then frozen solid among the ice blocks. Through the buildings she glimpsed the construction site under the raised rows of lights and the huge canvas sheets that shaded the south wall of the Palace. For three days the temperature had been climbing. Today it had reached forty-five.

Across the valley the north shoulder of Mount Massive glowed out of the dying light above the smoke and the dirty snow of the mining town. She wished herself on the pristine peak, away from desperation and worry and pain. She gazed down Harrison, toward the store. Suddenly the street looked alien and hostile, as if she did not belong on it. Where did she belong? Only with Thad, and he was in jail.

She shivered as the night air sank into the valley and the cold of the stone step under her seeped through her clothes. She should go back to Mrs. Eskitch's, where Larry lay in bed, having one of his weak days. She should go and see how he was, but the thought of his pale face in the midst of all her other worries made her feel trapped. And that made her feel guilty. Besides, she'd probably just blurt out the fact that Zeb was stealing money. Should she tell Larry? What could he do? What could either of them do? They could tell the police, but Woolsley would only think it was Thad's just deserts. And what of his customers? The certain answer to that question placed itself clearly in her mind. If word spread that Zeb was cheating, even Thad's regular customers would go elsewhere.

Should she go and tell Thad after all? Even if she had proof, it would break her heart to tell him when he had as much weighing on him as a man could stand. And beneath all her considerations lay a deep fear of Zeb, which she'd had since that one time their eyes had locked on the train and she'd felt like a rabbit trapped in the stare of a viper. She'd seen him look at Larry the same way, assessing his weakness.

Hunched forward, she rocked herself, her hands stretched as far around her waist as she could reach. But it was Thad's hands she wanted, his arms around her, his voice telling her everything would come out all right. That was impossible, of course, but she got up, went back to Fourth, and crossed to the courthouse.

When the officer led her to the cell, Thad's face didn't appear, as it usually did. He was lying on the thin straw mattress coughing, his face flushed under the week's worth of whiskers he'd grown because the guards wouldn't let him have his razor.

The last ton of despair crashed onto her shoulders, but for his sake, she couldn't give in to it. "Oh, Thad, you're sick!"

"It's just a cold. I can't seem to get warm in here." He sat up and leaned against the wall behind the head of the bed, pulling the quilt she'd brought him over his chest.

She knelt at his side. "This is such an awful place. Outside it was warm as spring today. Nothing penetrates here, does it?"

"No, you're my sunlight and my newspaper. Nothing but your love keeps me going."

She smiled and placed her cool hand on his forehead. "Well, you haven't much fever so far. Tomorrow I'll bring you some sage tea and a vapor rub on the way to work. Still no lice?"

Thad grinned. "No, thank heaven for that small favor. Come, Lettie, get up off that cold floor." He squeezed closer to the stone wall to make room for her.

"Have you decided about a lawyer yet?" she asked as she settled next to him, aware of the hardness of his hip through all her clothing and the thick quilt.

He shook his head. "That Mr. Grimes was in again, asking questions. He says there's a chance Dickson will set bail for me. I can't even think about a lawyer until I know how much bail I'll have to pay. I'm afraid it'll just have to wait. It's driving me mad. How's the store going?"

Lettie hesitated a moment too long.

He took her hand. "What's wrong? Is there a problem in the store?"

Lettie knew she couldn't tell him about Zeb, not when he was sick on top of everything else. But she had to do something. "Do you ever come up short of cash at the end of the day?"

"Why do you ask? Did you come up short?"

No, not I, she wanted to scream, *it's your leech of a brother,* but she said, "Once when I counted it, there was less than I thought."

"Well, write down each purchase amount on a piece of paper and total it at the end of the day so you'll have a cross check. That should clear up the problem. I did that a few times, but then I was able to keep a running total in my head. I'm sure you were just overly optimistic. There's rarely more than ten or twelve dollars over the fifteen that I start with."

"I thought about that," she said, "only . . ."

"Only what?"

"Nothing. That's what I'll do, then," said Lettie, wondering how she could keep a running check while Zeb was in the store.

"Are there any other problems? Did you find the forms for the week's order?"

"Yes. We got the order off. The flour and molasses ought to be here next week. And the representative from the souvenir company said the Palace tie tacks and brooches will be here by Christmas."

"How's Larry?"

"Feeling weak today, but it may just be the change in the weather."

"Tell him I asked after him and hope he's better tomorrow." Thad slid down a little on the mattress and kissed her hand. "Now, do, tell me some other news. Something cheerful. I'm bored out of my wits in here."

Lettie put her distress aside and searched for news that wasn't depressing. "Well, let's see. You know they're going to display Colorado-made products frozen right in the walls of the Palace?"

Thad nodded.

"The Coors brewing company down in Golden sent up a case of beer. I guess some of the workers thought it was a shame to waste all that beer."

Thad grinned. "They opened it and drank it?"

"Yes. Only it turned out Coors had feared the beer would freeze and break the bottles, so they filled them with salt water. Instead of drinking a round, the workers took one swallow and spat it all out again. They say Mr. Lambert spat the farthest of all."

Thad laughed and coughed at the same time.

"Oh, and you know I told you about the spraying of the Palace because of the wind. Wait a minute, what did they call that wind?"

"Chinook."

"Yes, that was it." Lettie forced herself to focus on what she was saying, when all she wanted was to give in to grief. "It's been blowing for a couple of days, made the valley very warm in the sun. I wish you could be out in it. It's so lovely after the cold spell last week. Anyway, the Palace is beginning to look a little funny with the added layers of ice."

"In what way funny?"

"Well, a little milky around the edges. Everybody says it's disappointing. But they've got the workers setting blocks 'round the clock."

"Right through the night?"

"Two twelve-hour shifts. They've got it all lit up at night now. The time that was wasted removing the blocks Old Marsh salted put them behind schedule. The teamster says they won't get it finished for Christmas, but he promises to be open for New Year's Day."

Thad shook his head. "It's an amazing feat, when you think about it, to build such a huge structure in such a short time."

"Five and a half weeks since the laying of the first block, if they're finished by the First. They say dozens of different groups from all over the state have reserved a day or two at the Palace." She smiled as a spark of hope flickered in the despair. "Oh, love, maybe it'll be such a success that you'll make hundreds and hundreds of dollars and everything will turn out all right."

He smiled wanly and took her hand. "Hold on to that thought, Lettie, hold on to it for me, too. It's hard to find any hope in this dungeon."

Lettie let herself into the store early Monday morning and took the ledger from the drawer under the tobacco counter. Zeb's awkward scrawl filled in the last eight lines, showing totals between four and six dollars. She thought of the customers who had been in since Thad was arrested. There hadn't been much business, but surely more than this. From the drawer she took a slip of paper and a pencil and laid them under the pile of fabric waiting on the sewing machine.

For the rest of the day she took them out whenever she knew Zeb wasn't looking and jotted down the last figures he had quoted. In the late afternoon, several customers and two uniform fittings prevented her from counting the money again before Zeb returned from the saloon, but on the next morning she compared her figures with his. Her scrap of paper showed $12.83. In the ledger he had entered $6.45. She clenched her fist, wadding her note into a ball. "Why am I shocked?" she murmured. And then, "I've got to stop him somehow."

Her mind searched desperately for a plan, but she knew if she confronted him, he'd deny it, or try to blame her or Larry. At the least, he'd spread rumors around town, and the business would fail. He was even ruthless enough to do them bodily harm, especially Larry, who was weak.

Thinking of him sent a shudder down her spine. She was afraid of him. But if she didn't stop him from stealing, Thad could go bankrupt. If she told Thad, it would only nag at him. Desperate and confused, she laid the ledger back and dated the note. Where should she keep it? At home? No, Mrs. Eskitch might find it and the news would be general knowledge in ten minutes. In the store? She looked around for something to hide it in. There was nothing here that Zeb might not touch. Even her sewing things weren't safe. She tried the storeroom. A bolt of fabric. She slid the scrap of paper between the layers of cloth and started out. No. Zeb might not be interested in the pink muslin, but a customer could ask for it. There was nothing she could do with the note but keep it on her person. The thought made her skin crawl, the way if would if Zeb found out and put his hands on her to get the note. Still, she fished it out again and shoved it in her skirt pocket.

.

CHAPTER 19

December 16, 1895

Following Officer Swinton to his bail hearing, Thad felt shaggy, unwashed, and pasty; and although there was no mirror anywhere to check himself, he knew that after two weeks in the cell, he looked capable of the crime he hadn't committed.

His wrists shackled in front of him, he climbed a stairway of City Hall that he hadn't even known existed. It was plain and dingy compared to the hand-carved mahogany stairway in the lobby, its air stale and dusty; but each step brought him into a warmer, friendlier light. He dared to hope that the day would bring his release. After all, Tom Dickson knew him; he would know the charge was ridiculous. Maybe he would just dismiss it.

They entered the second floor through a door labeled "prisoner's entrance." On his left as they went through the short corridor, he read a sign on another door: Judge's Chamber. The sign dashed Thad's blithe hope. This was not Tom Dickson, his occasional fishing companion, but a judge of the court, even though he would have nothing more to do with the case than presiding at the bail hearing. Suddenly the shackles were heavy as an anchor. There would be no dismissal in the face of all the evidence against him. The enormity and hopelessness of his situation overwhelmed him; he gasped and then doubled over in a fit of coughing.

Swinton shoved him from behind, propelling him into the

mahogany-paneled courtroom. The carved judge's bench loomed on his left. The stained-glass windows depicting Leadville's mining history glowed weakly into the chill, high-ceilinged room.

The buzz of conversation stopped as Thad stepped through the door. The spectator area was packed with his friends and customers, all wearing their overcoats. He tried to smile as a few of them waved.

Grimes already sat in front of the carved mahogany balustrade that divided the spectators from the court, a small stack of papers in front of him. To Grimes's left stood the empty defendant's table, and behind it he saw Lettie, Larry, and Mrs. Eskitch. He headed toward them. Before he reached them, the officer pushed him into a chair. The chain between the shackles rattled onto the tabletop. Thad turned and smiled as confidently as he could. Two rows behind them Zeb grinned at him, and at the back of the room Noah stood against the wall looking at the judge's door. He did not meet Thad's eyes.

"All rise," called the clerk of court. Judge Dickson entered and took his seat. The clerk announced the case before him. Dickson ran his hand over his trim gray beard and shook his head.

"I much prefer to see you with a fishing rod in hand, Thad," he began with a sad smile. "Where is your legal counsel?"

"I have none, Tom—sir—Your Honor. I can't afford to hire a lawyer until I know whether you're going to set bail for me. I only have the money I invested in the Ice Palace."

"I see. Well, how do you plead in this matter?"

"You know me well enough to know I couldn't commit murder, sir. I plead innocent."

"Uh-huh, I thought as much." Dickson leaned back in his chair with both hands behind his head. "Now, I believe the county attorney has already informed you I'm going to have to disqualify myself from the trial. Though not an investor in the Palace, I do know you, and who didn't know Old Marsh? Theoretically, I should even disqualify myself from setting bail."

Grimes stood up. "Your honor . . ."

Dickson waved him back into his seat. "I know, Grimes, it's on the border of legality, but then, I'm retiring at the end of the month and don't have any plans to run for political office like my colleague, Judge Wyeth. Thad, I'm afraid you're going to have to wait for the state circuit judge, Richard Maitlin, and his next stop is—let's see . . ." he sat up and checked his notes, "Friday, February twenty-eighth."

Stunned, Thad leaned against the table for support. He couldn't live with this hanging over his head for more than two months.

Dickson shook his head again sympathetically. "I'm sorry, Thad, there's not a single thing I can do about it. It's the law. Now you understand that this is a murder trial, and I can't just let you walk out that door without some guarantee you'll be back."

Thad put both hands out to the judge. "Tom—Your Honor, you know me, you know my word is good. If you could set some token amount, I'd sure . . ."

Grimes jumped up. "The prosecution demands a high bail, Your Honor. This was a brutal murder such as the county hasn't seen since the days of the Frodsham gang. We can't let Leadville revert to those days."

Dickson looked from Thad to Grimes and shook his head. "I don't think I can satisfy you both, but bail is set at five hundred dollars. Thad, I hope . . ."

Thad's knees gave way and he sank into the chair. He heard Lettie stifle a cry. "Sir, couldn't you just hold the shares in the Ice Palace as bond? It's only four hundred thirty-five dollars, but it's all I have."

A laugh started in Judge Dickson's throat, but he cut it off with a cough. "Even for me that would be too irregular, my boy. At this point no one knows whether the shares will be worth even half that come February. But I'll tell you what I *will* do. I'll reduce the bail to four hundred dollars. As soon as you sell the shares and get the money to the clerk of court, you're free till your date with the state judge. This all right with the prosecution, Grimes?"

Grimes turned his pasty face toward Thad and stared at him for a minute, his indecision written on his face.

Dickson didn't wait for his answer. "Fine, bail is set at four hundred dollars. My part in this is over. And good luck to you, Thad." He banged his gavel.

The sound stabbed into Thad like the last nail in his coffin. He was ruined; there wasn't even enough money left for a decent lawyer. The last glimmer of a hope he thought he'd purged from his heart went out. There was nothing for Lettie. Slowly he turned in her direction. She looked back at him, making no effort to stem the tears. A movement in the back caught his eye. Noah shoved himself away from the wall and moved toward the door. This time their eyes met and Noah smiled triumphantly.

He did it, thought Thad. *I swear, if it ruins me completely, I will get him to admit it.*

He looked once more at Lettie and knew that neither of them could find words for their grief. Swinton led him back out of the room, down the steps to the cold gloom of his cell.

Half an hour later the door opened and Lettie and Larry came in. Her nose was red from crying, and Larry's eyes were brighter than the fever usually made them.

Thad stood up and they all stepped into an embrace, struggling not to sob aloud. Thad released them with his eyes on Lettie's, and mutual despair passed between them.

"This is all my fault," said Larry, his voice catching.

Thad blinked hard and stared at him. "What? It most certainly is not. You had nothing to do with it."

"Not with the murder, but if it weren't for my damned stupid lungs—pardon me, Lettie—you'd never have invested that money in the first place."

Thad grabbed him by the shoulders. "Listen, Larry, I think of you as family, and what I did with my money was my choice, not yours. Don't you go loading yourself down with guilt for something you had no control over."

"But . . ."

"There are no 'buts' here. Now forget that and help me decide what to do."

Larry started to protest, but Lettie shook her head at him and turned to Thad.

"We tried to put the bail together for you," she said. "But even when we counted all our money with what Mrs. Eskitch could give you, we could only come up with about a hundred and fifty-three dollars. It looks like you'll have to sell the shares."

Thad put both hands in his pockets and began to pace. "To whom? Who has money anymore? Everybody who had a few dollars put them in the Ice Palace."

"Not . . ." said Lettie after a pause. "Not Noah."

Thad stopped in his tracks. "Noah! I wouldn't sell my shares to him." He looked hard at Lettie. "You know—what we decided. Besides, he wouldn't buy them."

"He might if I talk to him. He'd see it as another triumph. Thad, there's really nobody else. You could try to sell them to someone down in Denver, but that could take weeks. If you sell them to Noah, at least you're free of this cold jail. You can start trying to find who did kill Old Marsh. If you don't, all you can do is sit here and worry. Besides, the store—needs you. Let me talk to him."

"But we agreed . . ."

"I'll take Larry with me."

Thad turned to the small window near the ceiling of the cell and looked out at the sliver of sky above the building across the street. *There's nothing else I can do,* he thought. *Does it really matter anymore? She won't marry that murderer, but she can't marry me, either, so one more defeat makes no difference. And if I can find out how Noah killed Marsh, at least I'll get my four hundred dollars back. I can leave and start over somewhere.*

"All right," he said heavily. "Take Larry with you."

Lettie put her hand on his arm. He touched it briefly, put his elbow on the high sill, and laid his head on his arm.

Lettie slid both hands around his arm and rested her forehead on his shoulder for a minute. Then she let go of him. He turned from the window. She stood motionless beside him, head down, her hands balled into fists at her sides.

Behind them, Larry watched, equally desolate, his mind racing. *They're on the wrong track,* he thought. *They think it was Noah. Maybe it was, but my money's on Zeb. I have to get the proof somehow.* He started to tell them his suspicions, but closed his mouth again. There was no use saying anything when he had no idea how to go about catching Zeb. And even if they didn't protest his doing a little sleuthing, there was no use giving them hopes that might not materialize.

CHAPTER 20

December 16, 1895

Lettie knocked on the door to Noah's office, and she and Larry entered at his call. He smiled warmly, rose and came from behind his desk to meet them.

"I've come to ask you to buy out Thad's shares," she said without preamble, crossing the dark-paneled room toward him, already nervous. His presence had never been so intimidating. "You heard what the judge said. You know there's no one else in town who can afford to buy them." They met in the middle of the maroon Persian carpet.

Noah stared down at her, his brows knitted. His eyes narrowed and he shook his head slightly, as if shaking off disbelief. For an awkward moment no one said anything.

He walked her to a chair in front of his desk, leaving Larry in the middle of the floor. "Well, I'm willing to talk about such an unexpected turn of events, but I don't believe I want to discuss it with your brother present."

Lettie took the seat he offered and motioned for Larry to sit down as well. "I'd prefer to have him with me. Now, I know that you know Thad didn't murder Marsh. And since you do," she frowned pointedly, "I think the least you could do is help him out. After all, he is your friend—or was, before . . ."

"Just one minute, Juliet!" Noah sat down and rested his elbows on his desk with his right shoulder forward. "I'm really not willing to carry on this discussion. If your brother leaves we can continue."

Lettie looked at Larry, uncertain. At last she said, "Larry, could you wait just outside the door?"

"Lettie, I don't think . . ."

"It's all right. If I need you, I'll call."

When the door closed quietly behind Larry, she turned back to Noah.

His face had darkened, but now he smiled. "I really should be quite insulted, you know. Your reputation won't suffer from being with me."

"My reputation wasn't what I was worried about," she said quietly.

Noah either did not hear her comment or chose to ignore it. "Why don't you give me a chance, Juliet? Most people would say you'd finally come to your senses and married well."

"I'd prefer to marry for love, Noah."

"But I do love you. You know that."

"Maybe you want me. I know you're trying to *win* me. I don't happen to believe that loving and wanting are the same, but I'm not sure you know the difference." She rushed on before she lost her courage. "You told Thad you'd stop at nothing to have me." Her heart was racing now, and the frayed edge of nervousness crept into her voice. "I assume that included murdering Marsh and letting Thad take the blame. I hope you don't think I could ever love a murderer."

Noah's mouth fell open and he sputtered for a minute. "You think I killed Marsh?"

"Yes." She held her chin high and looked directly into his eyes, but nothing she had ever done had cost her as much force of will.

Noah's face went pale. He stared at her for a long time in shock.

Lettie felt her conviction begin to crumble. "Well, no one else had any reason to."

Noah's mouth opened and closed again. For a second she thought he was going to admit it, but his face only looked torn and then hardened into a bitter frown. He was sitting straight as a needle now.

"Did you come here to deliver false accusations or to get me to help your lover?" He spat out the last word with sarcasm.

Lettie felt her face go hot but checked the protest that was on her tongue. "Will you buy the shares?"

Noah sat back and considered for a long time, staring at her silently. "If I do," he said with a harsh edge to his voice, "it'll be on the condition that you consent to be my wife."

Lettie jumped from the chair. "No, you . . ."

He stood and looked down at her without blinking. His arms hung at his sides, and the quiet in the room seemed to emanate directly from him. "Whatever else I am, Juliet, I am *not* a murderer."

Lettie faltered. "I almost believe you, but I think . . ."

"What?"

She was confused now, and feared pushing the issue lest he refuse outright to buy the shares. "I . . . I don't know."

"But you *do* know you want Thad out of jail. I've given you my condition."

Images of her future flashed through her head: a ghastly wedding in white, a life of submission to a man whose very morality she doubted, help for Larry, loss of Thad, who was as much a part of her as her own heart. Everything inside her drew up into a knot. "You would still want me, knowing I love another man?" she asked, only stalling the inevitable.

Noah hesitated and Lettie regretted the question. It might make him change his mind. If he didn't buy the shares . . .

He nodded slowly. "I'm confident I can make you love me. Eventually. When you've been with me for a while, you won't even remember that poor failure of a shopkeeper."

"He's not a . . ."

Noah put up his hand. "Forget Thad. And forget the future, Juliet. That'll take care of itself. The present reality is this: you promise to marry me, move out of the store and the boarding house, stop seeing Thad *as of now*, and I buy the shares. It's as simple as that."

"I won't move. I can't afford to live or work anywhere else."

"I'll pay for . . ."

Lettie glared at him. "Don't even suggest it. If I have to be your kept woman, it'll be when it's legitimate, but not before."

Noah's head came up as if he'd been slapped and it was a minute before he said, "I want you away from Thad."

Away from Thad? Already? The thought was unbearable. Lettie stood and turned toward the door. "If you don't trust me to do what's honorable, I'll borrow the money from the bank."

"Juliet, be realistic. The bank isn't going to lend you a cent. You're a bad risk, living from week to week on income that will stop as soon as the carnival's over. And forget about borrowing against those worthless shares. The bank wouldn't give Thad more than a pittance for them."

He was right. Noah was her only hope, the only choice. The lonely future closed in on her. The huge weight of it pressed her back into the chair. She sat forcing the air in and out of her lungs until she could say through her tears, "If I agree to marry you, I stay in the shop and the house, but I won't see Thad socially, I give you my word."

Noah hesitated, and then his voice turned almost gentle. "All right."

"Will you help me pay for Larry's care?"

"Yes. Whatever he needs. As soon as we're married."

"Now. He's getting worse, Noah."

"Then we should have the wedding as soon as possible."

Lettie got up and walked to the window overlooking the rear entrance of the hotel, where garbage cans sat in the dirty snow of the perpetual winter shade. Tears flowed, and the image of Thad rippled in her watery vision, Thad under the aspen trees, Thad behind his counter, weighing out jerky for Old Marsh, Thad building her the bed-warmer tent in the front of his store, Thad with his warm hand on her face, smiling his love at her. Larry's face replaced Thad's, cheeks red and feverish, coughing in the night, waiting now outside the door.

She put her forehead on the cold glass and saw the last shred of hope flutter down into an ash can. In that moment she felt her life disconnect from Thad's forever, like an amputation of the heart. "I'll marry you," she said so softly that Noah came to her.

"Say that again." He put his hands around her waist from behind.

Lettie moved aside and kept her back to him. "I'll marry you."

"When?" He placed his hands on her shoulders and turned her to face him.

She couldn't think of setting a date now. Not until the pain lessened. "Soon." She looked straight into his eyes. "But I must tell you, Noah, I'll never love you. This is purely a business deal as far as I'm concerned. I'm selling myself to you to help my brother and to free Thad." Her voice caught and she choked the last words out. "But my price isn't four hundred thirty-five dollars, it's five hundred dollars. He has no money to hire a lawyer."

"It's done." He offered her his hand and she shook it.

"I need the money now so I can take it to the courthouse."

"It's in the safe. I'll take care of it."

As he led her to the door she wiped her hand hard on the side of her skirt.

★ ★ ★ ★ ★

Larry waited, leaning against the doorframe, where he listened intently but could hear only muffled words from Noah and nothing that Lettie said. A deep guilt settled over him and he bent his head under it. *I should just leave, go back to Baltimore, get out of her life,* he thought. *She wouldn't be in this position if it weren't for me. Noah will never simply buy the shares outright. He'll want something in return. But surely Lettie won't marry him. Not someone she suspects of murder.*

The door opened and closed. Lettie walked past him, head up, moving like a machine.

Larry knew what she'd done the minute he saw her pale face, straining for decorum, drained of all hope. He trailed after her grabbing at her arm. "You didn't agree to marry him, did you?"

Lettie jerked free and stalked through the lobby, looking neither right nor left.

"You can't do this, Lettie," Larry shouted.

Several men standing at the reception desk turned to stare.

"It's wrong, Lettie, you know it's wrong," he pleaded, following her through the doors onto Harrison Street. "You'll just make everybody miserable. I'm not going to let you do it."

She did not even appear to hear him. She walked blindly across Harrison, stepping right through a slushy puddle.

Larry stopped and watched her disappear around Seventh. He looked back into the lobby and down Harrison toward the store. *I won't let this happen,* he swore to himself. *I won't let Thad lose everything for me. I won't let her do this. I'll leave.*

If I leave, Thad still goes to jail. No one will ever find out what happened. But I'll find out. I owe him that. This all came about because of me. I'll set things right if it kills me.

CHAPTER 21

December 19, 1895

Thad stood for a minute on the steps of the courthouse, clutching the puffy down quilt to his chest, oblivious of its red, brown, and black patches or the lumpy books, clothes and toiletries folded in it. He gazed up at the early evening stars and took a deep breath of freely moving air, ignoring the smoke of a thousand chimneys. He should be grateful for any change from the rank air of the cell, but in nearly three weeks, too much frustration had built up in him to let him think of anything but Noah. The bile of anger rose and burned his heart. Noah.

Noah had framed him for murder and ruined him financially. Noah had taken Lettie away somehow. She had not come back to see him during the weekend. Only Larry had come, but Thad had sent him away almost immediately when he started coughing in the cold cell. Anger turned to fury, and he ran toward Eighth, the corners of the quilt flopping against his legs.

He ran into the hotel, banging the door against a snowshoe stand and shouting "Ralston!" He broke his stride for a second when the guests waiting for the dining room to open turned to stare, but they only made him angrier. Let their brocade and silk reproach his wrinkled coat and pants, his smelly shirt, and his floppy quilt. Let their tended hair and smooth faces disdain his shaggy moustache and beard. He left them to their startled stares as he rushed past them in small groups near the fireplace and around the maroon circular sofas. He ran to the desk.

"Where's Ralston?" he shouted at Bill Emmett, the clerk.

"Mr. MacElwain, I think you'd better . . ."

"Don't tell me what I'd better do, Emmett. Get Ralston out here this minute or I'll barge into every room in this hotel till I find him."

Noah opened the double dining room doors and froze with his arms out. "Get out of here, MacElwain," he said in a near whisper, glancing at the guests.

Thad started toward him, shouting. "You did this to me, Ralston. You killed him. I know you did."

Noah nodded at Bill Emmett, and the two of them grabbed Thad by the arms. The quilt with his belongings thudded on the floor. His comb and a pair of underwear flopped onto the carpet. The two men rushed him down the hall past the stairs. He struggled to turn back to the guests, who stood in bunches, gaping at them. "He did it, he ruined me. He's a . . ." Thad yelled.

Noah let go and struck him in the stomach. Stunned and thrown into a coughing fit, Thad sagged to the floor, but the two men forced him upright, dragged him into Noah's office, and shoved him into a chair in front of the desk.

"Get back out there and smooth things over," Noah told Emmett. "Tell them the wine is on the house or something. Just distract them from this. And get that junk up off the floor." He moved behind his wide desk.

Thad gasped for breath, putting a hand to the pain in his stomach. His rage rose again. He jumped up and leaned over the desk. "How did you do it, Ralston, how'd you get my knife?" he shouted.

Noah leaned toward him until their faces were only inches apart, his white knuckles clamping the edge of the desk. "Lower your voice," he growled, "or I'll have you arrested again for false accusations and disturbing the peace. I didn't kill Old Marsh,

MacElwain. You look me right in the eye, now. I'll tell you one more time: I—did—not—kill—Old—Marsh."

"Then you hired someone to do it. You're in this. I know you are. You told Woolsley it was my knife. Who else wants me out of the way? Who else stands to gain from this?"

Noah opened his mouth but closed it again. His expression hardened and his eyes stared back, giving no quarter.

Thad knew now. Noah would never admit any wrongdoing. "You just put this in your mind, Ralston. No matter how much you try to enjoy your triumph, I will always know. You did this."

Still Noah said nothing. He only stood straight, his arms rigid at his sides, the muscles in his jaw in knots.

Unable to read the hard face now, Thad slumped back in the chair, his rage spent. Grief rose where the anger had been. "My God, Noah, we were friends. If this had happened to you, even the way things stood, I would've tried to help you. I'd have done *something*."

Noah leaned toward him again. "You listen to me, Thad. I had nothing to do with the murder. And whatever you've gotten yourself into, I did help you. Juliet came to me. I made a bargain with her to buy you out so you'd make bail. I've kept my part of the bargain."

Thad was shouting again. "She came to you on Friday morning, Noah. You could have sent her with the money straight to the courthouse. But she never came back, so you didn't even give it to her. This is Monday. You could have brought it over yourself this morning. You let me sit through another three days for nothing." He looked in Noah's face for a minute and saw only a hardened stranger, whose eyes, however, were not those of a lying murderer. The last of the rage left him like a dying breath, emptying him completely. "I used to think you were a decent man," he said, pushing himself out of the chair to leave. "I don't care about myself anymore, Noah, except the good name I had in this town. I'll clear that somehow. You've taken everything else that matters away from me." Suddenly Noah's words echoed. He'd kept *his* part of the bargain. "What did you mean, 'bargain'? What did you demand of her?"

"That she become my wife."

The words ripped the away last scrap of his life. He fell into the chair, shocked. "And she *agreed?*"

"Readily."

"Did she say when?"

"Soon. She gave me her word."

Thad's breath stopped as he hung over the void of his future. She'd done it for him. She'd be unhappy the rest of her life and the blame was his. Guilt settled over him again, infinitely heavier than when he'd only had Zeb on his conscience. He stood and dragged himself to the door. With his hand on the knob he stopped and rested his head against the jamb, utterly defeated. "Just take care of her, Noah. Please," he begged, choking. "And Larry. She'll never be happy with you, but don't let her want for anything." He walked out of the office without looking back.

"Not while you're around, she won't be happy," mused Noah, watching Thad close the door. He sat down and leaned back in his chair, his jaw muscles clenched into pulsing knots.

Emmett handed Thad the rolled quilt on his way out, and Thad walked back to Mrs. Eskitch's, trying to concentrate on the sweetness of freedom. *I should be dancing these few blocks,* he thought. *I should be straining at the ropes to get back to the store tomorrow. Instead I'm like a skiff cut loose from its moorings. If things were different, I'd be dying to see Lettie, hold her.* His heart raced in anger again. Something more than a bargain had happened between Lettie and Noah, he was sure of it. He was scared to see her again, scared to read in her face what Noah might have done to her. The thought had driven him insane for three days.

He opened the door to the boarding house. The hall and the parlor were festooned with evergreen boughs and red ribbons; next to the fireplace stood a tree—far too early for the holiday—decorated with cranberry chains, small felt ornaments that Lettie and Larry must have made, and candles that glowed warmly. Above the mantelpiece they had hung a sign that read, "Welcome home, Thad!"

He looked at their faces and choked with love and despair. Larry came to him, looked down sheepishly for a minute, and hugged him around the quilt. Mrs. Eskitch shook his hand, then made a funny noise with her throat, wiped away a tear, and hugged him, too. Lettie busied herself moving Christmas cookies around on a plate. A painful heartbeat passed before she looked at him.

"I'm so glad you're home, Thad," she said, her voice unsteady, her chin quivering.

He dropped the quilt on a chair, went to her and put his arms around her. His heart sank as he felt her stiffen. He let go as if she had burned him and stepped back.

"Come on, let's celebrate," Larry said too loudly. "We've made a wonderful rum punch just for the occasion."

"If you'll excuse me," Thad said, pointing toward the ceiling, nearly sobbing. "Freshen up . . . wash that cell off me. I'll be back in . . ." He rushed away from them all, ran up the stairs and closed the door to his room.

A fire crackled in the small stove and his bed was turned back with fresh linens. They had prepared his return with such love that it took his breath away.

He leaned against the door and tried to cram down his grief. Finally he sat on the bed, laid his pillow over his legs, and pounded it until he feared the ticking would split. He bent over it with his hands behind his head and moaned. She was Noah's. He'd doubtless demanded things of her that Thad couldn't bear to visualize. He should have seen it coming, should have prepared himself better.

The promise he'd made her echoed in his head. He would step out of the way if she had to marry Noah. How foolish he'd been to think he could keep such a promise, how naive, or how much less in love with her then. The promise—oh, God—was a promise.

He stood up, stripped, washed in the cold water on his washstand, toweled off, shaved badly, and put on fresh clothes before going back downstairs. He stood at the bottom of the stairs, took a deep breath, and stepped back into the parlor.

"I want to thank you all for your kindness and your faith in me," he said. "You were what kept me going, all of you. Now let's have some of that punch."

"Oh, yes, it's all ready. I'll just get the glasses from . . ." Mrs. Eskitch bustled into the kitchen.

"I think I'll give her a hand," said Larry, hurrying out after her.

Lettie was sitting stiffly in one of the chairs that shared the lamp table at the front window, her back to him, her hands interlaced tightly in her lap. He sat opposite her, barely on the chair, leaning toward her.

"You can't do it, Lettie. I'd rather be hanged for murder than think of you married to Noah."

Lettie kept her head down, staring at her hands. "I know that. I knew it when I made the bargain with him. But it was . . ." She choked on her words. ". . . over for us, Thad, hopeless, and there was still Larry." She looked at him. "It was my only choice. *My* choice, Thad. Please don't carry this as guilt. The pain alone is unbearable. I couldn't live with it if I thought you blamed yourself."

"Lettie . . ."

She tried to smile, but her eyes brimmed. "It's all right. If I don't have you, nothing matters. I'll cope with it. You must do the same."

Thad hung his head. "I haven't forgotten my promise, Lettie." He felt he was choking. "I'll never stop loving you."

Her chin quivered. Tears flowed, but she seemed to have forgotten the handkerchief tucked in the bottom of her sleeve. "Oh, Thad, I . . . he made me promise to marry him and not to see you again socially. I love you so much. I just want to die."

Speechless, he laid his hand on her shoulder and she caressed it with hers. Their heartache flowed freely for a single moment, and then Mrs. Eskitch was back with a tray.

"Now that you're back, Mr. Mac, you really must go see the Ice Palace. You'll never believe your eyes. What they've done in the last two weeks since you've been—well, gone—I declare, and what with all the warm weather and whatnot. Why, it's truly amazing. I only wish my Mr. Es were alive to see it, God rest. He dearly loved a celebration, you know. They're already practicing for the opening ceremonies. There's going to be a parade with ever so many bands and costumed groups and the whole city's decked out . . ."

"Yes," continued Larry, though his frown showed his mind was on something else. "Lettie and I already cut out and sewed some decorations for the front of the store. They're just waiting for your approval. Maybe we can all hang them tomorrow. We can't wait for you to be back in the store, Thad, it just hasn't been the same without you."

"No, it really hasn't," said Lettie. "I didn't tell you . . ."

Thad waited, but she didn't finish. He couldn't read the look on her face—embarrassment? Fear? It didn't matter anyway.

They drank their rum punch while Mrs. Eskitch filled the silence. The celebration died after the first glass of punch.

"Well," said Larry, slapping his knees, "I think I'll just go out for a while."

All three stared at him in surprise.

"Larry, you know you shouldn't . . ." said Lettie.

"I'm just going to get some fresh air," he said. "I don't think it's cold enough to do me any harm. I promise I'll bundle up like an Eskimo." He turned and left the parlor, preventing further protest.

Ten minutes later Larry stepped into the Silver Dollar, and spotted Zeb immediately at the bar. He backed into the door he'd just closed, gripping the cold knob behind him and trying not to hear the nervous beating of his heart. It was now or never. He'd waited far too long already, giving in to his fear. Zeb was almost surely a murderer, and once a murderer, what difference would twice a murderer make? He shoved away from the door and headed for the bar.

Zeb turned to him and registered a caricature of surprise. "Well, blow me right out to sea!" he cried with mock enthusiasm. "If it's not our Little Larry Fauntleroy. What brings you out this fine evening, Little Larry?"

"A beer, please," Larry called to the barkeep. "A simple drink," he said to Zeb, with as much control as he could muster.

"You mean your sister lets you drink the grown-up stuff?"

"Leave my sister out of it, Zeb. I can do what I want. Despite what you think, she doesn't control me. And I think it's time I tried—another side of life." He waved his arm to take in the saloon.

Zeb's eyes were hostile, and Larry could sense the question running through his mind: why would Larry suddenly seek him out? But he only snorted and said, "How old are you now, all of seventeen?"

Larry coughed to give himself time to think. He would have to challenge Zeb. "So? How old were you when you started living . . ." He felt his face redden. ". . . the kind of life you keep bragging about? Unless, of course . . ."

Zeb glared at him. "You think it's all talk?"

Larry held his eyes but kept his hands on the bar to keep them from shaking. The barkeep set a mug in front of him, sloshing the foam over the side. Zeb's jaw jutted forward. Then he laughed in his mirthless way. "I know exactly what you want. You got a few dollars? I'll take you there."

Larry took a swallow to hide his stalling. The beer left a drop of foam on the end of his nose as its bubbles rose into his sinuses. It nearly made him sneeze. "Tonight I've got just enough to pay for the beer. Maybe another time." He sniffed and wiped at his nose. "Some Christmas money from my family should be here in the next few days. I'll go with you then. Let's just say this is a good start." He could feel Zeb's gaze on him. He looked into the face that grinned and the eyes that doubted and drank the rest of his beer as quickly as he could force it down.

Zeb watched him, his face full of ironic benevolence. "Your sister will certainly blame me for your corruption."

"If she ever finds out. I'm sure not even you would stoop so low as to tell her, Zeb." He forced himself to grin. He got through a coughing spell, spread his elbows out, and propped himself on the bar. His face stared back at him from the mirror behind the rows of glasses and bottles. The mirror was as long as the bar and framed in dark carved walnut.

"Never been in a real Wild West saloon before," he said. "That's what we Easterners always think, you know, the Wild West. Ride through a herd of cows all day, brand a few, hang a few *desperados*, ride into town for a whiskey in the saloon." He slapped the bar and raised his glass. "Then ride out again to your campsite. Sleep under the stars next to the crackling fire, wake up to the smell of coffee and bacon."

"Yeah? Down Savannah way we *Southerners* still think they milk the buffaloes. We don't need *banditos* 'cause we got darkies, and the whiskey . . . well, it doesn't count anyway because it's not a julep." He stared into space for a minute. "You ever seen a buffalo, Larry?"

"No."

"Me either. I hear it's against the law down there in Denver to shoot a buffalo from the rear platform of a moving streetcar."

Larry stared at him in the mirror.

Zeb's face stared back, devoid of irony.

Larry shook his head. "They have buffaloes running around the streets of Denver?"

Zeb shrugged. "Hell, I don't even know if they have streetcars!" Suddenly they were both laughing.

"Let's go on down there and shoot some from the *front* platform . . ." Larry was laughing so hard the bubbles of beer in his stomach rumbled up in a spasm and left his mouth in a hideous belch. "Oops, 'scuse me."

Zeb was still laughing. "You want to learn to control that. Drink whiskey. Doesn't repeat on you. Get some more experience under your belt." He poked Larry in the stomach. The laughter was hollow now.

Larry felt Zeb's eyes on him in the mirror, sizing him up. "I think I'll have another," he said. "I might have enough money for two. You want one?"

"Me? God no. Never touch the stuff. Whiskey man." Zeb picked up his shot glass, swirled the amber liquid in it for a second, and then downed the last sip.

"Well, I guess that cleaned out my pockets," said Larry after the second beer. "I'd better get back anyway. I'll let you know when my money gets here, Zeb. We can have that fun you were talking about." He started to the door and discovered he had to hold onto the bar for support. As the crisp air outside cleared his head, he congratulated himself for getting a step closer to Zeb.

Zeb was nearly alone in the saloon when the door opened and Noah walked past him to a table under the deer heads. Watching in the mirror, Zeb saw him order and receive a drink, all the while looking at Zeb's back. Noah downed his drink in three swallows, caught Zeb's eye in the mirror, and motioned him to the table. Zeb waved to decline the invitation, turned back to the bar, and then changed his mind. If Ralston wanted to talk, maybe he was buying. He sauntered over and slouched into a chair facing him and the mangy hunting trophies.

"Let me buy you a drink," said Noah.

Zeb smiled. "Any time."

"How was business with your brother in jail? I hear you took over the running of it."

Zeb gazed coldly at him, waiting. Ralston was shrewd and this was only parrying.

Noah toyed with his empty glass, moving it to widen the wet circle under it. "I can imagine there was a little less money in the till at the end of the day than when Thad was around."

"What's that supposed to mean?"

Noah gave him an ambiguous smile. "Why, just that times are hard, of course. People do all sorts of things they might not otherwise do. Things that could lead to trouble." He thumped the glass down in the middle of the wet spot.

Zeb stared at him without answering.

Noah shrugged and changed the subject. "The last couple of weeks must've been quite trying for Thad."

"Yeah, what with hoping to marry Little Miss Blue Bonnet and all. The bedding of the fair maid is your bailiwick now, I take it." Zeb grinned. "Congratulations. That is, if my brother hasn't already seen to it."

Noah's fist rose and flew toward the tabletop, but he caught himself. His hand stopped in mid-air, opened, and reached for the glass. "What're you drinking?"

"Thought you'd forgotten. Whiskey'll be fine."

Noah called the order to the bar and turned back to him, leaning on the table now, his face grim. "Let's be clear about one thing, MacElwain. Don't ever use language like that about Miss Corcoran in my presence. She's mine. I love the young lady. In my way. And I do intend to have her love me on my terms. She *will*, one way or another. I'm not one to give up." He sat back, keeping his eyes locked on Zeb's. "But there are easy ways and there are hard ways to get what you want, even with the ladies. When there's an easy way, it seems logical to take it, wouldn't you say?"

The barkeep set the glasses on the table, picked up Noah's empty glass, wiped at the wet ring with a corner of his dingy apron, and left.

Zeb took a swallow of his whiskey. "What're you getting at, Ralston? I don't have the patience for all this pussy-footing around."

"I'm just saying there are things you could do to further my cause. I'd make it worth your while."

"Sir, are you suggesting I add to my brother's woes?" Zeb let his mask of shock slowly contort into a smile.

Noah waited.

Annoyed now, Zeb stood up. "There's nothing I can do for you, sir. I've found it's best to work *for* myself and *by* myself."

Noah looked up at him, his face hard. "As I said, I can make it worth your while. Or I can make things difficult for you."

"Not interested." Zeb emptied his glass in a single swallow and went back to the bar.

CHAPTER 22

December 20, 1895

Thad left the house before the break of day and walked to the Palace site. His breath hanging briefly in the icy air, he stood staring at the brightly lighted, noisy chaos of construction: the men hoisting the huge ice blocks up on pulleys and ropes, those on the scaffolding reaching out in thick gloves to maneuver them into place, and those freeing new blocks from the great wooden forms. Nearly two stories high now, the walls rang with commands that the men tried to muffle for the sake of the homeowners around them.

Thad's mind, however, focused on another, darker scene: the murderer slipping up behind Old Marsh and stabbing him in the back.

Much as Thad wanted to force it, Noah's face refused to come into the picture, and the face of the murderer remained indistinct. Who had brought the elk-antler knife here and framed him? Under the ice and trampled snow there was surely no trace of the killer's boot prints left, but he could sense the frozen red reminder of Marsh's bitter person in the mud between the block forms and the ice walls. He shivered and suddenly knew Marsh's anger as his own.

He turned and looked around. He would go to every house and every business that surrounded the site. Someone must have seen or heard something. Old Marsh must have cried out when the knife . . . The thought brought a prick between his shoulder blades.

He stepped through the frozen mud that had washed down from the site in the last snowmelt and knocked at the first house where light shone from a window.

Mrs. Kelly came to the door holding a blue plaid bathrobe closed at the neck, a pancake turner in her other hand, her thick brown and gray braid falling over her right shoulder. When she saw Thad, she registered welcome and shock and a hint of fear in rapid succession. She narrowed the opening to a three-inch slit and put her right foot behind the door. "Why, Mr. MacElwain, I—heard you were out. I'm so sorry about this business. Everybody says, of course, that you couldn't have . . ."

"I didn't, Mrs. Kelly. You know that. I just thought you might have heard something that night. Or seen something. Please, I really need your help."

Mrs. Kelly shook her head sympathetically. "I didn't, Mr. MacElwain, and my husband didn't either. And our bedroom is here on the street side, so the children couldn't possibly have heard anything at the back of the house. I'm sorry." Her face softened. She straightened up and moved her foot aside. "And I'm sorry if I seemed inhospitable. Of course you didn't do it. Here, come on in." She opened the door wider. "We'd help you if we could."

Thad's heart sank, even though he'd told himself not to expect any revelations that would free him. "I won't come in, but thank you, anyway, and please forgive me for disturbing you so early in the morning."

He cut across the corner of the site to Eighth and the next house with a lighted window, old Mr. Paulson's. His response was the same as Mrs. Kelly's—doubt and fear, but without the assurance that no one thought him guilty.

Thad trudged to the west end of the block and a tiny weathered shack left over from the late 1870s when the lead-

and-silver-laden carbonate ore had given Leadville its name and its boom. Gus Winger, a wizened miner who'd prospected unsuccessfully in California and Colorado, answered his knock with a rusty pickaxe in hand. "What you want, young fella?" he asked in the creaky voice of the very old, his bowed back forcing him to look up awkwardly.

"Sir, I'm Thaddeus MacElwain. I guess you know I've been accused of Old Marsh's murder. I need to know whether you heard or saw anything back on the night of the First."

"You're the one, you murderer," he squawked, raising the axe to the level of his bowed shoulders. "Marsh was right, you know. They took what was his and when he tried to stop them, you killed him. Murderer! I hope they hang you." He slammed his door.

Thad reeled. No one, not even Woolsley, had ever actually called him a murderer to his face. It knocked the breath out of him. "I'm not a murderer," he said to the cracks of light in the old gray door. "Please, sir, did you hear or see anything?" he called.

"No. Get off my property." The axe banged against the wood.

Too discouraged to go on, Thad left the noise and lights of the unfinished Palace and headed for the store. It was a limbo time of day, neither light nor dark, unreal somehow, the streets empty, the way Leadville would turn out sooner or later if the Ice Palace floundered. If only he didn't have to be here in February, he could simply walk down to the station, buy a ticket to wherever he had enough change in his pocket to go, and try not to look back.

At the store he turned and looked out across the valley. He could barely make out the broad white peak of Mount Massive. It failed to lift his spirit. "Mount Passive. No, Mount Impassive," he said aloud. "Like me. I just don't care anymore. You hear?"

He entered the store from the front, missing the pride he usually took in the well-ordered shelves and racks. They were nothing to him, had no purpose in his life. He could board up the store and leave the cheese to mold with no regret.

No, he couldn't. He ran his finger over the closed sewing machine. He couldn't leave until his time with Lettie ran out. And even if every person he met accused him of murder, he still had to ask the questions that might clear his name.

He walked around the store as a customer might, touching a pair of ice skates, a kerosene lantern, a wool hat, wondering vaguely that things were not ordered the way he kept them. He stood for a minute behind the cash register in the dark and sighed. Finally he switched on the light, reached in the drawer and took out the ledger.

He flipped through the pages looking for Lettie's writing. Instead he found the jagged, crooked script of his brother. Cold ran down his spine like the scratch of an ice pick. Zeb? Lettie had said he'd often been in the store. His brow furrowed and he ran his finger down the totals from the first of the month. His breath caught and stopped. There was so little. Lettie hadn't said the business had fallen off so drastically. Could his steady customers really believe he was a murderer?

He dropped the ledger on the counter and leaned against the frame for support. When he paid the mortgage, the last order, and his room and board, there would be nothing left, even of the extra money she'd received for the shares, and no money at all for a lawyer.

The padlock rattled at the back door and he remembered he'd come in the front. He had to run out and around the building to let Lettie and Larry in, but when he reached the back door, only Larry was there.

"What's the matter, Thad?" he asked as soon as he saw Thad's face.

"Why didn't you tell me there'd been so little business?" Thad opened the padlock and they went in.

"What do you mean?" asked Larry. "The first day no one came in all morning, but after that things went back to normal, more or less."

"Are you sure?" Thad shrugged out of his jacket and hung it on a peg in the hall.

"Of course I'm sure. That is, I stayed home that one day, but I think Lettie would have told me if . . ."

"You mean to tell me you had normal business? Why are all the figures so low? Why are they in Zeb's handwriting?"

Larry hung his head. "Zeb sort of took it over, Thad." He shivered.

Thad's mouth fell open. "Zeb? What on earth . . ." His mind was reeling.

Larry waited for him to finish, shivering and rubbing his hands together.

"You're cold." Thad handed him the coal scuttle. "Here, let's get the stove going. Are you telling me Zeb kept the ledger the whole time? I don't understand."

"He just did, Thad. He quit his job."

"He did *what?* Why didn't anyone tell me?"

Larry looked him in the eye, and his face was full of shame. "I can't explain how it was. I—I think we're both half afraid of him, and he wouldn't hear any argument." He started for the storeroom. "Lettie didn't want to tell you while you were still in jail because she knew you'd just be more upset," he said over his shoulder.

Thad felt rooted to the floor. The lid of the coal bin squeaked and metal scraped through the coal.

Larry continued talking above the noise. "I don't know what he put in the book. He wouldn't let either of us sell anything, so I have no way of knowing how much money changed hands."

The bottom fell out of Thad's stomach. He braced himself against the cold pot-bellied stove. "Zeb was manning the register and keeping the books?"

Larry came back with the full scuttle. "Well, yes. He got right snarly if either of us came close to the register." He handed Thad a bundle of kindling wood. "I saw Lettie writing things down after most of the sales, maybe she was keeping track."

Thad stood frozen with the kindling in hand. Zeb. Could he have been so wrong about Zeb? He hadn't come to Leadville to be reconciled. He hadn't changed one iota. "Where did she put the notes?"

"I don't know. She should be here soon. She looked awfully pale this morning, but she said she was coming."

"Could you please open the sewing machine and see if anything is in there? I have to see those notes."

"Sure. Can we just start the fire first?"

They were searching the machine and the cutting table behind it when Lettie arrived.

She froze with her coat half off when she saw them. Her eyes were dark-rimmed above her pale cheeks.

"Lettie, was Zeb skimming my profits? Is this why you asked me about the money?"

Her face fell. "It wasn't I who came up short, Thad, I guess you know now."

Thad ran both hands into his hair and pulled hard. "Zeb did this to me? Why? Why did you let him, Lettie?"

"I . . ." She looked at Larry. "We didn't . . ." Her voice shook.

Thad looked at her stricken face. "No, never mind. If you were both afraid of him . . . But Lettie, you should have . . ." He stamped from the machine to the register and back with his fists at his sides, trying to calm his anger. "I don't blame you," he said slowly, putting his hands on her shoulders. "Larry says you kept track of the sales somehow."

Lettie nodded, reached into her skirt pocket and handed him the little bundle of papers. "Thad, I'm so sorry," she said while he compared her figures with Zeb's. "I didn't know how to tell you while you were still in—that awful cell. I kept track of the money he actually took in every day, but I didn't know what to do about it. I was afraid if I went to Woolsley, he'd just laugh, then word would get around and no one would come in anymore if they thought Zeb was cheating. Please, forgive me. I should have done *something*. I'll give you the money . . ."

The door jangled open and Zeb walked in. The stunned silence that followed was short and explosive.

"Well, did they finally let you out of the crowbar hotel?" Zeb asked, grinning as he threw his fur hat onto the notions counter. "Last I heard Noah was letting you twiddle your thumbs in the dungeon for the sheer pleasure of seeing you suffer."

Thad rushed to his brother and stood inches from him with his hands in fists, fighting the desire to tear Zeb's remaining good arm from its socket. Through clenched teeth, he said, "He doesn't seem to be the only one to take pleasure in seeing me suffer. How *could* you, Zeb? I'm your brother, for God's sake."

Zeb stepped back. "How could I what? Oh, you mean that little bit of money I peeled off? Well, I wasn't exactly operating on a salary, you know, and I still have expenses. Here I quit my job at the post office to help you out, and . . ."

Lettie moved to Thad's side and put a hand on his arm. "No one asked you to quit, and no one needed your kind of help."

Thad's shoulders drooped. The theft settled into the defeats he had already suffered and unspeakable despair joined his anger. "Did it ever, just once, occur to you that you might give me some of the money you were making instead of quitting your job and stealing from me? Just once in your life, Zeb, did you think about helping anyone else?"

"I did help you." Zeb was shouting now. "I spent every day in here, doing this stupid drudge work, even duller than walking all over town delivering stupid mail, and this is the thanks I get."

Thad moved so close to Zeb he could feel the rounded stomach against his own, see specks of soot in Zeb's eyebrows, and smell the staleness of last night's liquor. He spoke quietly. "I'll total up what you stole and I demand you pay it back."

"It was forty-nine dollars and eighty-seven cents," said Lettie.

Zeb blew out a small disdainful breath. "Not even fifty measly dollars. Well, I don't have it anymore. What do you think I live on, air?" He shoved at Thad's shoulder, knocking him into Lettie.

Thad grabbed Zeb's shirtfront in his fist and shoved him toward the door. "Get out, Zeb, get out of my store. I don't ever want to see your face again. I don't give a damn anymore about your scarlet fever or your useless arm. All you ever did was use them as an excuse for the miserable, lazy rounder that you are."

Zeb bent forward, squeezed his left arm between them, and shoved. "That's fine talk from you," he sneered, reaching around himself when there was room between them. He lifted his mottled, misshapen hand and waved it in Thad's face.

Growling, Thad slapped at the hideous hand. "If I had anything to do with that, which I doubt, all I can say is . . . No, I won't let myself feel glad. But you got what you deserved. Never come here again, Zeb. You're not my brother."

Zeb pressed forward until his nose nearly touched Thad's. His face turned the purple of rage, but his voice was calm and low. "Ever since I can remember you've been the canker sore of my life with your prissy, goody-goody ways. You never fooled me for one second in all that time. I hated you then, and I don't care one whit about you now. And I certainly don't take orders from you. You haven't seen the end of me by a long stretch. I'll be around till *I* decide it's time for the end of brotherhood." He turned and slammed the door behind him.

Thad staggered forward and leaned against the doorframe.

Lettie turned him to her and put her arms around him. "You did the right thing, Thad."

Thad groaned.

She rocked him slightly back and forth. "It *was* the right thing."

Larry came and put his arms around both of them. "If you ask me, you should have done it years ago."

CHAPTER 23

December 26, 1895

Larry left the post office and headed back to the store in the waning afternoon, taking in the new atmosphere of Leadville. He wished he could share it, but Harrison Street might as well be a foreign place with its evergreen garlands bedecked with red and gold bells and silver icicles.

Even Mrs. Eskitch's house, which they had helped her decorate with boughs and ribbons like so many other homes on the side streets, lent holiday color and cheer to the air. But the decorations were only part of the light the city seemed to bask in. The rest was the glow of hope. Money was beginning to flow into town; optimism rolled though the city like the waves on the Chesapeake.

Larry watched the smiling visitors who already crowded Harrison. Across the street a sleigh with tinkling bells pulled up to the Vendome Hotel, and a man with three children got out, laughing. His little girl, in a blue wool coat with a wide ermine collar, pulled at his sleeve.

"Daddy, now," she squealed, pointing at the toboggan.

Larry looked at the ride, which had been running at a pleasing profit since the middle of the month. A throng of small boys stood at the bottom of the support posts, jostling to be first up the stairs.

The little girl by the sleigh hopped up and down, and her brothers began pulling at the father, too.

"One minute," he said, laughing. "Let's go get your mother first. Then we can all ride together."

Larry watched them with envy. Their glee only made him sad, as did the general excitement, which was always *outside* Thad's store. Inside, though both Thad and Lettie were making a little profit, there was nothing in the air but resignation and dread and futile love. *And my stupid rattling breath that's caused all this,* he thought, yanking his scarf tighter around his neck. No matter how much he'd talked to Lettie, she was adamant.

"Don't you remember what we swore to each other when you were seven?" she'd asked when he'd argued with her the evening after she'd sold herself to Noah. "No matter what, we'd never break a promise to anyone. No putting another person in the fear and uncertainty we always felt when Father didn't return on the day he'd promised. Remember that? I've given my word now, and I'll never break it."

Larry remembered well. He could still smell and feel the salty wind that blew constantly around the widow's walk on their house, where they'd stood for days and stared over the water, always convinced that this time their father had been shipwrecked and would never return. It had been like that every time Father went to sea—days spent on the walk filled with agony and fear. *No, she'll never break her promise to Noah if I don't give her reason,* he thought.

The key to it all was Zeb, and Larry felt his skin crawl at the thought of the cad who'd clearly come to Leadville just to wreck Thad's life. *It's up to me,* he thought. *Thad's too decent to believe Zeb would stoop to murder, and Lettie's even more cowed by him than I am.*

Larry stopped dead at the corner of Ninth as a new thought hit him. His phony friendship with Zeb wouldn't be secret much longer. He'd already spent the evening with him twice since Thad got out of jail. "They'll hear what I'm doing," he muttered, and was startled by his own voice. *Even if Mrs. Es keeps her tongue in her head, Mrs. Kelly won't. No doubt she's seen me on the way to Zeb's both times through those lace curtains. I'll tell Lettie and Thad what I'm doing. No. They'll try to stop me. Besides, if Zeb found out somehow . . . No, Lettie, if you have your stubborn streak, so do I. I'm doing this my way. And if the town thinks I'm a rounder, too, well, when I catch him up, I'll make it clear what I was doing.*

Larry shivered, cold to his very marrow, and realized he'd stopped in the shade and was standing on a patch of ice. He crossed Harrison to walk in sun on the east side of the street and avoid the boys waiting at the toboggan. Even across the street he could hear them daring each other to stand up on the sled and speculating on how fast it would make the turn onto Leiter.

He ran his fingers over the red velvet ribbons streaming from the evergreen boughs at the entrance to the Vendome and took in the smell of Christmas that came from the branches. He sighed. For him, Thad, and Lettie, Christmas Day had come and gone in a pretense at gaiety, and they'd all been relieved when it was over. Only Mrs. Es's chatter about the first few wild Christmas and New Year's celebrations in Leadville had fluttered about the dinner table; then Lettie had joined Noah for the afternoon.

A group of boys his own age hurrying down Eighth toward the toboggan surged around Larry. As he turned to avoid them, the glittering walls of the Ice Palace two blocks away caught his eye and drew him toward them. He started down Eighth in the shadow of the slide, but moved under it to take advantage of the sun, shining obliquely over the top of the building across from Noah's hotel and through the support posts.

The sparkle of the ice danced along the walls as the angle of light changed with his approach. The milkiness that the nightly spraying had left around the edges only heightened the rainbows

playing in the blocks. Senior might have been a bad businessman, Larry thought, but he was right about this; it really was a
diamond in the sky.

Even from a distance he could hear the shouts of the workers. One electrician walked backwards along the parapets,
unrolling a spool of wire, while another squatted over a light
fixture to connect it. Flags already waved from the turrets on all
but the unfinished main towers. The north side, still waiting for
a few of the displays that would go in the blocks, would have to
remain boarded up for the opening.

Near the corner of Spruce, where the ramp was getting too
low for him to walk under the toboggan, Larry saw Noah and
Zeb standing near the posts. He was just behind them under
the run, about to raise his hand to touch Zeb's arm, when he
heard Noah use Thad's name in the same tone Old Marsh had
used the day he and Zeb had been in the store after the blast.

Larry shrank back into the cold shadow and went still as
death, the silhouettes of Zeb and Marsh against the store's front
window clearly before his eyes again. Clear too, was Zeb's voice
admitting setting the fire that injured his own arm. Now Larry
remembered standing in the storeroom, dizzy, fingering the
lump on his head from banging it on the coal bin, knowing
there was something he had to tell Thad but not being able to
keep it in his mind. The arm, Zeb's arm.

Noah's voice jerked him back to the present, but just over
Larry's head a sled whizzed by to the ecstatic shrieks of children,
shaking the posts. Larry stifled the need to cough. This time he
wouldn't forget what he heard.

". . . although I can't say I blame him." Noah laughed into
the silence that followed the sled. "I'd have disowned you long
ago if you were any kin of mine."

Larry breathed in quick, shallow puffs, lest the rale of deeper
breathing give him away.

"What makes you think it's any of your affair?" Zeb asked.

"I don't. It just sounds like you need a source of income. Your job at the post office has been filled. So this puts you in a position to reconsider my offer."

From behind the post, Larry could see the right sleeve of Noah's black coat and Zeb's whole left side. He heard Zeb grunt and saw his polished brown boot kick at a clump of frozen mud. His voice was barely audible. "What did you have in mind?"

"I want to be sure the jury is convinced he's guilty. Too many of us around here know he's not the type to commit a murder, don't we?"

Zeb didn't answer, but the tension building between the men seemed to engulf Larry. His throat was almost in spasm with the need to cough. He swallowed to ease the constriction.

Noah went on. "His jury will no doubt be made up of other businessmen, and at least some of them will believe his story about working on his books. Which was probably true, wouldn't you say?"

Zeb growled his answer. "How would I know?"

"Well, let's just assume it is." Noah's voice was conciliatory and tinged with sarcasm. "And if a jury doubts his guilt, he'll be a thorn in my marriage forever. I *want* him to go to jail. Everyone knows how things stand between Miss Corcoran and me, so I can't testify against him. But if his own brother were summoned as a reluctant witness . . ."

Zeb raised his head toward the sparkling Palace, and Larry thought he heard a smile in his voice. "You want me to place him at the scene of the crime."

Noah said nothing, and Larry could only assume he nodded.

Zeb continued. "You haven't said what's in it for me."

"I'll give you a hundred dollars."

Zeb laughed. "The trial is two months away. I can't possibly live that long on a hundred. In fact, I was thinking of leaving town, getting out of this Arctic hell."

It was a minute before Noah answered. "Two hundred, MacElwain, or go ahead and try to leave. I have another ace or two up my sleeve."

Moving just far enough for Larry to see his profile, Zeb stared at Noah and started to say something. He squinted and ran his left hand up and down his right arm. "Give me thirty a week."

"Starting on the First."

"Done."

Noah moved off without another word, past Zeb and down Spruce, probably to the courthouse to arrange for Zeb's summons, thought Larry.

Zeb stood looking at the Palace, his left fist obviously clenching and unclenching in his pocket. He gave a small snort and started walking toward the construction.

Larry watched him for a minute, then backed up quietly, stepped out into the sun, and stood shivering for a minute. "I have to tell Thad about this," he muttered, starting back for the store, still holding the cough in so that Zeb wouldn't notice him. He stopped before he even reached the south side of the street. He had no proof. All he knew for sure was that Noah had bribed Zeb to testify against Thad. Neither man had mentioned the real murderer. It was his word against that of a prominent businessman and a rake who would leave town at the slightest hint of trouble. The only chance to get Thad out of this was to prove Zeb had murdered Old Marsh. "I have to catch him somehow," he said through clenched teeth. "And at least I know about the arm. I'll confront Zeb with all of it when I have the proof."

He started again slowly toward Spruce but had hardly gone ten steps before realization struck him. Noah knew. Zeb had killed Marsh and Noah had found out. And he was using the knowledge to ruin Thad. The cough surged up from his lungs, a bass rattle that bent him at the waist. Larry let it pass, breathed for a minute, and turned to look at Noah's hotel. All he could see with the toboggan in the way was the top floor and Noah's apartment, where he'd been once with Lettie. His eyes widened and he sucked in a deep, rasping breath. The apartment looked directly over the Palace site. Of course. Noah must have seen something. "I *know* it, but . . ." he said half aloud. Suddenly he felt an arm around his shoulder and turned to find Zeb grinning at him.

"You 'know' what?" asked Zeb, staring intently into his eyes.

Larry's heart lurched as if Zeb had heard his thoughts. No one had ever frightened him the way Zeb did. He stammered an answer. "Why . . . that the winter carnival is going to be a huge success."

Zeb stopped without letting go and turned them both to face the Palace, his arm pressing Larry to him like a boa constrictor. For a minute they watched in silence, Larry's heart racing. Workers interrupted a sculptor chiseling away at the statue of Lady Leadville that would grace the entrance. He climbed off his ladder to direct them in unpacking another statue from a sled, a loaded pack mule carved from ice.

Larry took a deep breath. "The Palace really turned out fine, didn't it?"

Zeb shrugged. "Well, they got it up after all." His tone was flat, annoyed.

Larry looked at him sharply.

"After all Marsh's attempts to sabotage it," Zeb added.

Larry swallowed hard. He had to draw Zeb out. "Well, whoever killed him at least stopped him from doing any worse damage. I'll wager you . . ."

"You'll wager what?" Zeb's arm tightened and he stared the way he'd looked at the knife in Thad's store, the way a snake fixed on its prey.

Larry coughed to cover his search for something neutral to answer. "I'll wager . . . even you thought he was the meanest man in Leadville." The constricting arm relaxed slightly.

Zeb's face contorted to a humorless grin. "Second meanest. Remember that." He shrugged. "But so what? The old coot's dead anyway. Good riddance, if you ask me." The arm tightened again for a second. "Say, you got any of that Christmas money left?"

Relief flowed through Larry. "A little. It wasn't as much as I hoped, and I had to buy something for Lettie and Thad."

"How much?"

Larry reached into his pocket and counted. "A dollar and sixty cents."

Zeb frowned and his arm slid off Larry's shoulder. "Can't make much of an evening on that," he said.

"Well, it's enough for a whiskey or two, isn't it?"

"Maybe. You know where Lorna's is?"

"Back up there off State Street?"

"Right. Meet me there at nine. We can at least ogle the ladies over drinks." Zeb's eyebrows hopped up and down.

"Fine."

They parted, Zeb going back toward the toboggan and Mrs. McGuire's.

Larry waited till he was out of sight. He wiped at the spot where Zeb's left hand had curled around his shoulder and then shook his hand out, shuddering and cursing his lack of courage.

From his place at the back of the store, Thad rang up one purchase after another, but he'd been distracted all afternoon by short flashes of light from Lettie's left hand. He waited for Abby Marechal to leave and then strolled to the front.

Lettie was hurrying to finish the last of the skating team's uniforms, and her fingers darted through the light streaming in the window. He looked down at her hand pulling red basting thread from the gold woolen fabric.

"Did you talk to the rest of the people who live around the Palace?" she asked.

Thad nodded. "The last few were just like the rest. They're all sure I'm innocent—almost. They all want me to be acquitted. But not one of them asked me in."

"Oh, Thad, how awful for you."

"I have no idea where to turn now, but I'll keep trying, even if I have to buttonhole every person in town. I'm still trying to figure out how the killer got in. He had to have a key, but my keys were never missing. I'm giving myself no illusions." Thad rammed his hands in his pants pockets. "The worst part is feeling betrayed, Lettie. By my best friend for framing me, even if I don't know how he did it yet. And then my brother for stealing from me."

"I know."

"Zeb's actions shouldn't have surprised me, but Noah." His erstwhile friend. By far the worse betrayal. "I'll never feel right about selling the shares to him, and I'll never forgive him for demanding you in the bargain."

Lettie set the fabric aside and smiled up at him. "I think the only good thing to come out of all this was your getting out of jail." She put her hands on the edge of the machine and stretched her back. "Anyway, look out there. The way things are going, the shares'll probably be worth a lot more in a few weeks. He won't take any loss on them."

"More's the pity. May he choke on them." Thad looked down at her hand and took a breath. "Did he give you that as an engagement ring for Christmas?" he asked.

She frowned and put the hand in her lap. "Yes."

"May I see it?"

She hesitated a moment, then slid the ring off and placed it in his hand. The ring was set with five perfectly matched opals around a small diamond. The diamond glittered and opals flashed cheerfully in the sun, like tiny rainbows dancing with the motion of his hand. Inside the band Noah had had engraved: J.C.-N.R. 12/25/96. Between the initials and the date were two tiny entwined hearts. Thad's stomach turned. How could Noah be so blind?

He frowned at the ring. "It's beautiful, Lettie. It's what you deserve." He laid it on the machine and turned toward the door. "I would never have been able to give you anything like it."

"I know it's beautiful, but I feel dirty wearing it, and the inscription next to my skin eats at me like acid."

Thad balled his fists, his arms rigid at his sides. "Don't go through with this, Lettie. I love you. We'll work it out somehow."

"I gave my word, Thad."

Thad heard the pain in her voice and felt ashamed at his own unwillingness to keep his promise to her. He would never press her about it again.

After a minute she said, "He's after me again to move my shop to the hotel. He says I'd get a lot more customers that way. Of course, he just wants me away from you."

Thad's mood sank. He kept his back to her. "Are you going to?"

"Would it make this easier for you? Maybe it would be for the best. I feel like my heart's being ripped out every time I look at you."

He faced her now. "I know. But I think someday I'll look back and be grateful for every minute we had together, even if it wasn't as man and wife. Please, stay till you marry him."

Lettie smiled up at him as she slipped the ring back on her finger. "I told him I would keep my promise but not make new ones." She turned back to her work.

"I'm glad." Thad noticed a bit of green ribbon showing above the back of her collar. The medallion was hidden beneath her clothing. He looked away, his heart too heavy to bear. He had to focus on something else. "Did you see the man working on the statue of 'Lady Leadville'?"

"Yes. If that tower of ice is any indication, she's going to be huge. They say the arm that points east will be quite thin."

Thad nodded. "I'll wager it melts off before the middle of next month. Is that where Larry went, over to the Palace?"

"I don't know. I thought he was just going to mail my thank-you letters to Duffy and Mona. He should be back by now. Oh, here comes Mrs. Es."

Thad moved away and began counting the day's take.

Mrs. Eskitch bustled up the last block of Third, and in a minute she was chattering at them, muffled by the dark green stocking cap she'd wrapped several times around her neck. Its pom-pom bobbed up and down on her chest. "Well, I declare, that Ice Palace really is the most beautiful thing I ever saw. The north wall, let's see, I think it's north, that would be toward Eighth, wouldn't it, the one they didn't have to spray so much, and it really does look like a diamond with the sun shining through it. Tonight they're going to test the colored electric lights. Are you two going to watch it?"

"Yes," said Lettie.

"No," said Thad.

"Oh, what a shame, Mr. Mac. It's going to be a sight. I wouldn't miss it for all the rice in China. If you change your mind, you could walk me over. Maybe Larry would like to go back, too. I just saw him over there, with your brother, Mr. Mac. Isn't that nice they're getting to be such good friends? Having Larry for a friend ought to be good for . . . Oh, sorry, Mr. Mac."

Lettie turned and looked at him, her face showing as much surprise as he felt.

Mrs. Eskitch made a full circle, looking at the wares and unwinding the stocking cap at the same time. "Now, what did I come in for?" She fished in her flour-sack shopping bag. "Did I have a list in here? Hah, yes." She jabbed at the tiny corner of newspaper she fished out. " 'Parade.' Well, I declare, what on earth does that mean? Doesn't seem sensible to me to have a parade and an opening on the First when the Palace won't even be finished, but what does that have to do with my shopping list?" She scratched at her head through the stocking cap. "Let me see . . . Oh, I remember, I need a new pair of thick woolen stockings for the parade. It's supposed to last more than an hour, and then all the opening ceremonies and you know how it is when you just stand on the ice and snow. Your feet get cold all the way up to your . . ." She clapped her hand over her mouth. "Well, never mind how far north they get cold!"

When Mrs. Eskitch had gone, Thad tried to face the new betrayal. It was unthinkable. Larry knew how he felt about Zeb. "Did my ears deceive me, or did she say Larry and Zeb were becoming friends?"

Lettie's face showed her own shock. "Larry's been out a couple of times in the last week and won't tell me where he's going. When I asked him about it, he just said I should trust him to do the right thing. After that, I didn't say anything more because he's nearly a grown man and can make his own decisions. But if he's seeing Zeb . . . why?"

"I can't imagine." The saloons, gaming halls, and whorehouses of State Street came to mind. Lettie was right. Larry was nearly a grown man, and Zeb knew how to find cheap satisfactions for a man's needs. "Well . . ."

Lettie watched him, waiting. "Well, what?"

"I don't even like to think it."

Shortly after that Larry came back. Lettie stared at him from the machine and Thad from the register.

"What's the matter with you two?" he asked.

"Mrs. Eskitch says you've been with Zeb," said Lettie. "Larry, how could . . ."

Larry stopped her with his hand, palm out, and looked from one to the other. His mouth opened and closed. He coughed.

"I don't understand," Lettie went on. "You know how things stand . . ."

Larry smiled nervously. "It's really all right. I can't . . . could you just trust me?" he pleaded with them both.

Thad turned his back and began rearranging the reading glasses in their case at the far end of the store.

Through closing time, the three did not speak to each other again.

CHAPTER 24

January 1, 1896

"It should be starting any minute," said Mrs. Eskitch from the chair Thad had placed in front of the store window for her, her breath fogging the glass briefly.

Larry sat on an overturned bucket beside her. Between them and the sewing machine he had moved back, Thad stood, waiting, too, for the opening parade.

Mrs. Eskitch clasped her hands in her lap. "Mrs. Loomis said they've been lining up down at the Armory Hall since ten o'clock. So kind of you to let me watch from in here, Mr. Mac, instead of standing out there in all that new snow. How long do you suppose it'll take them to get from there to here?" She leaned forward till her nose touched the glass. "Ow, cold," she yelped, and wiped with her wool-swaddled elbow at the spot of skin oil she'd left on the glass. "Just look at those fine carriages down at the station waiting for all the out-of-town dignitaries they invited. Mrs. L. told me not one of them actually accepted the invitation. What do you suppose they'll do?"

Larry laughed. "Probably just take the first ten people who get off the train and shove them in the carriages. No one would even know they weren't the right people."

Mrs. Eskitch shifted and took in a long breath.

Thad sensed one of her long chatters coming on and couldn't bear to listen to it today. "Would you like to read the paper while we're waiting, Mrs. Eskitch?" he suggested, fetching the

Herald Democrat from the counter.

"Oh yes, thank you . . . why, listen to this, 'A Rainbow Rink of Roses, Pillars of Opalescent Hue More Beautiful Than The World Has Ever Seen Before,' now isn't that a fine title? 'With her fabulous Ice Palace, our fair Cloud City today will show the world her precious mettle.' Ha, so clever, the way they play with words. You know, metal, gold, mettle. I declare!" She let the paper float briefly in front of Larry's face and raised it for Thad, pointing at the pun before continuing. " 'Let the proud gentlemen of the Committee for Denver's Festival of Mountain and Plains, at which our contestants and our float captured myriad prizes in October, come and see a real spectacle . . .' "

Thad stopped listening and gazed across the street. On the other side of Harrison, Noah's imposing, bushy head caught his eye, bobbing through the crowd. The top of Lettie's hat appeared occasionally among the other heads as Noah steered her toward the edge of the boardwalk, and in a minute Noah shoved two visitors aside and drew her to the front. He stationed himself next to her, plainly embarrassing her and annoying the ladies he'd elbowed, who had to stretch to see over his broad shoulders.

Mrs. Eskitch began another article. " 'A Great Pageant of Leadville's Greatest Men Greet The Ice King's Bride . . .' "

Her erratic reading barely dribbled into Thad's consciousness. In front of the store children hopped and danced about to keep warm in the snow and the twenty-degree cold. The lowering sky obscured Mount Massive and hung oppressively into the valley so that the tops of the flags on the Palace nearly pricked the clouds. Still, Harrison Avenue glowed with gaiety, its storefronts, lampposts, and power poles decked with gaudy bunting and evergreen boughs. Spectators lined the whole length of the street, stamping their feet. Hawkers plied the crowd, selling tin replicas of the Palace, souvenir pennants, programs, cakes, cookies, and hot chocolate kept warm in hand carts with coal burners.

"Ooh, do listen to this one," rambled Mrs. Eskitch, " 'King Carnival Reigns In All His Crystal Splendor Of Imprisoned Colored Lights.' Now isn't that lovely, such a nice turn of phrase, don't you think . . ." She turned the page. "Oh, look, here's the schedule of events. The official lighting ceremony is at seven. You missed that last week, Mr. Mac, and it was such a sight, even unfinished. I just insist you go tonight. You can walk me . . . Hah! Here they come at last. I declare, this is so exciting! The Crystal Carnival is finally . . ." She jumped up from the chair, as did Larry from his bucket. Even Thad, painfully conscious of how it might have been to watch the opening ceremonies with Lettie, felt a spark of excitement.

A shot split the air. Near the station a cheer rose and made its way up Third and along Harrison. A father lifted his son onto his shoulders, making Larry shift his position behind the glass to keep his view. The first member of the parade started up Third Street, Grand Marshal W. R. Harp on a pure white horse bedecked with gold and silver tassels.

"Why do you suppose they didn't let Tingley Wood be the Grand Marshal?" Larry wondered. "He deserved it if anybody did."

"Maybe he can't ride a horse," said Mrs. Eskitch. "Oh, dear, no, that was a dreadful thing to say. I'm sure they had some good reason . . ."

"I think the parade picks him up at the Vendome, along with notables who arrive at the D and RG station and the South Park depot," said Thad. "And he makes one of the speeches at the opening ceremonies in the Grand Ballroom."

The parade turned onto Harrison and another cheer rang through the city. The onlookers waved flags, rattled noisemakers, and whistled. Behind the Grand Marshal came the city's entire police force, with barely contained elation under their sober expressions.

An "ooooh" followed them as the next entry rounded the corner, five-year-old Helen Marechal, dressed as mascot of the Leadville Hockey Club and holding a miniature hockey stick over her shoulder. She sat on a sled guided by her father Julius and pulled by two pug dogs.

Mrs. Eskitch put her hand to her heart. "Well, isn't she just the sweetest thing you ever saw?"

Already music was pulsing up the hill, but the Hockey Club preceded the band. They rounded the corner in their white wool uniform coats and trousers piped in red, their white buckskin moccasins, blue caps with red tassels, and red gloves, keeping their lines perfectly straight, their hockey sticks on their shoulders.

The Fort Dodge Cowboy Band, whose members had practiced twice on New Year's Eve to accustom themselves to the altitude, marched around the corner next, straining to keep together after the exertion of the hill. Behind them came a gift from the city of Pueblo, a bass drum so large it had to be pulled by four colorfully festooned donkeys. Each beat of the drum vibrated through the glass.

Mrs. Eskitch put her hand to her stomach. "I can feel that right here," she said.

"Me, too," said Thad. "I'll wager the drummer's ears will never be the same."

He looked over at Lettie in a break in the parade. She was looking directly at him, though he couldn't tell whether she could actually see him through the glass. Her face was full of longing. Noah glanced down at her, followed her gaze, and scowled.

Behind the drum came the skating team in their gold uniforms. Lettie looked up and said something to Noah, who focused on the passing uniforms she had tailored. Thad knew the feel of the gold fabric on the bolts he'd ordered for her, heard the snip of the scissors as she cut it, saw her pin it and guide it into her machine. His hands were suddenly afire with the feel of hers, the softness of her face, the silkiness of the hair he'd barely touched but never held, loose and flowing in his hands. He turned his back to the window for a minute.

The parade went on for another hour until the spectators were hoarse from cheering. Near the end came the workers who had built the palace: carpenters, sledge drivers, ice masons, electricians, carrying a banner that read, "We helped build the Ice Palace." The ice masons towed miniature ice blocks on small sleds, and all the workers carried their tools: ice tongs, saws, hoses. They received the loudest and longest cheer of all.

After the parade, while Thad stayed in the store, Larry escorted Mrs. Eskitch up Harrison in the throng that had fallen in behind the workers. They were soon separated and the crowd swept Larry toward the toboggan ride, where the official opening was just beginning. Grand Marshal Harp, Tingley Wood and two women Larry didn't recognize were at the top of the ramp, waving at the crowd. They sat down on the sled, the women securing their skirts as best they could. Mr. Dimick, builder of the toboggan, gave a signal, the workers shoved the sled forward, and it flew down the track to the screams of the women.

The crowd began moving toward the Ice Palace, carrying Larry with them. He was getting cold, even with all the bodies pressing around him. The coughing started. With difficulty, he pulled his handkerchief from his pants pocket and worked his way slowly to the right side of the toboggan. Hanging on to a support post, he bent over and coughed heavily. There were several bright red spots on his handkerchief when he took it away from his mouth. Larry stared, his heart racing, then closed his eyes to the significance of the blood. He hadn't much time left. A chill began at the soles of his feet and worked its way through his whole body. His fingers were stinging with the cold. It hurt his nose to breathe.

He thought of the way back to Mrs. Eskitch's. It seemed very long, especially bucking the crowd. Zeb lived closer, just up Spruce and Ninth. He let go of the post and let the crowd sweep him along, struggling to the right. On Spruce the crowd thinned to a few people headed for the Palace. Half a block from the toboggan he saw Zeb come down the steps of his rooming house with someone else and start toward him. Larry stopped to breathe and let Zeb get closer, bracing himself with one hand on his knee while he used the other to wipe at his mouth in case there was any blood left around his lips.

Zeb ambled nearer, escorting a painted woman dressed in a bright green coat with a black feather boa.

Larry straightened up. "Zeb," he said, "could you let me stay in your room for a while till I get warm?"

Zeb looked surprised and his mouth turned down in annoyance. "You ought to get on home, Larry. You look like a walking funeral."

"Please, Zeb, I need your help. I can't make it home, fighting the crowd like this. I'm freezing."

"Well, I'm busy. Just go on up to Tenth. You can cross Harrison there."

Larry stared at him, shocked at his callousness.

Zeb tsked and drew his lips into a thin line. "Oh, all right. I'll probably miss the first dances, though." He turned to the woman. "Wait for me at the entrance."

Her broad green hat rotated with the shake of her head, its peacock feathers swaying. "Not likely, sweetie. It's too cold to stand around outside. I'm going in and find someone else to dance with till you come."

"All right, I'll find you." He punched the air with his finger in front of her eyes. "Just remember who you're with, you hear me?"

She grinned, batted his hand away, and reached up to twirl his mustache. "All you have to do is wiggle this, honey." She bumped her hip to his and sashayed off.

"Didn't you watch the parade from the store?" asked Zeb, turning to look after her as they headed back up Spruce. "Why didn't you just stay with Thad?"

"I was trying to walk Mrs. Es . . ." *This is my chance,* he thought. *I've got to make Zeb think I've broken with Thad.* "Actually, I'm sick to death of Thad and his melodrama with Lettie." He stopped to breathe. "I wish she'd just move us into the hotel and be done with it. Sure be more comfortable." He breathed again. "But no, the two of them spend all day mooning over each other, both miserable. Makes me miserable, too."

Zeb snorted. "I thought Thad was your idol."

"He never was. Of course, I was grateful to him for all he did for us in the beginning, but after a while I could see through him. He just wanted my sister. He's too good to be true. I'm sick of Thad."

Zeb eyed him warily. In a minute he grinned. "I know what you mean."

At the lighting ceremony that evening, Thad stood in the middle of the crowd behind Mrs. Eskitch, alienated from the elation that puffed into the cold air from a thousand mouths. The sky had cleared, but few stars flickered down against the bright lights of the Ice Palace area. The temperature had dropped with the clearing sky, and his feet were freezing.

He hoped the ceremony would start on time. If Larry hadn't insisted that he accompany Mrs. Eskitch, he would have stayed home. Larry had been ashen and listless at supper, but when asked, he'd only said it was from the excitement. He wouldn't hear of anyone staying home because of him.

The lights around the five-acre site went out, and a hush fell over the eager crowd. They waited. And then the Palace lit up from within its walls: glowing emeralds, sapphires, rubies, and amber in a design that ran around the whole building from top to bottom. The crowd gasped with a single breath and fell silent as it took in the opalescent splendor glowing out of the dark. It was a minute before the roar went up, simultaneously from every throat; it shook the ground and pounded the stars. In the midst of the pandemonium the first rockets went off, showering the night with great balls of red sparks, white comets, and blue flares. Slowly, clouds of spent gunpowder sank through the frigid air.

The fireworks seemed to go on forever but finally ended with a continuous explosion of color in the sky. Most people stayed for a while staring at the incredible beauty of the Ice Palace, but eventually they began to stamp their feet, remark of the cold, and drift away.

"Oh, my dear, I'm simply speechless," said Mrs. Eskitch as she turned to leave. "I declare, I've never seen anything so beautiful in my life. Why, even the centennial Fourth of July celebration back in . . ."

Nothing of her speechlessness reached Thad's brain. He was still looking at the Palace, a stunning but hideous thing, colorful as Lettie's opal engagement ring, and as forbidding. Like his love for Lettie, the Palace was a beautiful dream that would melt in a few weeks and leave him far worse off than he had ever been.

At the top of the hill, two figures stood in the dimly lit window of Noah's hotel apartment. They were not touching.

CHAPTER 25

January 4, 1896

Lettie got up early and gathered a few clothes to wash before going to work. She would have to use the drying rack. If she hung the clothes on the line, they would freeze, and Mrs. Eskitch was predicting new snow by tomorrow. Lettie smiled at the memory of the landlady, taking her to the west window of the parlor back in November.

"See those fat cigar clouds floating in over Mount Massive?" she'd asked. "That means snow. Well, it really means change. And what else can a sunny day in Leadville change to but snow? You'll see, my dear." So far Mrs. Es had always been right.

If she waited, she'd have to get to the wooden platform under the clothesline by "post-holing," as they called it out here, which meant you sank to your knees in snow, getting your boots and the bottom half of your skirt all wet, and then tried to use the same holes to get back to the house.

She went into Larry's room. He was still sleeping, his breath a deep rattle, his cheeks feverish. She stood looking at him for a minute. The realization overcame her. She hadn't wanted to see how much worse he'd been the last few days, had ignored the fact that he'd stayed in bed twice since Christmas.

Her light mood sank into deep guilt. She shouldn't have put off getting help for him. She could no longer wait to set a date for the wedding, no matter how angry it made him. She bit her lip in shame. She'd used his threat of leaving to delay the ordeal

218

of being married to Noah—no, of not being married to Thad.

She pressed the laundry in her hands against her chest, as if to relieve the weight of her heart. She'd waited too long; she would talk to Noah today. A tear squeezed out of her eye. She wiped it off on a chemise and began taking things from Larry's clothes hamper.

There were no handkerchiefs this time. She looked around. Hanging on the towel rack next to his washbasin was one he had already washed out—badly. There were several brown stains on it. She snatched it up and stared. They were bloodstains. She ran to his pants, hanging on the ladder-back chair near the windows, found a handkerchief in the right pocket, and pulled at the edges. The red-brown stains reached up from the cotton and clutched at her throat. In his chest of drawers she found several more stained handkerchiefs he had washed. He was hiding the truth from her. For how long? She turned toward him. "Oh, my God, Larry, I didn't know it was this bad. Why didn't you tell me?" she whispered. He turned on his right side and the top of the quilt slid toward the floor. She pulled it up and tucked it around his shoulders, leaving her hand there for a moment.

Her heart pounded against her ribs, pulsing guilt and sorrow and fear through her. She dropped the washing on the foot of the bed and rushed to the hotel.

Noah was out. Mr. Emmett didn't know when he might be back.

"What's the matter, Lettie?" asked Thad, looking surprised when she entered the store from the front.

She almost turned and left, then leaned on the sewing machine. She couldn't bear to tell him.

He left the register and took her hand. "What's wrong?"

"It's Larry." She could hardly breathe. "I found blood on his handkerchief this morning. I have to get help for him, Thad. You know what that means."

"Oh, Lettie," he said, his voice choked. He turned her to him. "I have about ninety dollars now. Take that and get him to a hospital in Denver. I can give you ten out of the register to make it a hundred. And I'll get some more money somehow. I promise you. I'll borrow it. I'll sell the store."

"No!" Larry surprised them, coming in from the back, still disheveled from sleep. His face was pale and drawn. "I'm not going to let either of you make any more sacrifices. Thad, you will not lose your store because of me, and you will not marry Noah, either, Lettie. There are things you don't know." He joined them at the machine.

Lettie pulled his coat tighter around his chest. "I don't care what you think you know, Larry. We can't let this go on any longer."

He shoved her hands away.

"Larry, please." She urged him toward the stove.

"Stop fussing over me!"

She dropped her hands to her sides. "I know you've been coughing up blood. You're so sick. Do you think I can just stand by and let you die? I'll never forgive myself if I don't do something. You're my brother. I love you."

"And you're like a brother to me, too," Thad added.

Larry stood his ground, his hands on his hips. "Would you want me to go on, knowing your own lives are pure misery because of me? You think I could live with that?" He looked from Lettie to Thad and back. Slowly the anger left his eyes and turned to begging.

Silence filled the impasse.

Lettie felt the panic tighten around her heart again, knotted with her dread of marrying Noah and an awful guilt.

Larry grasped her arm and squeezed hard. "Please, give me

more time. Don't set a date with Noah till after the trial. It's only six weeks away. If you promise me that, I swear to you I'll hang on and I'll do whatever you want when it's over."

The door banged open and Noah dashed in. He looked at the three of them. Another tense silence filled the store as he stared from Lettie to Thad and back.

"My receptionist said you looked frantic," he said to Lettie. "What's going on here? What are you up to?" he asked Thad.

"It's . . ." started Lettie.

"Nothing," Larry cried, chopping through the air with his hand.

Noah ignored him and turned to Thad, accusation written across his face.

Lettie looked at the man she was betrothed to and suddenly hated him for his assumption that Thad was somehow at fault. "Leave him out of this," she said, her voice raw with desperation.

Thad looked Noah levelly in the eyes and said, "It's Larry."

Noah stared at Larry and his face softened briefly. "I haven't seen you since before the parade," he said. "You look awful."

Larry turned away from him.

Noah grabbed Lettie's arm and steered her toward the door. "I'll speak to you outside," he rasped.

She jerked away as the doorbell jingled. "No. If you have anything to say, say it here." She looked at him, furious, as the bell jingled a second time and the door closed.

Noah's hand came up fast, but only slapped the doorframe. He turned Lettie's face toward him. "Marry me now, Juliet. You do that one act of good faith, and he'll have every medication my money can buy," he said, his voice rising as he spoke.

"No!" shouted Larry, keeping his back turned.

Thad stepped closer to Noah and glared into his eyes. "If you loved her, you'd help him regardless of when the wedding is."

"You keep out . . ." Noah started.

Larry slammed his hand down on the sewing table. "No." He turned to her. "If you try to force me, I won't take anything from him now or ever. Or from Thad either. I'll go away. I swear it."

"Larry, please," sobbed Lettie. She looked at him through the tears, then at Thad, and at Noah.

"I swear it, Lettie."

Lettie turned her head from one to the next. The needs of the three men pulled at her until she felt she would snap. Why did Larry seem to think things would work out if she waited? Was there some small hope she could save Larry and love Thad? She looked hard at Larry and realized the determination in his face was no sham. He would leave if she married Noah now. But if he died . . . The thought was unbearable.

Noah waited, his face set, eyes hard.

Thad was still glaring at Noah, his fists clenched at his side. "Help her, for God's sake, man."

Noah's answer was nearly a growl, and it was directed to Lettie. "As soon as we're married."

Lettie put her fists to her face, weeping, and turned her back to all of them. "I'll marry you the minute the trial is over."

Noah slammed the door on his way out. He did not look through the window at them as he passed it.

Lettie stood for a minute and then opened the top of the sewing machine, seeing the faces of Thad and Noah on the oak lid. The one so kind and generous. The other hard. The brute force she'd just seen in Noah's eyes sent a chill down her spine and made her think of Zeb.

CHAPTER 26

January 15, 1896

Thad sold the last three pairs of ice skates to a man with two children in tow and wrote "sk." on his list for Friday's order, along with earmuffs. All morning visitors had been streaming in, buying souvenir postal cards, pins, programs of the day's activities and items they'd left at home. The opening and closing of the cash register drawer, which should have brought him satisfaction, only made him more keenly aware of how useless the prosperity was if he couldn't find a way to clear his name.

The store was quiet now. Lettie was sewing by hand, and even the visitors on the streets had found a lull in their merrymaking as they waited for the day's parade.

He went to the half-glass door and gazed out at the gathering crowd. There would be no more customers for a while now, with the parade about to start. Lettie looked up at him from the skirt she was repairing for a woman who had snagged it getting off the train from Denver.

He smiled down at her. "Why don't you stop for a while? She surely won't come to pick that up till after the parade."

"She isn't coming at all. I'm supposed to deliver it to the hotel on my way home." Lettie laid the work aside. "I don't have anything else to do, anyway, so I have plenty of time. I hope they're planning a lot more costumed affairs. What with all this commotion, no one's interested in ordering normal clothes." She stretched her back and looked out at the clowns, cowboys, kings, bullfighters, and frogs that blocked her view of the street. "Doesn't anyone else in Colorado work?" she asked. "This is beginning to feel like a continuous New Year's Eve party. I've never seen so many people in one place."

"Well, this parade is for Colorado Press Day and the 'official' opening."

Lettie cocked her head at him. "The 'official' opening? I thought they had that last week."

Thad laughed. "No, that one was the 'formal' opening."

"And the one on New Year's Day?"

"That was just the Grand Opening."

"Aha."

"I think this is the only one that really counts because the front entrance is finally finished. It is strange that they put all these parades on Wednesdays, though."

"That's what I mean. Doesn't anybody else work?" She gazed out at the merrymakers.

Thad watched the array of costumes for a few minutes. "I imagine the local children are furious, sitting in school with a parade about to start."

Lettie didn't answer. He looked down at her stricken face. She was staring at a tiny girl with a wand and gauzy wings sprouting from her blue overcoat. Suddenly he knew what was in her mind. She would never have his children. He leaned his head against the cold glass. "I'm sorry, my love. I'm so endlessly sorry."

She smiled at him. "You'd think we'd be used to this by now. Let's change the subject. Do you have today's paper?"

"Yes."

"Tell me about the activities."

Thad brought the paper from the back counter. "Hmm," he mused, flipping pages. "They took Governor McIntire and his whole entourage on a tour of the Little Johnny Mine this morning. And then to the vault of the Carbonate National Bank to see the hundred-fifty thousand dollars in gold bars that came from the Little Johnny. And tonight there's another parade, just from the Armory to the Palace, by torchlight and continuous fireworks. Then another lighting ceremony and a gala reception."

"My goodness! They're doing it up proud, aren't they? Is the proclamation Mrs. Es was chattering about this morning in there?"

"Yes, right on the front page. You want to see it?"

"Read it to me."

Thad glanced through the first few lines. "Well, I guess it's in keeping with a carnival atmosphere."

PROCLAMATION
Colorado Press Day
Wednesday, January 15, 1896
Hearken all Ye People!

Give ear unto the words of the Lord High Mayor of the city of Leadville.

Know then that I, Samuel D. Nicholson, the exalted potentate of the City of the Crystal Castle, do send word unto the people of the land, from Carbonate Hill even unto the uttermost parts of Malta, and to all inhabitants thereof, to obey and submit themselves to the will of the King Carnival, who will enter the gates of the Ice Castle on the 15th Day of the month known as January.

I ordain and decree, by the power vested in me by the Mystic Council of Seven, that on the day of arrival of the August King Carnival, ye shall not appear on the highways and byways of the city, between the hours of 2 o'clock in the afternoon and 10 o'clock at night, unless the face be covered by a masque. Nor shall ye enter unto the castle walls unless clothed in fantastic dress suitable to the majesty of his royal icicles, King Carnival.

And to him who fails to obey the decree will be meted out the lightnings [sic.] and thunders of the royal anger . . .

Lettie stretched again and got up to stand beside him.

"I don't think I can listen to any more of that," she said, shaking her head. "It's really a bit silly, isn't it?"

Thad nodded, scanning the remainder of the proclamation. "The rest of it goes on in the same vein. I'm sure it's just the ticket for anyone who hasn't a care in the world." He laid the paper on the notions counter.

The first band was heading up Third Street from the Armory. It was a dazzling parade to mark the coming of King Carnival, made the more resplendent by sunshine and mild temperatures. The bangled and bejeweled costumes sparkled in the sun, the acclimated musicians played with exuberance, onlookers responded with noisemakers of all kinds.

The first of the sled-floats glided by. "Larry'll be sorry he missed this," said Thad.

"I know. But I think he's planning to go to Zeb's for the fireworks tonight. He says you can see a corner of the Palace from his window."

The reminder of the friendship between Zeb and Larry annoyed Thad. He went back to the register, and Lettie picked up the torn skirt again. Neither watched the parade.

Larry sat at Zeb's side on one of the chairs they had dragged to the window, conscious of the air sinking off the cold glass and enveloping his knees and feet. He'd have stayed home tonight if Zeb hadn't invited him to come. But now that he had Zeb's confidence, he couldn't afford not to push on.

Suddenly Zeb reached across with his good arm and slapped him on the knee. "Come on, Larry, there's no point staying in the room when we can be out there where the real party is." He jumped up and threw Larry's coat at him from the bed, followed by the sable hat. "You're dressed plenty warm enough. It wasn't even that cold today."

Larry started to protest.

Zeb clicked his tongue and shook his head. "Don't be a sorry sister. Come on, the fireworks'll start any minute. Here, drink this, it'll put a fire in those lungs of yours." He held his flask out.

Larry shuddered at the thought of standing out in the packed snow of Leadville's streets. "Well, all right, let's go. Only you don't want to drink after me. Thanks anyway." He got up from the chair, struggled into coat jacket, and checked the pockets of his pants for an extra handkerchief.

"Here," said Zeb, handing him a small flat bottle. "You can use this. I rinsed the shaving lotion out of it this morning." He poured some whiskey into it from the half empty bottle on the table and handed it to Larry, his eyes challenging him to refuse.

Larry exaggerated his motions and took a small swallow. He coughed as the heavy odor of the lotion that lingered on the bottle irritated his nose and the whiskey set fire to his throat.

Before they reached Eighth, the first rockets went off, and Zeb pushed him along. They reached the corner just as the first marchers of the evening parade turned into the Palace grounds. At the side of the Palace a place had been cleared for the fireworks. A man stood on a platform and announced in every direction through a megaphone that Gloom and Melancholy had come to do battle with the King of the Castle.

Zeb took out his flask and prodded Larry. Larry took another swallow, larger this time, and found that it did, indeed, warm him as it went down. Internal cashmere, he thought. Nevertheless, it made him cough.

A rocket flew horizontally from the platform and shot toward the Palace. It fizzled and hissed the minute it hit the wall. It was followed by many others, all of which had no effect on the

Palace. The crowd applauded.

Zeb watched the show with one eyebrow drawn up in condescension, shrugged when it ended, and drew on the flask.

Larry followed suit with his lotion bottle, increasingly grateful for the warmth as it eased through his body. Sure wish it'd circulate all the way to my feet, he thought.

The man on the platform took the megaphone again and announced that the battle was over, the King had prevailed, and the visitors could now enter the castle. The gem-lights in the walls came ablaze, stunning the crowd to silence. Then the roar of appreciation joined a blast of fireworks that continued until the last of the two hundred couples in the grand march had disappeared through the huge octagonal front towers.

"I'd give my right arm to have an invitation to the goings-on in there tonight," said Zeb.

Larry giggled. "That'd be a fitting entrance fee for you."

"What do you mean?" Zeb glared at him.

"Cheap, I mean . . . with *your* right arm . . ." He grinned at Zeb and held his breath.

Zeb poured whiskey into his mouth without taking his eyes off Larry. He held the whiskey for a minute before swallowing it, and his face contorted into a fleeting, ironic smile. "You're right," he said with a hollow laugh. "Real fitting." He looked down at his shoulder, his face bitter. "Might as well cut it off."

"Your arm didn't seem to keep you from . . ."

Zeb's eyes narrowed to slits as he grabbed him by the collar. "From what?"

Larry couldn't go on in the force of Zeb's stare, which always straddled the thin line that divides malice from violence. ". . . from . . . having a good time," he finished, choking on the fist that pressed at his Adam's apple. Zeb let go with his fist but his eyes kept Larry paralyzed. Disappointment and failure overcame him. He could never quite bring himself to challenge Zeb, and

228

every time he tried and failed, he knew he'd let Thad down.

He sees through me, Larry thought, half panicked. He'd quit with me if I didn't buy half his drinks. I have to keep him trusting me. Someday he's going to make a mistake if I get him drunk enough. But if I have to match his drinks to get him there, I may make a mistake, too. And that'd be the end of us all. "I don't know what you're so touchy about," he said, annoyed that his voice shook.

Zeb cuffed him on the chest in a gesture that might have be manly camaraderie or vicious reminder of Larry's weakness.

In the resulting coughing spell, Larry didn't hear what he said.

CHAPTER 27

January 26, 1896

Thad sat in his armchair reading the Sunday paper by the light of his dormer window. Silence surrounded him like cotton batting. Loneliness and boredom drained his spirit, and he shrugged at the news that Stock Exchange Day at the Ice Palace had yielded a record-breaking trade of shares.

He flipped the page to an article about the Wheelers and their bizarre cycles racing around a board track on the skating rink. A shiver ran up his spine. His room was getting cold again. He dropped the paper on his lap and rubbed his hands. The slight thudding and clinking of Mrs. Eskitch as she prepared her lunch were the only sounds of life in the house. Suddenly they embodied his own life—a distant, insignificant noise in the emptiness.

Disheartened by the image, he threw the paper on his bed and turned toward the window behind him, its glass panes completely coated with ice, inside and out. The sun glinted weakly through it, but the day was bitter cold.

He threw off the wool blanket he'd laid over his legs, stood up, and paced semicircles around the stove near the inside wall. Little warmth was coming from the stove, and he hesitated to throw more coal onto the embers after only forty minutes. He could go down to the kitchen on the pretense of fetching more water for the tin pot he kept on the stove to raise the humidity. The kitchen was almost always warm, but even the thought of

Mrs. Eskitch's constant prattle wore him down. He should get some air and quit focusing on himself; find something to cheer him up.

A few muffled notes of music penetrated the window from the Leadville-South Park Station, where the noon train from Buena Vista must be arriving. A hired marching band still met the trains at all three stations to accompany visitors to the Ice Palace. From the store, he heard the music several times a day, and on cold days like this, it sounded brittle, thin, and out of tune.

He picked the paper up again and checked the day's schedule—no special group slated today. It might not be crowded. He put on another sweater, went down the stairs, put on his heavy coat, wool hat, and thick boots.

He approached the Ice Palace from the north side and gazed at the glassy walls sparkling in the midday sun. Centered in front of them stood the huge statue of Lady Leadville, her pedestal more than twice his height. She wore a crown with thin spikes radiating from it, each ending in a little ball. Her outer skirt was gathered at the waist so that the folds fell in graceful curves. Her thick right arm pointed toward the Mosquito Range. The index finger had already melted off. A slender icicle hung from the lowest point of the hand, the drop of water at its end a prism in the sun.

Thad looked at the tiny flash of color at the end of the icicle, cheerfully ablaze like Lettie's opal engagement ring and the colored Palace lit at night. All three made him feel cold, frozen in a block of time that ended in a trial. He looked away, taking in the spired turrets of the entrance towers and the sparkling blocks that topped the round turrets along the side walls. He moved with a few other people toward the turnstiles under the arched entrance.

He entered the huge tower on his left, staring up at the glassy, four-story walls. The tower housed the display of the Leadville–South Park Railroad, with photographs of its depots inside the ice blocks. He left the tower through another door and started up the steps that led to the ballroom. In the wall to the right of the door was a photograph of Tingley S. Wood, one of the first exhibits that had been placed in the walls, according to a plaque. Thad stopped to look.

"Hello, Mac. Good man, that Mr. Wood," said a voice behind him.

Thad turned to find his friend Julius Marechal, the baker.

"He surely is," said Thad as they shook hands.

"Did you know he insisted that tickets be sold cheaper to needy people so no one would be excluded from the Palace?"

"No, I didn't. Well, I salute him, then." Thad doffed his hat to the frozen photograph. "You just going in?"

Julius nodded. "I was here with my family a few weeks ago but never had a chance to look the place over. Too busy keeping the little ones upright on the ice. Thought I'd make that up while they're at afternoon church."

They stepped into the ballroom together, both surprised to find it slightly heated. They followed the walls to their left, past a scale model of a Denver and Rio Grand locomotive trimmed in gold. Beyond it, the front half of the wall was devoted to mining equipment, assaying instruments, and outdoor supplies.

"My word, I didn't know they'd practically made a museum of it," said Julius as they moved to the south side, admiring displays of musical instruments, leather goods, tobacco wares in the ice.

"I don't think I realized the size of it, either," said Thad, turning to look back across the fifty-by-eighty-foot room topped by timber trusses and a log roof and lit by hanging balls of electric light. The east wall was a dull glow now that the sun had moved to the west. Huge arched windows separated the ballroom from the skating rink so that the dancers could watch the skaters and vice versa.

They entered the skating rink at the back. Already skaters were carving their long ovals around the floor, some struggling with flailing arms to maintain their footing, others sailing confidently over the ice, keeping their steps to the Strauss waltz played by Leadville's little orchestra.

Immediately, Thad spotted Lettie and Noah on the ice toward the front of the rink. Noah was coaching her, skating backwards. Lettie looked miserable, bent forward, both arms out. She took a step and nearly fell. Noah reached for her, but she ignored his hand. She lifted her blue skirt slightly to show him that both ankles were turned and she was skating on the edge of the boots rather than the blades. Noah skated closer and put his arm around her waist to set her right on the skates again. Three steps later, she fell. Anger rose in Thad like a tidal wave and he started to run to her, forgetting the slick surface. He sprawled at Julius's feet.

"Don't, Mac," said Julius, helping him up. "You don't want to make a big show."

Thad straightened his coat and said ruefully, "You're right. It's not my place to . . ." He looked back at Lettie. Noah had already picked her up. She pointed back to the entrance, but he put his arm around her waist and guided her toward the rear. Thad saw her weak, red-faced smile, and turned his back.

He followed Julius along the rear wall, past displays of tiny electric lights, electrical appliances, small motors, overalls, fur coats, and fine soaps carved into delicate designs, all frozen in the wall.

In the corner tower the Singer Company displayed an electric sewing machine that could "embroider snowflakes without a flaw," along with amazing samples of needlework that had been done on it. He saw Lettie's slender, white-stockinged ankles struggling with her treadle machine. It would never be his place to give her an electric one.

They crossed into the rear of the heated dining room on the west side of the rink. The smell of beef and coffee thickened the air, underscored by the exhibits of hams, steaks, Kuner's pickles, fancy pats of butter, cheeses, breads, fruits, vegetables, fish, oysters, and delicate desserts.

Julius stopped and looked around. "Well, now I know why Miller only picked up twenty loaves of bread and a hundred rolls this morning when he had me bake three times that many. Just look at that." Picnic hampers lined most of the tables at the rear of the dining room, and a dozen families were enjoying lunch. Closer to the kitchen, only a few tables were occupied.

"I heard they come on the night train, bring their own food, and go back on the night train," said Thad. "No wonder we're not seeing them much on Harrison anymore."

They passed the beer displays near the kitchen, laughing over the tale of the salt water in the Coors bottles. They ordered coffee and drank it while watching the skaters.

They parted at the front end of the dining room, and Thad looked around the rink. Lettie and Noah were gone. Treading cautiously along the perimeter to avoid skaters, he looked at the ice sculpture in the first archway that separated the rink from the dining room. It was the loaded pack mule Larry had told him about several weeks ago. It stood in front of the ladder that led up to the windowed orchestra balcony.

He was about to move to the next arch when someone tapped him on the shoulder and then grabbed his arm, nearly throwing him off balance on the ice.

Startled, Thad turned to find Judge Dickson, whose feet were sliding in opposite directions.

Thad helped him right himself. "Tom, or should I say, 'Your Honor'?"

The judge clicked his tongue, grinned, and linked arms with him. "Certainly not when I'm likely to be an ignominious heap at your feet any minute. Besides, I'm retired now." He ran a hand over the mule's ear. "Amazing. Can you imagine yourself carving a thing like this?"

Thad let a bitter puff of air escape through his nose. "I can't imagine myself involved with this thing at all anymore."

"Not going so well, Thad?" The judge wobbled as one foot lost control. "Oops. Has the scandal hurt your business much?"

"Well, not since the first week. It's nice to know that most of the people here have faith in me. Still, I can't find a soul who knows a thing about the murder."

Dickson was looking at his feet, mincing his steps. "Let's just stand still a minute. I heard you'd been trying to solve it yourself. Who've you talked to?"

"I spent a couple of evenings going to all the buildings that front the site. After that I widened my circle. I talked to everyone near my store, and to the few people Old Marsh associated with. Almost everyone was sympathetic, but no one could give me any information." Thad's heart beat faster, hoping to hear the judge say he was sure the trial would end with his acquittal.

Dickson only held on to his arm and pulled him toward another exhibit, a miner at work. He laughed at the statue. "Well, that's romanticized. No miner alive ever had this much light to work in."

Thad hardly heard him. "I'm scared, Tom, to tell you the truth. I guess you know about the knife."

"I do." Dickson shook his head and moved on, stopping before a statue of a standing man wearing a straw hat and holding a staff. "Do you suppose this is Tingley Wood or Mayor Nicholson? Or maybe Edwin Senior, who thought the whole thing up?"

Thad could not let the subject of the trial go. "What do you think, Tom? Am I going to jail?"

Dickson hesitated a moment. "Well, look at it this way. If you don't have a witness who saw anything, then the police don't either. And it's up to the county attorney to prove that *you* did it, not someone using your knife." His tone did not convey the optimism of his words.

Nevertheless, Thad grasped at the straw. "You think a jury would let me go free on that?"

Dickson looked at him for a minute and shook his head. "I'm sorry, Thad. I know you want me to be honest with you."

Thad's heart dropped into darkness. "So I'm really likely to hang?"

"It's hard to say. You never can tell what a jury will do."

Thad reached for a last small hope. "You wouldn't take the case for me, would you, Tom? I can't pay you anything now, but if I'm freed, I'd get my bond money back."

The judge hesitated, but his face reflected something other than indecision. "It's like I said, Thad, I'm retired now. I'm not even sure about the ethics of taking a case for someone I bonded out. But come on, have you eaten? Let me buy you dinner. I'd buy you a beer or a whiskey, but they've never allowed any alcohol in the Palace. Probably wise, given this floor." He clutched Thad's arm more tightly and they stepped flat-footed toward the door to the dining hall.

Thad had heard the lie in Dickson's voice. It wasn't retirement or ethics that stopped him. He didn't think he could win the case. Thad felt the certainty take hold of his heart: he would be punished for someone else's crime. He wanted to run, leave this doomed life. Where could he go that they would not hunt him down? Where would he find meaning to his life again?

Dickson stopped and smiled sympathetically. "Come on, Thad. There's nothing you can do now but wait. The trial's still four weeks away. Anything can happen. Put it aside and try to enjoy the day."

There was nothing else he could do anyway. He forced himself to comply as they reached the plank floor of the dining room.

Dickson ordered beef stew and cherry pie. The food appeared quickly, since the meals were prepared in Miller's restaurant on Harrison or in his bakery on Sixth, where Julius worked. All the Palace's kitchen had to do was keep it warm.

Taking up the slab of Julius's bread that came with the stew, Dickson looked about the room and through the windows at the few skaters. "There aren't as many people here as I expected," he said.

"I hear the hotels aren't doing the business they projected, either, especially from the Denverites," said Thad. *And may Noah go broke in the end,* he thought, and then felt his face redden in silent shame. Noah's bankruptcy would only condemn Larry to death.

"You're right," said Dickson, spooning beef and potato toward his mouth. "Just look at that." He finished the bite of stew and waved the spoon vaguely toward the picnickers. "They spend almost nothing beyond their rail fare. My guess is, if it weren't for the different groups scheduled right through March, this thing would've folded shortly after the official opening."

Thad swallowed a bite of carrot and took a sip of coffee. "To tell you the truth, I'm tired of all the hoopla. I had a burst of business at the beginning of the month, but now, unless there's a parade, we don't see many of the visitors up on Harrison. I'm almost back to the old steady customers. I have a pile of skates I doubt I'll ever get rid of."

"I hate to say it, but the thing's basically a big, colorful disappointment," said Dickson, shoving his plate away and pulling the pie toward him. "Maybe it's just as well you had to sell your shares."

Thad nodded. *May Noah do what's necessary for Larry* before *he goes bankrupt,* he thought.

When Dickson left, Thad stood up but remembered he had nowhere to go but his cold room. He ordered another cup of coffee and sat with his hands around the cup, gazing at the changing play of light on the ice walls in the afternoon sun.

A commotion on the skating rink distracted him, and he turned to see Zeb and a woman in a heap on the ice. Her purple skirt was well above her knees, and her legs flapped in the air in her green and yellow striped stockings. She and Zeb were laughing raucously, their skates sliding out from under them every time they tried to stand. When a crowd began to gather, they turned their accident into a show.

Thad rose to go into the rink and upbraid his brother, and then remembered he had disowned Zeb. The whole town knew where things stood between them. It would do no good to make more of a spectacle. He left the Palace, embarrassed and more depressed than when he'd entered it. Where was Zeb getting the money for the unabated high life he led, for these women? Perhaps from home, though Mother or Father would surely have mentioned something in a letter. Why did Zeb even stay here? He hated Leadville. The muscles in Thad's jaw tensed as he walked, Zeb's coarse laughter still ringing in his ears.

And the friendship with Larry. What could he possibly want with Larry? Thad shook his head. More puzzling: what would Larry want with Zeb? They were apparently seeing each other at least once a week, and even though Larry had not changed in his attitude toward Lettie or Thad, he refused to talk to them about it. Something was very wrong.

CHAPTER 28

February 24, 1896

Shivering, Larry waited for a short evening parade to round the corner from Harrison onto Eighth. A small group of Negroes walked along between a sleigh carrying children and a noisy band playing their spirited music. Most of the faces he recognized from the small community of Negroes who lived in "Coon Row," out past the brothels on West State Street. The adults were dancing or sashaying rather than marching; the children were laughing, standing in the sleigh with their arms swaying above their heads to the music. No spectators lined the street to cheer them on. The carnival organizers should have put the Colored People's Day together with another group, Larry thought, maybe with the Red Men's Day and the Woodmen of the World a couple of weeks ago so they'd have a little support.

He glanced down Harrison toward the store. In the incandescent lights that lined it, the street seemed as jaded as he was with the carnival. Decorations on the storefronts drooped under the ghostly weight of heavy snow that had long since melted. Their colors were faded and streaked, even in the more cheerful light of day.

The Negroes danced around the corner to the rhythm of the band. Larry waved at the children in the sleigh, falling in behind them.

He glanced at the Palace as he reached Spruce. Its colored

lights were on now, but Larry pictured it as it looked by day. The building had aged quickly during the warm spells of February. The walls at the back had turned completely opaque with the nightly spraying; the blocks that had serrated the tops of the small turrets were shrunken and lopsided. Souvenir programs, used tickets and picnic trash often littered the grounds around the Palace. A boardwalk now stretched across the sometimes-muddy expanse from the street to the turnstiles.

Larry stopped for a minute to catch his breath and let his memory replay the town's excitement about the Palace and its stunning beauty when it opened. So much hope, so much disappointment. It hadn't long to live, just like him. He shook his head to dispel the thought and turned toward Zeb's rooming house, coughing as the incline increased.

Zeb greeted him without getting up from the table. He held the newspaper in one hand and a glass in the other. "You see this about the Colored People's Day?" he asked.

Larry laid his coat over the foot of the bed. "I not only saw that, I saw *them*. No one turned out to watch. It was pathetic."

"Damn right," he said. "Coloreds have no place in a white carnival, much less one for winter. Bunch of Africans. Let 'em make their own Ice Palace if they like the winter so much."

Larry was stunned for a second. "Well, don't worry about it," he said, throwing his sable hat onto the coat. "They seemed to be making their own fun. Got another glass for me?"

Zeb threw the paper onto the table. "Did you bring your own liquor this time, like I told you?"

"Of course."

"Well, here, then."

Larry took the shaving lotion bottle from his jacket pocket and poured the tea that he hoped looked like whiskey into the glass Zeb shoved at him. "Here's to . . . what?"

"I don't know. Who needs to toast anything? Just drink up."

Zeb half emptied his glass.

"You been down to the Palace lately?" asked Larry

"Saturday. I took Selena for a whirl around the rink."

"Did you see the arm had fallen off the statue?"

"Can't say I was making eyes at a frozen lady. The hot ones are more my style." Smiling tightly, he fingered the little black shark that hung from his watch chain.

"Well, it did. And all the little spikes on the crown. It's going downhill fast now."

"Old fool. Marsh was right after all. Some carnival." Zeb shrugged and refilled his glass. "Why should you care?"

"I don't. But they still have groups scheduled through the whole month of March. People are going to be furious if the thing's half melted by the time they get here. I read they're laying off the extra police that were hired for crowd control as of Saturday."

Zeb laughed and rocked on the back legs of his chair. "Hey, Saturday's the twenty-ninth. Anybody going to ask you to marry her on Leap Year Day?"

Larry laughed and poured himself another glass of tepid tea. "Several. Maisy, Belinda, and that new one, what's her name?"

Zeb half-choked in the middle of a swallow. "Zowee, she's a hummer, that Laurette. Drinks me right under the table." He raised his glass in salute and emptied it again.

Larry watched him slosh some of the whiskey out at the top of the salute and dribble a little down his chin. His eyes were already glazed and his speech slurred.

This is my chance, he thought. He sat down on the edge of the bed to make himself as unthreatening as possible. "You know, Thad's trial is Friday," he ventured.

"So?"

Larry could hear his racing heart above the rattle of his chest. "I heard you're going to testify against him."

Zeb lurched at the news, and the front legs of the chair banged onto the floor. "Where'd you hear that?"

Larry hunched over to make himself smaller, holding his glass between his knees. "Oh, you know how word spreads in a town like this."

"So what if I am? I thought you and Thad were on the outs."

"Oh, I see through him all right. I just don't happen to believe he did it. And I'd draw the line at lying to put him in jail, especially when I know he's innocent."

"You don't know that."

Larry's hands shook so badly his fake whiskey splashed onto his pants. It was now or never. "Maybe, but you do."

Zeb narrowed his eyes and stared. There was little of drunkenness in his face now. "What's that supposed to mean?"

Larry perceived the violent nature behind the glazed eyes and lost the resolve to accuse Zeb openly. He felt Zeb's bitterness, sharp as the cheese knife. Still capable of murder. With only one hand, Zeb could strangle him. "You . . . you know him better than anyone, Zeb. He's your brother. They could hang him. You can't testify against him."

"I can do anything I damn well please. He's got it coming, believe me. He may have everybody else fooled, but not me."

"Still, lying about your own brother . . ."

Zeb got up, bent over, and grabbed Larry's shirtfront. His face was so close that a mixture of spittle and whiskey sprayed Larry. He hissed, "This is the end of the discussion, you hear me? Why don't you go on back to the house and hold his hand if you're so concerned about him?"

"I'm not interested in holding his hand. I just . . ."

"Go on, get out." Zeb pulled him up by the shirt and shoved him toward the door. "I don't know what you think you're after, following me around like this, but you're not going to get it. I'm sick of you, anyway, with your constant bubbly cough and your pretense of having a good time. You think I don't see through that? Go on, and don't come back. I've had enough of you."

Larry grabbed his coat and the sable hat. He put them on in the hall, feeling defeated. Nothing in his whole life had prepared him to feel so powerless in the presence of another human being. He'd failed again and time was running out. There had to be a way to get Zeb to admit he killed Old Marsh. Or at least to prove that Zeb had stolen Thad's knife.

CHAPTER 29

February 25, 1896

Looking up from the paper spread over the tobacco counter, Thad watched Lettie for a minute. She sat at the closed machine, staring out at dust, dry grass, and bits of paper flying past in a stiff north wind. In a minute she went back to working with pale blue yarn that snaked out of a cloth bag on the floor. Thad missed the rhythm of the sewing machine. "What are you making there, Lettie?"

She turned in the chair and smiled. "It's a bed jacket for my sister. Her birthday is in March."

"I didn't know you could knit, too."

Lettie laughed. "I'm not knitting, Thad. This is crocheting, though I can knit, too."

"Well, you certainly are a lady of many talents." He tried not to think about the fact that she'd be an ideal wife and mother.

Mrs. Lambert passed the window, her skirts billowing ahead of her. She came in, pulling at strands of hair that had blown across her eyes. The wind gave the doorbell an extra jingle before she got it closed. "Morning, Miss Corcoran, Mr. MacElwain," she said as soon as the bell had silenced. "Do you have any travel bags?"

"Are you going on a trip?" asked Thad.

"How lovely," said Lettie. "Where are you going?"

Mrs. Lambert's face smiled, but her tight laugh sounded more like a sigh of resignation. "Not a trip. We're moving. My

Ed hasn't had work since they laid off the ice masons at the Palace. He says there's no point staying here with that work over and the silver mines closed and everybody clamoring for a job in gold."

"Oh, dear," said Lettie. "Couldn't he find something else?"

Mrs. Lambert shook her head. "He offered to do snow removal at the Palace, but it seems they're just letting that go these days. What with all the melting, maybe they reckon snow is better than mud. Anyway, we're going to California. He has a distant cousin out there near Salinas who's trying to start up a vineyard. I don't know what a miner-turned-mason can do in a vineyard, but there's no future for us here."

Thad nodded. "I'm real sorry to hear you're leaving, Mrs. Lambert, and not just because you've been one of my most regular customers." Immediately the inanity of that thought came to him. Beyond Friday, no customers would matter.

"I'm sorry, too," said Lettie. "I wish you the best luck."

Thad moved toward the storeroom. "Let me see if I still have a carpet bag in the back."

In a minute he came back, slapping dust from a flattened travel bag. He opened it and pushed the sides out. "It's not the latest fashion in luggage, but it's roomy," he said. "It's been here since I bought the store, and heaven only knows how long before that. I can let you have it for a dollar, if you don't mind that it's a bit faded."

"I don't have the money to be choosy, Mr. MacElwain. I'll take it and be grateful. We'll settle up with you before we go." Mrs. Lambert slapped at the bag again and tucked it under her arm. "Well, thank you, Mr. MacElwain, and good-bye. Good-bye, Miss Corcoran." She opened the door but closed it against the wind, and turned to Thad again. "I wish you good luck in your trial, Mr. MacElwain. I'm sure it'll come out all right. I wish we could be here to celebrate with you when it's over."

The bell jingled happily again.

Thad's heart raced, as it did every time he was reminded of the trial, only three days away now. He looked down at Lettie.

She gazed up at him, her lips quivering. "It's almost over, isn't it?"

He nodded. "I wish I could say I haven't given a single thought to Friday or any day beyond that. Without you, nothing beyond the trial matters. I keep telling myself I don't even care if they put me in jail or hang me. But deep inside, I'm terrified of both possibilities." He pressed his arms across his chest, trying to hold on to control when fear was racing through his arteries. He had to get his mind on another topic. "Whatever happens, Lettie, please, try to be happy. Maybe Noah didn't have anything to do with the murder. At least, he half convinced me. And I think, in his way, he'll try to do right by you. I couldn't go to my death or to jail knowing you'll never be happy."

"Stop talking like that. You're not going to jail."

"I don't know. The evidence is so strong."

"Well, I can't think that way, and whatever happens, Thad, I want you to be happy, too." Her voice began to quiver. She turned her face away, and her shoulders bowed. "Find someone else to love. Please say you'll do that."

Thad opened his mouth but couldn't force himself to make the sounds she wanted to hear. Instead, he took a deep breath and said, "Lettie, I saw Tom Dickson yesterday and gave him power of attorney to sell the store for whatever it'll bring. If I don't go to jail, I'm going to leave right after the trial. I can't be here when you marry Noah."

She nodded, her eyes welling over. She took his hand and laid it against her cheek. He moved behind her, as he'd done so often, and put both hands on her shoulder. They stayed that way, looking out at the windy sunshine of a too-warm winter, the sagging remnants of a failing carnival, and a future devoid of hope.

With his back to the wind, Noah stood at the corner of Eighth and Spruce and watched dozens of miners get off the noon train and spread out up the hill along Spruce and Third. The rock-drilling contest had attracted a good crowd, but for all the hundreds who came to the group days, maintenance of the Palace cost a good deal more than the income it generated these days. He wasn't going to get any kind of return on the $500 he'd paid for Thad's shares. Well, he'd simply bought himself a wife.

A sound like a growl escaped his throat. The thought of Juliet sent anger pulsing through him. She'd never shown the slightest affection for him, nor respect, nor even a comfortable toleration. She was more coldly polite to him now than when she'd first checked in to the hotel. With his head down against the wind and gloved fists balled at his sides, he turned up Spruce and shortly knocked on Zeb's door.

It took another, louder knock before Zeb's drowsy, annoyed voice summoned him in.

"What're you doing here?" Zeb asked, swinging his feet off the bed.

Noah turned his head at the smell of overnight breath, old liquor, and soiled clothes. "For God's sake, man, it's nearly noon. Is this how you spend every day?"

Zeb glared at him silently as he pulled on his pants and sat down on the bed again, running his hand through his pillow-stiffened hair.

Noah shrugged. "Never mind. I shouldn't ask when I'm the one making it possible."

Zeb looked at him with eyes still bloodshot and puffy. "I asked you what you're doing here."

Noah raised the window halfway, letting in a cloud of grit that blew up from the sill. He threw a rumpled shirt off the ladder-back chair near the bed and sat down. "What's your brother planning to do after the trial, assuming they don't sentence him?"

"How would I know?" Zeb slammed the window, pulled on a maroon dressing gown, and sat down again. "I haven't spoken to him in weeks. Why would they acquit him? I'm keeping my end of the bargain."

Noah just sat watching him.

Zeb clicked his tongue and shook his head. "Look, I'm going to say I saw him leave the store with the knife." He chopped his hand through the air, making a mobile check mark for each step of his story. "I just happened to catch him out of the corner of my eye from the Silver Dollar. I suspected something, knowing he's capable of anything." He shoved his right arm up as a demonstration. "I followed him. I saw him do it." He leaned back against the headboard. "I can read people. I'll keep going till the jurors are convinced."

"That's all well and good, but actually, it's your testimony I'm getting worried about. Yours wasn't the most savory of reputations before the murder. Since then, it's only gotten worse, especially after he disowned you. The whole town knows you for a ne'er-do-well."

"So? You knew that when you struck the bargain."

Noah almost laughed. The fool had no idea what was coming. "I realize that. But things have changed. The shock has worn off and the people are on Thad's side." He looked down and casually pulled a scrap of loose skin from his thumb. "I want to be sure that even if he's acquitted, he has to leave town." He flicked the bit of skin onto the floor.

"Why? She's marrying you right after the trial, isn't she?"

"My reason is not your concern."

"The whole damn thing isn't my concern except my testimony, and then I'm leaving this Deadville on the next train."

Noah looked him in the eyes now, ready to deliver the first shot. "Fine, after you set the store on fire."

"*What?*" Zeb jolted upright and his face blanched.

"You heard me."

"There's not a chance in hell I'd do that for you."

"I think there is."

"Well, you can just think again."

Noah was enjoying the interview. He let a minute's silence go by before firing the next salvo. "You remember the night you and Marsh set the lumber for the Ice Palace on fire?"

Zeb's mouth fell open.

"Don't bother to deny it," said Noah. "I saw the whole thing from my window. You were wearing a miner's light. You both poured the kerosene on all four piles, argued at the edge of the site, and then Marsh went back and lit only two of them."

Zeb considered a moment, his face full of desperate bravado. "You try to make that public, and you'll end up in as much trouble as me for keeping quiet so long. And I'll be long gone, no testimony."

It was time for the bombshell. "I don't think so. There's the little matter of the murder. I happened to see that, also."

Zeb froze and stared at him in disbelief.

"You tried to stab him once and only knocked him down. The second time you jumped on him and had to use your weight to get the knife in. You murdered him. That's not like some fire that hampered construction briefly. For murder they'll hound you to the ends of the earth."

"You're guessing."

Noah heard the ragged edge in Zeb's voice and knew he had him by the throat. "You know perfectly well I'm not guessing. And I'm not bluffing. Either you set the fire or I go to the police and pay whatever fine they set for withholding evidence."

"They'll put you in jail."

"So I'll spend a few days in jail. That doesn't cancel Juliet's promise."

"Listen, Ralston, I can't set fires. You saw me that night. Marsh had to go back because I can't get close to fire. If I lose the use of my left arm, too . . ."

"Then do it right this time. And you *will* do it." He took a box of matches from his pocket and threw it on Zeb's lap. "Do it in the middle of the night, when there's no chance Juliet is in the store."

Zeb snatched at the box. He started to throw it back but suddenly he was staring at it, fascinated. It represented a possibility beyond his dreams. The power contained in the little wooden box snared him. Its corners pressed into his palm. He shoved at one end and watched the tiny red and white tips appear at the other. The smell of sulfur rose to his nostrils and turned to smoke. He got up and paced from the bed to the washstand, staring in horror and fascination at the matches. Could he do this? Could he, just once in his life, deliver Thad a truly crippling blow after all the years of Thad's success and Thad's goodness and Thad's perfect little life? Did he have a choice? There was no doubt Ralston had seen him kill Old Marsh. And no doubt he'd use the information to get what he wanted. He had influence. But another fire. If Thad were in the store . . . Zeb visualized the flames licking at his brother, but he could not remove his own body from the picture. *No,* his mind screamed. His right arm burned in relived agony. His nose filled with searing smoke. Every organ in his body seemed to fuse with the others in a vibrating mass of fear. He had to stall, think of a plan. "I want a thousand dollars." That ought to give Ralston pause.

Noah shoved the chair back and went to the door. "You're

making me laugh."

"Come on, Ralston, this has to be worth something to you."

"Five hundred. I'll throw in a train ticket to Denver."

"Fifty now. I know you've got that much on you." He put out his hand. The way out of this would come to him later.

Noah dug in his pocket, peeled a few bills from a slim wad, and threw the money on the table.

"One hell of an expensive bride you got there," Zeb said with a sneer.

Noah grabbed him by the right upper arm and yanked his head close. "This is the last word I'll ever speak to you, you worthless lay-about. I expect you to leave town immediately after the trial. If anything goes wrong, *anything*, you'll find this useless arm handcuffed to a cell."

CHAPTER 30

February 27, 1896

Larry struggled awake, aware of pressure on his bladder. Good, it worked, the old Indian trick, drinking a lot before going to bed to make yourself wake up early. He wanted no one else around when he did a little sleuthing he should have done months ago. For a minute he listened to the silence of predawn. Lettie's breathing in the next room was even and deep. He stifled a cough, fearing to wake her.

He sat up, and the change in position caused the fluid in his lungs to shift downward—sluggishly, like corn syrup through a tea strainer. He breathed heavily, as deeply as he could, but it was never enough. Suddenly he was tired to his very marrow of the fight for air, the fight to stay alive when all he did was make other people's lives a hardship.

He hauled himself up. When he'd dressed, he took a lantern and walked to the front door of Thad's store. He'd let himself in the store any number of times with the front knob, but maybe there was something he just hadn't noticed. He snorted softly at the thought. The police had already examined the locks front and back and found nothing. He was surely wasting his time and breath doing this.

He shone the lantern directly on the key plate and bent toward it. Nothing. It wasn't scratched or awry, didn't show any unweathered wood around the edges. He'd waited too long. It could have weathered to match the exposed wood in all these

252

weeks. Still, it looked absolutely undisturbed. If Zeb had come in the front, he must have stolen Thad's key. Or he'd gone in the back. Impossible. The back was padlocked.

Larry shivered and it felt as if all of his body shook except the heaviness at the bottom of his lungs. He straightened up and went around to the back, knowing it was futile. Thad must have been mistaken about that day. He must have left the door unlocked or must not have seen the knife when he closed up. Zeb could have sneaked in at some time and stolen it.

The path to the back door had gotten narrower as Thad piled the snow he shoveled. Larry stepped through it, feeling the cold grab at him from the dirty layers of snow packed to ice.

He shone the lantern on the padlock. Nothing. He shifted the light so that it shone from the lower right. There, at the corner of the metal plate, he saw the faintest sign of wood that had once been covered. He bent over. Below the plate was a line of indented wood slightly lighter than the rest. It could be the result of the plate's having been removed, but it was so thin and faint he couldn't be sure.

He looked at the screw heads. In the lantern light they looked normal, but when he thought about how long they'd been there, he realized the notches seemed clean, as if an accumulation of dirt had been removed. The hardware at the end of the lock covered the other screws, so he couldn't compare them.

He lifted the padlock and shone the lantern under it. A short downward arc gleamed back at him, worn into the discoloration of the metal by the swinging of the lock. Larry bent and looked closely. There was a faint scratch. It started a fraction of an inch to the right of the arc and came out the other side. It was fainter in the middle, so the padlock had rubbed at it for some time. The plate had been scratched long after it was installed, and then subjected to the swing of the padlock again. Larry's thoughts raced. Why had no one discovered this? He reached for the lock again, and when he held his hand in the normal position to insert the key, the whole plate was obscured. No one had ever thought to look under the lock.

He straightened and smiled. *Now I've got you, Zeb,* he thought. But did he? He knew how the knife had gotten out of the store. But Zeb had only one arm. Zeb and Marsh could have done it together. Getting Zeb to admit it was another matter. Larry's hands shook at the thought of finally accusing Zeb of the murder to his face, and he almost dropped the lantern.

Zeb woke to a loud and insistent knock that crashed into his hangover. He tried to ignore the knock and go back to sleep, but it came again, louder. He threw back the quilt with an angry jerk of his arm and put his feet on the icy floor. The cold rocketed up his body and set the headache jangling against the top of his skull. Swearing, he searched for his slippers but found only one under the bed. He put on his pants hurriedly, buttoning them with his nightshirt bunched at the waist and hanging out the back.

He stumbled to the door and opened it a slit, half expecting to see Noah, back to remind him of his obligation. Instead, Larry stood with one arm outstretched, leaning against the doorjamb. Ghostly pale, he was breathing more heavily than Zeb had ever heard him.

"Good God, man, what're you doing here at the break of day, breathing like a dying elephant?" he asked through the narrow opening.

Larry shoved his way in and collapsed on top of yesterday's shirt on the chair. He rested his head and arm on the table, coughing and taking out his handkerchief.

Zeb glared at him. "I thought I told you to stay away from me."

Larry took the handkerchief away from his mouth to answer.

Zeb watched in shock as Larry folded a bright bloodstain to the inside, but molded his shock instantly into disgust. His left foot was getting cold on the wooden floor. He rubbed it against the back of his right leg, shuddered, and looked around for the second slipper.

"I came to tell you two things," Larry panted. "It *was* all a pretense. You were right about that. I never was your friend. You're the most despicable person . . ." He stopped to breathe.

Zeb turned back from looking under the dresser and barely checked his fury. As if this weak Gracie had the right to judge him. He put his hand on his hip and leaned toward him. "So what does that make you?"

Larry took a deep breath. "And the other thing is I know it was you who killed Old Marsh."

Zeb backed away, almost knocking over his spindly-legged washstand. This was incredible, two people telling him in the space of three days that they'd seen him kill the old fool. He hardly heard Larry's next words.

"I know how you got into Thad's store for the knife. You worked the hardware off the back door to circumvent the padlock. Or you got Marsh to do it on the pretense of getting the salt." Larry stopped again and looked as if he would faint. "It had a new-looking scratch under the padlock after that night."

The word *scratch* jolted Zeb to attention. He heard the scrape of the screwdriver across the lock plate again, so loudly he almost looked to see whether Larry heard it, too. Damnation. No one had even come close to figuring out how the knife got to the site. That moron Woolsley had just assumed Thad was the murderer and let it go at that. Now this sickly little worm had hit on it. Zeb stalled. "Oh, sure, you knew all the nicks and dents on that old building! You lying turncoat."

Larry nodded his head on the table. "I'll say I did."

"Well, if you think you know so much, why are you just now coming forward with it? That was months ago. You can't prove a thing. And nobody'd believe you now, even if you tried."

"But I *will* try. I'll make up a story so convincing that they'll *have* to believe it," Larry said, taking short breaths between each phrase. "And if they jail me for withholding evidence, it won't matter much. You can see for yourself, I don't have much time left."

Zeb stalled. "Let me see if I have this straight." His mind raced, searching for escape from new danger. "You're about to croak off, so now you're going to claim you can prove I killed the old dog?"

Larry propped himself up on his elbow and rested his head on his hand to look at him. "To put it with your usual finesse, yes. I'll say I saw you approach the store in the middle of the night and thought it suspicious . . ." He coughed into the handkerchief and brought it away wet with blood.

Zeb laughed. "Damn it all, Larry, get out of my room. I don't want you dying in here, and you're going to croak in the next ten minutes. You aren't even going to make it to the trial."

Larry flinched, but he went on. "So I followed you, saw you steal the knife and go up behind Marsh and stab him. I was too weak to run to his aid. And I *will* be at Thad's trial, Zeb. No matter what."

"You idiot. No one's going to believe you were a witness and waited all this time to say so. They'll take one look at you and won't even believe you were out roaming the streets in the middle of the night."

"Maybe they won't, but in the meantime everyone around here knows what a cad you are and how much you hate your brother. My testimony will be enough to sow the seeds of doubt in the jury so they'll have to acquit him."

"Aha. I see." Zeb sat on his bed and stared at him, his brain churning. After a minute he said, "So what do you want?"

"I want you to confess to the murder, of course. It's the only just thing."

Zeb threw himself back on the rumpled comforter. "Ha, don't make me laugh!"

"I'll get Woolsley to examine the padlock, see if it can be removed to open the door."

Zeb sat up and stared at Larry, knowing he would do what he said. He got up and looked absently out the window at the dirty snow in the shadow of the boarding house. Sudden clarity and a crafty smile flitted across the face reflected in the dirty, half-frosted glass. "All right," he said. He turned and put his hand up. "I can see you have me cornered at every turn."

Larry sat straight and twisted in the chair to look at him, his mouth agape, blood still on the corners of his lips. "I don't trust you," he said. "You wouldn't give in that easily." His eyes narrowed. "You'll get on the witness stand and testify against Thad, just like you planned with Noah. I heard you and him discussing it by the toboggan run." Larry was obviously tiring. His speech slowed with every sentence.

"Well, there you are then. If I lie, you can make Noah testify against me."

"Don't take me for an ass, Zeb. I heard what he said. He wants Thad out of the picture." Larry's breathing came harder. "Maybe the rest of Leadville believes he's a fine man, but I know better. He won't back me, even if he perjures himself." He paused to breathe, putting his hand up to show he wasn't finished. "But don't worry, I'll work that out myself. If you get on that stand and don't confess, I'll tell about your stealing money from the cash register when Marsh was in the store and plotting with him to set fire to the lumber. I *saw* and *heard* that."

Zeb looked at him sharply. He knew a bluff when he heard it.

The store had been dark and empty when he'd talked to Marsh. Hadn't it? He remembered the silence as he'd pilfered the register. Could Larry have been hiding in the storeroom for some reason? But Larry was rattling ponderously on, as if he had memorized his little speech.

". . . so I can also tell them you hurt your own arm back in Savannah when you set that fire and then let him take the blame. I know enough to make you look convincing as a murderer. And then there's the money you stole when Thad was in jail. That I *can* prove."

The last part was true. Everybody in town probably knew about that by now. "All right," Zeb shouted, slamming his hand on the washstand. The pitcher fell over in the bowl and water splashed onto the table and the floor.

Larry jumped.

Zeb forced himself to calm down, knowing the plan that was swirling in his head would crystallize into brilliance. "I know when I'm beaten. I give you my word, I'll be in court in the morning."

Larry pushed himself up from the chair. At the door he turned back and leaned on the frame. "I just don't understand how you can hate your own brother so much you'd want to see him hang for something you did."

"Yeah, well you didn't have twenty-six years of . . ." Thad. The thought of him made Zeb's right arm flame again, and the fire that had burned it as the culmination of hatred burned even now in his stomach. Fire. Noah's demand. The plan clicked into place in his head and Zeb changed his tack. "Still, I guess you're right. I should make my peace with my brother. Tell you what. I have some things to do this morning. I'll be down around closing time to make it up with him. 'Course, I'd just as soon your sister wasn't there. You get rid of her for me and I'll come in and talk things over with Thad. Just be sure she's gone and he's there."

Larry looked skeptical. "Right. I'll have her out by six. But see that you come. If you don't . . ."

"Oh, I'll be there, all right. You can count on it. Why don't you wait there till I come?" He held Larry's stare.

"I'll do that. Your word isn't much of a bond. So just in case you're lying, if you don't show up, I swear I'll have you arrested for stealing from Thad." He shoved himself heavily away from the frame, stepped out, and closed the door behind him.

Zeb reeled around with his fist in the air. He spied the toe of the missing slipper under a pair of pants on the floor, snatched it up, and hurled it against the door.

Thad shoved the last jar of beef jerky into place and went out the back to shake the dust from the rag he'd been cleaning with. He hung the rag on a nail in the storeroom and stood again for a few minutes behind the cash register. He looked over at Lettie. Her head was resting on her hands as she gazed out the window, elbows propped on the machine. She hadn't had anything to sew for several days, but she was better able to sit and wait than he was. He took the broom and swept the passageway past the storeroom to the back door for the second time.

Business had been so slow the last few days. Surely it was the slackening attendance at the Winter Carnival, but it felt as if the whole town was waiting for the outcome of the trial, holding its breath with him through the lowest point of his life. As the trial approached, his friends and regular customers had all let him know they were pulling for him. And the rest Leadville's people . . . well they just seemed to be waiting for something different to talk about at the dinner table. A hanging ought to do it.

He pulled the chain that turned on the light above the

register, and the circle of light swayed briefly from the dried food bins to the shirt shelf and back before the fixture settled again. Lettie sighed and turned to smile at him.

He moved to the front and they watched the last rays of sun slip behind the southern flank of Mount Massive.

"There goes the last day of my old life," he said.

She reached up and took his hand. He stroked her face, ran his hand over her hair and down to her shoulder, where it came to rest.

"Mine, too," she said.

"Noah's set the wedding for Saturday, then?"

"Eight o'clock."

Thad blinked hard. "There's nothing left to say, is there?"

Lettie sighed. "No. Let's not talk about the future anymore. It just hurts too much."

Thad nodded. "How was Larry when you went home at lunch?"

"He looked awful. The way he does when he overdoes it. But he was cheerful and said not to worry about anything."

Thad let a mirthless laugh escape through his nose. "Of course not. Well, if nothing else, after Saturday you should be able to go to Denver to get help."

She tilted her head so that her cheek rested on his hand. "There's no 'if' about the 'nothing else.' "

Larry walked slowly past the window, silhouetted against the dying light. He waved and came in, smiling at them. He looked happier than he had in weeks, almost excited, but his face was very pale, his lips almost blue.

"Mrs. Eskitch just ran into Noah . . ." He stopped to breathe. ". . . and she said he said he needed to see you right away, Lettie." He leaned against the wall and inhaled again. "Egad, I'm beginning to sound like her!"

Lettie's shoulders sank. "I suppose now he wants the wedding tomorrow, five minutes after the trial." She got up and reached for her coat. "I guess I might as well go home from there. Would you close the machine up for me and empty the warmer, Thad?" she asked, fetching her coat.

"I'll do it," said Larry. "Thad, why don't you walk up the street with her a bit. Maybe you'll run into—a pleasant surprise."

Thad looked sideways at him. "Why, what do you have up your sleeve?"

"You'll see."

"Well, I hope it's a miracle."

Larry laughed. "It just might be."

Thad went out in his suit coat behind Lettie and they started toward the hotel.

Larry let go of the control he'd exercised and slumped against the door, breathing with difficulty for a minute before closing the machine. He stopped when the lid was half down and listened, cocking his ear toward the back of the store. The sound he'd heard must have been the creak of the hinges he was moving. He craned his neck to see whether Zeb had appeared up on Harrison. Picking up the bed warmer from its place next to the treadle, he trod heavily to the stove, opened the ash pan door and drew the pan toward him. Still bent over the stove, he stopped again to listen. Must have been the scrape of the ash pan. He got up and walked to the front to look for Thad and Zeb returning together.

I knew I couldn't trust him, he thought. The other plan that had been floating at the edges of his mind suddenly presented itself squarely, and he frowned. If worse came to worse . . .

He went back to the stove, emptied the ashes from the bed warmer into the pan, and headed toward to the ashbin behind the store. He had not made it to the cash register when the door to the storeroom slammed shut, shoving a cloud of smoke before it.

Zeb opened the back door silently, heard Thad say something about a miracle, and sneered at Larry's simpering, teasing answer. He slipped into the storeroom just as the bell jingled to Lettie's exit. Peering around as his eyes adjusted to the dim light, he found a single can of kerosene. He took a deep breath and picked it up, trembling. The smell of dried kerosene on the lid was enough to cut off his breath. He tried to focus on the thrill he'd felt the day after the Palace fire, but only panic raced through his veins. He shook the boxy can. It was half empty. He swore silently, wedged it between his feet and tried to unscrew the lid. His hand slipped and the can shifted toward his heels. He wiped the sweat and dusty kerosene from his fingers and tried again. The cap came off.

Taking the can by its handle, he lifted it to a shelf, grabbed its rounded corners, and began spraying the kerosene about the narrow room. He nearly dropped it when his fingers slipped. The can tilted wildly, splashing kerosene on the cuffs of his pants. He looked at the spreading stain and his heart raced. He would have to keep himself far away from the flames. The walls and shelves closed in around him. This was not like the boathouse surrounded by water or the lumber on the Palace site, sitting out on the empty lots. He moved closer to the open door. His right shoulder knocked against the shelves behind it.

The sewing machine crate teetered on the edge of the top shelf and settled back into place.

His hand quaking, he set the can on the floor and took a box of matches from his pocket, not Noah's store-bought box, but one from the Ralston Hotel. If he got caught, he would tell the police Noah had paid him to do it. He set the box on the lid of the coal bin and took out a match. He looked for a place to strike it. The shelf edges looked too smooth. The wet soles of his boots wouldn't work. He rasped the end of the match over the coal bin and only broke off the sulfur tip. He could hardly breathe. The smell of smoke seemed to rise from somewhere inside him, closing his throat like a noose. He took another match from the box and held the wood in his hand. He ran the edge of his thumbnail over the sulfur head. A spark flew off and fell to the floor, but the match didn't light. His whole body was shaking, but he forced himself to focus on Thad, waiting stupidly out there with Larry for a miracle.

Desperately, he pulled another match from the box and scraped it under the nearest shelf. It came away ablaze, the flame almost touching his fingers. Panicked, he dropped it. It had nearly gone out by the time it hit the floor, but it fell into a drop of fuel. The small spot flamed up and spread instantly, and the tongue of fire grabbed at his pants. Suddenly his legs were on fire. He jumped back, slapping the flames on his pants out, but knocking over the can and slamming into the shelves behind him. The sewing machine crate leaped forward, banged into the door, and slammed it shut before crashing into the lowest shelf on the right. Its other side settled on the third shelf, knocking off a bottle of alcohol that smashed on a corner of the crate and splashed onto his clothing from behind.

Zeb screamed in panic, reaching under the crate for the doorknob and glancing behind him at the fire licking across the floor to the can of kerosene. The crate had bent the doorknob downward and now rested on it. Zeb pulled, but the door refused to budge. He tried to lift the higher side of the crate, but it was too heavy. He got under it and pushed up with the muscles of his legs and back. It was wedged too tightly against the lower shelves. The coal bin was ablaze, and the can was lying in the middle of the flames on the floor. Heat and smoke burned his eyes and lungs. He felt for an angle or corner he could use to pull the crate along the shelving, away from the door. He got his fingers under it and backed away, trying to pull. His calves were suddenly on fire, and the back of his coat. The fire was all around him, the room full of smoke. The pain seared him inside and out. He slapped at his clothing, screaming and retreating under the crate to escape the flames. His eyes smarted; his breath scorched his windpipe. He screamed again. The room exploded into flame. From the other side of the door someone was banging and yelling. Then he could hear only the roar of the flames. His whole body was on fire. He balled himself up in the small space, trying to escape the familiar pain. He screamed a last time.

At the storeroom door, Larry screamed Zeb's name. He grabbed the doorknob, but it burned his hand. Smoke was pouring out from under the door and rising to burn his lungs. He shoved at the door with his shoulder. It didn't budge. He heard the agony of the last scream and ran toward the front for help. He had not made it to the tobacco counter when the storeroom door blew out, rocking the store and knocking him off his feet. His forehead slammed into the side of the counter. He fell face first to the floor. He raised his head. The store filled with smoke that burned his eyes and lungs. In panic, he struggled to get up, fell again, and lost consciousness.

Thad watched Lettie walk away from him for a few seconds and started slowly back to the store from the corner of Fifth, his head down. He let the despair he'd try to fend off for her sake wash over him. Ahead of him he heard the sharp whoosh of an explosion and the clatter of debris. His head jerked up in time to see a column of yellow-gray smoke shoot up above the store. "Oh, my God, Larry!" he cried. "Get the fire wagon!" he yelled at a passing woman.

He ran to the front of the store. Through the window and the smoke he could see the blaze was still at the back. But where was Larry? He rushed in. The blast of heat nearly threw him out again. Flames were licking at the doorway to the back hall and along the ceiling, working their way toward the front. Through the glass of the counter he could make out the orange glow of flames on the floor.

Thad yanked the blanket from the tacks holding it on Lettie's machine and threw it over his head. He dropped to the floor and crawled about, looking under the cutting table and around the machine. Nothing. His back was so hot he began to wonder if the blanket was on fire. He lifted it for a second, but that only brought in a puff of thicker smoke. His eyes burned and watered. He felt around under the machine. The warming pan was gone. Larry would have emptied it into the ash pan from the stove. Thad crawled over the fallen shirt shelf toward the stove, visualizing the flames licking toward him through the floorboards. The door to the ash compartment was open; Lettie's warming pan lay to the side, empty. *My God, he'd gone to the back to dump it all in the ashbin.* He'd been right next to the explosion. Thad headed for the register and nearly crawled over Larry before he saw him in the thick smoke. "Oh, God, Larry, no!" he cried.

He threw off the blanket and laid it over Larry. He began pulling him out, taking only shallow breaths. The bells of the fire truck were clanging down Harrison now. His lungs were screaming to get away from the acrid smoke and the orange flames that seared the skin on his face and hands. Behind him the doorbell jingled with absurd normality against the roar of the fire. Someone's hands were on him from behind, pulling him away. "No," he shouted hoarsely, "I have to get Larry." He shook off the hands and reached for the body under the blanket.

"We've got him, Mac," said a voice.

"Let me take him," he shouted, rising to his knees and picking Larry up. He staggered from the store.

Outside a crowd had gathered on the opposite side of the street. Thad stood in the middle of the street and gulped air. The firemen took Larry from him and forced Thad to lie down behind the wagon. "Go get the doctor!" one of the firemen yelled at the crowd. They laid Larry in the blanket next to him. Thad raised himself to his elbow and lifted the end of the blanket. Larry was not moving. Coughing, Thad struggled to his knees and touched Larry's face. He began to pump the chest. "Larry, Larry!" he yelled above the roar of the fire and the shouts of the firemen.

Lettie broke through the crowd and dropped to her knees at her brother's side. "Oh, God, Larry, please, wake up." She shoved Thad's hands away and took up the rhythm of pumping. "This is my fault. I should have taken you away from here."

Larry's chest heaved. He coughed and sputtered, spitting blood and smoke.

"Oh, thank God," said Lettie.

"Lettie . . ." said Larry, then closed his eyes again.

Thad sat back on his heels, but exhaustion sapped all his strength. He lay flat again, still trying to cough the smoke from his lungs.

Dr. Loomis elbowed through the crowd, followed by two men carrying a stretcher. He knelt for only a moment at Larry's side before ordering the stretcher-bearers to get him to the office immediately.

Thad struggled to stand up.

"You, too, Thaddeus," added the doctor.

Lettie looked up. "Oh, Thad, your hair's all singed. Are you all right?" She looked at Larry and back at him, obviously torn.

"Go on, stay with Larry," Thad rasped. "I'm all right."

"You'd better come with me, Miss," said the doctor.

Lettie's face blanched at his somber tone.

Julius Marechal came to Thad's side and supported him with an arm around his waist. "Go on, Miss. I'll get Mac to the office. We'll be right behind you."

Lettie ran after the men carrying the stretcher. Thad turned back to the store, but Julius tightened his grip. "There's not a thing you can do now, Mac. Leave it to the firemen."

Thad let Julius steer him up Harrison, turning often to check the progress of the fire. By the time they reached Dr. Loomis's office, the flames towered through the roof and lit the streams of water in an eerie gold.

Larry came to again as the men lifted him from the stretcher to Dr. Loomis's examining table. It took him a minute to focus on where he was and what had happened. A hideous scream echoed in his head and he felt the heat again, the blow that had knocked him out. Zeb had been in the storeroom. He felt no pity for Zeb's agony. Zeb had to be dead, caught in his own fire. Again. *Now I'll never be able to clear Thad,* he thought. *It's my fault. Again. I should have known Zeb would lie, as usual.* Larry's heart sank. He had only one chance now, and he had to do it right. He smiled up at Lettie. "I'm all right, Lettie. Don't worry."

Julius and Thad pushed into the tiny examining room.

Larry started to sit up. "Thad, I . . ." The coughing racked his whole body.

"Stop talking," Dr. Loomis ordered, gently shoving him back onto the table. He turned to the others. "I can't have this many people in here. I need room to work and the boy needs air."

Thad moved to the foot of the table.

Julius backed away. "I'll go on back to the brigade now. I'll take care of everything, Mac. You stay here."

The doctor began examining Larry with a stethoscope, but Larry shoved at his hands. "I'm fine, Doctor, really." He coughed and smoke left his lungs. He grabbed Lettie's hand. "Don't let them keep me here."

"Stop talking," the doctor said, more forcefully.

Lettie bent over him. "Larry, you have to do what he says."

"No, I have to go home to fix things. Promise me."

"What do you mean, 'fix things'?" asked Thad.

"Sis, Thad, I *have* to go home." His voice was low and hoarse. "I'm really all right. It was just the shock." He tried to laugh. "Actually, I think the fire dried my lungs out."

Lettie looked at Dr. Loomis. He frowned down at Larry. "You'll stay here the night, at least, young man, so I can watch you. Otherwise, I won't be responsible. If you do all right, we can send you home on the stretcher in the morning."

Lettie took his hand. Tears flowed down her pale cheeks. "Please, do what he says, Larry. I won't know what to do if— you need help. I can't take the right kind of care of you."

Thad turned to Dr. Loomis. "Is he going to be all right?"

Larry spoke quickly, before the doctor could answer. "Everything will. You'll see." He nodded and smiled.

Thad put his hand on Larry's leg. "Do you know what happened?"

"Yes . . ." Larry coughed again.

"Never mind. You can tell me tomorrow. Are you sure you're all right?"

Larry nodded. *I'd tell you* everything, he thought, *if I just had the air for it.* "I'm fine," he managed to say. "Believe me."

Thad started for the door. "I've got to get back to the store, then, and help put the fire out."

"You'll do no such thing," ordered Dr. Loomis, turning his sharp blue eyes from Larry. "I haven't even examined you, but already your face is blistering. Besides, those firemen can do a lot better if they're not hampered by some storeowner constantly trying to dash in and drag things out. Now you just wait your turn here." He turned to Lettie. "Miss, take a rag and get some water from the basin there. Hold it against his right cheek."

Larry's chest heaved in an effort to stifle a cough. *I will hang on,* he told himself.

Lettie followed the doctor's instructions. "He's right, Thad. Your face is burned. And I'm so worried about Larry. Please, stay with me," she begged.

Thad hesitated and then nodded. He took the cool rag from her and put his arm around her shoulder.

The street door slammed, and when Larry looked, Noah burst through the waiting room and stopped at the door, staring at the stricken faces.

"You . . ." Larry started, but his breath failed him.

"There was a fire," said Lettie.

"In the storeroom," added Thad.

"It nearly killed them," said Lettie, looking down at Larry.

Noah's eyes darted from one face to the next. "Larry? You were there?" He blanched and looked back in the waiting room. "Where's . . . ?" He seemed to gasp for air. "I . . . I'm sorry," he choked, finally. He turned and ran out.

"Noah, I know . . ." Larry tried to call after him, but the coughing stopped him again. He lay back and let it run its course. Above him, Thad and Lettie looked at each other and then Noah's retreating back, frowning.

Larry sat up cautiously in the dark. The movement made his head reel. His breath came hard. One of the pillows fell off the examining table, and he glanced in alarm at Lettie. In the straight chair where she'd sat awake for hours, she now slept, slumped into a corner made by the back of the chair and the wall next to it. She didn't rouse as he slid off the table. He stood for a few seconds, dizzy and weak in the knees, before supporting himself on the washstand and then the doorframe to tiptoe into the hall.

The doctor had to have paper somewhere, something to write with. He stepped into the office, leaned against the desk, and pulled out the middle drawer. He felt around and found a stack of prescription slips. He tried another drawer, but it squeaked so loudly that he gave it up and decided to use the little sheets.

He reached over and closed the office door, lit the lantern, and let himself down onto the cracked leather seat of the swivel chair. For a minute he sat up very straight and breathed as deeply as his lungs would allow. His brain felt very heavy. He took a pen he found in the drawer with the tablet, dipped it in the inkwell and began to write, his head propped on his hand.

I, Laertes Corcoran, being of sound mind but finding myself shortly before my death, do hereby swear that on the night of November 30, 1895, I saw Zeb MacElwain . . .

He leaned back in the chair, arching his back to keep his lungs open. *No, Zeb was right. They'll never believe that,* he thought. *They know if I'd seen Zeb do it, I'd have come forward long before now. They'll think I'm just saying this to get Thad off when Zeb's already dead.*

He breathed again. Blackness closed in from the sides of his vision in spite of the lantern. He was running out of time now. There was no other way. He should have done it months ago. He owed it to Lettie to see that her life was with Thad. His arm was heavy as he dipped the pen in the inkwell again.

CHAPTER 31

February 28, 1896

Long before the first gray of dawn appeared behind the Mosquito Range, Thad was dressed and pacing his room. He'd hardly slept after Dr. Loomis had ordered him home, over his protests. He'd wanted to stay the night with Larry and Lettie in the examining room. He thought of going back now but feared waking Larry when he needed to rest. Instead, he would go to the store at first light to see if anything could be salvaged and then stop by before going to court. Maybe he'd have time to help them get home.

He wrote a note to Mrs. Eskitch about skipping breakfast, stuck it in the top of her coffee grinder, and left. In the predawn light he could barely see the puddles that had frozen overnight, and his concentration was too scattered to pay attention to his footing. As he rounded the corner onto Harrison, his feet slid out from under him. His hip landed on ice and went through to muddy water that sent a chill through his whole body. He scrambled up and wiped at the filthy wet spot with his handkerchief.

The entire intersection was a frozen mire, partly trodden into mounds of mud and debris from the store, partly sheets of ice. As the light grew, he could make out the black flows of ash that had streamed across the boardwalk into the street.

He looked through the broken front window. Scraps of roofing dangled into the store around a hole in the ceiling. Dark icicles hung from the shelves, the ceiling, the light fixture, and the jagged glass that remained in the tobacco counter.

Hanging on to the frame, he stepped past the door, which hung from its lower hinge, the glass in the upper half broken. The acrid smells of sodden, charred wood and sour ash stung his nose. His lungs, still burning from last night's smoke, screamed at him to fill them with clean air. The blisters on his face and the back of his right hand burned as if the fire were only inches away again.

Treading gingerly over ice patches and crunching broken glass beneath his feet, he made a round of the room. The shirts that had spilled from the fallen shelf lay trampled, torn, frozen in the ashes. The shelves behind the counters were warped beyond use, and all the glass jars had exploded in the heat. The cash register, its brass finish blistered, still stood on the listing tobacco counter. He looked through the broken glass of the counter and wondered inanely whether the firefighters had had a good smoke from the burned tobacco.

Behind him there was a scrape and a familiar jingle.

Julius Marechal was trying to set the door to rights. "I can't tell you how sorry I am, Mac. What a thing to have happen, especially with the trial hanging over your head today."

"Thanks, Julius. Don't bother with the door. I don't think a bit of this is salvageable, anyway. If I'm not in jail this afternoon, I'll just board it up and walk away from Leadville."

"You and a lot of others. Most of the Palace workers are giving up. I think the only reason a lot of us are still here is to see how your trial comes out." He shook his head. "Some Ice Palace boom this turned out to be."

Thad snorted a small ironic laugh and waved his hand about. "You can have *my* ice palace, if you want it."

Julius smiled wanly. "No thanks. I'm leaving, too. Miller said he was real sorry and fired me a few minutes ago."

Thad forced his attention away from the devastation. "I'm sorry to hear that, Julius. What'll you do now? You've lived here all your life, haven't you?"

"Since I was five. I'll just have to start over."

"I'm really sorry for you."

"Yes, well . . . somehow, I think I'm in better shape than you. How did all this start, Thad?"

"I don't know. I just got here myself. The storeroom was ablaze when I ran back last night, so I guess that's *where* it started. I was just going back there when you came in."

They picked their way through the frozen debris. The back of the store was a complete loss, the wall behind the scorched icebox open to daylight. In the storeroom the studs had burned to a cinder and the brick wall had collapsed outward. All of the shelves and their contents had fallen. Nothing remained of the sewing machine crate. Thad kicked at a few of the cracked and seared ends of shelving boards. Beneath them an ice-glazed, blackened skull grinned up at him. He staggered back, almost knocking Julius over.

"Oh, my God, there was someone here!" gasped Thad. They both backed into the charred wall on the other side of the passageway.

"Who could it be?" asked Julius.

"I have no idea."

Julius started toward the skull and reached for another board.

"Don't," said Thad. "I'm sure we have to notify the police about this."

Julius lifted the longest piece of debris with his foot and let it down again. "This must have been a hell of a hot fire," he said. "There's nothing left but the skeleton. It's all drawn up like a baby. You want me to go get Woolsley? He lives right next door to me."

Thad nodded and followed Julius to the front door. He went

out and breathed deeply to get the stench of the ruin out of his lungs. The grinning skull would not leave his vision. It prickled his back between his shoulder blades. Who could it have been? What was he doing there? Maybe trying to put out the fire. Or set it? Horror and desperation crushed him to his knees in the muddy, melting ice of Harrison. Someone had died in agony in his store. The store was gone; he wouldn't even be able to sell it. No amount of looking had led him to Old Marsh's murderer. Now he was on trial for a crime he hadn't committed. He would never have the woman he loved. Lettie. Oh, God, Lettie needed him now. She must be exhausted after sitting up all night. And Larry would want to go home.

He got up, took another look at the blackened hole that had been his store, and turned toward the doctor's office.

His friends and customers had gathered silently in the intersection. Mrs. Kelly stopped him to say how sorry she was. Everyone standing around him nodded and murmured their concern. Thad thanked them and started to push through.

"Just hold it right there," he heard from his left.

Officer Woolsley elbowed through the crowd, followed by Julius and Dr. Loomis, whose nightshirt trailed out from under his overcoat. The crowd parted and a number of people headed toward the courthouse.

The doctor stopped. His face was drawn and full of sympathy. "Thaddeus . . ."

"Come on, Doctor," said Woolsley, and pulled him to the store. "Don't you move, MacElwain," he added. "I'm going to want to question you."

Julius stayed by Thad's side, silent. Woolsley and Loomis entered the store. They emerged again after a long time, Woolsley wiping his hands on a grimy handkerchief, the doctor carrying a sagging, angular canvas body bag, too large for the remains in it, blackened where it had rested on the floor. Thad stood up as they approached, trying not to look at the drooping end of the bag or the lumps where bones poked at the fabric.

"You know who this is?" asked Woolsley.

Thad shook his head. "If I hadn't dragged Larry Corcoran out myself, I'd have thought it was him. As far as I know, he was the only person in the store when the fire started."

"Well, obviously, he wasn't. We'll have to do some more investigating. See you don't leave town, MacElwain. This is damned suspicious. If you aren't in jail by the end of the day, I'll probably be arresting you for a second murder." He put his hand on his billy club. "Say, aren't you supposed to be in court right now?" He pulled out his pocket watch and checked the time. He grabbed Thad by the elbow and shoved him in the direction of the courthouse. "Two minutes after eight. Get going."

Thad yanked his arm free. "Give me one minute, Woolsley. I have to look in at the doctor's office to see how Larry is."

"No time," Woolsley said sharply. He clamped his hand around Thad's arm again. "You're late for court now. You even try getting away and I'll handcuff you." He pulled out his club and held it at the ready as he propelled Thad through the gathering crowd outside the court and up the stairs.

Mrs. Marechal reached out from the crowd and patted Thad's shoulder. "For goodness sakes, Clyde," she chided Woolsley. "You don't have to treat him like a criminal. Every knows he wouldn't kill anybody."

Others in the crowd rumbled their agreement, but Thad knew popular opinion wasn't going to outweigh the evidence against him.

The front right section of the courtroom had been cordoned off, and Thad assumed the men sitting in it were the potential jurors. He gazed at them as Woolsley shoved him up the aisle, vaguely amazed at how many of them he did not know.

Already the prosecutor, Josiah Grimes, was at his table, holding a sheet of paper to the pale light coming from the stained-glass windows on his right. Thad sat down at the other one and looked around for Lettie. She was not in the first row, as she had been for the hearing. But she would come. Any minute. She'd promised; Larry had made her promise just before Thad left for home last night.

Thad waited, fearing the trial would begin before she came. The expectant silence of the spectators filled him with dread. In the barely heated courtroom, his wet clothing pressing against his hip and knees sent repeated shivers through his body. He ran his hands through his hair. His eyes focused on them as they moved down again, blackened from the charred remains of his store. A few ends of singed hair clung to his fingers. He wiped them absently on his coat sleeves.

He searched the crowd again. Larry, of course, was nowhere among the faces, but not even Mrs. Eskitch was here. Stunned, he realized something must be very wrong. He checked again. Julius came in the back and smiled at him. Noah was not in court, either, nor Zeb.

Thad started out the swinging gate that separated the participants from the spectators just as the clerk of court called for all to rise. Woolsley caught him by the arm and shoved him back to his place at the table. He forced himself to face the intimidating, raised judge's bench.

Judge Maitlin stalked in, tall and gaunt, a severe man, who looked as if he had forgotten how to smile decades before. He stepped up behind the carved mahogany bench, sat down, and checked his case sheet.

"The State of Colorado versus Thaddeus MacElwain," said the clerk from his small table at the judge's right.

"You're MacElwain?" asked Maitlin in a bored voice.

"Yes, sir," said Thad, then turned to see whether Lettie had appeared.

"Yes, *Your Honor*," Maitlin corrected him. "Where is your legal counsel, sir?"

"I have none, Your Honor." Thad searched the faces again.

The judge's voice was annoyed now. "Young man, you will face the court. Or don't you care about the outcome of this trial?" As Thad turned back, the judge registered his blistered face and muddied clothing. He sat back hard in his chair and his brow wrinkled with distaste.

"I beg your pardon, sir, Your Honor, I do care. I want to clear my name."

The judge looked at the ceiling and nodded. His downturned mouth showed he'd heard that line more times than he cared to. A flurry of talk circulated among the spectators. Maitlin banged his gavel and threatened to have the court cleared. The room fell silent again.

"Well, Mr. Grimes, are you ready to proceed?"

"Your Honor, in light of the fact that Mr. MacElwain has no legal counsel to advise him in the matter of impaneling a jury, the state requests that we dispense with the jury. It would save us a great deal of time in this open and shut case."

"Mr. MacElwain?" prompted Maitlin.

Thad looked up. Grimes probably feared a jury might free him while this stern, skeptical judge wouldn't. He tried to tell himself it didn't matter what happened to him, but Grimes's willingness to deal away Thad's life for a few hours of court time ran a spark of anger through him. "No sir, I want a jury."

The clerk seated the first twelve names on his list. Thad knew most of the faces by sight, including old Gus Winger, the miner who'd accused him of being the murderer when he'd canvassed the homes around the site. Gus hobbled with his bent back to the last chair and kept his eyes on the floor. Along with the others, he claimed not to know Thad. Five of the remaining jurors looked like miners, the others like businessmen.

When Grimes had finished questioning the men, Maitlin turned to Thad. "Do you object to any of these jurors, MacElwain?"

"Yes, sir, Your Honor. I had words with Mr. Winger there about the murder shortly after it occurred. He told me his opinion then. I object to his being on my jury."

"Very well. Mr. Winger, you are dismissed," announced Maitlin.

Expecting to have to argue the point, Thad blinked.

The clerk seated the next juror, a very young man Thad had never seen before, and neither Grimes nor Thad objected.

"All right, the remaining jurors are dismissed."

No one moved in the courtroom.

Maitlin looked surprised, but said, "Proceed with your opening argument, Grimes."

Grimes outlined the evidence against Thad, his resentment of Old Marsh for endangering his investments in the Ice Palace, his threat a few days before the murder, his unique knife used as the murder weapon when he himself could not explain how anyone else could have had access to it, his lack of alibi. Afterwards he called Woolsley to testify about his part in the investigation and two members of the skating team who were present when Thad threatened Marsh.

It was nearly ten before he rested his case.

"Well, MacElwain, present your case," ordered Maitlin. "Do you have any witnesses?"

"Witnesses? No sir, no one saw me working . . ."

Maitlin raised his eyes again. "You really should have hired a lawyer, MacElwain. Don't you have anything ready to present?"

"Just myself, Your Honor."

Maitlin wrinkled his brow and glanced at Grimes. "You realize that if you testify, the prosecution has the right to cross-examine you? This means you would have to testify against yourself. Didn't you even consult anyone about your legal alternatives?"

Thad stood and started toward the witness stand. "What? Oh, no, sir, I just couldn't afford it. But I want to testify. I did not kill Old Marsh, and I'd like to say so under oath. It may not save my life, but I would like to swear my innocence before my friends here." He motioned to the spectators and glanced around, looking for Lettie. She was still not there.

Maitlin glared out at the audience. "Let me warn you about any outbursts." He turned back to Thad. "Very well, take the stand, MacElwain."

Thad sat in the witness chair. "I swear that I did not kill Old Marsh."

The spectators looked at him expectantly. The judge waited through a moment of silence. "That's it?" he shouted.

"That's what this is about, isn't it?" Thad said, angry at the belittling tone. "I've sworn under oath that I did not commit this crime. I think my friends out there believe me. Now Mr. Grimes can ask me his questions."

Maitlin hammered a short spate of stunned talk to silence.

Grimes placed himself squarely between Thad and the jury, as if trying to block his testimony from them. "Tell the court where you were on the night of November 30, 1895."

"I was in my room working on my books, as I always do at the end of the month." Thad shifted to the side to look past Grimes at the jury. They were craning to see him, as well. "Most of you are businessmen," he added. "You probably . . ."

Grimes raised his hand. "Just answer my questions, sir. Explain to the court how your knife left its normal place in the middle of that night and found its way into the back of Lemuel Marshall."

"I can't explain it, Mr. Grimes. As far as I know, it was hanging where I always leave it at the end of the day."

From outside, a wave of shocked murmuring made its way up the crowded stairs.

Grimes walked back to his table and looked at the judge, as if waiting for him to demand silence again.

Maitlin was staring at the back of the court, as were most of the spectators.

Grimes frowned. He shouted above the voices. "The state contends you went back and got the knife, sir. You found Mr. Marshall salting the blocks, ran to your store, brought your knife back with you, and stabbed the old man in the back." He hacked through the air with his arm.

"No," said Thad, his concentration split between his defense and the stir at the back of the courtroom.

"No," cried Lettie, stepping into the room. Her hair was disheveled, she was wearing the same dirty dress she'd knelt in on the muddy street last night, and her face was red and tear-streaked. Her right hand, held at face level, contained several small sheets of paper.

Thad flew out of the witness box, but Maitlin shouted, "Sit down, MacElwain. I haven't dismissed you."

"No," Lettie repeated, sobbing. "It wasn't Thad." Slowly she walked forward. At the gate Officer Woolsley stopped her. She looked pleadingly at Grimes and held out the paper.

Grimes took it from her. She tore loose from Woolsley's grip, said something in Grimes's ear, and sank into a chair someone vacated for her.

Grimes read the note, blanched, and looked back at her. "I can't present this, Miss."

She was hunched over, her shoulders heaving. She looked up at Thad, tears streaming down her face. He leapt out of his chair again.

"You're in contempt of court, MacElwain," shouted Maitlin. "*Sit down!* Now, what is that, Grimes?"

"I don't think it has any real bearing on the case, Your Honor," said Grimes.

"*I'm* the judge here. *I'll* decide on its bearing. Bring that here."

Grimes approached the bench and handed the papers up to him. "I'm sure it's . . ."

The judge grabbed them, scanned the first sheet, flipped to the last. "What do you mean, *no bearing?*" he shouted at Grimes.

"Could someone please tell me what's happened?" begged Thad.

Maitlin turned to him. "There's been a confession, Mr. MacElwain."

Thad's mouth dropped open and he jumped up again. "No, that's not possible. She couldn't have done it. Even if she had the heart for it, she couldn't possibly have put that broken knife through several layers of clothing and into Old Marsh's back. I'll confess if . . ."

"Sit *down*, MacElwain! It's not her confession. It's that of a Laertes Corcoran."

The spectators gasped as one person.

"What?" shouted Thad. "That's even more absurd. He has consumption. He's too weak . . ."

"Mr. MacElwain, *will* you sit down and hold your tongue!" Maitlin commanded, banging his gavel.

Thad sat back down staring at Lettie. Her head rested in her hands and her shoulders heaved.

Maitlin banged again. "That's better. I'll read the confession."

Grimes rushed forward. "Your Honor, I object. I'm certain this confession is bogus," he shouted. "Under the circumstances, the State requests a continuance, and I don't think it's a good

Margaret Bailey

idea to read that into the record of this trial."

"It's a signed, sworn confession, Grimes. We can discuss whether the state should need time to investigate it, but I *will* read it into the record. I need to read it all the way through myself. Besides, it will get around whether I read it or not. We might as well have it accurately entered in the public record." He banged his gavel once more at the rising buzz of astonishment in the audience. "Now I want order here. . . . All right." He thumped the bottoms of the small sheets of paper on his desk to align them and began.

To whom it may concern:
I, Laertes T. Corcoran, being of sound mind but in the last minutes of my life . . .

Horrified at the words, Thad locked his eyes on Lettie, but she didn't look up.

. . . do hereby swear that I killed Lemuel Marshall on the night of November 30 last.
I heard him boasting to his cronies about salting the walls of the Ice Palace, and after the fire he set, I knew he would stop at nothing to assure its failure.
As my sister desperately wanted to marry Thaddeus MacElwain but felt constrained to marry a man who could assure her of medical care for me, I fell into a rage over such a mean-spirited old man trying to ruin Thad's finances.
I did not know when Marsh was planning to salt the ice. For several nights I unlocked the front door of Thad's store after he locked it. Then I would steal in, take the knife and walk over to the Ice Palace to wait for Marsh. It was bitter cold the night he came, and I was terribly chilled. My sister will affirm that after the first of December, my consumption took a turn for the worse.

Maitlin looked out at the courtroom. "Are you the sister of

282

this person, Miss?"

Lettie nodded.

"Is this true?"

Lettie looked up and frowned. "He got worse steadily, Your Honor. But I do know he was very much worse after the first of January."

"I see." Maitlin glared hard at her and went back to the confession.

> *I let him spread some of the salt so that the town would know what he'd done. Then I ran up behind him and stabbed him in the back.*
>
> *I swear this is a true and voluntary confession.*

"He signs it 'Laertes Corcoran.' " The judge shifted the last page of the confession to the back of the others and scratched his eyebrow. "Well, in light of this confession, I believe the state has to reevaluate its case against MacElwain."

Grimes was on his feet instantly. "Now, just a minute, Your Honor. This confession has to be false. It leaves too many unanswered questions. For example, why did this Corcoran person wait so long to confess? Why would he steal the defendant's knife and then leave it in the victim, which would only cast suspicion on his friend?"

Maitlin sat back and considered Grimes's objection.

He looked hard at Lettie. "Can you answer his questions, Miss?"

Lettie looked at Thad, and her eyes told him how painfully she was torn between love for him and loyalty to her brother.

She'd chosen him. Thad knew the cost of the choice. He could not let her do this, whether he went to jail or not. He spoke for her. "No, Your Honor, she can't. And I can't, either. But I did not murder Old Marsh."

The judge turned to stare at Thad.

Thad returned his gaze with what he hoped was his most honest expression. "I swear to you I did not kill anybody."

"Your Honor, the court can't . . ." started Grimes.

"I *am* the court, and don't tell me what I can do, Grimes. The State cannot simply ignore a signed confession," said Maitlin. He sat back and glanced through the sheets again, then rubbed his hand over the lower part of his face. Thad held his breath. The courtroom was utterly silent.

Maitlin looked up. "The court grants a continuance for the state to investigate this. MacElwain, you are continued on bond."

A shout of surprise rose in the courtroom and rolled out to the street. Judge Maitlin hammered angrily, but the gavel was hardly audible in the din.

Thad leaped from the stand and rushed to where Lettie was standing, her face a mixture of relief and anguish. "Oh, Lettie," he cried.

"He's dead, Thad."

"No," he moaned.

"We've been at the funeral home. Mrs. Es stayed there. I had to bring the confession."

Thad choked. "You shouldn't have. We both know why he wrote it. My God, Lettie, we can't send him to his grave as a murderer."

"It's what he wanted, Thad. His gift to you."

Their arms went around each other and they wept.

Thad took Lettie's arm and pressed through the crowd that lined the stairs, trying to return the good wishes of his friends with at least a smile. On the courthouse steps the crowd had begun to disperse, still buzzing with "continuance" and "confession." Thad stopped for a minute, took a deep breath of cool and only slightly smoke-ridden mountain air, and turned his face toward the warmth of the sun.

Before they reached the boardwalk, a small, gaunt man caught Thad's sleeve from behind. "Mr. MacElwain," he cried, "can you give me a statement for the *Herald Democrat?*" He walked sideways next to them, pencil and pad ready in his hands.

"I did not commit murder," Thad said, embarrassed at being the topic of a reporter's interest. "But anyone who knew . . ." he choked on the word, hardly able to accept Larry as being in the past. In the split second he paused, he realized what he'd almost said: anyone who knew Larry would know he only wrote the confession to get me off. But the confession was Larry's gift, and he dared not destroy it. Thad struggled for words to finish the sentence he'd started. "Anyone who knows me knows I didn't do it, even those who are hiding evidence."

The reporter raised his eyebrows and his pencil at the same time. "You think someone knows something and hasn't come forward?"

"I certainly do."

The reporter scribbled quickly. "Do you know who's withholding evidence?"

Instantly, several people who had been moving away turned back and surrounded them, silent now.

"I do, but I have no proof. Right now I have other things to deal with."

The reporter opened his mouth to ask another question, but Thad stopped him. "That's all I can say right now."

The little crowd fanned out toward home or work. Thad started to the left, toward the funeral home.

"Take me to the store," said Lettie.

Surprised, Thad said, "Don't you need to go back? Make arrangements?"

"Mr. Bailey was called out to one of the mines. He won't be back for a while. And I'm so concerned about the damage."

They walked down Harrison. As they reached the store, its

gaping, blackened window and door reminded Thad of the skeleton.

Lettie stared. "Oh, Thad, I'm so sorry. It's a complete loss, isn't it? Do you know how it started?"

"No. Lettie, I'm afraid the sewing machine is damaged, too."

Lettie paled. "I hadn't even thought about that." She shook her head as the news sank in. "It's all too much, Thad. I'm afraid I'll have to worry about that later."

"There's more." The black skull filled him with horror again, and he could hardly continue. "Someone was in there. Someone died in the fire. In the storeroom."

Gasping, Lettie stepped backwards into a black puddle. "*What?* Do you know who it was?"

"No. I'd have thought it was Noah if we hadn't seen him last night."

She looked up at him and away again. "Could Zeb have done this?"

"Definitely not. There was enough evil in him for this, but Zeb was terrified of fire after the accident in Savannah. I know Noah had something to do with it. Didn't you see how strangely he acted last night?"

Lettie nodded.

Clearing his throat, Thad kicked at a glass shard in the slush at his feet. "Speaking of Noah, forgive me, Lettie. I know it's a bad time to bring this up, but will you still go through with the wedding tomorrow?"

Lettie looked down at her hands, twisting the opal ring so that the stones were on the inside of her hand. The gold of the underside looked like a wedding band.

Thad felt a pang of guilt. He shouldn't have brought the wedding up at such a bad time.

She twisted it back. "No. Surely he won't insist when Larry's . . . I'll make the mourning period as long as I can. I'm ashamed to say it, but on the way to court I wondered whether Larry's death canceled my promise to Noah. Of course, it didn't." Suddenly she sobbed again. "Oh, Thad, it killed him to sit up and write that confession. And he did it anyway. On prescription forms."

Thad was overcome by grief and gratitude. "The smoke last night nearly killed him. He must have wanted to go home to write it."

Lettie's breath left her chest as if she'd been struck. "It's all my fault. I should have agreed to marry Noah long ago. I'll never forgive myself."

"Then you can never forgive me, either. It's as much my fault as yours."

"No, you weren't his brother."

"But I loved him like one. I should have freed you months ago. We both deserve whatever unhappiness waits for us."

"Nonsense," said Mrs. Eskitch suddenly behind them. "I'm sorry, my dears, I couldn't help overhearing." She gave them a guilty, sheepish look and waved a mittened hand vaguely up Harrison. "When I saw all that stir in front of the courthouse, I simply had to find out what happened. Mrs. Kelly told me, Mr. Mac. I declare, I simply jumped with joy to hear it. I'm sure you'll get this worked out now. Then she said you'd come this way, and I came down to see the damage, too. My, this really is awful, isn't it? What ever will you do, Mr. Mac?" Before he could answer, she turned her attention back to them. "I really didn't mean to sneak up on you. I even cleared my throat a minute ago, but you were so caught up in blaming yourselves you didn't hear me. Now, my dears, I simply can't let you do that. 'Course, I know everybody in Leadville thinks I'm just a silly, chattering old busybody, but I understand more than they think. And I won't stand by and see you take so much guilt on yourselves. You have to consider what Larry wanted, too. Such a lovely boy, wasn't he? Always so cheerful, in spite of everything. He would never have stood still for you to marry a man you didn't love so he could live a little longer." She looked sternly at Lettie. "You would have made him very unhappy. Why, I wouldn't be one bit surprised if he told you so himself."

Thad looked at Lettie, feeling as if a black veil had been lifted from his eyes.

Lettie was staring intently at the landlady. "He did tell me once he'd rather die than have me marry Noah," she said.

"Hah," said Mrs. Eskitch. "There, you see? I reckon he meant it, too. My Mr. Es, he used to say you should live your life so you don't have any regrets when it's your time to go, even if the reaper catches you by surprise." A tear started down her cheek. She wiped at it and spoke with a catch in her voice. "Ah, Larry. Maybe it was his lot to go now, and he used the timing to do some good. It would have been just like him, wouldn't it?"

Lettie started to answer her, but the flow of Mrs. Eskitch's thought wasn't finished.

"It's none of my affair, Miss C., but if you ask me, you should break your promise to Mr. Ralston."

Lettie looked at her in surprise. Hope and reflection and resignation passed across her face. It was a minute before she said, "I . . . I can't do that. All our lives Larry and I lived with words that were broken. Every time my father went to sea, he would give us a time when he'd be back. Our house on the Chesapeake had a widow's walk on the roof, and we went there day after day when the time came. Day after day we waited for the sight of his sails, terrified he'd never return, feeling betrayed even though we knew he could never be sure about the day. As we got older, Larry and I promised each other we'd never do that to anyone else. The fear and uncertainty were too painful. Larry knew that when he died. I can't go back on my word."

Thad started to protest, but Mrs. Eskitch stopped him.

She moved closer and put her hand on Lettie's cheek. "My dear, sometimes there just aren't any *good* choices open to us. You're going to feel guilty if you ignore your brother's wishes and your own heart and marry Mr. Ralston. That'll make you *and* him *and* Mr. Mac unhappy. And you're going to feel guilty if you break your promise. It just seems to me Mr. Ralston is the devil in this sad turn of affairs, and Mr. Mac is the deep blue sea. I declare, I'd take my chances on the water."

Lettie looked up at Thad.

Yes! his mind screamed. "Lettie, listen to her. Forget Noah. He doesn't deserve you, no matter what happens to me."

A man dressed in black with a stovepipe hat had stood at a respectful distance for several minutes. Now he took a deferential step forward, half bowing. "I'm sorry to interrupt. Are you Miss Corcoran?" he asked. At her nod he continued, "I'm Walcomb Bailey, from the funeral parlor. So sorry to have kept you waiting. Will you be coming up to see about the arrangements?"

"Yes, thank you, Mr. Bailey. I'll be right there." She turned back to the others. "Oh, Mrs. Eskitch, you're so kind. It was beautiful advice, even if I can't follow it. I don't know how to thank you. I had no idea . . ."

"That this old chatter-head could have a little insight?" Smiling, she laid her hand on Lettie's arm. "It just takes a little age and a little hurt, my dear. And there's no avoiding either of them, no matter how kind you are. We all hurt someone we love sooner or later, and they hurt us, too. All we can do is balance the good and the bad as best we can. If you ask me, the bad's been weighing too heavily on you for a long time and you deserve a stretch of the good. You think about that some more. But right now, you go on to Bailey's and then you come home and put on some clean clothes."

Lettie looked down at her skirt and grimaced. "I have to go

to the hotel, too, to let Noah know we can't get married tomorrow."

Frustration and anger that had been seething beneath the surface now rose in Thad's gorge and he said through clenched teeth, "No, damn it all. I'll tell him. I'm going to speak to him anyway. He was in this somehow. I know he can clear Larry's name, Lettie. I've just got to make him do it. And I'll make him release you."

She grabbed his hand as he turned. Her face showed a grief beyond words. "No, Thad. You know how desperately I wish it could be otherwise, but we only *assume* that Noah had anything to do with this. Besides, he kept his side of the bargain. He bought the stocks to get you out of jail and agreed to help Larry when I married him. If I'd done that when he wanted, none of this would have happened. It's my fault." She blinked hard and took a deep breath. "I gave him my word, Thad."

Thad walked to the hotel with his mind racing between fury and his unwilling acknowledgement that Lettie was right. He knew Noah was guilty of something, but wasn't sure what. And even if he did know, he was a long way from any proof. He opened the door to Noah's office without knocking.

Noah turned from the window where he was standing. He was wearing neither suit coat nor cravat. His shirt, unbuttoned at the collar, bloused out of his suspenders on one side. His face, sagging and reamed with dark lines, had aged ten years since he'd burst into the doctor's office the night before.

Stunned, Thad stopped at the door. "Larry confessed to Marsh's murder," he said, a little surprised that he wasn't ranting. The thought of Larry's sacrifice brought grief back and overwhelmed his anger and his shock at Noah's appearance.

"I heard."

"He didn't do it, Noah. That's obvious. He confessed because he knew I didn't either, which you've known all along. If you didn't kill Marsh, you hired someone to do it. Or at the very least, you saw or heard something. It's written on your guilty face like headlines."

Thad stopped, expecting a reaction, but Noah only turned back to the window.

"I could almost understand if you wanted me out of the way, but for God's sake, Larry never did you any harm. Clear his name before we put him in his grave. Please."

Noah said nothing.

Thad ground his teeth but said, "I'm begging you, Noah."

Noah's neck and shoulders tensed.

The anger surged, flowing hotly into Thad's arms and hands. He stepped behind Noah, wanting to strangle the man who had been his friend and then ruined so many lives. He was shouting now, his hands at throat level, fingers bent with the desire to maim. "What kind of man are you? Do it for Lettie, Noah. Don't make her marry you knowing you did nothing for her brother. All along you could have helped them."

Noah turned, saw Thad's stance, and brought his arms up like a boxer. "You heard what Larry said. He refused my help."

Thad's vision went red around the edges and he shoved at Noah. "Because you bought his sister."

Noah knocked his arms aside. "She came to me, Thad."

Thad was screaming now. "To save me! You know that!"

Noah's face reddened, his shoulders hunched, ready to deliver his own blow.

Thad stared at the hideous, contorted face before him and saw his own, full of the violence he'd foresworn years ago. Still, his hands and arms and heart ached with the need to strike out. Like Zeb. Like violent, despicable Zeb. If he let himself sink to Zeb's level, he would throw away the self-respect Lettie and Larry had given him back. There had to be another way. He clenched his jaw, took a deep breath, forced himself to put both palms outward. "She won't marry you tomorrow, Noah. Personally, I think your actions give her every reason to break her promise, but she's too decent to do it."

Thad waited, hoping Noah would soften somehow, but Noah simply continued to stare, his fists lowered only slightly. Lettie's face hovered suddenly in the space between them. "I gave him my word," the face said. Thad's shoulders drooped. He resigned himself to the hardness of his enemy and the finality of Lettie's decision. "All right. If you clear Larry's name, I'll leave as soon as I'm freed, even though Lettie can't marry you till after the period of mourning."

The belligerence did not leave Noah's face. "Get out of my office, Thad. There's too much . . . at stake here, not the least of which is the fact that I loved Juliet the minute I set eyes on her. In my way. I want her."

"I know that, damn it, Noah. You're not listening. You'll have Lettie. I'm asking you to clear Larry."

Noah went on as if he hadn't heard. "And I will make her happy in time."

"You're so damned blind. You never will. You don't love her. You only want her to beget your sons." Thad walked to the door. Turning back, he said, "She's too decent for you. My God, man, if you loved her, you wouldn't condemn her to a lifetime of misery. Release her, Noah, please."

Noah turned to the window again and shook his head.

In a few seconds Thad walked out.

Noah stood with his fists clenched at his sides as the door closed. He heard the latch click into its hole. His shoulders slumped and he leaned his forehead against the cold glass. His guilt swirled about his head, seeming to fill the entire room. He'd not meant for Larry to be caught in the fire. He hadn't even meant for Zeb to die, although Zeb's death left him indifferent. Larry was another matter.

Larry was dead. Noah had heard it from some guest this morning, who'd heard it on the street as he went to the post office. The boy had died. He probably wouldn't have lived long anyway, sick as he'd already been when he came. *But I sent him the messenger of death,* thought Noah. *I should have known Zeb would use my demands for his own ends, regardless of who got hurt on the sidelines. I could clear him, could even clear Thad. No, not Thad. But Larry. No, as soon as I clear Larry, Thad's cleared too. Juliet will denounce me and marry him.*

From deep under the guilt he felt the old need rise, the need to win, to get what he wanted. Fiona's happiness wasn't the first thing he'd sacrificed to it. The need went far back, to childhood. To being the neighborhood bully, to being first in every race he'd ever entered, to pushing himself and those around him to extremes only he could bear. Now he'd pushed Zeb and Zeb had killed himself. No great loss. But Larry. Noah knew the fevered face would haunt him forever.

CHAPTER 32

February 29, 1896

All afternoon Lettie stood by Larry's coffin as the people of Leadville came to the funeral parlor to express their sympathy. Not once had she been able to look down at his face, even knowing that if his spirit were still in the body, it was smiling at her from behind the lifeless face. Lifeless because of her. She'd put that body in the coffin as surely as she'd delayed her marriage to Noah. She would never outlive her guilt over Larry's death. Again and again, as waves of shame and sorrow overwhelmed her, she balled her fists at her side to keep from throwing herself publicly in Thad's arms.

By 6:30, only Thad still stood with her beside the coffin next to the windowless wall. Mrs. Eskitch, Judge Dickson, and Julius Marechal had taken seats along the opposite wall.

The loud brass rhythms of the Fort Dodge Cowboy Band escorting the parade of the Ancient Order of United Workmen to the Ice Palace battered the quiet grief of Larry's wake. The gaudy lights of the fireworks that followed the parade flashed into the gray and maroon showing room.

Near exhaustion, knowing the wake would be over soon, Lettie finally forced herself to look down. The tears flowed again, though she thought she'd shed the last of a lifetime's supply. She reached out, hesitated, and then touched the cold hands on top of Larry's only suit coat. She looked at his still, gray face, devoid of the fevered red spots. "Larry, forgive me," she whispered. "I'm so sorry. May you be happy and healthy where you are. And may you be warm after all the cold you've suffered. I'll miss you."

Thad's arm went around her and she turned into his shoulder. "I'll miss him, too," he whispered. "Come, Lettie, you've been standing here almost all day. Let's go sit down and wait. The fireworks will be over in a little while and we can go home when the crowd thins out." He closed the casket and covered it with the bouquet of evergreen boughs and white ribbons he had ordered.

She let him lead her to where the others were sitting. As they waited, Lettie tried to force herself to concentrate on the conversation at her side, but she could not take her eyes from the lightly stained spruce box that contained her brother. Now she wished she'd put his warmest coat in it with him.

"What do you think you'll do now, Thad," Dickson asked.

Thad shrugged and she felt the rise of his shoulder next to her.

"I have no idea," he said. "Everything's gone. I'm still not off the hook. It's like living in a void."

I'm here with you, she wanted to say. She let the little finger of her left hand touch his thigh, hiding the movement from the others, who might consider the action brazen. Thad moved his leg slightly to increase the touch, and she knew he had understood.

"Well, it looks like I'm heading to Arizona," said Julius. "I have a cousin there. He said Flagstaff is a growing town that doesn't rely on a single industry, like Leadville. I guess a baker has as good a chance there as anywhere. You ought to think about it, too, Thad."

Thad rested his head on the wall behind him. "Maybe I will. It'd be nice to start over in a place where I have at least one friend."

"Miss Corcoran lost her livelihood in the fire, too," said Mrs. Eskitch. "Such a shame, two businesses wiped out in one fire."

Dickson looked around her at Lettie. "Well, of course, I hadn't thought of that. I'm sure sorry, Miss."

Thad added, "The frame of the machine was so warped she'll have to have a new one, and I'm not even sure the machine itself is still functional," he said.

Julius said, "Maybe I could help out there before I leave. I'm a pretty handy fellow with wood when I'm not baking. I'd be glad to try, if you're planning to stay, Miss Corcoran."

Lettie tore her eyes from the coffin and turned to Julius. "Why, thank you, Mr. Marechal. That's very kind of you. I don't know whether I'll be staying here or not. It depends . . ." She did not want to finish the sentence, knowing she'd have to mention Noah. She looked down at her sodden, creased handkerchief. "Anyway, I don't dare go back to Baltimore. Larry had the consumption, my sister has it now, and my chances of getting it are that much greater back there."

"Perhaps Denver would be a better place for you," suggested Dickson.

"In any case, I have to stay here long enough to . . ." She'd almost said ". . . clear my brother's name," but the presence of Judge Dickson stopped her. What would he be obliged to do if she admitted she knew the confession was false? "Long enough to settle my brother's affairs," she finished. She hoped Dickson didn't know Larry had had no affairs to settle.

Mrs. Eskitch fidgeted in the small pause that followed. "It was a nice turnout for the wake, wasn't it?" she asked. "We never know how many friends we have until there's a tragedy. Such a shame. We ought to let them know we care all the time, don't you think?" When everyone nodded and silence filled the room again, she went on. "I just wonder that Mr. Ralston didn't come. Such a strange turn of events. Here it was supposed to be your wedding day."

Dickson and Marechal looked around at Lettie.

"I don't know why he didn't," she said. *He'd only have made it worse,* she thought.

"Or Zeb," said Thad. "I thought he and Larry had gotten to be such good friends."

Lettie noted the awkward silence that followed and knew what the others were thinking. When had Zeb ever done anything to help or comfort another person?

She heard little of the remaining conversation. Her thoughts wandered back to Noah and made her feel sick. Why hadn't he come? Not that she'd wanted him to. But why? More than ever her promise felt like a chain around her neck, pulling tighter. Larry had not wanted her to marry Noah, but Larry was dead and had taken with him her oath never to break a promise. No matter what she did, she betrayed him. Her shoulders heaved again.

CHAPTER 33

March 1, 1896

Thad stood at what used to be the door to the storeroom, trying to get a sense of who could have died there. The ruin told him nothing. Overnight the wind had blown through the gaping back wall, bringing a dusting of snow that outlined the wreckage in stark black and white. The scraps of shelving that had lain on top of the skeleton were scattered now, leaving a cleared space littered with glass, nails, and screws. Where the skeleton had lain in the frozen ashes, the indentations had filled with snow and looked more like a skeleton now than when he and Julius had found it. The ladder of ribs was there, a line of vertebrae, elbows, and a broad indentation that must have been the pelvis. At the end was an impression of a boot heel and several small dots that were toes in the outline of the sole that had burned away. All the impressions were white, the way bones are supposed to be. He stared at it in horror.

He stepped forward and dragged his foot across the white lines to erase them, but the ridges were solid ice and protected the snow. As he kicked at the slender rib imprints, something moved slightly, caught, and let go, leaving a small, curved black mark in the snow. It clattered lightly over the ice and came to rest in the print of the pelvis. He kicked it back toward himself with the other foot, thinking it a shard of glass. He stepped hard on it, expecting it to shatter. When it didn't, he bent down and looked closely. It was black. It must have been nearly invisible in the ash. He poked at it, picked it up. It was the shark, minus the tail and the dorsal fin. Zeb's shark.

Thad staggered back. He gasped, shoving out each breath of air as if it could expel his horror. He looked wildly around, feeling Zeb's dark presence in the ruin. Zeb. Zeb had died here. Why? And then the magnitude of Zeb's hatred struck home. Zeb had set the fire. He had hated him enough to ignore his remembered agony and his terror of fire. To ruin him. No, not just to ruin him. Zeb had thought he'd be here. Larry had said a miracle was coming. Larry had known Zeb was coming. Coming to see Thad. No, not just to see him. Zeb had set the fire to kill him. And Larry.

Thad stumbled from the store and stood in the middle of Harrison, trying to breathe, with the knowledge swirling about him, closer and closer, binding him like a shroud. His face toward the sky, his hands splayed at his sides, he reeled, turning and turning to find a place where there was not this knowledge. The knowledge of evil. So much evil. He ran both hands into his hair and pulled hard. Where was the knowledge of good to keep him sane?

Lettie. He needed the haven that was Lettie. He ran to the boarding house, barely conscious of slipping on frozen puddles and nearly running into a small boy pulling at a black dog on a leash. He tried to see Lettie's face, but Zeb's slid before it in a hundred versions of cruelty. Before he reached home, only the black, leering skull remained, screaming Thad's name with a syllable that elided into a thundering, echoing laugh.

"Lettie," he cried, slamming the door behind him.

A choked sob came from the parlor. Lettie stood with her back to him at the front window. Her shoulders were shaking.

His heart skipped a beat, and he needed a minute to refocus his thoughts. What more could possibly go wrong? "Lettie?"

She turned to him, her cheeks streaked with tears. "Larry

wrote a second letter," she said. "He left it in the desk drawer. Dr. Loomis found it and just brought it over."

Thad laid his arm around her shoulder. Zeb could wait. "Lettie, we'll get through this, whatever it is. We've been through so much already. This can't possibly be any worse."

"I almost don't want to show it to you. I'm afraid it's just sad news."

Thad took the bundle of papers from her, stunned at its thickness. "No, surely he couldn't have written all this after he finished the confession." He moved closer to the window and read the letter, also written on prescription slips. The handwriting was cramped and shaky, and in places the ink was blurred.

My dearest Lettie, dear Thad,

By now, Lettie, I hope you've freed Thad. I know you don't believe I killed Old Marsh. Just don't let the family hear I went to my grave a murderer. They wouldn't understand. You can't either, but I'll explain.

I hope your grief will be short and what I've done will bring you and Thad together. That hope compels me to set things right, since my mistakes caused you months of unhappiness.

Thad, you wondered why Zeb hated you. There was no reason. I think he was just born flawed. Like me. Only his flaw was being born without a conscience. Or maybe that fever burned it out of him. I do know his hatred came from within, not from you.

Zeb started the fire in Savannah, wanted to hurt you but got caught in his own act. I heard him admit it the day he and Marsh were in the store, but with the concussion, I didn't remember till later. I should have spoken then but didn't want you to be hurt anymore. I also sensed Zeb and Marsh were plotting something and decided to wait.

I'm fairly sure Z helped M set fire to the lumber, and I know he was the one who murdered him.

"Oh, my God. That, too," moaned Thad, sitting hard on the chair behind him. "Zeb. I should have known. I've been such a fool. I just didn't want to believe." He looked up at Lettie, but the grinning skull imposed itself in his vision. "My own brother. Lettie, it was Zeb . . ." He started to take the shark out of his pocket.

Lettie knelt in front of him. "There's more, Thad. Keep reading."

He unscrewed the hardware of your padlock to get the knife. Make Woolsley look again under the lock.

I pretended to be friends with Zeb, hoping if he got drunk enough he'd slip or confess. He never did, and finally he saw through me.

Noah knew about the murder, too. At least I know he had a hold over Zeb and paid him to testify against you. I overheard that. So, Lettie, break off the engagement. N doesn't deserve you.

Now comes the hardest part. I told Zeb this morning I knew about the murder. I made him agree to come to court tomorrow and confess. He even said he would come to the store and square things with you, Thad. And I, fool to the last, believed him. He set fire to the storeroom. N probably forced him to. I heard the door slam and then I heard him scream. The door was jammed. I ran for help, but something knocked me out.

Zeb must have died in the fire, Thad. I'm so sorry. He died of his own malice, and no amount of goodness on your part could've changed that. It's only left for you to forgive him for things he could no more help than I could help my lungs.

My only regret as I face death is that I didn't clear you sooner. I didn't think my word would hold up against Noah and your own brother. So I've done the only thing that might still work.

*I leave you both my love. Don't weep for me. I knew my time
was limited. Now it's over, and I go willingly. <u>Marry soon and
be happy!</u>*

Your loving brother,
Lar

The last words were barely legible. The pen dragged to the
bottom of the page from the r.

"Oh, Larry." Thad choked on his sobs. "My God, Lettie, he
pushed himself past the limits of his own life to write this. It
cost him his last exertion to hide it so it wouldn't cancel the
confession." He slid from the chair and they held each other,
kneeling.

CHAPTER 34

March 2, 1896

As Thad stroked Lettie's back, his eyes fell on the letter still in his hand. Rage boiled up from the pit of his stomach, jolting his whole body. He let go of her, jumped up, and ran out with the letter. When he reached the street in front of the house, he stopped for a second, took the shark out, and threw it as hard as he could into the empty lot next door. Three minutes later he banged through the Ralston Hotel doors, screaming for Noah.

Noah stood with several guests looking at a wall map of the Arkansas Valley. His face reddened in anger immediately. "Who do you think you are, coming in my hotel shouting like that?" He turned and hurried toward his office, away from the startled guests.

Thad raced after him, caught him by the back of the collar, spun him around, and slammed him against the dark paneling below the stairway with his lower arm pressed against Noah's throat.

"*You* killed Larry, Ralston! *You* killed Zeb. You set Zeb to ruin me completely and he burned himself into hell. And Larry, after months of trying to clear me, killed himself to get me off, when you might have done it all along."

Noah sputtered and struggled to breathe. His arms came up.

Thad was quicker. He slammed his left fist into Noah's stomach, feeling the force spurt from the hatred that filled his whole being. Nothing in his life had ever been so satisfying as the feel of Noah's flesh yielding to his fist.

Noah's body jolted, but the arm pressed into his Adam's apple prevented him from doubling over. His breath rasped in Thad's face.

Thad shouted, snatching the letter from his coat pocket and shaking it in Noah's face. "Don't tell me you had nothing to do with it. You're no different from Zeb. You're a murderer." He shoved Noah back to the lobby.

Emmett left the desk and started toward them.

"You keep out of this," Thad yelled with a savageness that startled even him. He pushed Noah to a small round table in the lobby and slapped the letter onto the polished top. "Read that, Ralston, read what you've done."

Noah tried to push himself up, one clenched fist on the table, the other already aimed at Thad's face.

Thad deflected it, grabbed Noah's cravat and yanked his head toward the table. "Damn you, read it now, or read it tomorrow in the *Herald Democrat*, Ralston."

Noah made a sound that might have been a choke or a snarl and picked up the first page. He read a sentence or two and looked up. "What the hell is this supposed to mean?"

Thad grabbed the page from his hand, looked at those on the table, and jabbed his finger at the bottom of the fourth page. "Read this, the part about you." He kept Noah's cravat in his fist.

Noah read and blanched.

"You're finished, Ralston. This *will* be in the paper tomorrow. It'll clear Larry's name and mine, and when it drags you down, I will shout for joy. Now tell me what you know."

Noah clenched his jaw and drew his mouth into a thin line as he tried again to rise. Thad shoved him so hard the chair tilted backwards. He jerked Noah back and lifted the fist around the cravat so that it held Noah's head where he could not look away. "Tell me what you know, damn you to hell."

Noah went ashen. He struggled to turn his head.

Thad grabbed Noah's salt-and-pepper hair and clutched the cravat until he choked.

"All right," he croaked. "Zeb killed Marsh."

"Louder," bellowed Thad. "I want witnesses. Tell me what you saw."

"I saw him from my window. He stabbed him." Noah's shoulders slumped, but his fists remained clenched.

"You forced Zeb to set fire to my store, didn't you?"

Noah stiffened.

Thad shook him so hard he felt Noah's neck pop. "Damn you, Ralston, you answer me. You sent Zeb to his death, didn't you? And you killed Larry in the bargain."

Noah looked at him wild-eyed and nodded.

"Say it, damn you, say it loud. I want everyone to hear it."

"I did," Noah screamed. "I blackmailed Zeb into setting fire to your store to get you out of my life. I still . . ."

Thad turned to the clerk. "Did you hear that, Emmett?"

Emmett nodded, his mouth agape.

Thad let go of Noah, vibrating with hatred. He raised his right fist above his head, wanting nothing more than to smash the face before him. An animal sound came from his throat. He spun around to remove the man who had been his friend from his sight. At the end of the turn Noah was in front of him again, starting to rise, his eyes flashing anger and desperation. Thad's fist came down and slammed onto the shining mahogany of the table. The table broke from the pedestal and the top slid into Noah's lap before crashing onto the rug. The pages of the letter fluttered to the floor. Thad grabbed Noah's shoulders and shook him. "Every muscle in my body is itching to strangle you, Ralston, and the only thing that's stopping me is that I don't want to stoop to your level. Instead, I'm going to have you arrested. I don't know what the police will do, but I'm finished with you. And Lettie is, too. You will release her or I'll beat you bloody."

Noah tried to stand. "Not that, I won't . . ."

Thad raised his right arm, every muscle burning for the impact of Noah's flesh and bone crashing into his fist.

"Stop," cried Lettie suddenly from the street door. "You don't need to do that, Thad." She rushed toward them, yanking the opal ring from her finger. "I will never marry you, Noah."

Noah growled like a cornered and dying lion. He leaped up and backed away from them, stumbling over the tabletop. He looked wildly back at the reception desk and around the room. His guests and his clerk gaped. Without saying a word, he bolted for the street.

Lettie held the opal ring toward his retreating back. As the doors to the street closed, she turned and reached to place it on the table. Only the jagged wood of the pedestal remained, and she stuck the ring in her coat pocket.

The guests, who had retreated to the corners of the lobby, began moving warily toward the desk, staring and murmuring to each other.

Breathing hard, Thad took her hand, and stood with his eyes closed and his head bowed. "My God, I wanted to kill him, Lettie."

"I wanted to kill him, too." She put her arms around him. "It's over, Thad."

Thad shook his head, his cheek brushing her hair. "I still want nothing more than to have his neck in my hands."

"I know, but the police can take care of it now." She reached up and stroked his face.

Thad took a deep breath, looking at the lobby's coffered ceiling. "I'll never rest until I know Noah's been punished. But I promise you, I'll let the police do it. I'm going there right now, and to the paper. Will you go with me?"

"Of course."

Thad knelt to gather up the prescription slips, the desire to kill still vibrating in his arms, the black hatred swirling in his heart. His breathing was ragged, but with each breath he lifted a page of Larry's letter from the floor, and with each breath something left him. He shoved the table top aside to retrieve the last slip. He felt himself let go of the poison Zeb had poured into his heart, poison Noah had intensified and Larry had freed.

CHAPTER 35

March 4, 1896

Two days later, Thad and Lettie were using snow shovels to pile the ash-mud and debris in his store for the trash bin, when a man entered through the listing front door. His face, with its bushy gray sideburns, was familiar. Thad had seen him with Noah from time to time.

The stranger doffed his gray bowler to Lettie, saying, "Good day, Miss Corcoran." He removed his suede glove and offered Thad his hand. "Mr. MacElwain. I'm Alfred Peary, Noah Ralston's attorney."

Thad scowled and rammed the shovel right into the baseboard. "That lying mur—"

"Thad," cried Lettie, "this is just an attorney. Not Noah." She untied the knot she'd made in her faded blue skirt to keep it out of the mud.

Thad straightened up and pulled at his old patched jacket and the sweater under it. "I beg your pardon, sir." Grudgingly, he extended his hand. "Where is that lying viper?" He gripped the shovel handle with both white-knuckled hands.

"Of course, I'm not at liberty to say. But I am here on Mr. Ralston's behalf. As you know, he left town immediately after his . . . ah . . . interview with you. He plans never to return."

"You tell him from me I don't care where he is. I'm going to badger the police into pursuing him until he's caught. Withholding evidence, they said, obstruction of justice, material witness. Conspiracy to commit arson, possibly murder."

Peary coughed but didn't respond to the accusations.

Thad's heart thudded with the memory of his desire to kill. He marveled that Noah would send his attorney here, adding gall to his treachery. "Just what is it he wants you to do?"

Peary looked around for a place to set his briefcase. Finding none, he let it drop to his side again. "It's the matter of the hotel, sir. Mr. Ralston has offered you the management of it in his absence."

Thad and Lettie looked at each other, their mouths open.

"*What?*" Thad shouted. "I'm not . . ."

Peary smiled and put a hand out to stop him. "Please. He said in his telegraph that you'd protest. Just listen to the terms, and think it over."

Thad waited.

"He will pay you fifty dollars a month with a guaranteed annual increase of ten dollars per month for five years. Of course, room and board in the hotel are free for you and Miss Corcoran if she chooses to become your wife. At the end of the five years, if you wish to stay in Leadville, Mr. Ralston will sell you the hotel at a fair price. It's a very generous offer, and one he hopes you'll accept. If not, he will sell the hotel elsewhere. If you turn the offer down, I'm to put it on the market immediately."

Thad snorted in disdain. "Is this how he thinks he can sidestep his guilt? I want nothing from Ralston, I assure you, except to see him go to jail for every charge that can be brought against him." He set the shovel to move debris again.

"Perhaps you'd like to discuss it with Miss Corcoran before you give me your final answer."

Thad looked at her, ashamed of having left her out of consideration.

Lettie stepped closer to the lawyer, her head high. "There's nothing to discuss, Mr. Peary. There's too much bad blood between both of us and Mr. Ralston. I doubt either of us could even breathe in that hotel again."

"I see. I quite understand, of course. I know this was simply a way for Mr. Ralston to try to . . . ah . . . set things right for you. I'll convey your answer." He turned to go but stopped and stared at the debris and the boards waiting to be nailed over the windows. "Do you mind if I ask what you'll do now?"

Thad looked at him and almost laughed. "We'll leave, of course, as soon as my bond money is returned. There's nothing to hold us here, and the town's prospects are too poor to consider starting over."

"I see. Well, best of luck to you both."

CHAPTER 36

March 6, 1896

Thad and Lettie stepped out of the house into a dazzling day with a south breeze whispering of spring. Already the light snow of the night before was melting and running down the streets in muddy rivulets. Last summer's matted grass showed through the snow at the bottom of drifted areas, and the sun was warm on their faces.

"Oh, Thad," said Lettie, "let's go by the Ice Palace on the way back. It's such a nice day. It'd be a shame to waste it sitting around in the parlor."

"You're right. Shall I ask Mrs. Es if she wants to join us there?"

"Yes, do."

Thad stepped back into the house while Lettie waited, breathing in air swept clean of smoke, her face turned to the sun. She started to whistle one of the old German tunes, but the void into which Larry's harmony should fall made her throat catch. She stopped and simply listened to the wind. When Thad rejoined her, they walked to Zeb's rooming house.

Lettie stopped for a moment before crossing under the toboggan run and turning up Spruce. "Another dull day for the Palace, from the looks of things." Only a few small groups were making their way across the boardwalk toward the entrance.

Thad unbuttoned his coat. "Today's temperature ought to take it down another notch or two. I have to admit, though, it's still beautiful. I didn't always see it that way."

Lettie gazed at the nubs of parapets and the subtle flecks of color caught in the blocks. "Strange, how our lives got tied to it."

Thad stroked her cheek. "We pinned so much hope on it, and that melted even before the ice."

"And now that the Palace is doomed, we have each other."

They both looked back at the gleaming structure before they were out of sight of it on Spruce.

Zeb's landlady, Mrs. McGuire, said little when they explained they'd come to move his things out. She demanded the last of the rent he owed and let them into the room.

Overwhelmed, Thad backed against the doorframe, away from the smell of stale liquor and tobacco, away from the memory of a brother who'd wanted to kill him. He turned, and went into the hall.

"Sweetheart, do you want me to do this for you?" asked Lettie.

"No, I think I need to do it myself. Thank you for offering. It just all came crashing back down on me for a moment. All the years of Zeb and his . . . his bitterness, like acid constantly dripping on my brain. I haven't found the peace of mind to forgive him yet." He closed his eyes to the hatred and hurt that were still ensnarled in thoughts of Zeb. Only the guilt was completely gone. He took a deep breath.

Lettie rubbed her hand down his arm. "What is it, Thad? Is something wrong?"

He shook his head to clear it, opened his eyes and smiled. "No, something is right. For years, I couldn't even think of Zeb without hearing the sound of his voice screaming at me, accusing me. It's silent now."

She smiled up at him. "Come, let's get this done and enjoy the warm air again." She pointed at the top of the wardrobe. "Is that his carpet bag up there? You said he came with one."

"Yes." Thad lifted it down and slapped the dust from it.

They opened the window for the fresher air and began going through the wardrobe and the dresser, ignoring the stale smell of the clothing. They made a pile of things that could only be thrown out and a smaller one of things they should send Thad's parents.

"Hm, look at this," said Lettie, drawing a miner's light from the back of a bottom drawer. "I wonder what on earth he had this for."

Thad turned it over in his hands and shrugged. "Maybe some previous roomer left it." He laid it on top of the wardrobe.

Lettie opened a chest next to the wardrobe. "All these bottles. I didn't realize how much he drank."

Thad glanced over from the pile of papers on the table. "Poor Larry. I wonder how he kept up with him."

"What are you going to do with Zeb's remains, Thad, when the medical examiner releases the . . . ?"

"The bones. Zeb's bones. I can't send them home, I'm afraid my parents would open the casket. I just wired them he'd died in an accident."

"You didn't say anything about the fire?"

"No. So I have to bury him here. Mr. Bailey said the bones would fit in a child's casket, but somehow I can't bring myself to put them in one."

They worked a few more minutes in silence, sorting things.

Thad stopped again. "Lettie, you know, when we've paid for both funerals, paid off the mortgage on the store, and bought the tickets to Flagstaff, there won't be much more than fifty dollars left of my bond money. We'll have almost nothing for starting over."

She tossed a threadbare slipper onto the trash pile and faced him. "You're wrong. We'll have each other, and that's more than we expected. More than we deserve." She smiled at him over the pile. "I don't know about you, sir, but I consider myself to be revoltingly wealthy."

Thad grinned back, fighting the surge of love that made him want to leap over the pile and carry her right to the bed. "And I'm the king of Fort Knox," he said. Suddenly, the disjointed flashes of insight he'd been having since the fight with Noah came together in two blinding revelations. His breath left him as if he'd been struck.

Lettie's smile disappeared. "What is it, Thad?"

"I just realized how much I owe Larry, Lettie. Not just for confessing to the murder. He gave me back something I thought was lost for good." Thad stopped and stared absently at the maroon dressing gown in his hands.

Lettie stepped around the pile and waited for him to continue.

"Even long before the fire in Savannah, my conflict with Zeb made me think I really was just plain bad. A person who deserved nothing. In the last few months I think I half accepted the thought of jail as somehow justified and didn't even try hard enough to clear myself."

"Oh, Thad, that's not true. You talked to every person in town . . ."

"I know. I mean I should have taken Noah more to task when I knew he was somehow involved. I wish I'd beaten the truth out of him sooner. Or out of Zeb. But I was afraid of my own capacity for harm. And then, when I wanted to harm Noah— no, *kill* him—for what he'd done to Larry, I couldn't." A sense of wonder crept into his voice. "I'm a good man."

She put her arms around him and held tight. "You always were, my love."

His arms encircled her, but his mind was still on Larry. "The second thing I realize now is that nothing in me compares with the goodness that was in Larry. But if I spend the rest of my life trying, I swear, I will live up to it."

Lettie leaned back in his arms. "I feel the same way, but you're much too hard on yourself." She paused a minute, as if looking for the right words. "I know Larry gave his life for us, and I'll thank him every day as long as I live. But what he gave was a life that had only a few months, maybe weeks, left in it, and he knew that. What you did was risk your whole long future. You invested everything you had for me, and when Noah refused to help Larry, you were willing to sell your store and give me your last cent. You wanted to confess to the murder when you thought I'd written Larry's confession. I don't know why you're surprised at your decency. Those are sacrifices that weigh equally with Larry's, Thad. Sacrifices only the best of men could make."

He kissed her long and softly then, and the weight of years left his heart, leaving him as light and clean as the breeze sweeping the foulness from Zeb's room.

Thad finished the work with a sense of detachment now. He carried the bottles, papers, and clothing out to Mrs. McGuire's trash bin while Lettie packed the few things for Savannah in the carpetbag.

"It's so light," said Thad, picking it up to leave. "All that's left of a wasted life." He closed the door and stood for a moment with his head against the chipped paint of the frame.

They walked back down to Eighth and set the carpetbag under the toboggan run, where they could pick it up later.

"Just stand here a minute," said Lettie. "Let the sun shine on your face. Breathe. The air's so beautiful today. I feel like I'm breathing in the future, clear of smoke and despair and grief."

He put his arm around her and they stood with their eyes closed. They relished the moment until a sled whooshed by, spraying slush.

"Do you think they'll build another one next year?" asked

Lettie as they walked on toward the Palace.

"I doubt it. Did you see in the paper what Tingley Wood said about another one?"

"No."

Thad blew out his cheeks and lowered his voice to a rasp. " 'If I had my way, I would have blown this one to hell.' "

They both laughed. They stood for a minute looking at the Ice Palace and the mountains west of it.

"I'm going to miss the view," said Thad.

Lettie nodded. "Are there mountains near Flagstaff?"

"Julius said there were, but I'm sure they can't compare with these."

"Well, we'll just get used to whatever's on the horizon there. Maybe Mrs. Es knows."

Mrs. Eskitch, coming up Spruce from Sixth, met them at the foot of the statue of Lady Leadville.

"Do you know anything about Flagstaff, Mrs. Es?" asked Lettie.

Mrs. Eskitch looked up at the flagpoles on the turrets. "Which one? Well, will you look at that! There's hardly a one that's not listing like some old drunk miner. They really ought to get up there and fix them, don't you think?"

Thad and Lettie laughed.

"We meant a town in Arizona," Thad explained. "Remember Julius said it's a good place for starting over? And it's supposed to have a dry climate for Lettie's lungs. We've decided to move there."

"Oh, my dears, how sad. I mean for me, of course. I'm so happy for you, but I'm going to miss you."

Thad and Lettie looked at each other. "Why don't you come with us?" Thad suggested.

She put both her hands on her cheeks and her eyes filled with tears. "Oh, no, that's impossible." She clucked her tongue.

"Aren't you just the kindest people I ever did know for asking me? But I've already had several letters from my sister in Houston, who's a widow woman like me, and she wants me to come down to stay with her. I don't know how I'll manage that. I declare, she talks my ear off, but it might be nice to be in a place where the winter doesn't last for eight months and I can breathe after I climb a hill. Of course, they don't have any hills in Houston, and come to think of it, they don't have any winters, either, but I've been thinking of going there for a while whenever the rooms were free . . ."

For the first time since Thad had known her, she seemed to run out of breath. With a rush of affection, he realized she was getting old. A move to lower altitude would probably be good for her.

A group of strangers with a picnic basket passed them, headed for the Palace entrance.

Lettie watched them and then pointed up at the statue. "Do look at Lady Leadville now."

Water ran down the front side, adding to an ice floe at the foot of the pedestal. The head tilted precariously. To the statue's right, the arm that had fallen off lay near the boardwalk, partially shaded by the pedestal. A small part of the hand was still visible, its stubby fingers merging with the mud.

Mrs. Eskitch put both hands on her hips. "I declare this Ice Palace comes up with things that try my mind. Could someone please explain to me why the sunny side of the statue isn't melting like the shady side. Is there some warm breeze blowing up there that we can't feel?"

"No, it's just that the ice transmits heat inward, and the melting occurs on this side," explained Thad.

Mrs. Eskitch shook her head and looked at Lettie as if concerned for Thad's sanity. "Now that makes about as much sense to me as pouring hot water on ice so it'll freeze faster."

Lettie laughed. "This time, I have to agree with you, Mrs. Es. In any case, it certainly is warm this morning." She unbuttoned her coat and took off her gloves.

The head of the statue fell off and smashed on the ice floe. They all jumped.

"Well, I declare! Imagine us being here when Lady Leadville lost her head!" cried Mrs. Eskitch.

Lettie shoved her right glove into her pocket. "Oh, I'd forgotten all about this." She pulled her hand out again with the opal ring in her palm. It glowed in the sunlight, its colors dancing happily, the small diamond flashing in the center of the five stones.

Thad and Mrs. Eskitch gazed into the fiery stones with her.

"I always thought it looked a lot like the Palace," said Thad, glancing up the sparkling walls.

Lettie looked up. "You're right. It's beautiful, but I always preferred this." She pulled the medallion on its worn green ribbon from under her coat. "I have no idea what to do with the ring now that Noah's gone. I suppose I could sell it." She looked at Thad. "Do we want to pawn it and take the money?" she asked, her doubt showing in a frown.

He shook his head. "I don't want even that from Noah."

She turned it over in her hand again. "I know. I'll give it to Lady Leadville." She stooped to lay the ring on a frozen fingertip. "When her beautiful Palace is gone, she'll still have this."

"Oh, child, that'd be such a shame," said Mrs. Eskitch.

"Why? I can't ever wear it. I don't want it anymore. I know it's valuable, just not to me."

Mrs. Eskitch protested. "Oh, no, my dear, it's not a matter of value. That's a thing of beauty, it gladdens the heart. Just look at the colors smiling up at you. Now, don't they make you smile back? If you leave it there, it'll disappear under the mud and be lost forever. There's little enough of beauty in the world, and what there is should be cherished and passed on. Don't you have a sister you could give it to?"

"You're right," said Lettie, stooping to retrieve the ring. "I give this ring to you, Mrs. Eskitch. To gladden your kind heart." She put it in her hand and folded the fingers over it.

"Oh, no, I didn't mean . . . I can't accept this." Her other hand fluttered up to her cheek.

Lettie hugged her. "Yes, you can, or you'll *un*gladden my heart."

"Well, then, I'll keep it and if you ever really need the money from it, you just let me know."

"We will," said Thad.

Mrs. Eskitch looked at them sheepishly. " 'Course, that means you'll have to stay in touch with me. Will that be all right?"

Thad read the genuine sadness of parting in her face and said, "We'll stay in touch no matter what."

Lettie grabbed both their hands. "Come on, let's all try our hand—no, our feet, at ice skating. Maybe I'll do better this time."

They turned and looked up at the Ice Palace, shining in thousands of tiny opals as it captured and exploded the sun's rays into rainbows.

"It really is a diamond in the sky," said Lettie.

"The diamond in the sky was Larry," said Thad.

ABOUT THE AUTHOR

Born by mistake in South Carolina when she really belonged in the mountains, **Margaret Bailey** moved to Colorado as soon as she'd received her master's degree in German from Johns Hopkins University. She taught German, English, English as a second language, guitar, and Spanish in the Denver Public Schools. She retired early to devote herself to writing and moved with her German husband to Frisco, a 9,000-foot town nestled among the 13,000- and 14,000-foot peaks west of Denver. She has three adopted Vietnamese sons. Her short story "A Measly Bottle of Oxygen" was published by Echelon Press, and other works have won many short story and novel awards. She would appreciate your visiting her Web site at www.margaretbailey.net.